ONEIRONAUTICUS

Peter A. Luber

Sageous

New York

2008

Sageous
Amsterdam, NY 12010 U.S.A.

First published in 2008
By
Sageous

Publisher's Note
This is a work of fiction. Names, characters, places, and incidents either are the
product of the author's imagination or are used fictitiously, and any resemblance
to
actual persons, living or dead, business establishments, events, or locales
is entirely coincidental.

Oneironauticus / Peter A. Luber

ISBN 978-0-6151-8290-2

Printed in the United States of America

CONTENTS

PART I

Awakenings

PART II

Lucidity

I.

AWAKENINGS

Chapter One

I had waited three years for the damn movie to be aired on free TV. It was an action-adventure film for which I was too cheap to pay to see in the theater, or even rent in video format. With martini in hand and two pot pies simmering in the oven, I settled into my tattered recliner, fully primed for two hours of commercial-strewn god-awful prime time viewing. Mindless TV bliss was imminent.

I was wrong. My long-anticipated night of empty entertainment was nixed before it began when the world exploded. It did so, as if on cue, the moment the film's opening credits scrolled off my dusty TV screen. It was not the fictional world on the tube that exploded; I would have enjoyed that. It was my world. I apparently was not meant to see that movie.

A thunderous blast shattered the empty peace of my suburban neighborhood. Hell of an establishing shot, I thought with elation before the clarity of the event signaled my baser instincts into action. I threw myself to the floor beside my chair in classic duck and cover form, admonishing myself for assuming even for an instant that my surround sound system was *that* good. My house became a boat awash in a twenty-second storm, bobbing on waves of roiling energy. After the rocking stopped, I held my prone position on the floor, hands over my head, and waited for the Emergency Broadcast System tone to fill the air. It never did.

Tentatively curious, I lifted my head. It didn't get shot off, or vaporized by an alien death ray, so I gathered myself to my knees to survey the devastation. Everything looked the same, save for my overturned martini glass and a couple of fallen pictures. I tried to stand, but my knees did not cooperate. They demanded a little more time than did my curiosity to recover from the blast. In a few moments they regained consciousness, and I crept to the window in a running crouch, arm still across my face, to investigate the anticipated mushroom cloud.

I lowered my arm, but, on the strength of a lifetime of images of people blinded by nuclear blasts, my eyes remained shut tight. Vocally counting, I whipped them open on "three," and gasped in terror when I saw two bloodshot brown eyes staring back at me. I fell to a seated position on the floor, and laughed nervously when I understood that it was not monsters or space aliens glaring through my window. It was my own reflection in the glass. The exterior pane of my window was black, much dirtier than usual. It had been rendered opaque by a thick coat of dust or ash from the attack. I swallowed deeply, held my breath, and did something every fiber of my being argued vehemently against: I slid the window sash open. I screwed my eyes closed again, and waited. I felt no heat or radiation (I was pretty sure radiation couldn't be felt, but I imagined there would have been some sensation, akin perhaps to pins and needles). I opened my eyes. Happily, there were no nukes over New York. No alien invasion. The explosion, though far from mundane, was local. It was extremely local – close enough to increase my heart rate. The house next door, the old frame two-family belonging to my friend and neighbor, Rudy, had been erased from its meticulously manicured lawn. It was not gone: I could see it all over the neighborhood and in the cloud that smudged an otherwise clear night sky. My neighbor's foundation remained, as well an irregular section of polished wooden floor upon which Rudy still stood. Startled, I leaned out my window for a better look.

Rudy's eyes were closed, but from my position fifty feet away he looked unhurt. Clean, even. He could have at least gotten dirty with the rest of the neighborhood, I thought. I decided, without rational deliberation, that I should rush to help him. I also opted to exit via a side door that opened, at ground level, on the narrow strip of lawn dividing my house and Rudy's. I pulled it open and was promptly knocked over by a river of dust and small debris. I covered my head as it flowed over me, but there was nothing bigger than a golf ball in the mess. It felt like warm snow. I had yet to register the lack of damage to my house, but I did whistle at the power of an explosion that could instantly convert a house to fine dust. I waded to the edge of Rudy's foundation.

"What the hell, Rudy?" I shouted to my best friend, who remained a painted statue atop his art-deco pedestal. He didn't hear me, or was ignoring me. Fine, I thought. That meant I had to go to him. I found an indentation that I recognized as Rudy's outside cellar stairs. I made my way down, carefully feeling each step through two feet of heavy dust that had the consistency of table salt. The black powder ended at the bottom step, flush with the inside wall. The floor of the cellar was clean, hard, shiny as marble, and unexpectedly cold. I could feel the chill through Nikes that I had expected would melt. The floor was still glowing bright orange in several spots, including that on which I stood.

Rudy's basement wasn't cluttered anymore. A hopeless packrat, he saved everything, and the damnedest things at that. Years of teasing and encouragement from me failed to convince him to throw anything away. Well shit, I thought, maybe I finally succeeded in a big way. There was nothing between me and the novel pedestal that supported Rudy eight feet above me. No old books, no useless furniture. No cases of unusual artifacts. No washer/dryer. No Sound Room. No walls. I carefully crossed the slippery expanse of vacant basement to the pedestal.

A conical pillar of ivory-smooth cinder block, thinner than my flimsy wrist at its base, held the last frayed boards of Rudy's hardwood floor. It fluted to the width of his stance, no more. I judged that there could not have been enough structure to hold him. If he moved he would certainly be in trouble. No problem there; Rudy hadn't twitched. Time to make contact, I thought. I leaned back and waved frantically. Rudy did not notice. I tried to give the pillar a shake, but it would not move. So much for my structural engineering skills, I thought. I waved again, jumping high so Rudy could see my hand. My landing did not go well. I had expected to touch down on concrete, not Teflon, and my feet whipped out from under me. I landed hard on my ass, twirled a couple of times before stopping. Rudy did not acknowledge my pratfall. I stood carefully, and crossed back to the base of the pillar.

"Shit Rudy, will you give me a hand or what?" I said. There was still no response from my static friend, not even the round of applause I had expected in response. He was hidden above the flooring that separated us. I worried that he had died, and the force of the blast had propped his corpse in an upright position. In a moment of altruistic panic, I leapt and found a handhold on the edge of the floor. Swinging wildly by one hand, I grabbed at Rudy's ankles for support with the other. I found one and hooked a wrist around it. A part of me was relieved Rudy was wearing socks. I waited for him to topple, dragging us both off the pedestal. He didn't; he took no notice of me at all. Frustrated, I crawled with clinical intimacy up Rudy's rigid form until I stood toe to toe with him on the tiny hardwood capital. I had to hug him to keep from falling back to the basement floor. His warmth hinted that he still lived, but Rudy still would not acknowledge my presence. His face was frozen in an expression of mild anxiety. Now what could you possibly be fretting, I thought impatiently.

"Rudy," I shouted through thick black hair into his ear, "It's time to go. I don't know if you can hear me, and I really don't care. Sorry about this." I pushed him off the floor. The effort required was enormous, and, with nothing to anchor myself to while pushing, it launched me off the opposite side of the pedestal. Rudy landed erect, without a bounce, and I was on my ass again. I shuffled to my feet and skated over to Rudy. That he was still a warm mannequin did not hinder my blind determination. I was getting his stiff butt out of his basement whether he helped or not. I tapped unknown reserves and managed to move my two hundred pound brick of a buddy up the cellar stairs to what was left of his front lawn. I held him until I had kicked aside enough dust to prevent suffocating him, and laid him in the shallow grave. Judith from across the street, her gnarled hand clutching a flannel robe tightly about her wrinkled neck, suggested calling an ambulance. The rest of the crowd that had gathered agreed, and little Bobby Clark ran off. His mother followed, sure he would forget.

"Anyone know CPR?" I shouted over my shoulder. My voice shook.

"That's okay," Rudy said, sitting up, "I don't think there's anybody hurt here. Thanks, Alex."

I watched him rise easily to his feet, straighten his spotless silk shirt, turn, and head for his car. He was unaware of any problem. I leaped after him.

"`Thanks Alex'?" I said quietly – we *were* in front of the
neighbors, "All I get is a `Thanks Alex'? What the hell happened?"

Rudy only sighed and said, "Boy, do I need a drink." He
stopped at his Porsche and searched his pockets. Finally he shook
his head, muttering to himself, and lifted the unlocked door handle.
"Want to come with me?" he asked.

"Sure, why not?" I said, ignoring an urge to find a clean
wall to bang my head against, "Movie's probably over anyway."

I entered the passenger side of his spotless Porsche. He
started it with the key that never left the ignition. Later I would
wonder why his car shined in a neighborhood buried in dust, but
for that moment I only wanted to know who totaled Rudy's house
and why he pretended to be catatonic.

"I really did appreciate your help back there," he said, once
we were underway, "I did need you. I had a feeling you might turn
up." His voice was soft, his tone as carefully measured as ever.
His gratitude would have been as vocal if I had just dropped a buck
into the collection basket at church in his stead.

"You did?" I seethed, "Well that's just fine. I'm glad I
saved you a few steps. Where are we going, anyway?" The road
was unfamiliar. Cobblestone, it wound downhill through blocks of
Swiss style houses. There were certainly enough houses like that
in Westchester County, but I'd never seen this street before. I
admired the way Rudy's car rode smoothly on the rough surface.
Always level.

"To a little place I know, just around the corner."

"Around the corner? From what?"

"A great little smoke shop." That silenced me until we
reached the bar and I saw the wooden sign swinging from iron
hooks outside a timelessly quaint German pub. The sign was
painted with German words.

"I've never seen this place before," I said.

"Probably not," Rudy said, "But it is a nice spot. You'll
love it here." He stopped just before he reached the place, parked.
We got out, headed silently down the hill to the pub. I could hear
the car doors lock behind us. As I rolled my eyes at such gadgetry,
I noticed the full moon. Odd, I thought, it was black outside last

night. I was not feeling conversational at the time, so I let such lesser thoughts lie. The strange neighborhood we strolled was a far more curious topic.

I could hear accordion music accompanying obviously German songs sung in English. I looked at the sign again, and saw that it said 'Fritz's Beer House.' I shook my head, wondering why I thought it was written in German earlier. We entered the smoke-filled room. My senses were ready for the usual acrid bar smoke that barely masked the stench of yesterday's spilled beer. Instead, I was pleasantly startled by sweet, full smoke from a dozen well-fueled pipes. Tankards and mugs of obviously good beer were everywhere as well, but it was the people that were most attractive. They had leapt directly from a travel brochure, singing and dancing, clad in the best of traditional Bavarian finery. I found it difficult to accept that I had never heard of this place. Some revelers spotted us and called to Rudy by name. He returned their greetings merrily, with a whispered joke or a slap on a back as he passed them by. I was stunned once more. I had never seen Rudy laugh before. He was a good-natured sort, no doubt, but stoically unemotional. In the years I spent with Rudy, he generally managed only the occasional smile at best. His deep, genuine laugh was probably the most disturbing novelty of the evening. So far.

Rudy found us a table. We sat, and soon the predictably buxom waitress, long blond tresses wrapped tightly behind her head, stopped at our table. Two huge mugs of gloriously dark beer swung from the fingers of one small hand. She smiled slyly at Rudy when she parked the beers in front of us. Rudy winked at her. Winked!

"Heidi, right?" I asked after she left.

"Of course."

We sat silently for a few minutes, enjoying the sensual, personal pleasure of the first sip of an impossibly perfect beer. I compounded this with the positive feeling in the room, and spent an extra long time soaking in this wonderfully warm tavern. Eventually the reality of the evening forced its way back into my reverie, and my gaze found only Rudy. He sat quietly, eyes half closed. He appeared to be thinking very hard about nothing, his empty concentration broken only by the occasional wordless wave or nod to a well-wisher passing the table. In time he lifted his eyelids. I raised my mug.

"So here we are," I said, "Wherever the hell, or Heaven I suppose, that is."

Rudy smiled, took a sip of his beer. He was looking at me, but his eyes were not. Clouded, they gazed through me, on to something far more important than a nosy neighbor.

"Seriously, Rudy, where are we? It said Fritz's outside, but --"

"You got it. It is called `Fritz's'," Rudy said, "I come here to get away from it all. Do you like it?"

"It's nice. How come I've never heard of it?"

"It's a bit off the beaten path." Rudy was saying all this without taking his gray eyes from whatever it was that held them. Then he finished the last half of his beer in one swig and slammed the mug on the table. Heidi set down another almost before the base of Rudy's mug struck the old table, but Rudy did not seem to notice. He was focused on me. His eyes were clear, perhaps tired, but clear. He continued, "I suppose you'll be wanting some sort of explanation."

"Some sort," I said, finishing my beer in equally dramatic fashion, and finding primal pleasure, as Heidi appeared once more to place a fresh beer before me. I took a sip, smiled, and said, "I guess they don't need pitchers here." Rudy seemed amused.

"I like you, Alex, you never manage to take a situation seriously enough."

"I try," I said, slightly hurt that he didn't recognize my dive into his basement as taking things seriously, "Especially tonight. Though I can't help but get real serious when someone makes me miss a good "B" movie." His bowed and slowly shaking head countered Rudy's casual smile. He ran a hand through his perfect black hair before forcibly raising his eyes to meet mine.

"Sorry about that. I had to drag you into this sometime. Sooner than I thought."

"Into what? Wasn't that just your furnace that blew up or something?" Of course it wasn't his furnace, I thought. My demolitions expertise was nil, but I knew furnaces do not vaporize houses.

"Of course it wasn't my furnace. I never had one. All you'll let me tell you for now is that someone made that explosion. A competitor."

"Remind me never to go into advertising."

Rudy's chuckle became a sigh, "I have other hobbies, you know."

"Not playing chess, I imagine."

"No, not quite," Rudy smiled, "But I have been finding myself in check a lot lately."

"You almost got mated for good tonight," I said, seeing in his eyes that his adversary, or whatever, hadn't come close. "What about your house?"

"It needed paint anyway."

"And the neighbors?"

"They must be a bit startled, I imagine," Rudy said, chin cradled in his hands, "They'll forget all about me before they finish sweeping. Count on it." His gray eyes flashed.

"They don't have popcorn here, do they?" I said, suddenly remembering that I left potpies cooking, most likely burning, in my oven. Rudy did not respond. His attention was elsewhere. Someone was shouting to him from the door of the tavern. He waved the person over. I turned, but a pewter stein blocked my view. In a moment a stunning young woman came to the table. She was wearing only black leather, arranged rather nicely around a wonderfully proportioned frame. Flaming red hair was everywhere. Huge green eyes glistened with emotion. Rudy stood and she hugged him in obvious relief. They said nothing for a moment, just stood there quietly, and then they sat down. She clutched his hands with both of hers. I tried tapping my fingers and clearing my throat, but their mutual trance could not seem to be broken. Finally the woman turned.

"Hello Alex," she smiled, revealing the obligatory perfect teeth.

"We've met?" I asked, too loudly.

"Oh, no. But Rudy's told me lots about you." Her voice was too low to be heard over the noise around us, but every word got to me. She turned back to Rudy, raising it.

"What now, boss?" she asked him. I had trouble picturing her as one of the secretaries in the firm.

"I don't know," Rudy said, "I've always said this is too big for me alone. He's getting to damn close. I'm not strong enough."

"Who's too close?" I asked. My query was ignored.

"Nonsense, Rudy. You know you're just as tough," she said. Her voice was excellent, soothing even while shrill. And the lips from which her words flowed so easily were flawless and bright red without lipstick. I wondered what her name was. She continued, "Trouble is, you've been wasting that strength on ridiculous things, like insisting on existing primarily on the other side." She was becoming more agitated with every phrase. This was clearly a subject she and Rudy often battled over. Rudy shook his head. I recognized the sigh; he had tried to explain before. He gestured to me.

"By the way, Alex, this is Max. Max, Alex." I reached to shake a hand, but Max didn't acknowledge. Max was actively ignoring me. She seemed to be preparing another attack, but then the anger left her eyes. They glistened again. She took a sip of Rudy's beer, sat back and folded her arms.

"Rudy, one of these times you won't have a way out. You've got to do something."

"I have. I brought Alex."

"He's still useless. Probably never any help."

"Thanks," I said, relieved to be useless in a situation I knew nothing about.

"Sorry Alex," Max said, glancing through the corners of her eyes in my direction, "I don't mean to be rude. Your friend here just drives me nuts is all."

"He's ready," Rudy said, raising his voice about one decibel. He was furious: "I know it. Now let me do this the way I've planned, and everything will work out." Max saw his anger and shrank away. She excused herself, heading for the bar.

"So what's the plan?"

"Be ready for whatever comes."

"Figures."

Max was not gone long. She skidded to a stop above Rudy and grabbed his arm. She was panting.

"Rudy! The bar is red hot," she blurted, "We must leave, now!"

"Shit," Rudy said, standing, "I didn't think that could be. Get up Alex, we're leaving."

I needed no prompting. I was seated facing the bar. Images in the mirror behind it were warping, and bottles adorning cut glass shelves against it had begun to burst. Some patrons witnessed the show and simply stared, transfixed. The rest did not notice.

We sprang to our feet, toppling our chairs and beers, and raced for the door. Max grabbed my wrist and Rudy followed, shouting something about fire, then "free beer," to the puzzled patrons. Most of the tavern had an orange glow about it, and the air shimmered with heat. We were five paces from the door when the floor began to boil. Molten wood was another new experience for me, but one I could have done without. People screamed in mixed surprise and agony as they leapt in the air to escape. Up, unfortunately, was their only safe route, but they could not fly for long. Tables, chairs, even other people were as hot as the floor.

Everything but us glowed like burgundy wine in candlelight. I felt warm; Max's hand was cool. Rudy wasn't even sweating as he pushed burning people toward the great oaken door that still blocked the panicked crowd's escape. The plaster walls around it had dissolved, effectively sealing it shut.

A dozen terrified wretches were pounding on the only exit, their hands sizzling with each thrust. When we arrived, Max gently but with alarming firmness shoved the pounders aside, and tended to the door. The seal broke with her initial touch. She whipped the door open, snapping it off its iron hinges with a deafening crack. Max pulled me out, dragged me across the street, and stopped. We turned in time to see Rudy come out with at least six victims in his grasp. A few more followed his cool wake to painful sanctuary. All but Rudy were smoldering, their clothes melted off, gasping for air through charred lips. Except for the anger that blackened his eyes, Rudy looked like he did at the Fair Acres clambake a week earlier.

I did not fare as well. Though unscathed physically, I shook violently. A mix of fear and revulsion that transcended my middle-class senses was about to overwhelm my shattered psyche. My feet were pawing the dirt, ready to carry me to safety, but nerve I could not name forced me to remain and endure the terror.

In time, my attention was drawn from the growing pile of licorice that was the remains of the former patrons of Fritz's back to Rudy.

He gently placed a shrunken carcass that had stuck to his leg down on the hot cobbles. I could not speak. I stood still, able only to passively watch the pub slowly sink into the ground, its molten wall gliding softly down the ancient hill. There were no flames, as if there were too much heat for fire. Only the survivors burned – all ten of them. Max, still clutching my wrist with a painful iron grip, was quietly weeping. Rudy did not move for about an hour. Something powerful stiffened his features long after the last rivulet of wood dripped by and the foundation began to cool. At last he moved.

He pushed through the crowd that had gathered to tend to the wounded and sort out the dead. He sat with them for a moment, touched them. He spoke to them in miraculously soothing tones whose mere echoes reached across the street and helped soothe my own battered soul. Though we all knew the target of this disaster, only respect and support were offered to Rudy. He brushed off both with noted indifference, or guilt. In time he rose to his feet. The weight of the patrons, the dead, the permanently scarred, rose with him. His gray eyes absorbed their pain, held it without reflection behind stillborn tears. He gestured, a movement of his head that was not much more than a nod, and Max and I followed him to his car, which had luckily been parked a safe distance up the hill. He drove out of town toward the Alps, and then took a side road to my house. Max got out with me, walked me to my door. She hugged me, kissed my cheek.

"Welcome to the club," she whispered, and pushed me through my front door. She shut it behind me. In a moment I heard the car door shut, followed by a quiet crunching as it made its way down the debris-ridden street.

I wandered robotically through my house to the kitchen, distantly noticing myself stopping to pull the battery from the screeching smoke detector in the hall. The thick smoke wasn't a problem, but I did shiver uncontrollably when I removed the charred husks of two potpies from the oven. I dropped to the kitchen floor and sat, dazed, until the last of the smoke cleared. I stood at last, threw away my dinner and pan. I shuffled to the living room, and fell into my recliner.

The closing credits had just begun to scroll up the TV screen. I felt drained, as though I had drunk three martinis, and never actually left. I wondered if I had, but was too tired to think about it. Exhausted, deeply confused, and completely interested in making it all go away, I went to bed.

Chapter Two

The black granite cliff, framed ominously between my bare toes, stretched its onyx smooth vertical surface downward for a full two miles before it violently punctured the surface of a passing green sea. If my cliff had a beach at its base it was invisible, shrouded in the mist of thundering surf. My heels, resting on the cliff's hard, cold, dirt-free edge, were my only connection to substance. My position at the high end of this wall of dense stone was familiar. I had enjoyed, or suffered – I was not sure – the precipitous point in my past, but the name of the place danced just out of my hazy mind's reach. A quiet thud shifted my gaze from my toes to squinting distance. The ocean spread away under the clear blue sky to all horizons. It was a solid green carpet broken occasionally by other monolithic fingers of gray rock. The source of the quiet disturbance was a nearby finger of black stone that had been taller than mine. Its altitudinal claims were now sadly moot, because the proud tower was crumbling to the sea. Its clamorous demise, amplified dramatically by my attention, raised a cloud of white spray, but the thick mist was not enough to conceal the cause of the mountain's fall. The mighty slab of ancient granite had been toppled by the impact of a single-engine private plane.

The Cessna, undamaged, banked toward my cliff, whistling madly as it dove below me. A redheaded woman clung to the leading edge of the plane's right wing. A long black cape that billowed in the wind behind her complemented her flowing mane. I knew her.

It was Max, from Fritz's.

She was staring intently through the little plane's windshield, witnessing a violent fight whose exaggerated energy warped the plane's cabin. Two shadows of men, identical in every thrust and parry, were beating each other mercilessly at the rear of the tiny plane. Their identities were concealed by heavily tinted glass. No one was working the controls, so without hindrance or heroics the Cessna's wingtip scraped my cliff hundreds of yards below my toes, loosing several tons of granite as well as Max. She started her descent to the sea. I dove after her.

I knew that I could plummet faster if I curled up into a cannonball, so I grabbed my bare calves and jammed my head between my knees. In no time, literally, I was racing along beside the striking little woman. She did not notice me, even after I flattened out and waved to her. Feeling a strong need to get her attention, I reached out and grabbed her wrist. She turned, startled, tried to shake me off. The contact caused her to recognize me. She looked past me and shouted a plea. I could not hear her through the heavy plastic of my motorcycle helmet, but I could see through my dirty visor that Max was pointing to the plane. It was circling wildly, and was about to pass behind my cliff. I gasped, lifted the visor and backpedaled my legs. As planned, the frantic effort ceased my descent. The plane continued racing seaward and hurtling into the shadow of my cliff. I paused in mid-air to carefully consider the situation. I knew that if the plane left my sight, it would be lost. The cliff had to go away.

The ancient granite wall soundlessly vanished, allowing the plane to remain safely in clear view. Cool, I thought as I dove after it. Max hitched a ride with me, her long fingernails digging into my ankle like angry butter knives as she clung to my ankle.

When I hovered, relatively, within an arm's length of the spinning plane, cold spray from the disturbed placid sea stung my face. The wet, wispy pins and needles signaled the proximity of the icy water below. I knew that I had to act immediately, or this scene would not end well. With gripping determination, I wrapped all ten of my outstretched fingers around the leading edge of the Cessna's tail. Then, with Max's arms now firmly around my neck, I dug my bare heels into the air and forced the plane to a cartoon-quality screeching halt. My utterly painless heroic act brought the plane to a stop less than a hundred feet above the ocean. Through the back windows I saw the fighters. One turned to me. It was Rudy. The other remained a silhouette of solid blackness. I vomited at the sight, and noticed upon looking back at the plane that the shadow was leaning heavily against the flimsy and buckling cabin door. Feeling quite clever, I ripped the door off the plane, expecting the shadow to tumble to its doom.

My plan failed: the shadow did not fall out. I had managed only to break the plane. Pissed, I crouched over and grabbed the plane's landing gear, and flipped it to an inverted position. The shadow clung tenaciously while I shook the plane like an empty saltshaker (I hate empty saltshakers), but the rules were mine, so the villain cloaked in a flexible silhouette of perfect darkness eventually fell out. It didn't fall far, though, as it was able to latch an ethereal black hand onto the slowly spinning propeller. Annoyed, I threw the plane straight down at the river below, knowing that the shadow would fear death and flee. It initially maintained its grip on the blade, comically orbiting the plane at the end of the propeller until the last few yards of the rapid descent. It suddenly seemed to sense impending doom, and emitted a frozen shrill and vanished. The plane settled gently on its back in the clear calm river.

We sprawled on the expansive belly of the flipped Cessna, breathing heavily but smiling gratefully at each other, much relieved. We relaxed, our torn-t-shirt clad stomachs heaving still from the excitement. In time, though, the hypnotic warmth of the plane's gently undulating soft flesh compounded our shared sense of euphoria. I was between Max and Rudy, each of them a comfortable body length away on the soft white aluminum. I gazed up at the New York Skyline as it passed slowly by under fluffy white clouds, but movement to my left distracted me. Max had raised herself on an elbow, and was speaking to Rudy. I missed what she said. I glanced at Rudy in time to see his response. He made one, but I couldn't hear it. Apparently I was either deaf (though the sounds of the babbling river and distant city traffic denied such an affliction) or underprivileged. I was at first nervous, then embarrassed, by my inability to participate in their easy exchange. I was practicing my sign language in order to share my concern when I noticed that we were headed for a new obstacle.

The river was destined to end in a few hundred yards. I couldn't see the majestic waterfall yet, but I knew it was there. I also knew that it dropped a thousand feet into a shallow pond studded with very pointy boulders. My suspicions were confirmed when a crowded school bus driving a short distance in front of us tilted forward and disappeared over the horizon (I wondered, as I listened to the bus's occupants sing Amazing Grace to herald their descent, why these things always happen to church groups). Rudy and Max didn't seem to notice, or care, even though I waved and gestured frantically. They continued their exclusive conversation, oblivious to my warnings. I noticed through my panic that their discussion had become quite heated – Max's face was bright red, protruding veins on her forehead marring perfect skin, and Rudy's eyes squinted ever so slightly – but I had no time to care. Our lives needed saving, and apparently the chore of rescuer was mine. The roar of the falls was deafening. The river's edge was just feet away when I finally stumbled on a remedy for the woeful situation. Without taking my eyes off the waterfall, I rolled over, onto my back. Rudy smiled slyly as the cascade bent one hundred and eighty degrees about and our canoe was flung vertically up instead of down. The deep blue maelstrom swept us skyward through black clouds to the street above.

The chauffeur, whistling a happy tune, pulled the limo to a stop beside the roof of my office building. I was less amazed by a car parked fifty stories above the sidewalk than I was by the thrilling fact that my office was in a tower in Manhattan again, rather than in that tired suburban low-rise in Westchester County. The chauffer, a thin black man with impeccable taste in uniforms, hopped out of the long car. He sprinted fifty yards to my door, and opened it with a flourish. I got out, waved to Max and Rudy, who remained huddled in the tiger-furred back seat. They returned the wave, appeared a bit puzzled, then disappeared behind the tinted glass of the closing window. The limo drove away from the roof, hovered for a moment, and then dropped out of sight. A few seconds later I heard a spine-wrenching crash, followed by the horns and shouts of angry motorists whose days had been rudely interrupted. Attracted by the alarm I strolled, hands thrust deep in bathrobe pockets, to the edge of the roof. I peered over, and was

rewarded with the spectacle of legions of lemmings attacking my
building. They were armed with M-16's, and were spraying the
glass below me with rat shit bullets.

The president of the company, Leland "The Beaver" Olson
himself, arrived on the scene aboard a Caterpillar bulldozer. His
normally pasty wasp face was dark red, and he was shouting orders
at a convoy of trucks, demanding that they move their asses, dig up
the dirt.

I woke gradually to the steady vibration of heavy
equipment outside my house. I absently wondered who was
getting a new pool. As I waited for my sunny bedroom to come
into focus, I reflected on the vivid dreams I endured the night
before. The faded ghosts of my recent adventures raced across the
white expanse of my ceiling until I shook my head to clear them. I
folded my hands behind my head and sighed. The intensity and
general strangeness of my dreams had been very much on the rise
over the previous few weeks, and last night's were the nastiest yet.
I swore as the bar scenes reentered my mind, their clarity
disturbing. I wished my dreams would go back to being the barely
noticed intrusions on a good night's sleep that they once were.
They were monopolizing my time off from consciousness with
annoying, and exhausting, consistency. How could I catch up on
my sleep if my dreams were more taxing than reality?

Still, it was fun making that waterfall bend up.

I stretched, considering whether to summon the strength to
pull the blankets away and haul myself out of my warm bed. A
glance at the clock helped revive me. Either it was an hour fast or
I had ignored its alarm again. I sprang to my feet, grabbed fresh
underwear and bolted into the shower. The warm water and soap
helped allow reality to soak back in. I set aside the dreams,
forgetting them. All except Fritz's; I couldn't shake that image.
That, or the surreal afterglow of Rudy's basement. And Max.
Since they made it to the shower, these images had transcended
their gossamer existence. They were all memories now,
inescapable. By the end of the first shampoo – I was a slave to
"lather, rinse, repeat," – I was pondering the symbolic significance
of melting German beer houses, cobbled streets, the tidy hole
where Rudy's house once stood, and his unlikely survival of the

terrific blast. Why had I imagined this stuff? Any introspection was complete before the last of the shampoo was in the shower drain, though. I had no interest in interpreting my dreams. There was a time that I had, during the dark ages of my life, when I attended college. I even bought a dream dictionary once. When I still did not get money the third time I dreamed about a dog, I threw away the book.

I skipped breakfast to save time, and had the side door, the one made for people, not cars, to my garage open when a knock sounded at my house's front entrance. I considered answering, then went into the garage with a gesture of dismissal. Nobody worth talking to had been at the front door in months.

The garage was dark. Sighing profoundly, I resolved for the third time that month to wash the windows. I bent down and grabbed the handle on the garage door, and almost wrenched my back when it resisted my firm pull. I yanked harder, attributing the problem to my lack of breakfast instead of a broken door. It is much easier to eat better than it is to fix a broken garage door. It yielded with the extra effort, and I inspected it as it opened, just in case it needed more than an extra helping of Cap'n Crunch. I noticed its heavy wooden sections were warped, like something had twisted it in its tracks. I immediately jumped to the conclusion that my garage had been the victim of an attempted break-in, but I realized that I was too late for work to indulge in such needless domestic anxiety. After all, the door was still closed, so the attempt clearly failed. My Weedwacker and Ford Beater (a.k.a. Escort) were safe.

When I lowered my gaze from the damaged door I nearly swallowed my tongue, choking off the latest version of the "I'm late for work" rant that had begun to flow. I thought it best to hold back the curses as long as the cop that had appeared in front of me was, well, in front of me. I could not prevent my pulse from tripling when my eyes came in contact with the cop's bloodshot baby blues. He did not appear very pleased to be alive that morning, and, in a manner peculiar to law-enforcement officials, he gave me the impression that his bad day was my fault. I forced myself to relax, and struggled to hold his gaze, preventing my eyes from darting suspiciously. I knew I hadn't done anything wrong.

Besides, he was probably there to check on a thief that had attempted to break in through my garage door. He was on my side. He'd better investigate quickly, I thought, or else I'll have to bring him to work to vouch for me.

"Morning, officer," I said in attempted cheer.

"Right," the tired cop rasped, glancing at the clipboard in his hand, "Why didn't you answer your door mister, uh, Creaux?"

"Sorry sir. Thought it was just a neighbor looking for a cup of sugar. I'm late for work."

"I think your neighbors are minding their sweettooths today, sir. Cleaning up."

"Cleaning up what?" I asked. The sharp twitch of his stiff jaw illustrated the error of my question.

"Look buddy," the cop snarled, "I'm too tired for games. I've been at this scene the whole damn night. Now let me ask you some questions so I can get the hell out of here."

This guy was serious. And dusty. I hadn't noticed earlier, since I had been unable to see past the shield and gun. He was enshrouded in a veil of fine black powder. I glanced past him, hoping he didn't think my eyes were darting suspiciously. My driveway sported a matching coat of gray dust. Gray dust, I thought, closing my eyes. That's odd. Suddenly I felt my pulse begin to race again, and this time not because of the cop. I was waking up. I grabbed the officer's upper arm, pulled him close.

"Is my neighbor's house -- the one on the left there -- is it all right?" I whispered into his ear.

"You don't sleep as deep as I thought, mister," the cop said, shaking off my grab, thrusting me out to arm's length, and thankfully not shooting me, "But you got no idea what happened, right? Thought so. Go take a look for yourself. You've answered all my questions. But don't get too close to the site. We don't know how safe the surface is under the dust," he said. He left my garage, then turned, and forced a smile, "Oh. Thank you for your time, *sir*," he finished, emphasizing `sir'. He walked away, raising a cloud of dust in his wake that remained suspended in the still morning air long after he had waded to his patrol car, climbed in, and slammed its door closed.

When his dust finally settled, and the sound of squealing police car tires left my ears, I registered that I was still standing in my garage, frozen in uncertainty. I was not sure about what was real anymore, and wondered if I were still dreaming. They, the dreams, had been this vivid before, I knew. I spun on my heel once, turning 360 degrees in place. When I returned to my original position, everything was where I had left it, including the dust. Someone once told me that you cannot turn around in a dream. If you do, then everything will be different when you come back to where you started. That's what I had been told, anyway. As things grew more real I became less interested in leaving the garage. I opened the car door, felt the cold steel of its rusty handle. I slammed it. It was real. I was real. I was awake. I sat on the hood, considered rationale options that might allow the events I experienced the night before to passage into reality.

I shook my head, determined to deny. Of course I had had dreams that seemed as real as this before. But how could I have thought up that cop? This is real, I decided, but it couldn't relate to my dreams from the previous night; that was impossible. Yeah, my manic reasoning continued, maybe the cop was here about something else. He didn't specify. Besides, all my neighbors were in the dream. If it were real, they surely would have told the cops that I was the one who pulled Rudy out. Clearly they hadn't. I snapped my fingers in a shallow attempt to firm up my conclusion. It had to be, I thought. I was associating my dream last night with the cop's appearance this morning. I was sure I had misunderstood the dust thing. I slapped my thigh, looked at the time and said, "Hell with it, I'm late." I got into my rusty Escort and backed into the driveway.

The car skidded to a stop before it cleared the garage threshold. I leapt out and sprinted toward Rudy's foundation, my heart beating two paces ahead of me, pulling me along. I decked two cops on the way, not noticing them. Others grabbed me before I could hurl myself into Rudy's empty cellar in disbelief.

The morning sun glinted off Rudy's cellar floor, which was dotted with policemen doing apparent forensic work in the empty space. Their primary activity involved squinting closely at nothing, followed by much head shaking and brow scratching. Five investigators were crowded around an aesthetically appealing pedestal near where the front door once was. A sixth was atop the pedestal, jumping up and down, apparently testing its impossible strength using the most scientific of methods. Rudy's yard was cordoned off against the small crowd leaning across the yellow tape. Patrol cars and news crews were everywhere. So were bulldozers, garden tractors, and snow blowers. The neighborhood was gray, coated in a thick layer of dust. Trucks with canvas tops had already begun to cart it away in quantity, but a dent did not appear to have been made yet. I looked back at the pedestal. The gnarled patch of hardwood floor glistened in the morning sunlight. Just enough room for one, unless another clung to him.

The two officers turned me, dragging my limp, confused form to my car. They mechanically muttered soothing words, as if they had dealt with my reaction before. They dumped me into my driver's seat and left me, legs still outside the car. I sat, mindlessly tracing patterns in the dust with my toes. In time I stood, still a little wobbly, but mobile. I marched stoically, eyes straight ahead and carefully avoiding the police officers' annoyed glances, back into Rudy's yard.

I considered pinching and slapping my cheeks, to confirm once more that I was dreaming, but that probably would have pushed my budding relationship with the police right over the edge. I knew the effort would fail anyway: it was still there. Or rather, it was still *not* there. The reality of last night's blast severed my mind. It had happened. I did not want to believe it, but Rudy's house did blow up. Where, I wondered, was Rudy?

The memory of Fritz's flashed through my mind again, but I quickly discarded the horror. No, that was a nightmare, I thought. It had to be. It must have been a reaction to the explosion. I was tired last night. Yes, it was the shock of the blast. In my fear for Rudy I must have blacked out. Maybe a piece of shrapnel hit my head. Where was Rudy?

It wasn't like him to miss this. I asked; the cops could tell me nothing. They apparently were ignorant of the fact that I had dragged Rudy out of the cellar, and I did not volunteer what was probably my own private image. The understandably excited fire chief mentioned that he could not expect a body to survive such a blast, even partially intact. He said there was little hope that Rudy's body, or even a trace of it, would be found. I silently disagreed. I had a feeling Rudy wasn't home last night. He wasn't the type to get himself vaporized. He also was home for a total of about three nights in the last month. Business trips, he said. A big account in Germany. His car was gone, too. Rudy always parked his Porsche in the street. He joked whenever I asked. Said the street was safer. If the car was gone, he was gone. With that reassurance, I shed the situation for the moment and trudged through the dust back to my car. Rudy was okay. He was in for a surprise, but okay. And I was late for work again. Fletcher would not believe my excuse this time.

The somnambulant occupants of the Beaver Toys Building, an ancient brick edifice situated on the corner of 200 acres of lush gardens, were unaffected by my midnight trauma. No one noticed, knew about the incident, or cared. I sat motionless in the fifty square feet of litter that was my windowless third floor office, and somberly reflected on the tired reality of the moment. It would be easy, I was sure, to just fall back into work, lemming-like, and forget about Rudy, his house, and the dreams. My little steel desk was buried in plans for toys, a couple of working models, some drafting tools, and an obsolete PC, all of which I had been successfully ignoring since I sneaked in an hour earlier. Writing assembly instructions for toys was not very high on my list of life priorities that day, but with concentration, I might have brought it back up. In doing so, I could restore sanity and prevent further confrontation, two items very important to the preservation of my boring life. While I brought my psyche back to Earth, I wondered why I thought of lemmings.

I glanced at the day's undone tasks. If I had arrived at work on time I would be half done with the instructions for Magenta Man's racer. I wasn't interested in explaining to the boss why it was 11:00 and not a word had been written. So far luck was with me. I hadn't seen Fletcher yet. I hoped to be able to avoid seeing him all day, which was a fortunate possibility in this company. I did not feel like writing about, or projecting the image of writing about, the assembly of pedalcars. There was still too much to try not to think about. I sat back in my swivel chair, stared into space.

As I considered the grimy ceiling tiles above me, I caught some peripheral movement nearby. I casually pulled my gaze down, refocused out my open doorway. Nancy sat at her desk across the hall, waving frantically. Her brown eyes, wide with mock terror, were betrayed by a bright smile. I liked Nancy. She was smart, reliable, and dull, the right kind of person to work with to get something done. She was helpful, too. I caught the sign, thrust half the paperwork under my desk, grabbed a pencil, and mussed my hair. Mr. Fletcher's belly appeared at the edge of my doorway, paused for a moment. Then it moved, and was followed a moment later by the rest of the Vice President of Product Development. He glanced into my office as he strolled by. I struggled to avoid eye contact and the commensurate pleasantries, and hoped to look as busy and boring as possible. It worked, and Fletcher continued on without comment. After I heard him start up a loud and useless conversation with Ira Jones down the hall, I leaned back in my chair and sighed. Another morning in Disneyland, I thought. My neighbor's house blows up, I'm late for work, and the boss sees all is fine.

Chapter Three

I hate it when I forget to shave.
I had been at work for two hours before I noticed that I neglected my sprouting nubs during my semi-numb flight from home that morning. While rubbing the coarse bristles with an almost detached curiosity I decided, for the fourth time in twenty minutes, that it was okay to be unkempt that day. If what happened the night before really did. Happen.

I sighed and resumed the random shuffle of meaningless work about my desk that I had repeatedly attempted to begin since my belated arrival that morning. I had actually tapped a few viable words into my computer, but the morass I was trapped in that morning did not leave much room for the mundane. The simple reality of a day's labor was not enough to quell memories of the complex, unreal stuff I had endured the night before. Even the hollow creativity needed to write the instructions meant to help hapless parents assemble outdated toys that precious few kids wanted failed to mask or even shadow the images that continued to dance just an inch behind my eyes. The busy work should have done the trick, but not this time. Whether it was a dream, real, or a psychotic episode, last night happened in my mind. My memory was adamant. I saw what I saw; endured what I witnessed. I was reluctantly acquiescing to my battered instincts.

As a rule, I always believe what I see. Always. Except, I prayed, for last night. No, I repeated to myself, I did see it. It was true. My half-hearted attempt to keep my head submerged in the soft, insular sand that was my life had failed. My world could not keep out last night's drama, and its portent. A big hairy monster was tapping on my shoulder, encroaching on my comfortable, empty little life. The shock of rough stubble on my twitching chin lent credence to my apparent break from my heretofore Sargasso existence.

For the hundredth time, I asked myself why the hell had I come to work at all. I had known when I wallowed my car out of the dusty driveway that work wouldn't help. I perhaps should have called in sick. Or insane, maybe. Oh, well, I replied to myself again, I'm here; it's best to deal with it.

I carefully reviewed the headlines on CNN's website again, still slightly disappointed that the explosion next door hadn't made the big time. I absently hit the "refresh" button once more, but no new news had been uploaded in the last three minutes. I spent some time staring at the draft of the instructions I was being paid to write, but that day my work could not rise above its status as a bunch of inconsequential lines that I simply could not care about. Then I felt my chin again. That cycle had persisted repeatedly, until I rubbed my itchy eyes, fatigued by my memories' incessant clamor to be heard.

I had been able to avoid my co-workers all morning. I hadn't spoken to anyone, not interested even in a typical empty greeting. Nancy had retired her questioning looks an hour earlier. I could have sat down and told her all about it, I was sure. She was the type. I also knew that I couldn't. If I did, I would not have ended my tale with the hole next door. I would have continued, describing the dreams. Fritz's. Max. Nancy would either have lost interest or shied away from my apparent mania, never to return. I desired neither, so I ignored her until she finally shut the door to her office. I had forgotten that she had a door; it had been open so long. I assumed that in time she would muster courage to come to me, demanding an explanation. She would be deeply, sincerely concerned, and would bear an offer to help, or at least present a shoulder to support my pains and catch possible tears. But she would wait until tomorrow, maybe Friday. A nice girl, Nancy. Always caring. Too bad we never got together.

Well, not really. She probably would become quite dull should higher levels of intimacy be approached. Fundamentally dull, like the work I could no longer internalize. I massaged my neck, wondered: Why the hell did I ever take this job? Hunger, I figured. I had to take it. It was all I could do after Cassie died.

The *Times* couldn't keep my catatonic carcass on the payroll forever.

Why did she try to fix the oven? Why didn't I? The new one was on order; three days away. Shit. You'd think that after two years, and Fritz's, I would have had some new questions with which to wrench my soul. I suppose I didn't need any; the old ones still worked quite well. I forgot to shave then, too. For weeks. I rubbed my beard.

I hate it when I forget to shave.

Some poor child's dad was destined to lose his mind on the few instructions I managed to write that morning. Tab `A' would never meet slot `B' in that pedal car. The rest of my assignments lay untouched. Mr. Fletcher had presented himself just once, seconds after I shoved another quarter of the pile of never to be finished projects under my desk. He smiled, shook his head at my shadow, and continued down the hall. That was his job, to continue down halls. I wondered how he maintained the beach ball under his vest. He should have sweated it off years earlier.

By 12:30, I noticed that people were making special trips past my office to watch me slouch over my desk, diddling with my office supplies. Strange, what people find interesting. Of course, Beaver Toys was it for the wretches. They had to take advantage of any excitement, or hint of it, that crossed their horizon. That day I desperately wanted to join them. If a hairy beard made their day, God bless them for it. I would have gladly traded their mediocrity for Rudy's hole and my dream. Fritz's left my thoughts only when the shadow in the Cessna crowded it out. I absently punched Rudy's number on my telephone. Silly thing to do, I thought; what was left of the line must certainly have fried off at the pole.

My hand jerked on the first ring, forcing the plastic receiver to bounce against my temple. A rush of panic swept over me before I smiled. It must have been the wrong number. The telephone was inches from being safely back on the hook when Rudy answered.

"Hello?" he said. Whoa, I thought. This can't be.

"Rudy?" I said, bruising my ear with the receiver.

"Of course," he said in his usual easy tone, "Who else would answer my phone?"

"But you don't have a phone, Rudy. Or a place to use one," I said. My voice was steady. Oddly, there was no panic, "Am I asleep again?" I rubbed my beard. It did feel a little numb.

"Alex, if you were asleep you wouldn't have been able to call me. What did you want?"

"Nothing. Sorry, I over reacted. I must have dialed your cell phone…"

"I have a cell phone?"

"Shut up. Just shut up and let me believe."

"That's fine with me," Rudy said. I could almost hear the slightly condescending smile I knew he wore. Silence followed. I was about to hang up when I remembered that I had told him to shut up.

"I guess here is the point where I'm supposed to look for some answers," I said, "But I have no questions."

"You will. You will… Listen, I'm free for the next hour, how about some lunch?"

"That means you're alive enough to eat something?"

"Of course I am, Alex. I'm not the type to be vaporized. I'll pick you up out front in a few minutes."

"Fine," I said, listening to him hang up. I disconnected, then immediately dialed his number again. A tinny recording suggested I hang up and try again. In a moment, I put the wet receiver down. I looked at my watch. It was 12:40. Time had passed for the call. I did not imagine it. I was all too awake. At least I thought I was. It was hard to tell the difference. I gave my cheek a pinch, to the amusement of Bates from Printing, who had come by to see my beard.

By 1:00, I was ready to see Rudy. I remembered that we had barely mentioned his house. I assumed he might not want to talk about it. I decided to hold back inquiries about it for the time being. There had to be a good chance that it was too much for him to discuss so soon. I stood outside the Beaver Toys building, nodding to the smokers assembled, as always, by the large ashtray set outside the door. They weren't interested in my haggard demeanor – the smokers had their club, something important to do. I liked that. I leaned against the brown cinderblock wall, soaked in the warm sunlight while I waited for my good, and happily not dead, friend to arrive.

His car glided noiselessly to the curb. The passenger door swung open as it stopped. I got in.

"So Rudy, what the hell happened to your house?" I asked before I had completely fallen into the soft leather seat.

"Thought you might ask again. You know I told you last night." Rudy said. I looked at him. His eyes searched straight ahead. He was saying, "Where to? There's that Italian place right around the corner. Their garlic would suit your beard." I didn't hear him. The blood that was roaring in my ears blocked him out. I shook my head, turned to Rudy.

"Jesus Christ, Rudy!" I cried, "That was a dream last night. How the hell would you know what I asked you?"

"Or we could just go for burgers. Nothing fancy," he said, taking no apparent notice of my outburst. That was all he needed to say. I understood what he meant, and calmed myself. Answers would come.

I was silent as Rudy pulled into a McDonald's. When we climbed out, the car doors closed and locked behind us. The restaurant was packed, but we were at the front of our line almost immediately. Rudy always picks the correct line. While we waited at the counter for our Mac-whatever's, Rudy flirted cheerfully with the chubby young woman who took his order and money. I remained silent until we were seated at the table and the french-fries had been salted.

"Was last night real?" I asked, fiddling idly with a soggy bun. Rudy looked up, chewing. He smiled Rudy's smile, 10,000 smiles old—one corner of his mouth curled slightly more than the other, a few teeth showing, and gray eyes that never acknowledged his projected pleasure.

"Real? Depends how you look at it, I suppose. Was *what* last night real?"

"Everything. The tavern. Fritz's. The fire. Max. I know your house really went up, I saw that this morning. But what about everything else?" I wanted to stop mid-sentence when he clouded at the mention of Fritz's, but I could not hold back my thought. It was a good decision. He was placid before I mouthed the last word. He tilted back in his chair—not an easy trick when you consider that McDonald's bolts their furniture to the floor.

"It all happened, if that's what you mean. That doesn't mean that you can watch the six o'clock news to see Fritz's destroyed again, but it did burn. You were there, weren't you?"

"Yes. No. I thought it was just a dream."

"Don't ever put `just' in front of that word when you're talking to me, Alex. I might find some very un-just vantage from which to sway you."

"You may already have," I said.

"True. By the way, I neglected to thank you for the rescue last night."

"From your house? It seemed like you could have walked out without my broken back thrown in."

"No, I didn't mean my house, though I am grateful for that shove too; I did need it. I meant the Cessna."

I don't remember if I excused myself from the plastic table or if I simply left. I found myself a mile closer to my office before I realized I was gone. Rudy, my dreams, or Rudy and my dreams had gotten me into something I knew nothing about. I wanted to know no more.

I knew he wasn't in advertising. Ad men enjoy talking about their work, and I never heard him breathe a word about it. Rudy did not even watch TV. I always knew he was into something very different, but consistently chose not to investigate. I felt it wasn't my business. That held true at least, until his basement hobbies moved into my life. He tried to tell me a dozen times what he was doing in that room in the cellar. I called it a sound room. He called it a desensory room, a word with which Mr. Webster certainly is unfamiliar. I never listened. I never prided myself on openness to ideas. He usually said, apparently in understatement, that I would get it all, in time.

Once I thought he was dead. I had barged into his house one summer afternoon, looking for a ride to his beach house. I shouted for him, but got no response. Rudy did not appear to be home. I knew he was around somewhere, though, because his black Porsche was parked outside. I descended the carpeted stairs to his room in the basement. Remembering what he told me, I followed the narrow hallway past the spotless laundry room, and stopped halfway to the workroom in the back. The wall appeared to be unbroken wood paneling, but I remembered the trick. I felt around the veneer, and found a slight dimple. I filled the dimple with my thumb, and pushed. Part of the wall slid out of the way, revealing the steel door that opened on Rudy's sound room. I turned the knob, was mildly surprised to find it unlocked. I peered in. It was dark inside. Not dark. Black. There's a difference. Utterly silent. I listened for him fruitlessly. I couldn't even hear myself breathe.

I found the light switch behind some padding near the door. The Velcro rip set my nerves dancing as I triggered indirect lighting somewhere in the padded ceiling. Rudy was reclined in that chair I lusted after. It was a thin chase lounge, built to Rudy's form, and upholstered in a two-inch thick velour. It could change temperature as he did, and he said it would subtly and constantly alter its shape to allow proper blood flow. Under the chair was a small, impossibly silent fan that worked air down through baffles in the ceiling, somehow not breezing past him to the padded floor and vents beneath that carried on to a sort of French drain, finally to a vent outside. The setup helped his dreams, he had said. Funny, I had noted, my dreams never needed any help. I know, he had said quietly, head bent.

He had looked dead that summer afternoon. Pale, eyes upturned in his head. I knew the look, and he had it. He did not smell dead, but that could have been the fan sucking his scent away. When I greeted him from the doorway, he did not answer. I approached, shaking my head at the lack of sound from my own steps. I yanked his blue T-shirt, and shook him softly. He didn't wake up, didn't even react. I touched my violently shaking index finger to his neck, felt for a pulse. Some searching revealed a faint murmur. My medical knowledge was and is minimal, but he had seemed comatose. I shook him violently, tried mouth to mouth, and then shook him again. I started slapping him, hard. He caught my third slap mid-swing, and calmly thanked me. We went to the beach house with two six-packs, without ever discussing the incident.

Now he had me walking, probably running before I realized where I was, back to work from McDonald's. I was retreating from a truth about which I wished to know nothing. Rudy needed me. He said nothing to verbalize this need, but I was getting the hint clearly enough. He could not manage with his fancy closet and cool chair alone anymore. He had to draw me into his work, as he had always hinted he would. He needed me in the dream, apparently my only dream, last night. I helped him, and was glad to oblige. Hell, I really didn't even know I was putting myself out. I remembered my easy confidence in the dream, and that I didn't question my role, or my innate ability to fill it. I had unbridled confidence in myself throughout the Cessna scenario because it was a dream. There is no doubt in dreams. Reality, however, had plenty of room for it, and for fear.

I increased my pace, resisting the urge to run blindly again. Like Rudy's house, my world was collapsing around me, and doing so excessively fast. Normally I required time to absorb new problems, get familiar with them, and then act. A week or two, maybe a month would pass before I dealt with any new situation, especially the tough ones. Normally, after a comfy buffer of lapsed time I could sit down with Rudy and discuss what he wanted. And that normalcy, I decided in the security of my solitary pace down the sunny suburban street, was what I would have. A nice gap between last night and my next encounter with Rudy. He might be able to draw me in; I might even invite his conscription, but it would be on my terms.

Suddenly feeling quite dignified, I tucked in my shirt and strolled back into the Beaver Toys building. I stretched casually in the lobby, and then headed for my office. An afternoon of hard work writing things that just didn't matter would encourage clarification. Who knows? I thought, maybe I'm still dreaming.

Chapter Four

My last afternoon at the office passed with no further surreal events, and precious few real moments worth noting. Though the hours passed in a general blur, I did remember carefully drafting a vertical waterfall and telling Nancy to shove her compassion up her ass. I also remembered apologizing profusely, and carefully wiping a tear from her eye, moments later. I whiled away the hours by doodling, refining my Free Cell skills, and avoiding Mr. Fletcher's frequent surveillance swings. Since I could no longer feign labor and was simply sitting at my desk, staring into space, I was consumed by guilt each time I saw his vested belly appear at the edge of my doorway. I attempted several times to rationalize my guilt into exile. I thought I could do so because my behavior at work, and the job itself, had lost any semblance of priority that they might have once had. However, I had been trapped in the world of middle class labor far too long to immediately rise above the base feelings that laborers must endure when their bosses wander unannounced into their workspace. It was a territorial statement, a reality check made and transmitted by the employer to helpless employees that clarified both who was in control, and how easy it was to forget that when the boss was safely ensconced in his office.

The act of containing my basal fear of Fletcher exposing my thinly veiled lack of productivity was about as close to thought as I could venture that afternoon. Thought is an exercise I find easy to refrain from at the best of times, and recent events had convinced such painful activity to take a back seat to cozy numbness. The combined forces of the empty purgatory of work and my innate ability to run away from intellectual review successfully anesthetized me to my recent past. I was actually placid during the short drive home that began at exactly five o'clock. I was even humming a tune until I approached my neighborhood. Normally the humming would get louder when I saw the traffic light above the intersection to my street. As usual, it changed to red before I could make the last left turn. When I slowed my car to a stop, the tune faded from my lips. I tried to revive it, but the sound I produced was contrived, and I let my last gasp at nonchalance slip away. The time for that was probably over anyway. My hands shook a bit as I waited to turn onto my street. I craned my neck, but couldn't see past Nate and Ruby Sturbridge's ramshackle Victorian that dominated the corner. Everything that I could see through the leafy veil of their busy garden appeared fine. From this happily obscured viewpoint my neighborhood was clean, even inviting in the golden light of the late afternoon sun. Since Rudy's yard was out of my line of sight, I knew I could cling to yesterday's world for a few more seconds before the truth would smack me upside the head once more. I still coddled a tiny fantasy, that my last sixteen hours really were all a dream. I convinced a portion of my mind to believe that I would turn the corner and, bing-badda-boom, there would be Rudy's perfect old house with the perfect car out in front of the perfect lawn.

The light changed. Reluctant to proceed, I waited to make the turn until I was jarred by the angry honks of the impatient sport-ute driver in line behind me. Once moving, I tried to focus only on the road, but I registered that the house next door was still missing as soon as the Sturbridge house no longer eclipsed Rudy's hole. Though the city had done a fine job cleaning the neighborhood, their efforts did nothing to clear my confusion about what was, and what was not, real. Indeed, the official cleanup was so thorough that I was able to allow myself to imagine that someone had simply picked up Rudy's house and carted it away.

I slowed as I passed Rudy's recently vacant lot. If I didn't I would have overshot my driveway, but the pace still felt significant. I forced my eyes to the right. I could feel their resistance to my desire to scan Rudy's yard, but it had to be done so that I could be sure. Of course I was sure.

The low sun scooped light from Rudy's cellar, creating triangles of darkness that had nothing to conceal. The cops were gone. Kids were playing in the hole. Some seemed to be fruitlessly searching for souvenirs of the blast, others were jumping their bicycles off the lawn and into the basement's empty shadows. I shook my head slowly, drove into my driveway. The Escort's tires chirped when I absently skidded to a halt inches from the garage door.

I paused for a clammy minute or two, staring intently at the section of garage door that loomed inches from the Escort's dirty hood. I struggled to coax from my fraying nerves sufficient strength to exit the safety of my car and re-enter the manic vortex that I still longed to somehow sidestep. It was out there. The bizarre intrigue I faced was beyond the steel confines of my car. Adventure lurked nearby, perhaps inside Rudy's hole, or even in my garage. But it was outside the car, a safe familiar place that I was now reluctant to exit. I did not want adventure. I just wanted the potpies that I had burned the day before. I realized sullenly that my encounter with Rudy at lunch I had depleted all of the resolve that I had previously convinced myself I possessed. He had tapped my strength, and diminished my ability to cling comfortably to the mundane world. What an asshole, I thought, though I was not sure to whom my slight referred.

When I did manage to fling open my car door, I discovered that the journey from familiar security to all too familiar fear was still incomplete. My rubbery, uncooperative knees forced me to swing my legs to the ground like an invalid, and shuffle clumsily to my feet. It was embarrassing, but I was moving. I trudged along my weed-ridden (but clean!) path to my front door, never once looking over my shoulder into Rudy's yard. My keys jingled as my distant, quivering hands tried to work one into the lock on my front door. When the correct key finally slid home and the jangling stopped, I paused to listen to an odd noise that had been obscured by my clamor: the Escort's engine was still rattling in the driveway. Having grown up in the 1970's, I at first sighed at another wretched car dieseling long after I shut it off. Then I remembered that new cars don't usually run without keys in them. Though it was old, this model was not from the 1970's. I stepped toward it, but the car shut off before I could get closer to it. I regarded it silently, wondering if I had imagined the phenomenon, and slightly angered by the little car's betrayal. I used the moment as an excuse to postpone reentry into the house. I rubbed my hair, sat on the front steps, and hid in the late afternoon shadow cast by my house. I didn't mind the obscurity, sure that I looked better when masked by gentle darkness. My tapping feet remained in the afternoon light, cut off from the rest of my body. They seemed normal enough. I wiggled them, scuffed marks on the slate walk. I sighed, and rested my head in my hands.

I had forgotten to shave. I imagined my car was still running. I verbally abused one of the few people I knew who still wanted to know me. I avoided the reality/nightmare that Rudy had thrust into my face. I deserved to be lost in shadows. My hands were actually strained from shaking. They had never stopped, all day.

Except at McDonald's. And when I sketched that weird waterfall.

My disheveled reaction confused me. I'd always been a difficult person to excite. The explosion next door was earth-shaking, yes. Literally. Shattering? No. I had certainly dealt with calamity before, from the devastation of Cassie's exit to the final abandonment of hope that accompanied my job interview with Beaver Toys. Cassie had rattled me, nearly to death, but my hands had held steady then. So why did they shake now? Thinking about it from my perch in the shadows on my cold concrete stoop, I wondered if the only respite from quivering that my hands enjoyed since yesterday came when I was with Rudy. It was as though his absence, or something about it, unnerved me.

After the evening shadow had engulfed my shoes, I stood up and resigned my self to venturing into my house. The move was bold because it initiated my attempt to have a normal post workday evening, but I could not feel pride. The fact that I trembled while opening my own front door implied that there would be little domestic activity that evening.

I made a vain attempt at a typical dinner, but I couldn't stomach the Salisbury steak TV dinner. Who can? I threw it out the window, still frozen, for the squirrels. Dismissing dinner, I gathered my martini materials (Bombay gin, dry vermouth, a plastic shaker filled with ice, and my oversized martini glass) and parked myself in front of the TV.

Upon switching it on, I was pleased to see that the TV was already tuned to a re-run channel. I left it there, happy to know that I would have to do nothing but stare at material I'd seen countless times before. I would have had to pay attention were it the History Channel, or one of those learning channels from which I regularly surfed away. No, the re-run channel was better than Prozac, especially in combination with a good martini. I generously dumped the Bombay on the ice, waved the open bottle of vermouth over the shaker, shook, poured, and looked at the clock.

The TV was unfortunately not able to provide the solace I sought. It instead became a backdrop for my memories, a reflection of the dreams. I guess anything would have at that point. I left it on, too comfortable, too tired to drop my finger on the power button, perhaps too frightened of the silence that would ensue. If I still had my shoes on I would have thrown one at it to at least make a gesture.

In my quiet haze I spent some more time wondering about the source of my fear. Rudy had explained what could develop out of his sound room work a dozen times. I had listened marginally, picking up enough to be startled, yes, but not terrified. I sighed, realizing that if I had shown an ounce of trepidation then, I would probably not be as disheveled as I was today. Hell, if I had really thought about it, I probably would have moved.

I finished martini number three, tossing the glass to the carpet. Three tries with no results is a waste of good gin. I leaned back in my recliner, pulled the afghan Cassie made for me three years earlier snugly against my chin, and settled my heavy eyes on a familiar episode of the Honeymooners. Ralph was begging Alice for money, insisting that his scheme couldn't fail. He only needed a forty-dollar investment. Alice was starting her standard degradation speech when a familiar sharp knock sounded on their door. As usual, Norton entered before they responded. At least, the guy that walked in was sporting Norton's clothes, gestures, and lines (he was poking fun at Ralph's dream). It wasn't Norton, however. It was Rudy.

The scene around Norton/Rudy froze. He tilted his head toward me, touched the brim of his cap and stared for a moment. Then he smiled, waved, and shouted, "How ya doin' Alex-boy?" and stepped out of the screen. His right leg came first. Then his hands reached through and grabbed the edges of the screen. For a flash he was an arm's length self portrait snapped through a wide-angle lens, then Rudy was standing in my living room with me. My dreary walls were gone, replaced by a panoramic view of Earth from a few hundred miles in space. Rudy smiled and pointed to a meteor that screamed past, chased by two lovesick elves.

"Nice touch," he said.

"Thanks," I replied, shaking his outstretched hand. It was still grimy from the sewer. I continued, "Am I ever to have a dream to myself again, Rudy?"

"Not if we can help it," Max called from behind me as she swung into view aboard a winged Chrysler. Real, feathered, wings. She leapt off the hood, landed on her feet, long legs spread. Her red hair splashed in the sunlight, showered over her loose blue silk tunic. Boris Vallejo would have a field day with this woman, I decided. She brushed a lock from her high cheek, said:

"Rudy thinks he can use you, so we keep bothering you."

"I know he'll help," Rudy corrected.

"How do you get in my dreams?" I asked, feeling a silly answer coming.

"You must think you're useful too." Max said. Not so silly.

"What the hell can I do?" I asked.

"We don't know yet," Rudy said. He was floating above me, suspended by steel cables that were bolted securely to a fancy leather harness he wore with style. The cables met at a single ring high overhead, and that ring was welded to the underside of Rudy's Porsche.

"You can talk to us in your dreams; that's something," Max added, heading gleefully toward a glittering Ferris wheel.

"That is something, Alex," Rudy repeated, releasing the cables with a single strike of his fist against his chest. He retained his elevated stature, though, and continued speaking while buttoning worn chaps to his thighs, "Now if you'll excuse me, I've a roundup to see to." He leapt on a rocket-powered wombat, waved his white ten-gallon hat at me, and disappeared into the Sun. I never realized before that I knew what a wombat even looked like.

"Wait," I called after him, my voice echoing, "What the hell has to be done that I'm useful for?"

The Sun exploded on Rudy's impact. The expected flash of supernoval radiance compelled me to turn the other way. As I did I caught my foot on a willow root. I fell onto cool moss, nearly sliding into a small babbling brook. Sunlight, filtered by the thick oak canopy overhead, dappled the ground and water. As I sat on the ground brushing the green turf from my denim thighs, I heard a familiar giggle nearby. A still pool of black water had appeared, just upstream from my soggy but not unpleasant position. Centered in the pool was Cassie, feigning embarrassment at my accidental voyeurism by flattening her bare breasts with open palms and squatting in the water. Then she smiled, rose swiftly from her liquid modesty with a delightful splash, and walked slowly out of the stream. Crystal water spilled down her shimmering body. Her smooth skin was clean, pink, and nothing like the shade of purple I had last seen it possess – it was completely alive. She hovered over me for a moment, and then shook her head at my reticence. She held out her hand, releasing one of her breasts with a hormone-wrenching jiggle, and waited for me to wrap her slender fingers in mine. Not being completely stupid, I did. She helped me up. I held her. She was warm, and I could feel her flat stomach rhythmically pressing against mine as she breathed. She breathed! Her presence felt real – completely real. I held her tighter. Our naked bodies felt right together. They always had.

"Alex," she whispered, her lips brushing my ear, "I want you back." I held words back, sure that anything from me, any question, would break the spell. I knew that this was a dream, a painfully fragile dream, but I easily ignored the thought. I was content to clutch the moment instead, for as long as it would last, without daring, or bothering, to question it. Cassie then put her hands against my chest and straightened her arms, forcing a space between us. She stared into my eyes, and tried to smile through her misty eyes. Finally her shoulders sagged, and she turned away, head bent. She gently walked up the riverbank, without turning back.

I tried to chase after her, but my distant feet were locked in thick black mud, preventing pursuit. I noticed absently that I didn't shout her name. I knew there was nothing to prevent her silent walk up a mountain path to a great castle that loomed above us, so I just watched for as long as I was able. Her red satin gown billowed in blue moonlight, glowing before the blackness of the open gate. She disappeared into the shadows of the tower. The tower retracted with an electric whir into the black mountain, which in turn sagged slightly before it folded up and fell into the trunk of Max's Chrysler. I could no longer feel Cassie's presence. I wanted to follow the scene's morbid example and fold up myself.

"Captain!"

"Yes Scotty," I said, turning to the engineering station of the Bridge.

"Captain, if we push her any further, she'll blow!"

I watched the view screen. Cassie, clad in blue jeans, my old T-shirt, and plastic gloves, was crouched near the oven. A hand rested gently on my shoulder.

"She's dead, Jim," Bones said.

I started awake to the sound of phasers and dying Klingons. I retrieved my glass, filled it again. I sat back in my chair, sighed deeply. This double life not two days old was wearing thin. I resolved to sit out the remainder of this night. I would watch the rest of Star Trek, then perhaps read a book. Or two. I was asleep before the next commercial, and rested undisturbed until morning.

As far as I could tell.

Chapter Five

I leaned my forehead against the cold, hard, and happily very real glass of my bedroom window, and gazed through groggy eyes at the world outside. A chilly early spring rain had fallen before I had wrestled my burning eyes open that morning. Though it must have been brief, the weather did wash away any dust that the Sanitation Department had missed in the amazing cleanup they had performed the day before. I had to smile, knowing that somewhere a sanitation "official" was looking out his bedroom window, scratching his head, and wishing he had waited a day to assess the cleanup.

The morning was gray and cool, but blessed with enough sunlight to create those sharp contrasts of brilliance and shadow peculiar to the moments of first light. I found the ambience fitting for my mood. I had called Mr. Fletcher before dawn to tell him I was sick. Though I had intended to safely leave a message, he was already at his desk and picked up his phone. He insisted I do my work assignment at home. I agreed before I hung up on him. He actually cared about those instructions. Odd man.

I had spent the last few waking hours waiting for dawn, looking for things to do (that did not include watching TV) that would pass the time until there was enough daylight to explore Rudy's foundation. I spent an unusual amount of time dressing, and then enjoyed a two-week-old Sunday Times over my protracted breakfast of Sugar Pops and coffee. I felt good about myself, and my newfound resolve, at least until the cereal was gone.

Had I been my usual sensible self the day before, I would have had the sense to stay home and investigate the phenomenon then. An immediate study of the aftermath may have made the last

24 hours slightly more bearable, or at least believable, and I could have avoided wasting time at work. My denial had cost me a day, and more pain than I felt comfortable remembering. I had decided, before dawn, that I was through with denying and escaping. I resolved, at dawn, to open my eyes slightly – a weak squint, perhaps – to Rudy's world. It seemed I had few options, from the standpoint of my dreams. I felt secure after that decision, though I knew it had been based on words only. I felt obliged to bolster my bravado with action. Since I had no idea where Rudy was, I opted to search his place. It was a nice idea; since there was virtually nothing to search, I would be done by lunchtime. I peeled my face from the window and coaxed suddenly leaden legs to begin the expedition.

The neighborhood to the right of my front door had regained its composure. The quiet street was once again clean, inviting, comfortable, and littered with kids. Some of them stood at the corner of Dayton Street, waiting for their school bus. Though I was hesitant to look, as if the view from outside was different from what I saw through my window, I was relieved to see that the left side was about the same. There were kids on the corner of Elm, waiting for another bus. Suburban systems are amazing.

The street was clean, normal, and apparently as refreshingly dull and as packed with middle class security as ever. A robin chirped in my crabapple tree. I picked up the morning paper, thrown unerringly on my front porch at seven a.m. daily. I wanted to toss it into the house before I began my investigation of Rudy's place. Leave a paper on the front porch too long and someone from a bad neighborhood might steal it – middle class security and honor only go so far. An absent glance to the front page revealed what could have been my neighbor Fred's distinctive belly protruding in the lead photo. I paused, scanned the caption.

It was Fred's belly, all right, and his pipe. They were the foreground of a four-column photo of Rudy's place. The Banner headline read:

LOCAL HOUSE MYSTERIOUSLY DESTROYED
ARSON SUSPECTED

No surprise that the Bugle took a day to get the story to print. I sat down to read:

The home of Rudolph Frisset, 111 Scenic Drive, disappeared in an explosion Tuesday night, according to neighbors. The explosion came suddenly, startling the quiet neighborhood. Frisset's two-family home was completely destroyed. The rest of the neighborhood suffered no damage, except for a shower of black dust that took crews all day Wednesday to remove.

"I was walking my dog at the time," said neighbor Frederick Johnson, "Then there was this explosion. I thought it was the end of the world. Funny   thing, though. I was right next to Frisset's place when it went, and all I got was dirty."

Other eyewitnesses also mentioned minimal damage. Many cited a lack of flame, or heat, though some disagree. No damage was reported beyond Frisset's lot. Frisset himself managed to escape unaided and unhurt. He was unavailable for comment, as he left the scene immediately.

"He managed to be standing on the only part that remained intact," said Fire Marshall Jim Curren, "Truly amazing." When asked about the mystery of the explosion he responded, "No mystery. Furnaces go up like that sometimes. Especially gas."

Curren stated, however, that the cause of the fire is still under investigation. Arson is suspected.

Arson. If they only knew. And what the hell did they mean 'unaided?' I was not the type to seek glory, but it would have been nice if someone noticed me. I bit my lower lip at that thought: the cops never mentioned my daring rescue either. Not even to me. All of the neighbors couldn't have forgotten that I was there. I looked up and down the street in retrospect

Yes, they could have.

I looked past Fred's grizzled neck to the picture of the hole again. It looked like an excavation for a new dwelling; clean and hopeful. That thought helped fortify my morning's mission by lending a positive flavor to it. A new house would be a more comfortable place to search than a bomb crater. And again, there would be nothing to be found. I was not without hope, or anxiety, that something was there, however. Occasionally a builder draws figures or small diagrams on rough walls of what he has in mind for the finished product. Perhaps I would find a picture. I left the newspaper inside. Hands in denim pockets, I strolled to Rudy's foundation.

The low, distant sun bathed it in shadow. It looked like the footprint of a square-pawed behemoth. I stood for ten minutes at the edge, pondering once more the merit of my endeavor. I touched off my fingers as I listed the reasons to go home: the cops had spent the previous day down there, they must have retrieved any useful debris that remained; then the children took over. Kids are experts at finding anything worth trading or treasuring. They miss nothing. I would not find anything on the black marble floor. Therefore the floor became the ideal place to search. I would enjoy finding nothing. And, since I had only used two fingers, I was unable to rationalize my way home. So, I would continue, for a while. Then maybe I could grab a nap after a hard morning's work. At that point I would risk the dreams with Rudy. I felt secure in them anyway. I was in charge. I laughed at my bravado again.

My hesitance to continue my journey lagged for about an hour after I had reached the cinderblock rim of Rudy's former residence. I sat dangling my legs into Rudy's cellar, watching my legs slowly emerge from shadow. I had just finished studying the walls, and found myself unable to picture the old colonial that had so recently rested on the shiny blocks. I supposed I simply didn't pay enough attention, that nothing was important enough for my time, or, more important, my energy. If that were the case for all things, I asked myself again, then why didn't Rudy take control in my dreams? It was his department. He had to have the capability to dominate my sleep, to draw this "contribution" from me without these party games. And I certainly couldn't have cared about it as much as he did – nobody blew up my house. I made a mental note to inquire the next time he appeared.

The sun had arced higher in the clear morning sky. Its heat burned off the morning dew, and its light illuminated Rudy's cellar. Mysteries lifted with the waning shadows. By noon the basement resembled a drained swimming pool with a custom island near its center. Any exploratory zeal still burning in me began under the bright sunlight's revelation that there was simply nothing left down there. I gathered my resolve anyway and, without another thought, dropped off my perch into Rudy's hole. My feet skated in two directions on the slick surface, and I landed, howling in pain, in a groin-wrenching and ungraceful split. I bit my lip. I was not interested in attracting the attention of my neighbors. I writhed quietly for a moment, then pulled myself to my feet.

I hoped nobody had witnessed my gaff. Except for the occasional cup of sugar, I rarely spoke to the neighbors, but there was a certain suburban decorum that had to be maintained. Rudy must have broken fifteen rules when he blew up his house. Of course, neighborhoods like mine have a disaster clause, and appropriate procedures. Someone would be by soon to collect unwanted clothing for him. They would do this whether they wanted to or not; it was the rules. They probably hoped he would fail to turn up, to save them some trouble. I shook my head of such empty thoughts and set about my inspection.

I found nothing, including my balance. I steadied myself against the thin, but remarkably strong, fluted base of the pedestal. Gripping the base with both hands (it was cold to the touch, like steel, though I knew it could only be plaster), I hauled myself to my feet and reestablished my bearings. I centered my view on a six-foot wide indent on the nearest wall, and decided that that was the space that the front entrance once occupied. From there I imagined the path to the cellar door, then the flight of stairs down to my level. As I was facing, Rudy's sound room would have been a left turn from the base, a few paces—there. I skated to the spot. There was a slight dimple where the ducting had been channeled beneath the cement floor. The force of the blast had fused the duct's foam grate marble-smooth, consistent with the rest of the floor. But it had left a dimple.

It was a shame to lose that chair, I thought. Rudy was probably done with it by now (and he most certainly was at this point), and that meant that it could have been safely stashed in my house. A year ago he said I could have it soon, if I needed to be that comfortable watching TV. I never pressed him, and he never mentioned it again. If I had bothered him, he probably would have given it to me. I laughed, amused by my simple greed. I was behaving like a child scavenging a recently deceased great-uncle's attic. I carefully leaned my back against the pedestal, then slid slowly to the floor. I smiled, feeling strangely at ease in thinking about comfortably materialistic things for a change.

A shadow swept over me, tempting me to involuntarily duck. A crow lighted on the oak floor above me. I had never been so close to a crow. They are sizeable birds. Its call — "crow" — brought me to my feet. It did not leave when I skittered on the floor just below it. It cocked its head to regard me with agitation. I wondered if it was Rudy in disguise. It would be like him to turn into a bird. He was of the Livingston Seagull breed.

"Sorry Alex, that's not my style," Rudy said, hand on my shoulder, "Birds are too dirty, and not terribly bright. I'd probably fly into a picture window on my first possession."

My pulse paused, but I remained outwardly steady. I turned nonchalantly, rolling my eyes. Rudy was next to me. His hand still rested lightly on my shoulder. His touch steadied me on several levels, but I was not sure if he understood that. I was also strangely certain that that sort of steadying was not his purpose.

"Rudy," I said, smiling, "Good to see you. Am I dreaming again?" Of course I wasn't. Rudy was stealthy and had an uncanny sense of balance. What a shock.

"You can't tell? Not a good sign, Alex. Maybe you'd better pinch yourself?"

"I tried that last time. It doesn't work." Rudy was simply dressed in new jeans, a red T-shirt, and running shoes. His black hair was freshly cut, as usual. He was smiling, of course, but his ancient eyes were not. Of course.

"What brings you back to the scene of the crime?" I asked.

"You. I had a feeling you might be here, after you didn't answer your wide open door. I also wanted to check out the damage. Not much to see, is there?"

"Not anymore. The Hoovers came through yesterday."

"You wish I had given you that chair, don't you?" Rudy asked. His eyes were fixed on the dimple in his floor.

"Damn straight." He looked up at my wistful response, into my eyes. For a moment I held what they held. My shoulders sagged. I said, "But damn you I would only have used it for watching TV."

"Perhaps," he grinned, "I should have stuck to Gilligan as well?"

"At least you would still have a house to watch it in."

"Not for long, Alex."

"What's that supposed to mean?"

"It means there was a reason for that chair. A reason for these ruins. Everything ties together. I came today to tell you that, and to ask you plainly to join me in a mighty struggle. Together."

"Why does this feel like the first reel of a Conan movie? What the hell are you talking about? This is all dreams." I already knew that wasn't true. Fritz's was real, as real as the hole in which we stood, and there was probably more. I knew that, but the phrase seemed like a decent trigger to get my old friend talking.

"Yes," Rudy said, walking easily as he spoke, touching the walls with reverence, "It is all dreams. Or dreams are all it is, depending on your viewpoint."

"What?"

"The world itself is what an individual would call a dream: a series of random events occurring in a seemingly unending and unstoppable stretch of time. Yet we know that somehow our unconscious minds control it all. The World is the same." I heard the upper case `w'.

"A series of random actions?"

"That seem to have nothing to do with each other," he said.

"And?"

"And somehow its unconscious mind has a handle on things."

"And you're going to tell me now that somehow this mind has lost its grip, and it's up to us to save the world? Like interplanetary therapy?"

"You're no fun, Alex. This dialogue was just getting good and you had to figure it all out before the tenth line. But you need not be melodramatic, this isn't Buck Rogers."

"Could've fooled me," I sighed. Then, "Well, then, what is it we have to save?"

"Why, the World," he said, his chiseled face impassive. He looked up, toward the area his bedroom once occupied, and continued, "Actually, we have to keep it from being saved."

"What?"

Rudy turned, shook his head, said, "First, Alex, I need to know if you're with me."

"Do I have a choice?"

"The decision of my presence in your dreams has always been yours. You merely had to wish me gone once and I would never have returned. You kept calling me back."

"I wish I had known that."

"Are you with me?"

"I could make you go away for good, just by wanting it?"

"Of course. And the World would soon follow my path."

"Why?"

"Are you with me?"

"Is the world really at stake?"

"Are you with me?" Rudy's brow was slightly furrowed. I was pressing my luck.

"I can make a difference?"

"Are you with me?" The floor may have quivered slightly.

"Yes, I'm with you," I said, spreading calm over Rudy like a blanket. For him, my words were a balm. For me, they were just words. Not a lie; just words.

"Yes, then," he whispered, "The world is at stake, at least the one we're acquainted with. And yes, you can make a difference. You are the difference." I would have laughed if those words came from anyone else. It was something Jor-El would have said to a young Superman. But Rudy meant it. I shivered in the cool cellar, though the Sun hung directly over us. We should have been melting in that black hole.

"How can I be the difference?" I asked, absently rubbing a hand through my thinning brown hair. Rudy paced for a few minutes, apparently lost in a heavy debate with himself. At least I assumed it was only with himself. At times I thought I saw shadows of light shimmering near him. I wondered quietly if he weren't debating with specters that did not possess enough strength to be seen completely. In time he turned back to me.

"I've told you fifty times what I've been doing in this cellar," he said.

"More like a hundred," I said. We both smiled easily.

"A hundred. I've been at this longer than you can imagine, Alex. Lifetimes. Eons. Not just me. Others like me. Ancestors that exist now, in the World. Our quest has culminated in me. I've been able to tap into ten thousand years of dreams in that chair. To push through to the World. To the greater whole, the combined efforts of every unconscious mind in all the ages of the Earth. One mind. In that chair, I've seen that mind, been one with it."

"Sounds like a lot of work," I said.

Rudy sighed, "You're telling me."

"I'm sure it all must've been a helluva rush, Rudy," I said, gesturing at the remains of his home, "But what have I got to do with any of it?"

"What all our combined minds didn't stop to consider was the possibility that you might emerge, Alex. Your connection is innate. That's seriously infuriating, by the way; I sweat for ten millennia to do what you do in your sleep."

"Huh?"

"Alex, you don't need a chair," Rudy sighed. He rested his right hand on my shoulder, stared at a spot about two inches behind my eyes, and finished, "I hate and honor you for it. You do not need a chair." It took an effort for him to offer words that were so painfully important to him. He paused between each one, possibly waiting for the vital truths to sink into my well-insulated skull. None did. I raised my hand like a kid in class.

"Forgive my stupidity, but what the hell are you talking about?"

Rudy sighed, "I've told you enough for now. Suffice it to say that in your dreams you can help us win." Now we were using words I understood.

"Win what?" I asked. Rudy took my arm and led/carried, me to a wall of his cellar. We sat down. Well, he sat. I slid to the door like a damp towel, bruising my coccyx when my ass slapped the marble.

"There's a cancer in the World's mind, Alex. At about the same time I pushed through to the oneness, another single entity did as well. In as much as I was overwhelmed by it all, this being was thrilled. He felt the immense potential for power, and sought control. Such control is akin to attempting to poise a battleship on your bare shoulders, if you'll forgive the awful analogy. He's convinced himself that he has seized control, but the World is crumbling around him. What used to seem to be a random pattern has indeed become a random pattern. This being either cannot see the chaos he's unleashed, or he ignores it. Or revels in it."

"And me?"

"You? I can only remotely experience the Whole. My power of influence is miniscule. I work with many—"

"Max?"

"She's one. I work with many who can move within the Whole, for one reason or another, but they can have no influence at all. And they know little of our world of individuals."

"Why not?"

"It's their world. The influence I'm looking for would be like you moving Everest in this world. With your bare hands."

"That's serious influence."

"A tiny fraction of the push you might have."

"I sound mighty impressive. How do I do all this?"

"I was hoping you would be able to tell me," Rudy said. I laughed out loud. He smiled. Then we considered each other in grave silence for a time. Finally I slapped my thigh, stood, fell, and stood again. Once up, I scratched my nose, shook my head, and looked down carefully at my very old, or very insane, friend.

"I don't know if I can be any help," I said, "I don't know what to do. I have a degree in English, not metaphysics. I'd be lost in your World," I felt myself say it with a capital `W.'

"As far as you know. Remember, you saved my neck three times already. And you barely lifted a finger." Rudy stood to join me, without effort. Yeah, I thought, but I saved your neck, buddy. Three times.

"I thought they were just dreams."

"To you they were," he said, his eyes locked on mine, "Keep that in mind." I nodded, pretending to finally understand all that was being thrust at me. I said:

"Now that I'm in this up to my neck, what's my next move?"

"I couldn't imagine. I will be back, of course, perhaps in a dream, perhaps not. Now that we've enlisted your help consciously, you might have more sway unconsciously. We'll see."

"We'll see," I repeated, emphasizing 'we' and hoping Rudy caught my skepticism. He showed no sign that he had, but that meant nothing when interpreting Rudy's glacial reactions. He smiled, took my hand in an extremely unusual, for him, formal shake.

"Thanks Alex," He said, "I knew you would be with us freely. Again, forgive me for sounding like a partisan, but the dramatics are necessary." He started to walk toward the cellar stairs, but stopped. He turned.

"I'm glad I didn't have to use the special lever I had set aside."

"What's that? Fame and fortune?"

"Something better. Cassie."

I gasped, skated up to him. I had to grab his arm to keep from falling, but I appreciated the emphasis my grip provided. He supported me effortlessly.

"What about her?" I demanded, my face inches from him. I felt the blood rush to my cheeks. I felt no anger, though I probably appeared ready to throttle Rudy. It wasn't anger; fear, hope, dabbles of anguish, yes, but not anger. Rudy understood, hooded his eyes as he nodded.

"I'm not sure. Maybe answers, maybe more."

I pushed Rudy away, regarded him for a moment. I chuckled softly.

"You were wrong, Rudy," I said.

"What do you mean?"

"You should have used your `lever' in the first sentence. Then you wouldn't have had to talk so much." Rudy said nothing, letting go of me. He turned back to the stairs, walked up three of them. He stopped, faced me again.

"I know," he said. Then he was gone.

Chapter Six

After my monumental, epic, and sacrificially heroic decision to join Rudy in his crusade against the evil of evils, he abandoned me.

Okay, so he didn't exactly abandon me. It's not as if Rudy stranded me on some blasted plain somewhere, with mortar rounds bursting on all sides. He didn't ride off into some cinematic sunset in his black Porsche, Max's red hair billowing through the open passenger window. No, he simply didn't come around to pick me up.

I spent my soldierly vigil at home, alone. I did little more than sleep, and occasionally keep watch at the living room window for some sign of Rudy. I procrastinated all things, even meals, in the name of being ready when he finally summoned me into the ethereal fray. Instead of getting magical, world-rending action, mixed with the feeling that I finally was doing something useful, all I managed to get were several good nights of sleep.

After Rudy left his cellar, just one week earlier, he never returned. A lonely week filled with the gritty reality of dreamless sleep, TV, and cold food was eating voraciously at my resolve, and my imagination. I was beginning to lose heart in the game. Game. It may have been that – a game I played in my dreams. It was no coincidence that Cassie was the dangling carrot. What fantasy of mine would be complete without her as the finale?

The kitchen, happily concealed in early evening shadows, was a shambles. I had redecorated it over the last week with empty cereal boxes, milk spilled Saturday, a plague of crumpled paper cups, and the random placement of every dish I owned. I noticed the night before that I had taken to feeling my way around the room in the dark, reluctant to turn on a light and have my sloth physically presented to me. The malaise came upon me gradually, and was a surprise – I am usually quite tidy. Initially I was reluctant to leave my house, fearing that Rudy might make an appearance in my absence. Then I was unwilling to do anything. I relegated myself to lounging, waiting to respond to the trumpets of gods.

No mystical summons sounded, no apparitions beckoned. There wasn't even a humble rap upon my front door. The Powers of All There Is must have been on holiday. By Sunday I was assuring myself that I was a complete fruitcake who had no home in the world of sanity (with a small `w,' of course). I toyed with the grounds at the bottom of my third cup of coffee that Monday morning, pushing them about with my spoon. I formed shapes of airplanes and cliffs to be destroyed by the roiling waters of the next cup.

Coffee was the last ingestible item in the house. I reheated another cup of it in the microwave, but my rumbling stomach did not subside. I sensed that my body was suggesting that I turn back to reality and forget Rudy, at least long enough for a trip to McDonald's. I was inclined to agree with my, um, self, and considered abandoning my lonely vigil. After all, the entire life-altering experience was contained in just three days of the week before. Rudy and I were close. Our friendship could have coaxed creation of the surreal situation. I laughed vocally. It was easy to stage an imaginary scenario of my breakdown. However, my decision to pursue the madness left me with no option but to see it through. Fine. I was either mad or trapped in a world utterly alien to me. I banged my fist on the table and rose to pour another cup.

The thick stuff at the bottom of the coffee pot slipped into my cup, and was enough to push me over the edge. I hurled the empty pot, shattering it against the wall –the debris from its impact was instantly lost among the mess in my kitchen. I gasped for breath, and tears clouded my vision. I was becoming furious at myself, finally, for allowing myself to be suckered into committing myself to Rudy's veiled master plan.

I should have known he wouldn't return. He probably didn't want my help after my pathetic display of abject gullibility. What normal person would accept the story Rudy tried to press on me? Shit, I thought, smacking my forehead with a dirty palm, it was the truth; at least as far as I could tell. And I was confident that I could 'tell' fairly well. One thing I learned early in life was how to spot truth from a distance. One thing I learned later was how to ignore it and believe whatever was interesting.

That contradiction, I decided, was the little monster that currently tore at me. It wasn't Rudy's absence, or my confusion about what to do. It was my unnatural urge to do what was right instead of what was easy. Engulfed in the wisdom of my self-induced epiphany, I realized that the best way to cure this pain was to simply ignore it. I would get on with my life, not Rudy's, but be willing to help him if he ever did turn up again. Suddenly resolute, and slightly euphoric (though that may have been light-headedness due to hunger), I collected myself. I brushed several magazines off a chair, and sat at the kitchen table to sip, and occasionally chew, my last cup of coffee before cleaning up.

I showered and shaved for the first time in days, hoping that the refreshing action might help me come to a final decision. Decision. The word allowed clarity to drift into my happy little world again, but I fought it off. I had thought that I only needed the one decision to wait for Rudy. Wrong. I was on my own again. Rudy had left the ball bouncing lazily in my court, looking for action. It was my choice to decide not to decide. Trouble was, I would eventually hate myself for my laziness, cursing the briared path over which my phlegmatic ways consistently dragged me.

"Why don't you go to work today Alex?" I said aloud to my reflection in the misty mirror. Glazed eyes stared back incredulously at the statement, lips formed a little round island in the generous sea of foam. "Might do you some good," I continued. My reflection shrugged.

As I washed unused shave cream from my face, I caught myself humming the Mr. Grubber Rubber Roundup song. It was the latest jingle from the company, pumped relentlessly over the office public address system in a sort of subliminal pep rally. Though I endured weeks with the insipid tune tap-dancing nonstop between my ears, I had managed to exorcise it just before Rudy's house blew up. Now I welcomed the awful song.

I smiled. I would enjoy work that day. I felt sure that the meaningless exercise of writing instructions for a second-rate toy company would take on new meaning. Strengthened by resolve, but still very hungry, I finished dressing, locked up the house, and climbed into the car. I held my breath while turning the key, because the Escort rarely started after sitting for a week. I was pleasantly surprised when it roared to life in an instant. I accepted that as a good omen, and backed out of the driveway happy.

I felt good about going to work for the first time in years. I actually looked forward to a day of mindless hard labor tapping a keyboard to produce useless, and unreadable (and generally unread) assembly instructions. The drive to work through the hazy morning sunshine was pleasant. Traffic was light enough at the midmorning hour –about 10:00 – so there were not enough idiots sharing the road to overwhelm my tolerance threshold, or my good mood. As I turned into Beaver Toys' long, tree-lined drive, I felt good about my "decision" to return to normalcy. I even thought that I would have little trouble explaining my long absence to Fletcher, who had stopped calling a few days earlier. I probably realized that I was kidding myself at least a dozen times during the commute, but I was successful in quelling the onset of reality by loudly humming the Mr. Grubber Rubber Roundup song. My self-deception, and the car, came to a screeching halt just after I turned into the crowded parking lot.

Showing up for work may not have been such a useful idea, I thought, scratching my smooth chin. Lately things were not working to my advantage. When I pulled in I glanced, as was my habit, toward the front door to see who was outside smoking. I always found a moment of envy for the smokers, because they could escape for a brief respites every few hours (or minutes, in some truly carcinogenic cases), and enjoyed automatic membership in that special outcast smokers club. However, I would remind myself that their habit was cutting their lives short, and wasn't worth the pleasure and camaraderie. I felt a sickly confirmation of this when I saw that there was no one there. I moved the car slowly to the fire lane near the front entrance, knowing that no one would mind my violation. That was because no one was there. No one and no thing.

A plume of soft blue smoke rose from just beyond the spot where the smokers once congregated. Though it was inside the building's perimeter, it was easy to see. This was because there were no obstructions between the interior of the building and me. There was no entrance, no door, no building. Beaver Toys had been reduced to a twenty- two thousand square foot hole. It was similar to Rudy's, only bigger. I stood there for a few moments, feeling Nancy's short-lived terror. I had always told myself that my work there was meaningless, and I always carefully ignored what it meant to the rest of the staff. Now I knew that arriving for work today had meant everything to each of them. And that meaning, that end, was somehow my doing. Without looking back, I got into my car and locked the door. I wondered for a moment whether to alert the authorities, but then wondered as briefly what the point of that would be. Then I just drove away.

I drove in a haze, letting the car find its own path on the Westchester back roads. It did this well. The first coherent thought that entered my clearing mind was one of self-preservation. He, it, they, whatever, was after me. The lack of fire trucks or police at the scene must have meant that the destruction was recent. No one got there yet. No one noticed yet. It must have been sudden, quiet. There was no dust. The attacker was gaining proficiency. There was probably no flame or sound, either.

I marveled at myself calmly reasoning the demise of my last friends – okay, acquaintances – on earth. I should have been consumed by guilt, riddled with loss. Loss was easy, but paranoia overwhelmed tears for the moment. Though I intensely believed that this catastrophe would not have happened if I weren't involved with Rudy, I was able to force myself to understand that it wasn't my fault. There was more at fault here. I was a pawn. I had to subscribe to this logic just to keep the car from veering into a tree at very high speed.

A silhouette emerged from the haze, still far away but solidly in the path of my hurtling car. I slowed, both curious about who or what it was, and not interested in creating more casualties. As I closed, I could discern that it was definitely human, but oddly shaped. It was either a hitchhiker or a hunchback. When he was just a few feet away I could finally see the outline of a backpack, a couple of legs, and an arm outstretched from the other side. No doubt there was a thumb sticking out as well. Not in the frame of mind to consider hitchhikers (when I do consider, I still never offer them a ride), I passed him, careful not to look. His presence remained peripheral for only a heartbeat, but that glance was enough to leave sixty feet of skid marks as I forced the car to the shoulder. I looked over my shoulder, threw the lever to 'R,' and spun the wheels as I headed back to Rudy.

He pressed his nose against the passenger window, pointing to the lock. He was not smiling. I reached across the interior and unlocked the door. I had assumed that it would have been open for him, but was not in the mood to question the assumption, or why I was wrong. He got in, gently shutting the car door. He then sat still, eyes forward, focused on nothing as I pulled back onto the road. Driving was difficult; I was unwilling to take my eyes off Rudy for fear that he would disappear. I said nothing as I drove, assuming that he would speak when he was ready. We rode in complete silence for a few miles of country road, and then he turned to me.

"Sorry, Alex," he said, "I didn't know he was on to you. I would have given you a warning, but you knew it happened before I did."

"I knew what happened, Rudy?" I said. In a useless attempt to portray an appearance of total ignorance, I tried to smile. Rudy didn't bite.

"Alex. You must know your office is gone. Why else would I be here?" he said.

"Gone? Where did it go?"

"Come on Alex, you know bloody well. It went the same route as my house. Don't feign ignorance. I'll tell you anything you want to know."

"You only come when something blows up?"

"No, I only come when you want me here. Sort of like a butler." Neither of us smiled at that. I suppose I should have, to uphold my façade of ignorance, but I wasn't very good at facial deceit. Rudy continued, "And I know you were just there. You still have his scent on you."

"Whose scent?"

"Our enemy's. I've learned to recognize it."

"Why the hell did 'Our Enemy' vaporize the toy box? Why not my house?"

"He probably hasn't figured out where you live yet," Rudy said, ignoring my guffaw at such bad logic, "But he will, you don't have to worry about that."

"You can see its something I'm real concerned about."

"You should be," Rudy said, in a tone that made me feel that he was taking my hand, "But you're not. I can't figure that out about you Alex."

"Ask Cassie. With her went all reason for anxiety."

"All right, I will."

Well beyond considering what I was doing to my brakes that day, I locked them, bringing the car to another noisy stop. I turned to face Rudy, expecting him to cower under my look, or at least be concerned about the sudden change of color to my face. That was what I hoped. Rudy, however, does not cower, or even recoil. He didn't even notice my thumping carotid artery, though it felt to me that it grew larger than my neck with each high-pressure pulse. He simply sat there, feathers in mouth, waiting for me to say something. I did.

"Dammit Rudy, I wish you would stop talking like that."

"Like what?" Rudy asked sincerely, his tan face impassive.

"Like my dead wife is your new neighbor! Jesus!" I started the car rolling again, needing some activity to keep from either fatally strangling or hugging Rudy. Neither would make a difference anyway: Rudy was strong enough to hold off a division of crazed Nazis, and aloof enough to shrug off the most passionate hug. In time he responded, taking my hand with his mind again.

"I did say that you might be able to reach her again."

"Stop it Rudy, I don't believe in that stuff. I don't even read Edgar Cayce. Besides, we're supposed to be dealing with the destruction of my last portal to the real world, not to mention a few hundred unsuspecting souls."

Rudy turned to me when I said that. The winding road and my high speed prevented me from looking back, but I felt his gaze. It had softened. I had actually spoken words powerful enough to soften Rudy. That was not a mean feat. I drove silently, wondering what button I had accidentally pushed. I chewed my last sentence nearly beyond recognition before my addled brain finally spit out the key. I sighed. It wasn't the pathos that got him. It was my choice of words.

"Is that what I am, Rudy, your last portal?" I tried to ask tactfully. This must be a difficult area for him, I thought. I represented his last grasp on reality, or at least his home world; it must have been humiliating for him. I felt sorry for my friend, "It must be heartbreaking needing me to help you come home."

"Be serious, Alex," Rudy smiled, "I'm not so far out of this world that I need a medium to pay cab fare. You forget that I am more a part of Everything now. Not less."

"Oh yeah, sure. But still, shouldn't we be concerned about my dead co-workers?"

"Absolutely, and we are. I am amazed at how well you handle these things. Any other man would be groveling under a rock by now, and I wouldn't blame him."

"Like I said, ask Cassie."

"Okay."

"Cut that out!"

"Right, I forgot. Cassie is dead."

"That's enough, Rudy. Any more of this and I'll start believing you." It was too late for that, but I thought it best to let Rudy hold the notion that his grip on me was complete.

"Right," he said, "Sorry. But there is nothing we can do about your office. It's gone, like Fritz's. Just hope they didn't suffer as much. They probably didn't. Suffering is profitable only in the presence of witnesses. My main concern was for your own mental welfare. I know that sounds cruel, but there's more than an office building's worth of lives at stake in these attacks. Let's hope there won't be too many more casualties."

"Why do there have to be any?" I asked. He did not respond in words. He only looked at me and shrugged. We drove in silence for a few more minutes. The comfort I felt with him returned, and I began to feel as though we were headed for his hunting cabin in the Catskills. In time he looked around, stretched, and sighed loudly.

"Well Alex, I must be going again. If you'd be good enough to stop anywhere so I can leave."

"You can't leave yet, you haven't told me what to—what our next move will be. When will you appear again?"

"Have I needed to tell you anything like that yet?" He asked. Good point, I thought. I drove in silence for a while, then lifted a finger off the wheel, said:

"Wouldn't you rather have a ride somewhere? It must be a long walk—"

"Do you even know where we are?" he asked. I hadn't thought of that. I lost track of where I was when I left the office. I stopped the car, looked around at decidedly strange surroundings. It could have been Connecticut.

"I may be lost, but I do have wheels and a map. It'll be easier than walking."

"Oh, I hate walking," Rudy said. He got out of my car and shut the door. After adjusting the straps on his backpack, he tapped on the window in farewell. With no further gesture or word, he turned and walked in the direction from which we had come. I put the Escort in reverse and looked back. I decided that I would insist that he come with me, at least back to his car. I never let my foot off the brake, though. I turned back, swore softly, and drove forward again.

In a few seconds Rudy passed me, alone in his black Porsche. He waved as he blew by, and then disappeared over the next hill.

Chapter Seven

Cold rain soaked the brick Parisian street, drowning any sound that challenged its own incessant chatter. Early morning's blue sheen glazed the slick sidewalk I paced. I set aside my frantic paranoia long enough to appreciate the great age that permeated the scene – this street was as old as it was wet. Suddenly I hid in a doorway, knowing that the man following me was around the next corner. I had shaken him for the moment, but he would be back, perhaps with help. I stretched, adjusted my trench coat, and leaned against the thick stone arch. I searched for comfort in anticipation of a long vigil before the arrival of my contact, whose tardiness seemed to prompt the rain to fall with greater ferocity. Indeed, I looked down between my soft-soled shoes and saw that the rain was actually falling with enough velocity to dissolve the granite step on which I balanced. I noticed too late, however, and swore when I realized that the step would no longer support me. I slid through the viscous gray gel of the French stoop, careful to hold my breath while my head passed through the granite step. I hung in blackness for an instant before I dropped beneath the stoop to the pasture below. I wasn't sure if I had landed on my feet, but I must have since I was standing on them. I surveyed my new surroundings without surprise, or even much looking.

The red sun, low on the close horizon, flashed behind the spinning arms of a monstrous windmill like a celestial strobe light left switched on at very slow speed. I walked toward the windmill that towered miles away, dominating the distant shore that defined a rippling sea of hip deep ruby grass. I was careful to step only when the sun shone between the tattered blades to avoid tripping in the complete darkness that each interfering blade created. Small furry creatures nipped at my bare toes, forcing me to balance atop the blades of grass. From that height I could see that my pursuer had found my contact, eaten the poor raccoon alive, and was after me. A snarling emerald vulture made a pass, missed, and tore a screaming scar of grass from the Earth. The windmill was still miles away. I decided that that simply would not do. The thought brought the windmill to me immediately, but someone had recently laid fresh asphalt in the empty parking lot that surrounded the whirling edifice. My Nikes sank into hot tar, their soles gluing me in place. I untied them and waited for the next flash of sunlight. When the world lit again, I deftly leaped from the shoes' white leather clutches, over the molten road, and through the threshold of the windmill.

I was thrilled to reach the windmill, because I knew that the enemy, Rudy's enemy, was mere seconds behind me. I turned at the door long enough to see him swimming powerfully through a seven-foot chop of roiling black water, with no land in sight. The male pronoun I affixed on him was purely arbitrary, as I did not see him. I felt his presence as I would that of an oncoming storm. When I turned away, I noticed an old barn door rotting against an unpainted cinderblock wall. It was barely more substantial than tissue paper, but it was all I could enlist to help hold the enemy back. I flipped the edge of the door in the enemy's direction before I completed my turn.

The thundering resonance from the steel door slapping home brought out the tuning fork in me. After I finished vibrating (a novel sensation that I thoroughly enjoyed and hoped would repeat sometime soon), I reviewed my latest surroundings. I was in a narrow tunnel that stretched for miles in either direction. I flipped a blue quarter, saw heads (Washington winked at me), and went straight. The tunnel ended in about six paces. It opened on a lavish chamber with gilded walls and a ceiling that soared hundreds of feet above me. A crystal fountain dominated the center, with park benches facing it and mermaids splashing in its still water. A wino was sleeping on one of the benches. He woke as I passed him, wordlessly offering a sip from his brown paper bag. He dissolved to sticky gray dust at my refusal. Poor guy. I pressed on, knowing to ignore the mermaids' song-styled entreaties for me to join them in their sensuous bubble bath. I lamely chose to give in to their comely temptations after a few paces, and turned back to the fountain. They were gone. Instead, a wall stood three feet away, decorated with a mosaic of frolicking nymphs. I could still hear their pleas. I wanted to pat myself on the back for originally making the right decision, or at least taking a long enough time to make the wrong one.

The badly carpeted floor dropped away like a rogue elevator, swaying to the left as it did. I grabbed the open door of the DC3's cramped control cabin to steady myself. Fine, I thought, another plane. Rudy occupied the pilot's seat. Taking no notice of me, he flipped switches, consulted gauges, and turned dials with at a hand-blurring pace. If he missed anything, and he did with alarming regularity, Max caught it from the co-pilot's seat. I approached them, looking through the tinted windshield at the battle outside. Four mammoth ships – two salamis, one egg roll, and a sinister looking beef jerky – hovered above Manhattan, less than a mile from our nose. Their vast shadows cloaked half the city in darkness. Occasionally a windmill blade would slowly pass the glass screen. I gripped the backs of my comrades' seats, the excitement of the ensuing conflict stretching my veins. Rudy looked up from his controls and shook his head.

"Alex," he said, "This is the silliest battle I've ever been in. I suppose they use sauerkraut as cannon fodder."

"It is unusual," Max interjected, fingering the deflector control to ward off a volley of relish with mustard tracers. She continued, "Are you hungry, Alex?"

"Sorry about this, folks. It's the best I can do on short notice. Remember, I am new to all this," I heard myself say. I had no idea what I was talking about, but I liked the sound of the words. As I began to recognize the threads of this universe I battled in, I felt comfortable, if amateurish, as its creator.

"Here they come," Max said, "And they're moving at frank, I mean flank, speed!" The meat group turned in formation and approached us at an alarming rate.

"No problem," I said, watching me produce a foot-wide antacid tablet from the hip pocket of my jeans. It was heavy, but with an extra effort I was able to hurl it through the liquid windshield. The tablet was the size of the salamis when it ricocheted off them. They exploded with a wet thud before showering the city streets below with bacon bits. Max scored a direct hit on the egg roll with her grease gun. The egg roll sucked the stream of grease, savoring every drop until it could draw no more. Bloated, it dropped to Earth, landing squarely on Cleveland. No one noticed.

"Now for the real action," Rudy said grimly, pointing to the shadow astride the jerky, "Dammit Alex, why the hell can't you have nice sedate, pastoral dreams? This action-adventure stuff is wearing thin."

"So I'll stay away from Leo's Deli," I said. I had intended to offer a stronger defense of my choice of culinary adventure, but my attention was taken by the jerky. It rolled up on itself, paled, and thickened into a giant ball of freshly baked dough with a tiny saddle mounted at its flaky crest. I squinted, and my vision telescoped enough to confirm that a perfect black shadow filled the fancy western saddle. It held the saddle's horn with one sinister hand while the other waved a Stetson. I pointed, speechless, but my failure to warn my comrades was moot. A windmill blade passed through the creampuff and caught the shadow unawares. It launched the enemy skyward, out of the frame of my vision. We breathed a sigh of relief, and then Max stripped off her clothes and leapt into the steaming lagoon in which our schooner was anchored. I admired her perfect body as she executed a two-minute swan dive into the clear water a few feet away. She disappeared when she hit the surface.

"Nice," Rudy said, hand on my shoulder.

"That goes without saying," I said, "And so did she. Are we done now?"

"Done? We haven't yet begun. This is still a dream. Nothing has really happened here. Don't take it wrong, you were a real hero against the refrigerator stock back there, but nothing was accomplished."

"What are you saying?" I asked.

"How should I know?" Rudy said, "It's your world. Funny. Max is usually pretty shy."

I started to respond to that, forgot what he said, and glanced up toward the source of the thundering roar in time to see the last few cars of an endless freight train pass over the blackened railroad trestle above us. Rudy and Max were in the caboose, Max still naked, jiggling in enticing rhythm with the motion of the clattering train. Rudy was dressed but was also clearly thrilled. I could tell. They were waving merrily at me, their idle arms stretched around each other's waist. I tried to mimic their enthusiasm when I waved back, but my extra energy only forced my outstretched right hand to sink more deeply into the cold green slime that layered the cave. I pulled my hand down. It was enveloped in the stuff. I tried to wipe it off, succeeded only in getting slime on my face. The thick goo spread its cold-snot tendrils across my mouth and nostrils, threatening to smother me. I noticed before the green covered my eyes that my hands and feet were deeply embedded into the cave walls. I attempted to panic, to wildly thrash my head about until the slime shook free. My efforts did not match my intentions, though. I moved slowly, as if in a pool of molasses. I recognized the danger, and its context, and went into the automatic wake-up function that I reserved for the worst of nightmares (those of which I was sure were not survivable).

I failed to end the dream. Instead, I merely felt more awake, and conscious of being in a deadly place. I resumed my struggle to escape the slime, but I moved ever more slowly with each renewed effort. Oh, I thought to myself, I get it now. At least, I hoped I did. I was indeed still in a fight, but not with the standard monsters I usually faced. This beast was a new force that wielded new rules, or at least twisted those to which I was accustomed. Since I was losing strength in my traditional battle, but gaining understanding in my, and Rudy's, new realm, I decided to go with a familiar instinct, or rather habit. I backed off. I relaxed and held my breath.

My eyes sprang open to a strange vista of mottled squares joined together in a perfect geometric pattern that was broken only by the occasional blotchy brown galaxy or black tear in the pattern itself. This was a good thing, I realized after my intellect caught up with primitive focus, and I welcomed the mundane sight of my motel room ceiling. I sighed, stretched a bit, and noticed I was lying on top of a made bed, still dressed. I must have been more tired than I thought last night, I decided. I had spent it driving. I knew better than to go home, if there was still a house to return to, so I simply kept driving into the night. I wasn't sure how far I got, or when I stopped. I didn't care, though. An anonymous motel in unknown territory would do just fine until things settled down. Or ended.

I rolled over, tried to absorb every photon of the safe morning daylight that streamed into the room, animating passing dust. I knew the mild pleasure would be short lived, though. Something in last night's dream had made me nervous. What it was, I did not know. The dream had already slipped from my memory, its misty shards scattered by morning brilliance. I didn't fret the loss. The details would come to me later. They always did. I rolled back to follow the water stained contours of the cheap tile ceiling. I could spend the entire day buried in a meaningless task to escape the problems that were sure to arise. I was a master at sidestepping work, truth, or obligation through meaningless tasks.

But it wasn't right that day. I sat up, tossed the pillow to the floor. I had enough. Rudy offered me meaning, and it was time to collect. He left me little choice anyway. With some effort I rolled my legs over the side of the bed. I stood up.

I stood for a moment on the dirty brown linoleum floor. I looked around the room, wondering at my penny-pinching ways. I deserved a better place than this dump, especially if I was going to stay a while. I would have liked to have imposed on a friend, but Rudy's place was gone and the rest of the people I dared call friend were at Beaver Toys. Nancy would have been a great host. The room was frigid, sub-zero perhaps. Odd, I thought, considering the season. They forgot to shut off the air conditioning, no doubt. I planned to complain on my way out. The room was ugly too. No TV, no dresser, not even a picture on the wall. It was a room even the Giddeons would have snubbed. The missing bureau would have confused them.

It was also the first motel room I had ever rented that was not carpeted. I was surprised that a night lapsed before I acknowledged the point; surprised and more than a little curious. Suspicious now of anything unusual, I started a careful scan of the entire room. I turned in a full circle to take in every detail. The single complete spin was also confirmation to my racing mind that I was awake, since things always change when you fully rotate in a dream. Before I was halfway around, I spotted a patch of tattered wallpaper close to the floor that was glowing red. Nearby was a shard of salami. I had no time to realize their significance, however, because on attempting to take a step I encountered a more immediate curiosity. My feet were buried to their ankles in the linoleum. "Oh, yeah," was the only thought that entered my head.

I felt no pain from the floor's grasp. It was actually warmer than the room, so some shock was masked by comfort. I studied the oddity calmly for a moment, saw no immediate, rational causes, then I swore at myself for bothering with confusion. First I should excavate myself from the floor, I may have said aloud, and then I can worry about how it happened. Hell, I thought, still scrabbling for simplicity, I probably checked into a condemned building. I successfully tugged my right foot out of the paste, and set it on the hard floor nearby to force the other foot free. It wasn't easy—the stuff held tight. After one painful lurch incorporating every muscle in my body, the floor reluctantly released my foot. In reaction I flew across the room, hitting my head hard on the far wall. I sat, dazed, for a moment, holding my throbbing brow. The floor by the bed resumed its original unkempt but solid form. I was not relieved, however. There was something else wrong that I hadn't identified yet. I was confident that it would come to me in time. I stood, gingerly feeling my way to the only door in the room. It opened on a bathroom. My mind stopped racing, but my pulse did not. There was no outside door.

I had no time to panic. As soon as I fully understood the meaning of an exit-less room, the liquid floor swallowed me whole. In an instant I was surrounded by nothing but utter darkness. Finally, while drifting in distraction-free liquid oblivion, I was able to step back (as it were) and realize that I was still dreaming. I laughed, the terror of the moment draining through battered spiritual pores. My laugh was muted, perhaps only imagined, in the heavy liquid matrix, but I still felt the ironic humor. I was amazed and slightly humiliated that I had overlooked so many obvious clues: the salami, the floor; the fact that I hadn't checked into a motel room in five years. I began to concentrate on changing the scene, to bring about a more placid and illuminated situation.

I remained in the dark liquid, breathing easily. My hands and feet writhed in a vain search for something to grasp or even touch. There was absolutely nothing; even the sensation of liquid faded. Perhaps, I reasoned dully, my senses were dimming, and my mind was becoming as empty as my surroundings. Coherent thoughts were swirling down an unseen black maelstrom whose presence disappeared with them. I could no longer concentrate on creating a more agreeable scenario. I could visualize nothing. My thoughts were stark whispers of cold night. I tried to summon Rudy, but he too had diminished to a distant memory. I could concentrate only on blackness, though even if I could still focus on my mystically estranged friend, I still had no idea how to reach him. My mind finally matched my body's dearth of feeling. I felt no fear, no comfort; I had lost the ability to identify them. I could still feel alone, and did, becoming sure that I had a universe to myself. It was not a nirvanic experience. Instead, my world was an abysmal, boundless emptiness. I forgot my name. I felt what was left of my soul slipping into oblivion, devoid of all that made it human.

Then I thought no more.

I landed in an ungainly heap on the marble sanctuary floor of an old church. I knew it was old because the ornate white altar faced away from where the people would stand. Plus it smelled old. Smelled?

I stood, hugging my body, playing with my fingers. I took a deep breath, did some arithmetic in my head just to feel it work, then I laughed loudly. Holy shit, I thought, I'm still alive! Stimuli were touching my mind again. Returning memories made me no longer alone. The marble was cold and my bare feet knew. I could again feel my skin through familiar cotton clothes, sense the movement of my eyes, and neared rapture at the sensation of musty air wafting into my nose and lungs. I found myself jumping up and down like a very bad ballet dancer, just to dispel some of the excitement, the rush of still being alive. After this behavior started getting silly, I calmed myself enough to explore my surroundings, and look for a possible way out.

My search did not extend beyond the marble altar, though, because Cassie, dressed in her wedding gown, was tied to it. She was alive and watching me. Her brown eyes flared with fear. I ran to her, but slammed into blue steel bars that materialized between us. One of the four hooded monks near Cassie tittered. Another stepped forward.

"You continue to thwart us, Alexis Creaux. It has become inevitable that we meet to solve this difficulty," the monk said, its bass voice filling the sanctuary. Cassie's presence readily cleared my timorous throat.

"Let her go," I thundered, "Who the hell are you to do this?" The monks laughed. A hideous laugh, a bizarre mix of stopping trains and fingernails on chalkboards.

"Who are we? Who are you to meddle in the affairs of the World?"

"I know nothing of this!" I cried.

"Then you conspire against us in ignorance. You are a fool." The word `fool' violently ricocheted around the church, nearly knocking me over. Cassie's bound presence compelled me to maintain my erect stance against the blast, though I trembled uncontrollably.

"Why do you take a fool seriously?" I shouted, clutching the bars. I knew if I could concentrate long enough, the bars would leave the scene. The monk apparently knew that too, and continued to distract me.

"Fools must be dealt with," he hissed. The bars glowed, sending waves of searing heat through my hands. I hung on. Defeat was mine if I let go. The monk pulled a jeweled scimitar from a sheath at his side, raised it over his head. The rest chanted, filling the chamber with incoherent but frightening echoing elephant banter. I ignored them, concentrated on the white-hot bars. I emptied my mind of the molten steel obstacle, but struggled to leave the rest of the scene intact. No mean feat, considering the damage the bars had inflicted on my palms. I paused, sensing with relief an approaching wave of enlightenment.

In proportion with the pain, the air should have been rank with the smell of burning flesh. I sniffed, but could sense only ancient, musty air. I smelled a tomb, and all that comes with it (not that I had ever been in one before), but no smoke or anything else that could be considered unusual or related to intense heat. I looked at my hands again, and realized that the pain had no doubt been my own creation. I tried to work on that concept, but my concentration was further contested by a black scimitar inching down to Cassie's heaving bustier-clad chest. I displaced the distraction without fully dismissing it, and I felt a change in the bars. The blade was an inch away from Cassie's breasts when I stumbled through cool jelly bars. I stepped forward, imagining what I would like to add to the scene. As my confidence grew, I decided to remove first and then add.

The monk howled when its scimitar disappeared. Its cry of anger sounded like a buzz saw gone mad. Black silk robes flowed everywhere as it turned to face me.

"You have earned my wrath, single creature!" it shouted, incredible volume flowing from the empty hood. Not empty: bottomless. I smiled, folded my arms.

"Oh please. Leave us alone," was all I could say. Not very dramatic, I supposed. The coven vanished before my words stopped echoing. The church was silent. I could hear Cassie's breath. I went to her. She looked unhurt, beautiful, and so alive. She sat up, looked around with very wide eyes. Then she saw me, as if for the first time, and smiled. She extended her unbound arms toward me. The wispy white fabric of her sleeves hung nearly to the floor, shimmering in soft yellow candlelight. I sensed another distraction, and refocused on Cassie's eyes. She locked onto my gaze and leapt. We grabbed each other, held on tight. I could feel sweat through her thin gown.

"Alex," she whispered into my T-shirt. Cassie always whispered in church, "How did you get rid of them? Don't you know who they are?"

"No, and maybe that's how I did it," I said, "I couldn't let them hurt you Cassie."

"But they're so powerful," she said, looking up at me. She believed what she was saying.

"Tell you the truth, it was a piece of cake after getting rid of those bars. That must have really pissed Monsignor Black right off." She smiled at that. A thin, polite smile. A gesture she never made when she was alive. I dismissed the thought. My existence on this particular stage seemed to depend on my ability to dismiss thoughts. I sure was glad I was good at it. I pushed her back from my chest, cupping her elbows in my palms. She was as soft and pliant as ever -- no more, no less. I could not avoid that distraction.

"What now, Cassie?"

She shrugged, "It's your dream, Alex, or at least it is now."

"It was your dream before?" I said hopefully; only living people dream. Nonsense, I thought, I buried her.

"No," she sighed, looking deep into my eyes, "Alex, before; it was real before."

"Real?"

"Yes, until you put him on your level. Now we're back to a dream."

"You were real?" I asked, rubbing her soft bare arms. She sure felt real.

"I don't know, Alex. I can't tell. Last I knew I crossed the wrong wires, and then I started turning up at the damnedest places with you, but only for a moment. It scares me. Please, no more." A pearl slid from her eye. I held her, promising never to let go. She shook her head, looked at me again, and faded. Another tear dropped before I found myself desperately gripping my own elbows. I was alone in the sacristy. I touched the altar, felt the warm stone where she had lain, then laid on it myself and cried, bitterly.

I looked up to the sound of steady tapping beside my head. A concerned old woman was knocking on my car window. I put a hand to my wet cheeks, and gathered myself. I smiled, assured her through the foggy glass that I was fine. She shook her head and walked away.

I straightened, wiped the condensation from my windshield with my hand, remembering. I had tried fruitlessly to find a vacant motel last night when I finally made my way back to town. I had eventually given up, and stopped at the next parking lot to camp until morning. The wet blanket I had found in the trunk to keep me warm had fallen around my feet, and the Dutch deli in front of my car was just opening its doors.

Chapter Eight

I had been driving all morning. In the early stage of my listless journey, I was content to roam upper Westchester County, easily lost among the contrived country roads that connected hidden estates, gated communities, and the occasional small town where the help lived. Sometime around noon I stumbled upon the Taconic Parkway. With no decision in place, I merged into southbound traffic, and began a mindless commute into Manhattan. I wasn't familiar with the route, but the big green signs, traffic flow, and some serious pocket change for the bridge toll helped me gain access to the center of the material world, sans map. I wandered midtown because the grid was easy, though I got a bit confused in Times Square. I wondered why I wasn't more nervous. I was not a city person, and visited only on the rare occasions when I needed to feel vitality. New York is a living beast, its energy not dependent on the dull world around it. I also came when I needed a new toaster or stereo equipment.

My visits were also always by train, never by car, so I was a bit tentative as I cruised Forty-Second street slowly, taking in the sights of the West Side. The place never changed. The streets of New York are eternal, locked in a stasis of constant flux that leads inexorably to the same end: no change. The city was not decaying. It was aging, shedding old skin for the sake of new, different skin. If an urbane traveler were to return in a hundred years he would look around, see different buildings, different people, and still acknowledge that the city hadn't changed. It would feel the same. The same riff-raff would still be there, mingling with the denizens du jour of business, political, and gang-related circles. The same streetwalkers, homeless, grifters, and ticket sellers would visibly infest the streets, energizing the pavement with the threat of their interference, the fact of their existence. They were always there; but the powers that be simply moved them closer to the Hudson each year in an attempt to make room for the more tourist-friendly Dysnified "attractions" that promised to reform the unchangeable.

Ticket sellers?

Without even a precautionary glance, I halted my car to an ensemble of horns and utterances. Transfixed by what I thought I had just seen, I was unaware of the outrage expressed by my fellow victims of traffic. To compound my emotionally ignorant affront, I tossed the Escort into reverse and drove backward until I returned to the address that had caught my eye. A taxi standing at the curb behind me lit its tires and fishtailed out of my way at the last moment, forcing a lesser vehicle across the street. I didn't hear the horns or complaining tires from the oncoming traffic.

Damn, I thought, all these theaters look alike... there, to the left of that twenty-five cent movie sign... I knew I saw her... but it couldn't be. I looked again, feeling confident that 'it couldn't be' was a cliché that I no longer should carry in my verbal repertoire. My scan paused at a particularly sooty ticket window. My eyes started to hurt as they strained to confirm what they had previously sensed. In a moment, they did: behind a grimy window, selling tickets for an unnamed movie theater, lurked the object of my death-defying driving.

I parked the car in front of the theater, too much a stranger to the city to register such a miracle. I rushed out, slammed my door, and then heard it lock behind me. I paused, smiled, and fished in my pockets for ten dollars. I forgot to check what film was playing before I stepped under the marquis. I hoped it was not something embarrassing.

"That'll be ten dollars please," she said, not looking up. Her voice projected through the little hole in the glass at a substantially higher pitch than I had expected. I stood for a moment, trying to hide my smirk while I waited for her to recognize me. Her height was betrayed by the way she had to slouch slightly to be heard through the hole. I paused briefly, remembering that there should have been plenty of room for her in the booth, but then dismissed the doubt – it was her. Her purplish

hair was matted in a sticky punk style, its original color lost to
years of dye. The sharp lines of her face were hard to recognize
behind the orange make-up, but the leap was not impossible.
Something had to be right, to allow me to spot her from fifty feet.
I had assumed that she would know me on sight, but all my
presence brought to her face was a twitch of apprehension.

"You coming or going creep?" she asked.

"You don't know who I am?" I asked.

"Sure. You're Brad Pitt. I'll get your autograph later. Ten
bucks." She spoke in a tough Brooklyn dialect. After Max's
perfectly neutral diction, I wondered, fleetingly again, if I was
mistaken.

Nah.

"Is your name Max?" I ventured.

She pursed her glossy lips as if deciding whether to get ol'
Leroy from the back to take care of me. She looked behind me for
a line, apparently to determine whether she had time to waste on
me. There was nobody near the window but me. She smiled.

"Sorry Bob, name's Mary. You're close, though, I'll give ya
that much. What'ya want to know for?" she asked, pulling an
unwrapped stick of gum from the breast pocket of her purple
blouse. Not lavender. Purple. She tore the gum in half, offered
me what she did not put in her mouth. Though the gesture spoke
volumes, I declined with a wave of my hand, gave her the ten
dollars. With a friendly smile and no more, I took my ticket and
entered the theater, strangely ambivalent to my abrupt retreat. A
clean seat was surprisingly easy to find in the empty, well-lit room.
I plopped down and watched, as happy for the excuse to escape as
I was pleased that I had found Max.

The movie, of the Fists of Fury variety, passed blankly
before me as I contemplated the portent of Mary's existence. I was
convinced that she did matter, and also that she was Max. Max
was a unique figure of a woman, and Mary could not completely
hide such structure behind all that make-up, a few extra pounds,
and maybe a couple of inches in added height. Besides, no one can
see ticket sellers from the street, and I wasn't looking. And I was
not in the market for vitality or stereo equipment that day, so why
else would I have been on that street? I settled into a smug little
euphoric slouch, pleased both by my deductive ability and the

apparent support of unknown supernatural origin that I was enjoying.

I endured the film, and a foul stench that had been emanating from the front rows since the big fight scene, until the credits rolled and the lights became slightly less dim. I followed the rest of the tiny audience from the theater, maintaining a slow pace while I searched my meager social lexicon for a telling parting word to give Max – Mary. When I reached the lobby, I couldn't see her in her ticket booth. Nervous, I looked around, and spotted her across the tattered plaid carpet, speaking to a heavily jeweled black man near a frightening drinking fountain. Their discussion appeared heated, but was inaudible to my distant prying ears. I waited until the man slammed through the glass doors to the street before I approached. Mary put her cigarette out in the fountain with the others, and mumbled something under her breath. When she saw me approaching, she squelched a smile, looked away. Feeling unusually confident in my knowledge of her secret identity, I smiled openly. I wanted to take her hand, tell her what she looked like under all those layers of tacky clothes. Of course, she probably already knew.

"Hello again," I said casually.

"You back? I thought I seen the last of you, Bob."

"Alex. I have to come out of the theater too, don't I?"

"Oh yeah," she said, "Listen, Bob, that blue Escort out front yours?"

"I know it's not a Mercedes, but..."

"Is it yours?"

"Yeah. Why?"

"Cause some brothers have been trying to get in it for an hour. It usually only takes them a second. Funny, they can't even get the hubcaps off."

I panicked first, nearly succumbing to one of those fears of the dangers of the big city that are embedded by social decree into every suburbanite's psyche. Then I remembered the unusual circumstances surrounding my recent life, extended those experiences to my Escort (a la Rudy's Porsche), and relaxed. Indeed, I nearly giggled when I imagined the frustration that had to be accumulating among the thieves. I did not, though, assuming that such a sound would be counterproductive if I wanted to impress Mary/Max. I did grin broadly, though: associating with Rudy seemed to have some redeeming material side effects.

"What?" she asked, perhaps unnerved by my cheerful reverie.

"Nothing. Just hadn't realized I had hubcaps. Are they still there?" I asked, heading for the door without fear. I felt confident that a car that was able to lock its own doors and drive for days without refueling could hold its own in a street fight. Mary nodded, smiled, and walked with me to the exit. I wondered with faint hope about why she wanted to join me, but then assumed that she was looking for some excitement, maybe even the opportunity to see me have my skull crushed.

I had to push through the small crowd that had gathered around the scene of my car's attack to see that there were four young men gathered around my car, each armed with an implement of destruction. They were feverishly, and still fruitlessly, seeking entry. The one with a tire iron appeared fatigued. His repeated attempts to break my passenger side window found the only thing broken was the sweat pouring down his face. Though his tool merely bounced off the glass with barely a thud after each swing, the thug continued, incredulous. I whistled, impressed by this show of Rudy's influence in the real world. One of the youths looked up, seemingly at that thought. He saw me through the glass from the other side of my car, dropped his club and backed away, eyes wide. He was a huge boy, capable of breaking my back with a gesture. When he was across the street, he opened the throttle, pumping his feet madly for the nearest subway with nary a backward glance. The other three continued pounding, still trying to jimmy the door, pry the hatch, or discover anything that would solve this unexpected reality puzzle for them. All they learned, though, was how creative their comments regarding their failure could be stated. They also probably improved their physiques, too, since each blow on the Escort was harder than the previous whack. I stepped clear of the crowd, into the circle of curious life that had formed around my car. I felt oddly prepared for a confrontation. Mary grabbed my upper arm, tried to pull me back to the safety of anonymity among the crowd to which she clung by not moving her feet.

"Stay here where it's safe," she said in a hoarse whisper, "They'll get in soon. I think. Then they'll take your radio and leave. But they'll kill you if you try to stop them. I know 'em." I shook her loose, sauntered to my car. The three looked up at once. Their sweaty glares caused my arrogance to falter. I resisted the urge to turn and run, still clinging to the confidence Rudy and the Escort had instilled in me.

"Dis your wheels?" the taller of them demanded. I steadied myself, struggling to ignore the two-foot screwdriver he wielded.

"It is, and what the hell are you doing to it?" I shouted. Two of them stirred at my volume. They seemed ready to flee, though probably more to avoid arrest than me. Their leader held them with a glance.

"Why, we was detailing it for you, suh, and we only wants to clean out the inside too, but you got it locked real tight. Now why don't y'all open the mo' fuckin' car up so we can take care inside too?" They took a step toward me. Primordial forces again lapped at my legs, urging them into motion. I caught myself mid-turn, tried to make it look like I had to twist for a reason. I saw that Mary had provided one. She stood beside me, hands on her yellow spandexed hips.

"Man," she cried, "Leave this one alone Cleavus. He ain't done you no harm." Wrong, Mary, I thought. I ruined Cleavus' day. I embarrassed him in front of his gang. That had to be more harmful than a broken jaw in this neighborhood. The tallest, darkest kid looked at her in apparent agreement to my thought. But he did pause, and bared his yellow teeth in what might have been a smile, "Why should I hear a tight-pussied white bread bitch like you, Mary Mary?" She had no response. Her face flushed through cakes of Mary Kay. She turned her back to them

"Aren't you even going to give them the finger?" I asked. The boys laughed.

"Man, that girl don't know shit, but she do know better than give Cleavus Brown no shit. Where your keys, asshole?"

"They're in it," I said. I searched for more words to spill before my voice froze, and my cowardice surfaced. Mr. Brown filled that gap for me.

"Don't fuck with me boy," he said, crossing to me. He held his face inches from mine, so I could taste his spit.

"Look, man, that car is a fuckin' safe. Why, I really wanna know, too. Who puts those kind of guards on a fuckin' Ford P.O.S.? Now don't you tell me the keys is in it, too, asshole."

"They are," I piped, "Look inside." I dared say no more, lest my voice shake completely apart. We stood together in silence while Cleavus scanned the street. Then, without a signal, his cohorts formed a circle around me. Though I felt sweat on my nose, an adrenaline rush made me shiver. Cleavus smiled. I smiled, feeling my lips curl the wrong way. He was not planning to thank me for my time and move on to the next car. I prepared for his attack in the only way that my flabby, untrained soul could imagine: I tried to treat the immanent attack as if it were a dream.

My plan felt good at the outset, because I noticed myself looking directly at the hand that Cleavus chose to swing first. As if time slowed down, I ducked his blow by simply stepping out of the way, and let Cleavus fly by under his own inertia. I turned to face one of his buddies in time to block a kick with the edge of my wrist. The impact brought unprecedented pain, but I was able to use the same dream trick to find time to wrap my hand around the kid's sweaty ankle and twist it with all my strength. The second assailant yelped in surprise as he spun to the ground. I stepped back and squatted against a wall, ready, when the three of them shouted something to each other in an indiscernible tongue. They ran off in three directions. I saw why in a moment. A cop swinging a billy club had sauntered on the scene.

"About time you got here," I said.

"You're lucky I came at all, I think," Rudy said, tipping his cap with the stick, "What the hell are you doing here?"

"Look who I found," I said, reaching into the clear glass theater doors behind which Mary had retreated. I grabbed her wrist, gently pulled her out to the sidewalk, and presented her to Rudy.

"You came all the way into the city for this?" Rudy asked, grinning at Mary's sneer. He seemed amused that his costume was effective.

"Doesn't she look familiar to you?" I asked, shaking her in front of him.

"Not in the least," Rudy said, rubbing his chin, "Though I may have run her in a few weeks ago for soliciting."

"No way man," Mary said, shaking loose my grip, "I'm clean, cop."

"If you say so, miss," Rudy said in a perfect Bronx/Irish brogue, twirling his billy club like a twenty-year veteran, "But I'm sure not going to test that theory, am I? Sir, could we have a moment?" He pulled me aside, leaned me against a particularly slimy brick wall.

"What are you doing here, Alex?" he whispered.

"Don't you know who that is?" I asked.

"We'll talk about this later," he said. Without another word, he turned and disappeared into the disappointed crowd that had already begun to disburse. I sighed. I failed to understand Rudy's behavior, and wished he had hung around to explain it, but I wasn't shaken by his enigmatic ways anymore. I walked out on the street and opened the unlocked passenger door of my car. Mary stood where I had left her. I gestured to the seat.

"Want to go for a ride?" I asked.

"Be serious Bob," she said, "I work an honest living."

"Name's Alex. That's not what I meant."

"Al. Bob. Sound the same to me."

"Fine. Listen, just how mean is Cleavus?"

"He's got a collection of teeth at his place. He rips them out of old people for fun."

"And you want to be around when he comes back?"

She stamped her foot, turned a little circle, and folded her arms. I assumed she was reasoning this out, but also turned up my collar in case of rain. Oblivious to my reference, she bit her lip and said, "Listen Al, I work here, you know. I can't just take off. What'ya want with me anyway? You some sort of spy? Is this candid camera? Yeah. That's what was with your car. It was a trick. Right?" I suddenly had severe misgivings about my decision. This was not Max.

"Candid Camera isn't on anymore. Look, I just want to talk to you for a minute. We can just walk around the corner to a bar or some..."

"We'll drive," Mary said, getting into the car. She slammed the door. I looked through her window at her, confused. She pointed in front of the car, behind me. I looked, and in an instinctual burst of motion threw myself over my hood to the driver's side. I whipped the unlocked door open, hurled myself into the driver's seat, and almost slammed the door shut on the fingers of a slim kid, the first of a gang of thirty crazed thugs. He hit the car with a thud, those fingers immediately working the door latch.

"We'll drive," I said. And we did. To New Jersey.

"Listen," Mary said an hour later, biting into her second Big Mac, "You gotta know by now we never met before. Who the hell you think I am?" She had softened quite a bit since I fed her. MacDonalds had seemed a good destination, again. It felt safe. Sort of homey.

"You're sure you don't have a sister?" I asked for the fourth time.

"Of course. I mean, I would know if I had family wouldn't I? Of all people? I had a mother once. She disowned me when I moved here."

"Where are you from?"

"Levittown."

"Oh, well, I guess I can understand that."

"Why d'you think I have a sister?"

"I know another girl that you look like, sort of."

"Really?" she smiled, batting her eyelids, "Same eyes?"

"No, hers are green."

"Same hair?" she paused, running a finger through her faded purple tuft, "Light brown?"

"Red."

"Same face?"

"No."

"Body?" she asked, mouth full as she stood and turned for me.

"Well, no, not exactly," I sighed.

"What the hell man?" She yelled, slamming her Big Mac into its carton, "You makin' all this up er somethin'? Shit, you're just playing a game to get in my pants, ain't you?" The fire in her angry, frightened eyes flashed confirmation of her connection to Max, but I had no way to communicate that truth to Mary. I just shook my head, and held my voice steady.

"Believe me," I said, "That's the farthest thing from my mind." I grabbed her wrist before she could storm indignantly from the plastic dining room. Without getting up, I brought her gently back to the table.

"Then what?" she asked, sulking. She was able to hold her sulk yet still munch on a handful of French fries.

"I just don't know, Mary. I could try to explain, but it would take too long."

"Why? I'm not stupid," she said.

"Of course you're not," I lied.

"Then tell me what's goin' on."

"I can't. I'm not sure myself," I said. I took a moment to finish my Coke (and my lunch, since that was all I had) and continued, "Listen, I'm sorry I did all this to you. It must have all been a mistake. I'll take you back to your theater now and we'll forget any of this ever happened. I'll try to explain something to your boss if you need me to"

"No need. What about Cleavus?"

"You can rest assured that he has forgotten all about me, literally."

"Literally?" she asked, puzzled.

"For real. He might not even bother you any more, if I know my friend. The cop."

"'Friend?'" she asked, hand limply set on her hip.

"Just a figure of speech," I said. I stood, primarily to distract her from an inane attempt at piecing together cop show plots in an effort to place my true identity. I continued, "Come on, let's go now." She stood obediently and followed me out, uneaten French fries in hand. I drove her back to her theater, getting lost twice on the way. It was much harder reaching midtown Manhattan when I wanted to get there, and Mary was no help with directions. I pitied the girl, yet grew more fascinated as well. I longed to find the Max that I knew I saw in her. Better to leave things be for now, I thought, until I talked to Rudy about it.

There were no street gangs waiting for us upon our eventual return, though that greasy old man I imagined to be Mary's boss stood at the doors with his arms folded. Mary got out of the car, shut the door and stuck her head in the open window.

"You're really not gonna try nothin'?" she asked.

"Nothin'." I smiled.

"Huh," she said, sounding a little disappointed, "will you be back?"

"I have no idea. I don't get into the city much."

"You from outa town?" God help us.

"Westchester."

"Wow. You really might never be back."

"Who knows?"

"I hope so... you know, now that I look real close, you do look a little familiar."

"I do, do I?"

"I never lie. Really." She waved good-bye and ducked past the angry bloodshot glare of her boss, who had grunted for the third and obviously final time. I left the curb, headed home. As I wandered about searching for a way out of the city one thought lingered in my shopworn mind. Were Mary's last words merely a lie to spark interest?

Chapter Nine

The crayons looked delicious. I rubbed my hands in gleeful anticipation while the plain waitress slowly set the crystal tray of wax delicacies on the table. The crayons, each with a bit of its paper sheath slightly torn to facilitate peeling, were sorted in appetizing concentric circles: green around red, gold around green, blue around them all. In the center a single purple crayon stood on end. The culinary display of tempting Crayolas reminded me of the view from those overhead cameras in a 1930's extravaganza. I was very excited, but tactful enough to be sure the heat from my rubbing palms did not melt too many crayons. Cleavus, across the booth, smacked his lips and adjusted his thin leather tie. Rudy smiled. He was satisfied that he had ordered a fine dinner. Max sat next to me, her pleasantly strong hand on my thigh. She was smiling at me. I smiled back, feeling like I was at the soda shop with a varsity cheerleader. Everything was cool. I was content.

The three of them began speaking to me at once. Their words overlapped, syllables rattling against each other in an indecipherable staccato clatter. I eyed each of them, quietly respected their privacy, and relaxed. I found it much easier to admire the view from the diner window than to attempt uninvited interjections into clearly private conversations. And the mountain scenery 20,000 feet below certainly was glorious. I sipped blue juice, mildly surprised but not dissatisfied that it tasted just like sky.

"Alex, are you still there?" Max whispered in my ear, her lips gently brushing it. I turned, startled by the abrupt silence. They were looking at me, waiting for a response.

"Of course I am," I said, "I've been having a little trouble understanding you is all. I wish you wouldn't all talk at once. It's real confusing."

"At once?" Cleavus said softly, "Why, we have been speaking separately, Alex, enjoying attentions to all of our individual thoughts. You may not have comprehended, however."

"He's right, Alex," Rudy said, "Your timing is just a little off. You're supposed to listen to each of us separately, not all at once. Like you are now."

"You mean you haven't been talking simultaneously?" I asked.

"Of course not," Max said, "If we did we'd never know what we were saying, now would we?" She spoke in a condescending tone, similar to my words with Mary.

"Do you know Mary?" I asked.

"We've never met actually," she said, "But I do know of her. She's sort of home base for me. My starting point."

"Is she you?" I asked.

"Let us not get personal Alex," Cleavus warned, shaking a green crayon at me before tossing it whole into his mouth.

"It's okay, Clive. Alex, in your world Mary *is* me. The trouble is, our personality bent a bit too far toward my experiences here, and I became me and she was lost to a lifetime of—"

"Abject stupidity," Rudy finished, casually waving the gold crayon that he had speared with the end of his fork, "The tender balance was broken. Alex, didn't you ever wonder why there are so many consciously comatose people in this world?"

"No."

"Too many for it to seem unusual, huh? It happens because their consciousness for whatever reason gets locked into the greater whole of the World, and it loses touch with everyday reality. A split forms, though the halves can never truly be separated."

"Or joined," Clive cut in. Clive. Go figure.

"Is that what happened to you, Rudy?"

"No. My action was quite voluntary. I can be in both places. Not at once, but I am complete wherever I am. I can experience everything."

"Whereas I can never be in your world outside Rudy's influence," Max said rather sadly, playing with her Crayola.

"You walked me into my house once," I said.

"Or yours," she added, grinning.

"Mine. Now wait a minute, I never made *myself* complete."

"There's the rub," Rudy said, "All that time, all that work we put in to get me to understand, and all you had to do was be born."

"Sorry Rudy," I said, containing a sudden flush of pride. I again rejected asking him who 'we' was, sure that I would receive an incomplete response.

"That's all right, Alex," Rudy grinned, "I am here. That's what's important."

"Not true," Clive said, "The true imperative is that Alex is here. Alex, you must join us."

"Haven't I done that already?"

"No," Max said, "Anything you've done so far has been an accident, or Rudy's work."

"We need you to be able to move among the united consciousnesses of the World," Clive said.

"Sounds like a charity group," I quipped. They ignored me.

"That way you'll be able to exercise real power," Rudy continued, "Out of your dreams but still your dreams."

"We need you to understand us," Max said. Hers was the last sentence I caught before their voices became one again. I sighed, munching on a gold crayon, sans fork. It tasted like gold crayon.

"Alex," Rudy's voice poked through, "You still with us?"

"I'm not sure I ever was. But then, I'd never thought I'd like the taste of gold crayon, either. Look, I want to help you, believe me. I've certainly got nothing better to do. I think you and your enemy have seen to that. In spite of all that, and maybe even a distant urge to do some good, I'm still having trouble moving into your world. It's like trying to drive from Maine to Baghdad."

"Without a map," Max finished, her emerald eyes flashing.

Rudy sighed and lowered his fork to his plate. He looked out the window for a few minutes before he spoke. It was probably for dramatic pause, but I'm guessing that he also wanted to finish chewing his crayon before he spoke to avoid any embarrassing images or spray.

"Alex, it's not like walking through a door into our world. This isn't Star Trek. There is no transporter. There is no other world. There is only the one we all share. You have only to adjust yourself, your vision, to include Max's home as well as your own. It's not that hard. I've done most of the work for you."

"Gosh thanks Rudy."

"Hey no problem. What I'm saying is, it's up to you to join us. In your dreams you aspire to us, but dreams aren't real."

"They're not? That's not what you've led me to believe in the last few weeks."

"They're not real because they hold no tangible experience. I didn't say you couldn't live or die in one."

"What?"

"The news on TV is never real until they report that a house has blown up in your neighborhood."

"Do I get what's behind door number two if I figure that one out?"

Rudy shrugged, "You can't exercise power in the World until you make that power real. Take it out of your dreams. Wield it in the same manner."

"You make it sound easy."

"It is, after you get the knack of it."

"Why doesn't everyone do it then?"

"If they could accept the possibility, they might," Rudy said, bottomless eyes meeting mine. No Rudy, I thought, no one would try, if they had one look into those eyes.

"How do I get that knack?"

"We're not sure," Rudy said, "I did it by concentrating for a few hundred lifetimes. You seem to have innate ability. I suppose you only have to consciously combine dream experience with real moments. A neat trick, but possible for you."

"I have no idea what you're talking about Rudy," I said. That was probably because I wasn't listening very hard. Explanations usually pass right over me, especially when a beautiful woman is rubbing my thigh.

"You'll catch on soon enough," Rudy said, "For now let's enjoy dinner."

We resumed eating. I allowed my friends to fall into incoherent conversation again. However, I found that if I concentrated hard enough I could separate phrases. It was a matter of timing, in the truest sense of the word. I had to make my personal time hiccup, thus reversing my sense of time a bit for each one of them. Then I could hear what was said, fast-forward to the next speaker, and hiccup again. I juggled the moments for a few rounds of conversation before retiring, exhausted. I settled for enjoying my dessert—iced earwax—and waiting patiently for the dream to end, or at least for some change that I might enjoy.

I passed the time watching Rudy, Max, and Clive dine. They were animated, appearing almost joyful. This must have been a great moment for them. Rudy was smiling, almost laughing at unheard jokes from Clive. Rudy wore a simple khaki jump suit, open at the neck to reveal his tan chest. Of course he did not open it for that reason. Not Rudy. Clive was more difficult to digest than Mary had been. The man who was ready to kill me hours ago for not opening my car door was now dressed in a black Italian suit, picking carefully at his food, one hand clutching a folded napkin; a gentleman by every account. I sighed, not surprised. Rudy had more impressive shows than this. The lack of subtlety in Clive and Max's counterparts was puzzling, however. I remembered that I had not mentioned yesterday's motel dream to Rudy. Odd, since it had rarely left my mind since I had once more lost touch with Cassie. I raised a finger to speak, but then kept my silence. They were enjoying themselves. There was no sense in ending a good time for information I could pick up later.

Rudy broke from their conversation to signal the waitress. I smiled at this detail. Surely the waitress would come if he – or, rather, I – thought about it. But I hadn't. Everything was so concrete that I hadn't taken the time to think about creating details. This was a first in a dream with Rudy. Another first was the crayon dinner, I thought, smiling. The crayon dinner in the floating diner was the same as it was an hour ago. I halted at that thought, sensing something intrinsically wrong in it. The same? Impossible. Nothing in my dreams had ever remained intact for any length of time. Yet there we were, floating in space in the same diner after seven courses. I nervously drummed my fingers on the Formica table. The knife scratch that I had noticed during chalk soup was still there. I stopped drumming.

"What the hell is happening here?" I shouted, resisting an urge to stand and slam my fist on the table. They looked up as one, politely smiling at the interruption.

"What do you mean?" Rudy asked.

"This dream I'm having. It isn't one, is it?"

"Whoever said it was?" Clive asked. Before I could respond I felt Max apply pressure to my leg. She stood up.

"If you men will excuse me, I must powder my nose," she said uneasily, leaving the table. Clive rose as well, and took Max's seat after she left. His move seemed natural, and mannered, enough as not to upset me.

"Well," I said, "I had assumed—"

"I thought you would have cast your assumptions aside by now, Alex," Rudy said.

"You mean this isn't a dream?" I asked. They shook their heads. I began to feel boxed in, and glanced nervously about me for an exit. I asked, "Then what is this? Where are we?"

"In a diner," Rudy said calmly.

"And where's the diner?"

"Somewhere over Innsbruck, I think."

"Is it real?" I asked.

"Depends on how you look at it, I guess. To me it is real. Like Fritz's was. For you, who knows? You have the capacity to make real anything that you wish."

"Or perhaps the other way around," Clive added.

I heard none of this as my agitation at being in a place that was not a dream increased. The last two places I had experienced this, Fritz's and the sanctuary, did not end pleasantly.

"How do I get out of this?" I asked.

"Simple," Rudy said, "You have only to assimilate the situation into your mind as a dream, then manipulate it to your whim. It's easy. I do it all the time. You've been practicing with your car for days."

"That was me?"

"You didn't know?"

"Of course not. I thought you were giving me a hand."

"Nonsense. I told you that I couldn't help. I don't need to anyway, it seems. You've already got the methodology cold unconsciously. Now all you have to do is know what you're doing. No problem."

"No problem," I sighed, dejected.

"Maybe a small problem," Clive said, looking at Rudy.

"Just tell me what to do to get out of here." I pleaded, "I'm starting to feel a bit trapped."

"Well," Rudy said, trying to smile, "There may be something we can do for you there."

He and Clive exchanged glances for an interminable moment. Then Clive calmly, and with great speed and power, pushed me through the glass window to cold free fall outside.

Chapter Ten

The chromium bastion of suburban comfort wafted quietly above my outstretched fingers. I could see the broken window through which I had just passed – three small heads peered out from the jagged-rimmed blackness. One waved. In a few seconds, and several hundred yards, I imagined, the people I had assumed to be my compatriots in this bizarre new world were too small to see. Only the diner remained, and it had already shrunk to a size that could be eclipsed by my flailing hands.

The floating diner was hopelessly beyond my fingers' grasp, regardless of my sincerest effort to believe that it was a tiny thing nestled between white knuckles. I began my silent and involuntary descent. The shock of being tossed through a window by allies still clogged my senses, but I was aware enough to assume that there had to be a purpose to their unexpected actions. I felt that I could cling to the wholly intellectual concept that this fall could have a finish that did not include a bone shattering impact.

I also had enough of my wits on tap to admire the surreal wonder of a 1950's-era food emporium suspended in the air under a balloon whose vast Pepsi-logoed surface area rivaled that of a football stadium. When my descent had reduced the diner and balloon to two tiny specks in the clear blue sky above me, I rolled over to see if landfall was imminent. It was not. I was still several miles above a rugged snow-capped mountain range. I had an instant of hysterical pleasure when I realized that I had a few extra minutes of living to do, but the sensation did not last more than a few hundred feet. I was falling, and I was alone.

Given my extreme altitude, I expected to be cold, and perhaps out of breath; I was clad only in jeans and a gently luffing gray T-shirt. But the air, though crisp, had no real bite and was quite breathable. The absence of any wind let me believe I was falling gently, with no acceleration. I clung to that group of improper stimuli with the iron grip of desperate hope. Such anomalies implied that what was happening possibly was not real. Of course, I had never actually experienced free-fall at 50-odd thousand feet, so I could have been wrong about what to expect, given that my only experience with such extremes was gleaned from the Discovery Channel.

Reality was having another form of sway on my battered psyche as well, by presenting the rocky terrain that was rushing inexorably to greet me. That terrain, and the impact it predicted with granite surety, was not helping my metaphysical struggle. Still, mine was not a standard cinematic tumble with me, the victim, spinning to my death, arms and legs swirling in the wind. It was a simple drop, a casual change in direction of many thousands of feet. I remembered news photos of bodies thrown from airplanes. I imagined the sensation as every bone in my body was pulverized simultaneously. But those people accelerated to over 175 mph. I was barely moving. At least I thought I was barely moving. Again, I never did this before. I could have been mistaken.

That new thought did not settle me – or rather, elevate me – so I discarded it. I clung instead to the oddities of my fall. Thoughts about anomalies worked almost as well as a very large net may have toward reducing my anxiety. The questions also came easily, given my situation: Why did Clive push me? I muddled over that for a few hundred feet. It was no accident; he did not just happen to sit next to me when Max left. And why did Rudy let me fall? Surely he had the capacity to prevent it. If he was not behind it in the first place, which I deemed in less than a thousand feet that he was. Why was I moving so slowly? Why didn't anything change? Somebody had to have a hand in this; the dream was too well choreographed. A dream, I called it. But it was real, according to Rudy and my amateurish observations. Perhaps, but a dream made this drop far more acceptable, and the snowcapped mountains below much less final. I wondered if it was a test to see how well my untapped talents could adapt to an unknown situation. I scrawled a mental note to remember that, if

my abilities did indeed adapt, I would adapt a few changes to
Rudy's face on our next meeting.

I continued to fall. Regardless of my intellectual leanings
on the subject, I still battled naturally ensuing panic as the ground
loomed twice as large as it had when I was enjoying sticky dessert
moments earlier. My mind raced against my instincts for a
conclusion to this plummet that did not include going splat, or
dying en route because my body went into shock (I was suspicious
of that fate, having only heard stories about it growing up, but I
couldn't chase it from my thoughts). Conclusion was the wrong
word; I was in search of a solution. There had to be one: natural
law, and logic, had been far too defiled in the last few hours to
permit me to assume that I was doomed. If it was a dream I was
experiencing, then my only option was to ride it out. Perhaps I
could enjoy the descent, confident that no harm would befall me
upon contact with the mountains below. I laughed, wondering if
there was a bridge I'd like to sell myself. It was a high-pitched
laugh, bathed in sweaty, unavoidable fear.

I began, unconsciously at first, to concentrate on my
passage, to focus on the physical details of my descent. Though I
had no source for inspired comprehension, I understood that I
could grasp the reality of the moment in a complete context, in
Rudy's fashion. I could form this fall into a dream in order to
manipulate it properly. Perhaps I could put the earth above instead
of below me. I laughed again, my concentration broken.

My fall had progressed to the point where I could discern
individual trees in the forest below. They were pines, starkly green
against the virgin white snow of the Alps, and each came to a
menacing point at its top. Menacing trees? I struggled to
concentrate, to transform finite linear surroundings and actions into
the noncommittal randomness of a dream. It was not an easy task,
given the alarming nature of the situation that I was attempting to
warp. I closed my eyes, felt no change. I opened them, and saw
that everything was indeed the same, only closer. I closed my eyes
again, and tried a lot harder. This time, instead of just
concentrating on an abstraction like "change," I pictured simple
concrete images of comfort. I chose safe, indoor images, like the
sofa in my TV room. I opened my eyes again, expecting to find
myself in my recliner, watching the re-run channel with a bowl of

buttered popcorn in my lap. Wrong. I was still falling toward the same cold granite. My efforts, which I thought had encompassed the gamut of my knowledge of Rudy's reality circus, had failed to soften or slow the approaching landscape.

My heart leapt into my throat when I passed near and below the tallest peak in the area. Its passage gave me hope, however, because it confirmed that I was not falling as fast as nature had intended. Instead of plummeting at almost 200 miles per hour, I was moving at probably about fifty or sixty miles an hour. Of course, I thought, anything over thirty is no doubt academic.

My thoughts were shaken by the abrupt presence of a huge raven flying with me. It was diving, wings extended but with no visible effort, at a speed that matched mine. It must have recently arrived. I had been scanning the skies for Rudy to magically appear since the diner faded, and they remained consistently clear. The huge bird cooed gently. It seemed to want me to hop on its back. It confirmed my impression by dipping its wings slightly in a gesture of welcome. Birds don't do that, I thought. Of course, ravens don't coo or boast twelve-foot wingspans either, so I was already wary. I did not want to miss an opportunity, however, so I reached for a giant ebony wing. That wing seemed large enough to enshroud me. I imagined it providing a quilt of warm black down that would support me safely to the bottom of the gorge that loomed a scant two or three thousand feet below. I touched the feathers, and rejoiced when I felt their downy texture. The bird was not a product of my panicked imagination; at least not an intangible product. I clamped my hand on a clump of trailing feathers, each as long as my forearm. The bird's beak seemed to twist into a smile, one gray eye studying me with intelligent interest. The feathers were ice cold. I would not have minded if they were on fire.

Something deeper did mind. My hand let go suddenly. Its release of my last perceived chance was fully independent of what I thought had been my heartfelt wishes. My body seemed to be shunning the aid. I felt, to the pit of my already churning stomach, strangely repulsed by the presence of the big bird. Though I normally refrain from argument with instinct, I made another attempt to snare the wing with an open palm. The bird flew closer for me, gently lapping my back with frozen feathers. I flailed my unresponsive arms, terror welling from just above that gushy spot in my gut, but succeeded only in batting the wing away. I screamed. My eyes remained fixed on the bird, rather than the boulders that were mere yards from my head. Then, in the instant before impact, the frigid nature of the feathers filtered into my terror-clouded mind and I recognized it. It was the same cold that had stabbed at me when I faced that shadow in one of Rudy's epic dream battles. My body's reaction to this bird had elicited the same feelings. In my fear of becoming a coat of warm pink paint for some desolate boulders, I almost deflected my own instinct and leaned on the potential source of my demise for help. I laughed aloud once more—a full, easy laugh this time. Things were coming together.

I let the panic bleed from me, replacing it with an easy calm. The bird was still with me, squawking madly, properly. It had become much smaller, almost to scale with its surroundings – a young eagle could have kicked its ass. I laughed at it as it blundered into a nearby cliff, bursting into a ball of flame like a WWII fighter plane. I felt good, confident. The mountains were as solid as ever, I knew, but now I felt that I could move them with a thought, as I had done in dreams past. The rapid growth rate of the boulders below no longer filled me with fear. It was the bird that had coaxed my most primal fears to the surface, causing me to ignore the truth of my fall. The guise of safety it carried on its hellish wings led me to believe in my descent, and that final impact would guarantee my death. The bird appeared at the moment that I would have decided to trust Rudy and live with the fall. I congratulated my unconscious sensibilities, happy that they had outshone my terror. My last thought before I made contact with Mother Earth was that at least if I were wrong I would never have known it. I would die happily, rewarded with final faith in myself.

I hit the rocks. Nothing happened. They were not crushed, and I did not splatter.

Instead, the nominal light and wind noise were replaced by darkness and a sound akin to sugar being poured into a pie tin. Because I felt no deceleration I guessed that I was moving through the ground at the same rate as I had through the air. Cool, I thought, there *was* another solution. I put my hands behind my head, enjoying the peace and tactile security of the situation while I could. Something would certainly happen soon to banish this moving blanket of stone, and the relief I could not help but feel would be replaced by some new fear.

No, I thought, that isn't true anymore. That was the purpose of the big bird. I was in my own province, and whatever happened would be my fault. Perhaps it had always been that way. A faint yellow glow grew below me and to the left. Interested in the warm change, I drew it to me. The dim circle dilated until I could define the lines of a cave around it. A meandering stream divided the floor of the cave, glistening with the reflection of unseen light.

I was in the stream. It was warm, shallow, and peppered with chunks of vegetables and noodles. I laughed while scooping a handful of chicken soup to my lips. I slurped a bit of it, allowing the warm liquid to languish on my tongue. The soup was a little salty, but good. I had no time to savor it, though: The cave mouth was upon me. The rushing soup, chest-deep and hot, was forcing me through and down a hundred-foot broth cataract to a patch of clear water far below. Though the soup emptied into it, the water seemed very cold. I avoided getting dunked, and hypothermia, by grabbing a tree limb that appeared a few yards off the ground, just within my reach and just before I would have entered the still water. The branch bent under my weight, becoming a giant wooden spring that gently set me on my feet, ankle deep in soft blue sand. I adjusted my T-shirt and surveyed my new surroundings.

I was in a standard movie-studio tropical paradise. A mountain stream dashed down a narrow cleft into a crystal lagoon. Lush greenery abounded. Colorful monkeys played in blue treetops. I settled into a plastic chaise by the beach, and sipped a cool drink that was waiting on the awful rattan table beside it. I could not identify the drink. It was one of those tropical blends that taste like suntan lotion, served in a hollowed pineapple. A pink parasol perched on the pineapple's rim. It was good.

I serenely surveyed my new world, intrigued by the busy animated scenery: a purple pterodactyl snatched a monkey from a tree; fish jumped into the lagoon from a nearby bluff, also on which orange palm trees swayed to a hula breeze. I leaned back and closed my eyes. This was nice, but it was also quite wrong. Sure, it was all real, but it was empty; a façade with no depth, truly mimicking a movie set. And it was empty. This paradise was tangible, as Rudy put it, but there was nobody there to share it with me. I was utterly alone. I was accustomed to company in my dreams. To experience all this without people just felt wrong. I put my palms behind my head, and wondered, after what I had learned that day, if there wasn't something to be done about my solitude. It did not take me long to fall over the edge.

On an impulse from whose talons of self-deification I should have run, I decided that I would just have to make my own company. With little more than interest in doing so, I `caused' some sand to mix with water and air on the beach near the water, imagining instructions in unrepeatable flowery text. I then watched, fascinated, as lumps of the stuff quickly formed into discernable shapes. I rose from the lounge chair, probably because I felt a need to stand above my newest creations, and stepped closer to the shifting piles of sand. The sand had sculpted itself into three perfect human statues: two men and a woman. In a moment the statues acquired the flesh tones of white people tanned bronze by years of sunbathing (a part of me worried that I had only made people from one race, but I ignored it – I would not allow myself to be bogged down by such petty ethical disputes as skin color). I then took care to dress them in appropriate clothes (linen suits for the men, a sarong for the woman). Once dressed, I stepped back in awe. They were beautiful. Statues of people one might encounter on Fifth Avenue. They were beautiful, but they were also still lifeless sand casts that were no better company than photographs of strangers. I tapped the tall, blond woman's arm. Her soft skin dimpled under the pressure of my finger. I moved closer, amazed, but not surprised.

They were no longer sand. I bent the woman's bare arm. It moved like a corpse, not a mannequin. I lifted one of her eyelids, gasping slightly when I discovered a dull, blue, perfect eye behind the soft curtain. I lifted the lid of her other eye next. Though she seemed to stare placidly into my own, I knew that those new eyes regarded nothing yet. I released her, stepped back. This is way too much, I thought, there's no way I should, or even can be doing this. My new power tempted to overwhelm me with imagined potential. It felt like a static charge that I could not ground. For a single sane moment I feared it, desperately wishing to flee. Then I wanted more.

Feeling my chest swell in anticipation, I decided that it was time to breathe some life into my creations. The thought had barely, irrevocably, left the sanctuary of my fantasies when the men opened their eyes, wide. Those orbs were not blue and handsome, but rather red with the blood that filled them. The men screamed in agony, though there was no life defining their ghostly visages. They were horrendously invigorated for a fraction of a second, and then they began to decay. The dissolution from flesh back to sand was very fast, very violent, and possibly very painful. Their feet went first, changing from perfect flesh to bloody bones to swirling sand in a heartbeat. The legs crumbled, and the decay continued upward. Green mucous-blood formed a pool that the torsos fell into as they thrashed in pain. Finally, their empty heads gasped for breath after their necks were gone. In just a few seconds, my living beings were primordial ooze sans life.

I stood in silence over the green muck that remained of my creations, uncertain of my initial reaction. My first thought, after the mind-rattling tremors of terror and shame faded slightly, was that I might have stepped on some mighty toes. I was horrified that my mind still searched for some practical reason behind my failure. It should have been obvious that I was not spiritually equipped to supply souls to sand. I shuddered when I imagined what substitute for life I had tried to breath into my statues. It obviously could not have been the real thing, the true breath, or word that drives genuine creation. But it *was* something. Something else. I looked at the woman. She was still poised for life, unaware of the fate of her two brothers. She was beautiful: her tall, bountiful body swept with long, flowing flaxen hair. Her high-cheeked face lacked expression as she stared at my contemplation. She resembled no one I knew. I stroked her hair. It was soft, full. I grabbed a handful and pulled very hard, ripping that masterpiece of a head from sandy shoulders with unchecked violence. With my vision blurred by tears, I kicked the rest of her down without pause. After she had been reduced to a few piles of multicolored sand, I retreated a few paces, stumbling over a fallen log.

I numbly climbed onto the log, and raised the lagoon's water level by a few feet with a gesture, burying my horrors beneath a blanket of liquid clarity. I stared at the spot where my "children" were born and died until the bottom was ground smooth by many tons of moving water. Then I sat on the log and wept, carefully preventing my feet from touching the surface. I had found my limits of power in the sightless world of dreams. I hated myself for having the nerve to discover them so soon after my initiation.

In time I stood, distrusting the false peace of the lagoon. The vegetation around me was brown, dry, and the monkeys were gone from the trees. It was time to leave. I knew I had to move back to the real world, be it Rudy's, mine, or both at once. I had enough of this nonsense of creating my own surroundings and audience. Rudy said I would find great power, but he should have asked if I would be able to curb it. I hoped that I would be able to perform less arrogantly in a place that was not of my making. I wondered for a moment if it wasn't safer to simply be afraid.

I walked through some brush near the waterfall and got into my waiting, running, Escort. I drove silently through the forest. Gloom and the guilt at what I had done crowded me in the small car. I passed a familiar oak tree, pulled onto Route 9 a mile south of Croton. I drove north to the first exit, followed 9A to that Greek diner on the right. A black Porsche with German plates was parked in the lot.

Chapter Eleven

"...lex. Alex!" A familiar feminine voice called from far, far away. That voice was attempting nonchalance, but betrayed embarrassment, and perhaps mild panic. I could hear it clearly, closely now, though it still seemed strangely disconnected, as if I were across a stadium from the speakers issuing its summons.

"Alex! C'mon man, wake up!" the voice cried again. Eyelids heavy, I tried to concentrate on the blur that was shouting at me and apparently shaking my shoulders vigorously. The pale image I could view was not all that was out of focus – my disorientation was complete. I remembered that I was conscious earlier when I walked into the diner, moments before a finely woven curtain dropped in front of my mind. I assumed first that I had blacked out, but that did not feel right. I had never fainted before. If I had, I was sure I would have been able to remember my last moment of consciousness and associate it with my first moment of waking. Plus, I was sure I would have less trouble opening my eyes.

My face felt sticky, like it had been recently coated in Elmer's glue. Perhaps I had been sloppy with dessert, I thought, feeling a smile flash across my face. That positive movement felt encouraging, and helped me realize that I was beginning to regain muscle control. I was waking, but was still numb. My original panic abated, however, and I grew comfortable in my warm glue mask. I was unperturbed by the spasms of nervous pain that crushed my chest, signaling my body's basic reaction to the fact that it was no longer breathing.

"Alex! God damn it. Wake up. You can't stay like that." Hands shook me firmly.

"Yeah, and you look ridiculous lolling in your soup," a heavier voice said. That helped. I forced myself awake with a method I employed when trying to exit a disagreeable dream; I simply shook my head until I saw a sign of reality. That reality was usually something basic, like my alarm clock or familiar ceiling cracks. With some effort I could feel my head shaking vigorously, and when that sensation was concrete I could concentrate on the rim of the soup bowl that seemed to hover inches from my forehead. That was enough. Suddenly I was awake, seated in a red leatherette booth at the diner in Croton. I was encircled by the icy stares of several strange patrons who had suffered the rain of cold chicken soup that I had hurled off of my truly shaking head. I heard someone quietly call me a drunk. The old woman at the next table more verbally voiced her opinion of unordered soup fouling her dinner. That was it, though; the people of Westchester County are reasonable, polite, and wary of the actions of strangers. I stopped my still swaying head, looked around at them all. I smiled, feeling blood rushing to my cheeks. Wiping their faces with paper napkins, Rudy and Max were seated across the table. The dirty window beside our booth looked on a street lit parking lot, not a Nepalese postcard. I grabbed Rudy's wrist, wildly relieved.

"You wouldn't believe the dream I had," I panted. I continued to clutch his wrist, unwilling to release him. I feared my hand would shake, I would knock something over, and the management would boot this drunk out. I continued, "Where's Clive?"

"Right where you left him before your great fall," Rudy said with empathy. My fingers tightened. Though I knew what was coming, I asked anyway.

"In the dream?"

"What dream?" he asked.

"The one I just pulled out of. The balloon. The crow. The lagoon...the people."

"Alex," Max said, wrapping her two slender yet powerful hands around my wrists to pry open my vise grip. She dug half-inch-long red fingernails into my unyielding flesh, and continued, "You walked in here five minutes ago."

"No. No, I never left. Really. It all must have been a dream."

"Then when did you get here?" Max asked. I looked at her. Her eyes were wet. I did not blame her. Mine would have been, too. I was flustered, sure that my recent experience had been a dream. I must have appeared truly pathetic. I paused, and, after consciously reviewing my memories, I did notice that their details were a bit too clear. This clarity was disturbingly similar to that of my memory of the demise of Fritz's tavern. Rudy drained his glass of yellow American beer and spoke.

"Alex, I'm guessing that you're having some trouble with your transition. I know, it's happened to me. You've traversed two existences without leaving either, and, more importantly, you've realized that you can. That's a hell of a concept to absorb, on any level."

"I think he can see that," Max said sharply.

"Right," Rudy said, "I suppose you can."

"Yeah?" I snapped, "Well what I can see is that this is all totally nuts! I was in my car. I know I was in my car. Before that I was falling from – no wait, I was in the diner first. But the whole time I was there I was here..." I drifted off, realizing that Rudy was being gentle in his diagnosis of my rapidly deteriorating sanity. I knew I was present at the (real) diner, and I knew I was never asleep to dream, so I was able to rationalize that there was no dream. But then, I thought (to myself, in a lame attempt to conceal my obvious confusion), if there was no dream, the fall, the lagoon, and the soulless lives I had created were real, in some arcane way. An inner fog that no doubt existed to protect me from my own guilt began to lift, and I was able to string together the events that brought me to this diner. Or, I was able to realize that there were events that led to this diner, though they all had begun at another diner that my mind's eye had trouble separating from the more believable current one. It was as if I had never left, yet my mind insisted that all my recent experiences did happen, though they may have done so out of time. Oh, my, I thought, I can't believe any of this, and yet I must. I released Rudy and rested my forehead in my sweaty palms. I closed my eyes, but nothing went away.

"It's not a straight line anymore," Rudy offered, hinting that he had somehow followed my train of thought. I ignored that possibility, but lifted my head and looked across the table at my old friend. He was the same as ever, not godlike at all as he munched a French fry and thoughtfully rubbed his wrists.

"More like a pile of unraveled cassette tape," I said, forcing a smile, "So I really did all that I dreamed—did?"

"You sure did. I don't know what you might have tried after you didn't hit the ground, but if it was anything like my first time, you no doubt did some dastardly deeds."

"Dastardly in all but the hands of the proper authority," I said pointing my thumb to the sky.

"Whoever," Rudy acknowledged, "Now you can begin to fathom the power we face, and the potential for its corruption by real evil. You're part of an elite group, Alex."

"A club of three."

"Three?"

"Three," Max repeated, "You, Rudy, and the guy without the, um, moral fiber to leave well enough alone."

"The shadow?" I rasped, feeling melodramatic.

"If you will," Rudy said, "And you might understand from what you may or may not have done moments ago why we're committed to curbing the evil."

"I think I got a pretty serious hint, but I was a bit too busy enjoying the special effects to register just how much shit I was really in. Until it was too late."

"You're a good man, Alex," Rudy said, clapping my shoulder as he stood, "I always knew that. Now let's go." He left a fifty on the table and walked out. Max and I followed. The old Greek at the register by the door smiled at us as we left. If I had dined alone, he would have chased after me for payment.

"Wait," I said as we strolled out the glass door that Max held open for us, "You never finished explaining my dream. My trip. My fall. Whatever the hell it was. Hell, you never even started. Am I going to get this dream dyslexia every time I venture through the World?"

"Nah," Rudy said over his shoulder, "It gets easier; clears up. You'll be able to designate a starting point, a clean slate, soon enough. It only took me about twenty years to get the knack."

"Fine."

"And that's really cool that you learned how to say World with a capital 'W.' That takes real talent. Oh, do you mind if we ride with you? Max hates the back seat of my car."

"Not at all. Where are we going?"

"As long as you're primed tonight, I thought I'd take you on my rounds with me."

"Rounds?" I asked, once more feeling my personal freedom, and sanity, ebbing, "You actually go on rounds? What the hell for?"

"Never mind," Max smiled, "Just get in the car."

We drove in silence, with Rudy at the wheel. Max had taken the seat behind me. She was careful to shove all the CD's and newspapers to one side before she sat. I made no objections when Rudy offered to drive, since I was more confidant that he would take us in a better direction than if I were driving. He turned onto Route 9A and headed south. He drove with traffic, and the ride seemed like any other evening commute along a heavily traveled suburban corridor until the road surface suddenly switched from smooth asphalt to rumbling brick. Startled, I looked around, but could not get my bearings. I could not identify the town we had entered, but it certainly was not Ossining. It was probably foreign, though; everyone rode bicycles. At that point I noticed that Rudy was speaking. He had been for quite some time, but I had not been listening. Why ruin the surprise?

"...to do is re-adjust what was done by the enemy in his attempt to inflict mayhem on the world," he was saying. I shifted mental gears, and imagined what he was talking about.

"Still sounds like a comic strip to me," I said, "Does this enemy shadow have a name?"

"Forgive the melodramatics," Rudy smiled, "His real name was Freuzre, about eleven centuries ago. You won't hear it used much. As I was saying, the enemy, Freuzre, if you must, thinks he is doing the right thing. In fact, he's brimming with righteousness. Righteousness can fuel some pretty huge steamrollers, and his is particularly hard to stop. So, whether he is evil incarnate or simply unaware of his actions, he sees no reason to be stifled. If he does not see what he is doing, then this is all a mistake. That is a bit farfetched, though."

"For our sakes we hope that all this is an accident." Max said, "That means that there is a solution to his invasions that is not based on insanity, or our own concession to evil."

"That is what we hope," Rudy added, "Because that makes for a workable situation."

"Situation?" I asked.

"Anything that you ever saw as unreasonable, bad, or a behavior that defied rational explanation was probably a twist Freuzre added to your environment."

"You mean just in my dreams, or in all of reality?" I asked.

"Everything. Freuzre's fingers may have been in all of the nasty chaos that this world endured over the last century."

"That's crazy," I said.

"Or simply an accident that a well-meaning villain inspired."

"Right," Max said, maintaining the syllable for a moment.

"So everything that goes wrong in the world is because of this one incredibly old man. Am I supposed to believe that?"

"If you want, though the term 'man' might be a stretch," Rudy said, "But of course you'll always think there is more to it; it's only human to do so. How can one person be responsible for everything wrong in the world? I'm not sure, and I know that's a tough concept to wrap your mind around, but it does work that way."

"What about random chance?"

"Not in a neatly packaged World where every cog must mesh, however distantly, with all others to make reality tick."

Max leaned over my shoulder, whispered loudly in my ear, "Don't believe him. Rudy is a firm believer in loose ends."

"Then none of this is true?" I said aloud, facing Rudy.

"Of course its true," Max said, "But there are some factors that can cause, or prevent, random occurrences. Like people that can operate in all facets of the system."

"Right," Rudy interjected, picking up where he had left off, "It's sort of like time travel. You must be careful where you step, lest a misplaced toe change destiny for all."

"You sound like you are quoting the Law."

"I'm glad you hear it that way," Rudy smiled grimly, "The third member of our club considers such caveats an invitation rather than a recognition of higher purpose. And that, my friend, is the one difference that makes him so damn dangerous. But enough talk for now, guys, there's work to be done. See those feet sticking out from under the limo over there?" He pointed to a Mercedes parked around the cobbled corner of the quiet intersection we had entered. After a preliminary squint in the dim evening light I spotted two denim-clad legs protruding from beneath the car. They wriggled occasionally as their owner adjusted position or needed leverage. Rudy stopped my Escort in the middle of the street. There were no other cars out at this hour, so no one minded. Rudy lifted one finger from the wheel to point at the Mercedes.

"Belongs to an Arab diplomat. The guy underneath thinks he's doing something good, for whatever reason, but his bomb will trigger an intifada, encouraging a bloody and completely useless war. This is an accident that we can't allow to happen."

"Doesn't seem like a random event to me," I said.

"Far from it, but then I never said anything about random. No, this is a result of cosmetically twisted reality, and we can't let it happen."

"Are all car bombings a result of twisted reality?" I asked.

"Of course not. Usually they are necessary, sad but important, dollops of grease that help keep things running smoothly. All peace and no war make a dull, and evolutionarily stunted, world." The man pulled out from under the car, looked both ways and ran into an alley. He was middle-aged, blond, and decidedly non-descript. He wasn't at all the textbook Arab terrorist that I had expected. I was not surprised when he ran down a darkened street, away from his 'noble' deed, without noticing us parked a few yards away. My indoctrination into Rudy's World had already led me to understand that he was seen only when he wanted to be seen.

When the bomber was out of sight, Rudy got out of my car. He strolled to the Mercedes, his hands thrust casually into his pockets. When he got to the car, he turned, and leaned against it with almost comical nonchalance. Then he walked back to us. Before he reached my car I saw something drop from the Mercedes. Rudy started the engine and drove.

"So this is rounds, huh?" I asked after we were a few blocks away, and the pavement had become asphalt once more, with the air above it rippling in noonday desert heat.

"Yup," Rudy said, "And they rarely get more exciting than they did just now."

"'Cept when you're in the mix, love," Max whispered in my ear. She kicked my seat from underneath for emphasis.

"Thanks. Rudy, how do you know that guy wasn't just your basic loony out for a good time?" I asked as we drove into a purple sunset.

"A feeling," Rudy said softly, eyes fixed forward.

"You'll find out soon enough," Max said firmly, preventing my volley of follow-up questions. I sat back in my seat and stared out the window. I figured I had time to be patient now, since I was in this conflict completely now, and Rudy and Max apparently weren't going anywhere. I changed the subject in my mind, wondering briefly what happened to Clive, or if he had existed at all, while we turned left off the two-lane highway onto a palm-lined lane. A bay of blue water glistened in the distance. Rudy was quiet. His face had become passive, his expression grim. In Rudy's case this meant that the corners of his mouth had dropped a millimeter. I started to say something, but then suppressed it when I felt Max's foot press firmly against the bottom of my seat once more. I cleared my throat and resumed my review of the fascinating flux of the passing scenery.

The road curved away from the distant ocean, and aimed us toward a distant range of rough beige mountains capped in yellow snow. Fine, I thought, more mountains. They were very far way, though, and it became obvious that they would not be an obstacle when the road abruptly dipped down into a tunnel whose circular face was flush with the surface of the wide treeless plain. As we entered the round crimson tunnel, Rudy accelerated, but did not turn on the lights. There was no need, since there was plenty of ambient red light seeping from the walls. We followed the red tunnel without event or conversation for what seemed to be several miles. I wondered why I had never heard of this route, and wondered even more solemnly why I was not in awe of its vast and apparently alien dimensions. In time the cylindrical tunnel fluted out on all sides, including the floor below us, until it was a quarter mile wide. I could hear a distant thump that vibrated the car and lifted the smaller hairs on my neck and back one or two times every second. Those hairs became permanently erect when I noticed that the tunnel was not filled with air, but with a thick ruby-tinted clear liquid. Oh, I thought, so maybe it wasn't alien. Rudy swore under his breath as he quickly maneuvered the Escort around a man who was anxiously floating in the plasma. His outstretched arms and legs were scrambling for a nonexistent solid surface. The man was old, perhaps in his sixties. He was well dressed, and his ruddy features were familiar, though I couldn't place him. He was someone political, I decided, though I was thoroughly disconnected from current events. Max must have perceived my thought, because she leaned forward and said softly:

"He should look familiar. Remember, people dream subjectively. We're seeing the President the way he sees himself."

"Of the United States?" I hissed, "Oh man, this is definitely comic book material."

"Well, love, either you came along on the right night, or Rudy figured an extreme example might help clarify his position."

Rudy was still silent, oblivious to our banter. A small bead of sweat had formed on his clean-shaven upper lip. Wow, I thought, that had to mean that he was using a great deal of energy to do whatever it was he was doing. I had played hour-long full court pickup games of basketball with Rudy, and never saw him sweat once. It used to drive me nuts.

Other people began to flow past the President as he continued his frantic tumble through the giant throbbing vessel: the First Lady; his children, his dog; strangers, no doubt his close friends. In just a few beats of the distant heart, the artery was clogged with throngs of screaming, whining people. They were running towards the President across a long flat field of freshly mowed grass. Their eyes were wide with terror, though that was difficult to tell because their heads rarely faced forward. Their screams were deafening, but did not eclipse the steady beat of the distant pump. The artery's distant translucent walls blackened briefly before erupting like torched paraffin ahead of a rapidly approaching wall of fire. People at the rear of the mob began to graphically disintegrate in the heat of the firestorm. Though they were reduced to charred skeletons, their screams continued, and the pace of their sprint toward the President did not slow.

A new obstacle floated in front of the President, and it stayed before him, regardless of the direction in which he repeatedly tried to swim away. It was an ornate wooden podium capped with an array of blinking lights and LED readouts, like the control panel requisite on any science fiction show. Not only did the panel remain fixed in front of him, it also consistently remained between the President and the mob. A red button as big as the President's fist comprised the center of the control panel. Oh, I thought, this is so subtle. I was not amused by the intellectual shallows in which America's highest elected official waded.

Though trite, the image was all too meaningful to the President. His eyes were filled with terror as his hands hovered over the red button. The ornate console held two locks fitted with keys, one red and one green. The left key was green, but the President was reaching to the right. The screams of the people escalated with his motion, but the hand continued inexorably. At that point Rudy leapt from the car.

I had expected a torrent of blood to flow in through the open door, but I should have known that was too sloppy for Rudy. We stayed dry. Rudy, also dry, floated beside the President, who did not acknowledge his presence. The President had his middle finger and thumb compressed against the red key. His knuckles were white. The twisted and tearful nature of his unguarded visage betrayed his distaste for this particular grip. His disgust was not going to inhibit his action, though. Neither would the thousands of burning souls who still approached but came no closer, their cries bleeding with dismay. They could not stop him either. Rudy, however, simply touched the President's wrist with the gentlest of pressure, and the fingers released the key without turning it. Rudy guided the world leader's wrist to the green key. The President mindlessly followed, not seeing or feeling Rudy, and touched the green key.

He turned it. The people stopped running, their flames were extinguished. They disbanded, going about whatever business that they may have had before the alarum. They oddly offered no thanks or acknowledgement of the President's decision; they just left. The podium dissolved into a spiraling catwalk with a sturdy wooden rail that the President gratefully grabbed. Rudy got back into the car before the now clear artery faded to a healthier scene of the President dancing merrily with scantily clad cabinet members on the floor of the Senate. Rudy sighed, rubbed his lip with the back of his hand.

"Oh," I said, "And here I thought it was humanity, conscience, and maturity that held the politicians in check all these years. Silly me." Rudy ignored the comment, and drove us over the Brooklyn Bridge without slowing.

We rode on into the night, passing easily and constantly between dreams and reality, adjusting a street fight here, ignoring an aerial dogfight there. At one point we broke up high school lovers in the back seat of an old Chevy by throwing a spotlight on them and suggesting they move on. It seemed trivial at the time, but when Max said something about the dictator they would have sired, I made no jokes about the action. I reminded myself once more that Rudy had his reasons, and I was merely a passenger. At no point did we encounter the shadow – Freuzre – who seemed to dominate my earlier dreams that also included Rudy. I asked about that.

"Alex," Rudy said softly, using a tone he should have reserved for telling a six-year-old that the world is indeed round, "We've been in Freuzre's domain all this time. He is everywhere. In a sense we are just bacteria giving him a stuffy nose. I've been making these rounds for what would seem like centuries to you, and I swear I haven't made any progress toward cleaning his stink from the World. He's here all right, but I can honestly say that the first time I physically met Freuzre was in that Cessna, when I was trying to contact you."

"Freuzre seemed to think that your presence was important enough for him to congeal into something tangible to personally try to stop Rudy from talking to you," Max offered, though her speech sounded more like a Gregorian chant than a point of fact.

"So instead I stopped him," I said, "That must have really pissed him off."

"To no end," Rudy sighed.

"How do you know?" I asked.

Rudy faced me, for the first time all night. Those bottomless gray eyes considered me for a moment, allowing me time to see dark secrets yearning to be free. Rudy looked away.

"Trust me," was all he could say.

We turned a dusty corner in the center of a Louisiana bayou under harsh sunlight, covered a few city blocks, made a left at the third light, found my street bathed in the placid orange tones of a Hudson Valley dusk. It was early fall, about the time of year that Cassie and I had bought the place. I remembered pleasantly that we had liked the fullness of the trees, the smell of fresh cut grass, and the spectacle of neighborhood kids playing capture the flag on the biggest lawn on the block, regardless of its owner's wishes. We once planned to raise five children on that street. Max dabbed a tear from my eye with the loosened tip of her purple silk glove as Rudy rolled into my driveway. I did not look at her, tried not to look at myself when it occurred to me that this was my first thought of Cassie in days. Why hadn't I tried to conjure her in the lagoon?

"She probably had a hand in preventing me," I said aloud. Max looked at me, smiled empathetically. Rudy allowed the Escort to squeal to a stop, threw the shift lever to park, and said, "What?"

"I said, why are you parking next to the garage? Is my car safer out here now?"

"No," Rudy smiled, "I needed to leave room to get my Porsche out. I hope you don't mind that I borrowed your garage."

"No, no. Not at all. In fact, I don't even care anymore about *how* it got into my garage in the first place. Care to stay for dinner?" I asked, knowing the answer. It was a bluff anyway, for my cupboard was bare, or rotten at best.

"We'd love to Alex," Max said, "But I tend to fade if I hang around too long in this world. I forget things too."

"I hope you can understand," Rudy said sarcastically. When we climbed out of the car, Rudy and I glanced simultaneously to the right, to where his house once stood, eons ago. There were already changes evident in the fading light. A new foundation had been laid, and some carpentry erected.

"They don't waste any time, do they?" Rudy said.

"I guess this means you surfaced and sold the place," I said.

"Yep. Had to do it sometime, I suppose. I hear they're a nice couple. Plan on raising quite a litter."

"You sound like a farmer," Max said.

"But I can see that they'll be a happy family," I added.

"Whatever," Rudy said, clasping my shoulder, "But for now, we had best be going. Thank you again, Alex. For everything."

"'Tweren't nothin'," I said.

"Wrong," Max said as she kissed me good-bye, softly on the lips. Rudy lifted the garage door open. I could hear the doors unlock before the door was all the way. I had to smile. He was still a bit of a ham.

"When will I see you again?" I asked as Rudy held the passenger door open for Max.

"Sooner than you'll want to, I'm sure," He said before dropping into his seat. Without another word, or a sound from the car, they pulled out of the garage. I stepped out of the way, waved as they made a left at the end of the driveway. He even used his indicator. What a ham.

"A week ago I would have thought that," I shouted after them as they drove down my street and out of sight.

Chapter Twelve

Something smelled bad in the kitchen.

I had been tossing and turning in the secure, streetlighted gloom of my bedroom for hours, trying to ignore the stench that had wafted into my nostrils with startling, eye-watering clarity at around 10:00, just after I dragged myself from the TV and into bed. I was kept awake as much by the stink as by the nagging guilt I felt about my complete domestic negligence that had allowed all the wrong stuff to accumulate with pungent abandon. I rolled out of bed, tripped on my shoes, and grabbed my ratty terry bathrobe. I resolved to get real for a moment, and go downstairs and investigate. Afterward, I might even consider doing something about the odor.

I felt my way down the cluttered stairs, wishing I had replaced the bulb in the hall light that had burned out several months earlier, and successfully crossed the unlit living room to the kitchen door. Then I stopped. Some primordial instinct barred me from crossing the open threshold to my kitchen. I shook my head at my silly fears. I had decided to accept the challenge of dealing with my own refuse, and I was not going to let primitive fear negate my resolve. I will do this, I thought, admiring my bold stance in the face of such opposition (I would have thumped my chest, had I thought of it). I wasn't completely stupid, though, so before entering the kitchen I cautiously stretched my arm into the room, and fumbled around the wall for the light switch. Though I was sure there was nothing in the kitchen but garbage, intuition insisted that I beware of what may have spontaneously generated from the half bowl of Fruit Loops I had left unattended two weeks earlier, during the hurried breakfast before my last day of work. Or my work's last day, I supposed grimly. I found the switch, threw it, and then peeked inside. No horrible creatures lurked near the range. The kitchen, like the rest of my disheveled house, was as I had left it. I took a deep breath and walked in, cheeks bulging with a reserve of air that I hoped would sustain me until I found the source of the stench. I determined that the cereal had become too solid to stink, so I tossed it on the already overtaxed trashcan and resumed my search. I risked a short sniff.

The aroma of one suspect item lurking on the counter inspired me to retreat, maybe even move to a new home, but I held my ground, and a dishtowel over my nose, to inspect it. A quick watery-eyed scan hinted the object was of alien origin; one of those biological mind-control devices that invading creatures attach to unsuspecting beautiful spacewomen in the movies. It was nothing so glamorous, however, as distant memories returned. The bizarre creature lurking before me was once a freshly opened package of hot dogs. I was sure of it. I had left them out to thaw for dinner after work that day. I could discern ten pink tips huddled under the brown and green mass that enveloped them. I left the kitchen and went to the garage. I pulled a set of very long tongs hanging beside the barbecue. The tongs, like the battered charcoal grill, were rusty from disuse, but they would do. I returned to the kitchen with it, and in a few moments had the pungent mass as far from the back door as my thin arms could heave it. During the decayed food's flight into darkness (and the neighbor's back yard), I wondered why my house hadn't adopted the supernatural babysitting skills that my car administered almost naturally now. I dismissed the thought before the hot dogs landed in an unseen bush, however, deeming that such explanations, and perhaps the power behind them, were still well beyond my novitiate ken.

The first battle over, I walked around, turned on all the lights that still worked, and set about cleaning the place. Cleaning consisted of depositing every errant object in sight into a large plastic trash bag. I started with the kitchen, filling the first bag in minutes with old food from the refrigerator, the kitchen trash can (container included), and dishes from the sink that were beyond washing. Some of them had languished in the sink for weeks *before* Rudy's house erupted.

The rest of the first floor got the same treatment, and I had four large bags filled before I was done. I looked up the stairs to the dark second floor landing. A single sweat sock was draped over the top step, no doubt the tip of the iceberg of the mess I had so carefully avoided noticing when I came home from the diner that evening. I sighed, returned to the kitchen and trudged down the creaking cellar stairs to search for another box of trash bags.

The light switch for the cellar was of the pull-string variety, situated in the center of the basement ceiling. I never liked the arrangement. It forced me to abandon the safe pool of light that emanated from the kitchen and scurry four paces in blackness until the metal ball tied to the end of the string struck my eye. I was accustomed to the problem, however, and rarely noticed how my pace accelerated when I left the kitchen's glow.

Deceleration was the operative word this time, however, when my nose came in full contact with an unexpected wall. My body recoiled involuntarily to absorb the impact, taking some of the pressure off my face. I yelped, retreated a pace but stayed in the dark section. I stood silently for several moments, deciding whether to submit to the tug of curiosity. My eyes were becoming accustomed enough to the dark to discern a wall and eventually a darker splotch on it. I reached for it without moving my feet, found a double switch, threw both.

White indirect light surrounded me, filling the basement with soft, unprecedented luminescence. A wall stood where one had not been last month. I was instinctually annoyed at whoever had invaded the sanctum of my home to install a room, but curiosity sifted acid from my thoughts. The extraction of anger was not hard, since I felt no fear or humiliation. Recent events in my life had carried me way beyond such trivial pursuits.

The addition occupied the center of my basement, in the space I vaguely remembered was once filled by my boiler. The walls were paneled in mahogany, polished mirror-smooth, and about ten feet long per side. I walked its small, familiar perimeter. My face muscles tensed into a smile as I finished my inspection. Holy shit, I thought.

Only the brass switches I had just used broke the surface of this fine box that ranged from floor to ceiling. That barely slowed my entry, however, because I knew what this new place was. I pushed confidently on a warm, smooth, but otherwise nondescript area two feet directly to the left of the light switches. A two-foot wide panel that ranged from floor to ceiling clicked in half an inch. It exuded a long, airlock like hiss, and then it became a very thick door that swung outward to reveal a red interior. I entered Rudy's sound room.

Rudy's mystical dream chamber was as I remembered it, to the finest detail. The switch outside operated the distant blowers as well as the light, so the temperature and humidity inside was more agreeable than the usual wet cellar chill. I silently thanked Rudy for the minor improvement in controls, having never liked digging behind foam panels for the fan and light switches. I rubbed my chin, noticed that I was still smiling, and sat in the scarlet chair that resembled a cross between an oversized recliner and a chaise lounge, but aesthetically transcended both. The light dimmed as I settled into the chair's luxurious padding. I could feel the chair adjusting itself to my body's contours – it probably even made room for the bathrobe I still wore. In a moment, I remembered, the door would be sealed. Once that happened, I knew, the blackness and silence would be complete. I closed my eyes, I think, and relaxed. My amused relief that Rudy contrived to save his beloved chair helped me settle into the mood as well. He's human after all, I thought. Or desperate.

"I thought you said I wouldn't need it," I said aloud. The walls absorbed my words, leaving only their hollow echo in my skull as confirmation that I had issued them. I was not certain about what I was to do at that point; Rudy had left no instructions pinned to the headrest, so I sat and waited for whatever might happen. I sat for what could have been hours, feeling nothing. I wasn't simply numb, or subdued emotionally, I was truly experiencing nothing at all, in the strictest of definitions. All of my senses, even taste somehow, were neutralized. I was alone in my own black universe, unable even to discern a real sense of time. I was not paralyzed. I knew empirically that I could sit up and walk out, whenever I wished, but that truth was difficult to believe. The pure emptiness was beginning to take its toll, draining even my thoughts. I did consider leaping off the chair before all was lost, but a sense of the potential power and freedom in the nothingness subtly tempted me, inviting me to give pure escape a chance. I stayed put.

I decided to apply what I had learned in my recent adventures to the chair. This time I was able to relax, however, and feel myself moving into the dream instead of involuntarily becoming part of it. The level of control and confidence that the chair appeared to offer was invigorating, and uniquely calming. I was finally entering Rudy's world with poise, rather than with the awkward and surreal tumble that had been the norm to date. Even without instructions from Rudy, I understood how the chair's potential could be exercised simply by being there, and knowing from often tragic experience what potentials hid in the void in which the chair allowed me to float. This is going to be fun, I thought. If I could find them, I would have rubbed my hands together.

At least, I assumed it would be fun. After what felt like another half day (though it could have been five minutes), I was becoming impatient. The lack of stimulation that was originally enthralling had become a nuisance. Bored, and wary that perhaps dropping into my own dreams on cue would be tougher than I had originally thought, I experimented with my physical world. I probably would have been wiser to continue my happy vigil, though, because my tests did not go well. First, I tried to touch my face with my hand, but I could not find my hand. I felt no blood coursing through my veins; they may have been empty. I thought I joked aloud about being dead, but heard nothing. I was beginning to panic, perhaps. I was not sure, because none of the physical symptoms that accompany the malady were evident. Nothing was evident. I tried to move my hand again, with more negatively neutral results. I tried smacking my lips, shaking my head, even crossing my fingers. I sensed no movement. My commands were either not making the journey through my nervous system, or else they were being ignored. Or perhaps my arms were flailing about as my head shook violently, comically grimacing, and I simply did not notice.

Eventually the shock of this new, well, shock of senselessness settled in, and I was able to resume rationalizing my way through the sound room's indoctrination. I decided that, if nothing was physical for me, I should try doing something physically easy, but not in the usual mundane manner. I opted to try to touch my nose in an unreal way. I imagined my hand by carefully drawing its outline in three dimensions against the backdrop of my blackened mind. In time I could see misty shadows of my fingers approaching my face from six o'clock. The presence of my hand, or anything at all, hovering in my empty space was exhilarating. I was again filled with the confidence I had enjoyed when I initially sat in the chair. I boldly imagined that I felt my nose being tweaked, instead of actually trying to touch it. In response I felt a sharp pinch in the space I was sure my nose occupied. I stepped up the assault on oblivion by picturing myself rising from the chair, finding the crease in the wall fabric that hid the door, then exiting the room. After I had a decent, though still quite hazy, picture in my mind of the outside of Rudy's sound room, I created the image of my hand reaching to the brass switch and flipping its toggle.

I blinked as the lights came on, full brightness. I shook my head, moved my hands from their positions on the arms of the recliner. After confirming that all my parts were still in the condition in which I had left them many hours, or minutes – I still wasn't sure – earlier, I grinned broadly. I was elated at my success, but also mildly embarrassed. In retrospect, I should have known there was a way out of the chair. Rudy designed it. I stood up, looked at the chair, bewildered by its impossible ability to sweep away all sensation. It sure didn't look like anything more special than a souped-up Lazy-Boy. In the glow of warm real light, it appeared harmless. Of course, no harm was done. I cracked my knuckles, rubbed my neck, and sat back down.

      The room blackened again, and this time I was ready. Using the same expectations that I would have were I dreaming, I calmly forced a picture of a lighted sound room into my thoughts. The room brightened instantly. I laughed, not surprised that Rudy would have it work that simply. He would have known how nervous I get when I lose control. I settled deeply into the chair, making myself comfortable for another round of nothingness. Why I did this I didn't have a clue, since I knew my body wasn't going to feel anything in a moment anyway. For a brief instant one last wave of panic did pass through me when I wondered, irrationally: what if the lights coming on, everything I just thought and did, was an hallucination, a dream brought on by the chair? I had the good sense to quickly dismiss such a question as irrelevant, and relaxed. What did it matter if it was all hallucination or not? To me it was still happening. I, of all people, should have realized that by then.

After a few seconds, or several hours, the blackness became less complete. I could see thousands of faint shadows, specters, of people or things hurtling past me, inches beyond the touch of my extended ethereal fingers. They slowed, but before I could discern who the passing people were, their images lost resilience and blended together into a bright purple maelstrom that held me, sans chair, in its calm eye. Though I didn't like the effect, I felt oddly secure within it, so I made no attempt to alter it. My patience was rewarded when the maelstrom slowed and settled softly until the slow swirl had stopped. I then stood upon an empty purple plain.

Glass smooth, but vinyl soft, it stretched in every direction, forming a sharp horizon with a pure white sky a truly immeasurable distance away – the edge of this world could have been fifty feet or fifty miles away, I had no way to judge. The white sky was not brilliant, like sunlight. Instead it was diffuse, evenly spread in a soft glow wherever the plain was not. That light also had had no effect on the plain; there were no shadows, no spikes of glare. My surroundings made me feel like I was under a giant overturned mixing bowl on God's kitchen counter. I fittingly realized from nowhere that what I was in was a blank slate of sorts. This flipped-over bowl was a dream, I mused, but my consciousness had rudely interrupted the normal creational phase by its presence. Now I was left with an empty world, waiting to be filled.

"This is so cool," I said.

The texture of this world, the feeling it elicited, both tactile and emotional, was subtly different than the reality of the lagoon. This, I knew, was definitely a dream. Though the plain's presence was without question, there was enough lack of tangibility about it to confirm that it was the stuff (or non-stuff, in this case) of dreams. I felt more comfortable with that conclusion, and in complete control. Now, I thought, perhaps I would finally get a clear idea of what Rudy was talking about, along with some hands-on training to help me avoid the mistakes I made at the lagoon.

The purple plain was a blank canvass, waiting for my mind to paint it, to lend it form. Unfortunately, I still did not understand how to bring my consciousness to the forefront, so, even though I knew this was a dream open completely to my guidance, I needed a vast amount of unconscious input to help me create. My consciousness had not matured in the dream department enough yet to create the thousands of stimuli that my unconscious mind handled routinely.

I decided that I should work with the tools I knew I had at first, and then mull expanding my consciousness later, when I had picked up a few more skills. So, I gave some thought to my unconscious mind. I sensed that there was activity there, however, and did understand that I was not in a separate reality, only another phase of my own. My unconscious mind had to be present, and ready to work for, or against, me. I just needed to prod it into action to help me forge complete dreams. I would allow it to create the background for my activities, so the myriad details of the worlds I visited would form "naturally," while my conscious mind focused on simple actions like direction, speech, and inviting guests. The things it knew. I sensed that to prod my unconscious mind into action no doubt meant simply to quietly wait while bearing no creative thought to interfere.

"How the hell am I thinking of all this?" I asked aloud, then said to the sky, "Wait, don't answer that, because I'm sure that I do not want to know. Let's just let the fun begin." With my rules for a change, I added silently.

The purple faded, replaced by the front lawn of the Eastland Tennis Club. Eastland was a snooty little upper class redoubt in Scarsdale, littered with wealth, pomposity, and very little good tennis. Cassie and I were occasional members there. Joining was her idea; she had played for the tennis team in college, and proved willing to endure the empty sort of people she deplored for the sake of the excellent facilities. The facilities were excellent, and so was Cassie's game. I personally had consistent trouble getting the ball over the net, but still enjoyed helping her practice. Anything was fun when I did it with Cassie. Oh, and we scored the membership because of connections in her family, not mine.

I crossed the lawn, careful to avoid the club's front entrance. I chose this route both because I didn't feel right arriving without Cassie and to avoid the gauntlet of two dozen elegant servants flanking the glass front doors. I walked in through the kitchen, which looked correct but appeared as though it hadn't been used in years. I found my way to the expansive, satin-lined formal dining room, which was also empty. It had been occupied far more recently than the kitchen: I caught a glimpse of a figure darting out a side door before the kitchen door slapped shut behind me. I made the wall around the door the figure used disappear, but there was nobody on the other side. I crossed the dining room to the pool.

The kidney-shaped, slate-lined monstrosity that I would never go near was not filled with the usual eye-burning over-chlorinated and under-heated water. Instead, it was topped off with Burgundy wine. A duck floated at its center, its green head below the surface in search of food. It found some and took off, flapping into a green sunset with a tiny human wriggling in its beak. I laughed. I left the pool area, still unable to find any other, full-sized people. Passing through an abandoned locker room, I tripped over a broken wooden bench, and rebounded noisily off some rusty lockers to break my fall to the dirt floor. An old oaken door, flapping loosely on its broken hinges, appeared before me, and I eliminated it to save time lost securing it. I passed through the stone arch and found myself back outside, near the orderly rows of leaf-covered tennis courts.

The asphalt surface was golden in the noonday sun. A modern graphite racket was balanced, handle up, on the other end of the baseline I straddled. I was at it without a step, and picked it up after tapping it a few times to admire the precision of build that must have been required to get it to stand like that. I hefted it, took a couple of practice swings. It had that comfortable feel of my old racket: a bit heavy, with that extra weight in the head. It may have looked like my old racket as well, but I saw it in a haze because my eyes had filled with tears. I pulled a tennis ball from my shorts pocket, bounced it a couple of times on the clay. I batted it lightly, and poorly, across the net, impressed with how well dreams can imitate reality. I laughed at my snobbery, realizing to myself that I had not been able to discern one from the other quite frequently of late. I pulled another ball from my pocket, served it over the net as best I could, then reflexively set myself for the return shot. There was none. I had no opponent.

At that point it dawned on me why I was having the dream. It was, of course, to contact Cassie! The club was a place where we spent much time together, a happy place well removed from our daily lives. Feeling electrified, I snatched yet another ball from my pocket and served it.

It was returned immediately, to my backhand corner. It got by me, as Cassie's returns usually did. I dried my eyes and refocused my gaze across the net. She was indeed there, standing across the court in her sexiest tennis whites, with that suppressed smile of victory livening her sharp features. I laughed, feeling nothing unusual as I pulled a fourth ball from my shorts and briskly served it to a woman two years dead. She returned my respectable serve gracefully, and with ease. Prepared for her, I backhanded her return cross-court to her weak forehand. She was at the net, waiting for my shot, and slammed it off the court well beyond my reach. She backed up to her baseline. I walked to the net.

"Alex!" she cried, as I lifted a leg over the net, "Don't come any closer."

"Why not?" I laughed, "This is my dream, I'll do what I want."

"No one has complete domain over their dreams," she said softly, her tone bleak. Her voice was still sweet music to me. I felt like starting an argument just to hear it again. Instead, I chose to pursue a higher priority: I wanted desperately to touch Cassie in this, my, realm, to make her real to me again.

"I'm not nobody," I said, lifting my leg higher to clear the net that was now level with my neck. I forced it down with a wave, but was then unable to lift my leg over it. My limb had become extremely heavy, but only when I tried to step over the net. I knew I could walk away any time I wished. "What the hell?" I asked aloud. When I tried to grab the top of the net in order to jump it, climb over it, or rip it to shreds, the nylon was white hot and I had to let go. "I'm beginning to see what you mean," I shouted to Cassie, who still stood nervously at her base line.

"Can't you talk to me from there?" she asked.

"I need to touch you."

"I thought you had had enough of that. I haven't felt your presence in ages."

"I always want you, my Cassandra, but obstacles have arisen." I had given up climbing over the net at this point, began to walk around it. I was puzzled by my inability to make the net vanish.

"Obstacles?" she asked. I had no response, unable to determine or attempt to describe (to her or myself) what obstacle might be more important to me than Cassie. I shed the thoughts, increased my determination to touch my dead wife, and soon found that I was running along the net. After several minutes of a strong pace I stopped, seeing that the post to which the net was attached was as far from me as it had been when I started toward it. I turned around and ran the other way, yielding the same results. My frustration growing, I turned to Cassie and shouted at her:

"Cassie, come to me."

"I can't," she replied, her voice faint. Her baseline, with her still standing at it, had receded into the distance. The opposing tennis court now appeared miles long as it stretched over the horizon, threatening to take Cassie with it.

"The net won't let me pass," I called, "But don't worry. This is my dream, I can bring you to me."

I could see her face pale in the distance. She shouted, "Alex, please. Don't try. I'm here, isn't that enough?"

"No," I said softly, my guilt demanding that I touch her somehow. I couldn't let her drift away again; she would have thought I did so on purpose. I concentrated on her lightly clad figure in the distance, willed it to grow. She grew rapidly, responding to my strength. She shook her head anxiously as she approached. Irrevocably bent on seeing her again, I ignored her anguish. In a moment her baseline was regulation distance again. She stopped.

"Alex, really," she pleaded, "Don't."

"It's all right, Cass, this is my dream, I know what I'm doing."

"Doing, maybe. Dealing with, you haven't a clue." I ignored her whispered sentiment and pulled harder.

"Come to me!" I shouted, my hands held high like Moses parting the Red Sea. She moved again. I concentrated, pooling my conscious and unconscious thoughts to create an unstoppable concept of a reduced distance between Cassie and me. It was working. In a second she was two yards away, her face contorted with pain, eyes wide.

"Stop!"

Finally I listened, seeing belatedly that something was wrong. I could not stop her approach. I could slow it to a crawl, which only stretched the time in which I was able to watch as she bloated, her body growing as if being inflated by some unseen air pump. In my arrogance I had mistaken my perspective of Cassie as a change in position. I was wrong. She hadn't come closer; she had grown larger just to give the impression. At first I hadn't noticed, because she maintained her excellent proportions as she grew, but now she was growing huge, and I could not stop her rapid expansion. When she burst out of her clothes, Cassie loosed a scream that froze my blood. Her skin stretched until she was twice her original size, then she cried out my name and exploded. The concussion floored me, and I slipped on her liquid remains when I tried to stand. The tennis court was crimson. Then it was gone.

I stood once more on the purple plane, my unconscious activity spent. The plain was not an empty waxed floor this time: a hazy figure stood several paces away from me. When I focused on it I recoiled. It was the monk I had defeated in the sanctuary. It lifted a billowing sleeve to point an unseen, accusing finger in my direction.

"You see, boy, you are not confined to your own plane. Now you know. But know this as well: neither am I. Bear this thought when next you meddle with my work," the monk hissed, then released a volley of hideous laughter.

I awoke in the lit sound room. My entire body trembled, though I could not feel it. The cackling echoed softly in the silent chamber.

Chapter Thirteen

Preempting potentially violent anguish over what I had done, I removed light from the sound room and prepared to undo my arrogant misdeed. Like a veteran in my urgency, I leapt back onto the purple plain. I paused at my imaginary base of creativity just long enough to establish a beginning to my quest for redemption. Then I dreamed. I was consumed by the intent to create every makeshift world, every memorable situation that I could imagine, which might include an intact Cassie.

I returned to Dartmouth College, where we originally met. I was alone as I followed the familiar wooded walks to her dormitory, and took the stairs to the third floor. The long hall was empty, though my memory was able to fill in the sounds of music and conversation that usually bathed the hall. Her room, the year we met, was 325. The wooden doors, all closed, passed my fluid gaze. I remembered that the odd-numbered rooms were on the left, so was careful to look in that direction only. I fully reviewed each polished brass number plate as it passed...317, 319, 321, 323, 327.

I wasted no time pacing the hall, seeking absent coeds for directions, or rechecking all the numbers. I had missed her, and it was time to move on. Without returning to the base purple plain, I shifted immediately to Cassie's hometown in Vermont. Her family had lived for generations in a well-insulated tiny hamlet on Lake Champlain. The scenery was perfect, but none of the avatar townspeople that I made sure existed this time remembered her, not even the immediate members of her close-knit family. I visited the antique clothing boutique she had managed in Greenwich Village right after we got married. Sheryl, the dark-haired woman who had helped her establish the store, was at the counter. She looked at me with no sign of recognition or discernable emotion, and said woodenly that she had never heard of Cassie.

"This isn't working," I shouted at Sheryl, grabbing her limp shoulders and shaking her. I held my face close to her non-reactive visage and screamed, "Nothing is working! Why the hell not?" I swept out of the store in anger, vaporizing it behind me, and returned to the neutrality of the purple plain. I fell without looking first into an old wingback chair that appeared behind me, and put my feet up on its tattered ottoman. I lifted a glass of scotch from the table beside me, and settled into staring out at the plain and brooding. After an indeterminable amount of time spent pouting, sipping, shouting, and finally scheming, I threw my arms in the air. How could I reverse my mistake, I asked myself, when I have no idea what I really did or for that matter, whether what I did was ever real? This confusion, and the severe discomfort I felt just behind my eyes, hinted that my mind was almost ready to make a sudden departure. It was time to try something a little different, perhaps an option rooted in concepts I could get my untrained hands around. I decided that, rather than continuing to let my unconscious mind do most of the work, I would set about creating a situation in which my dead wife would be obliged to participate.

My purple home base and comfy chair drifted into the shadows of my bedroom. Our bedroom, actually – I chose to return to the night before her death, and our last time together. It was a memory I could not erase, a vivid image whose detail would remain etched in my mind forever. It may not have actually been the best sex we had, but the event of the following day caused it to evolve into the only sex that I could remember clearly.

The small lamp on her dresser, the one I had purchased, for one dollar, at a garage sale for her, dimly lit the room. The windows were open, though winter's chill still gripped the night air. I had entered the memory with us already in bed, and near climax. Why wait? The bed shook from our efforts, and I even heard that familiar squeal from the box spring that often coaxed uncontrollable giggling from Cassie. I was on top, my muscles quivering from the lengthy workout. I savored the delicious odor that I felt sure was unique to our lovemaking. I could feel her writhing rhythmically against me, under me, her supple body easily supporting my weight, happily absorbing my thrusts. Though I knew every detail of the room and moment, my eyes were as closed as they had been that night. I prepared to open them to catch her in the ecstasy of her last orgasm ever. I knew that she would smile at me, embarrassed that I caught her during such a disarming moment.

When I slid my eyes open, I felt as though the last two years had never happened, and Cassie was alive. My mind had already begun its attempt to keep this moment real, like I did as a child after waking and discovering that the ice cream cone was just a dream before my eyes were fully focused. When they were, my mind stopped, because I was greeted not by the expected vision of an ecstatic Cassie, but instead by moonlit white sheets gently shifting six inches below me. Cassie was not there. I felt her motion, her warmth, and her moans for another instant, and then they too were gone. I screamed, my soul blowing out across empty satin. The bed crumpled into a little paper ball, then disappeared into a singularity that sucked all of my furniture, hopes, and desires into an unseen oblivion.

I stood once more on the purple plain, still alone. Well, I thought, that went well. I paused long enough to regain my composure, stop shaking, and then realize that I was again forcing this pursuit down a wrong path. It was time to stop this extreme, guilt-driven quest. I had blown up Cassie, again, on that tennis court by doing exactly what I had attempted in the bedroom. I had to accept that episode of naiveté, admit to pushing too hard for something, someone who I knew was dead, and step back from these attempts at self-deification. In short, I thought, I have to chill, big time. Cassie was nowhere. She was supposed to be nowhere, and I had to take that as truth until she, Rudy, or God Himself proved otherwise.

I sighed and blinked my eyes once, very slowly. When they opened, I was back in the sound room. The lights had come up and the door was open. I was bathed in sweat. "What an asshole," I said aloud as I swung my legs over the edge of the chair. I sat for a moment, contemplated the wall's pattern of finely woven red cloth, stood, and stretched mightily. As I left the sound room, I was sure I caught the unforgettable aroma of the roses that died at her first funeral. I turned around at the door, sniffed again, but could smell nothing but the odor of dank basement wandering in from outside of the room. I eyed the chair for a moment, instinctively longing to get back to the plain, then left. The door clicked shut behind me, but the lights outside the room stayed on. I was relieved for that detail, since I was not interested in standing alone in the dark again.

"Man," I said while ascending the cellar stairs, "That thing can sure as hell get addictive." The lights around the sound room were off before I reached the top step of the rickety wooden flight. I thanked the darkness for closing up behind me, reducing further temptation at least until morning. God, I thought, how the hell can I do all this stuff and still be afraid of the dark?

I walked through the kitchen, my rekindled gloom able to mask the filth I had begun to clean the night before (I was right about the time confusion; though it felt like only a few minutes had passed in the chair, I had spent most of the night under its spell), and set about numbly repeating the actions that I took after Cassie's funeral. I entered the living room, left the lights off, grabbed the remote control and fell into the Lay-Z-Boy in front of the TV. I flipped on the set, hoping that the empty euphoria television can provide would flow into me, dissolving my unwanted thoughts into a nice, safe mush. I had attempted to obtain that state for weeks the first time she died; I had a feeling that I would repeat the same failure again. I was right. I merely grew more sullen. My mind was a gray cloud, its haze broken occasionally by a clear and unwanted replay of Cassie exploding. I had killed her twice. Both were accidents, yet both were completely my fault. Space did not exist in me to contain the grief, the guilt, and the overpowering fear that I had no control over my desires. To be numb was to survive. I sighed and continued watching without seeing or hearing.

A distant voice invaded my selfish solace. It was uttering things that sounded familiar, though I wasn't really listening to its words. Curious, I forced myself to focus, and found that I was watching CNN's headline news show. The cookie-cutter anchor was reporting that the President of the United States had made an abrupt change of plans: it seemed he intended to meet with the

Russians to discuss nuclear disarmament after all. Immediately following was a piece about an unspent bomb found by children on a street in St. Denis, a suburb of Paris. An American submarine captain turned himself in as a spy.

Fog lifted.

My interest was piqued as the TV retold stories that could be remotely connected to Rudy's recent "rounds." That kind of verification was exhilarating, and almost got me out of my funk until I rationalized that, if what we had done was real, then what I had done to Cassie had to have been real too. I had assumed that, but I did not care for the humiliating affirmation. I stared dully at the screen as the headlines continued:

"In other news, an upstate man inflated his wife to the bursting point last night."

I lifted my head.

"It seems he yearned for her in a dream, but wanted more than his fantasy's allotment provided. Authorities say he broke the rules. The assailant was unavailable for comment."

By then my attention was complete. My mood fought to swing to the positive when I realized that I was watching Rudy reading headlines to me. Part of me wanted to laugh, but was quickly overridden by more basic emotions. I leaned forward enough to fall off the chair and onto my knees. I crawled across the dirty carpet to the old Sony and shook it on its plastic stand. Inside, Rudy grabbed his desk and held on. My vision blurred by tears brought on by emotions so mixed that I was unable to identify them, I shouted at him:

"Rudy! How could you do this to me?"

"You blame me," Rudy said, his grin gone, "I had nothing to do with it, you can rest assured of that. Now calm down so I can try to get you to understand what really happened." I sat back in my familiar, personally comfortable chair and adjusted the TV's volume with the remote that had managed to stay in my hand. He was a bit loud.

"Did I kill her again?"

"Did you kill her the first time around?" Rudy asked.

"No," I answered quickly, "What I meant was, did I destroy her living remains?"

"Living remains?" Rudy asked, lifting an eyebrow.

"Her soul, I guess. Whatever it was that was communicating with me. In the dreams."

"Maybe it was all just figments of your lively imagination," Rudy suggested, adjusting his striped necktie. He hated ties.

"That would be best," I reasoned, "Then none of this really happened. Of course I don't like that either, because that means that she is actually dead."

"You buried her."

"But what I saw was all so real."

"Dreams get that way."

"But what about the sanctuary?"

"What sanctuary? The dream?"

"She said it wasn't a dream."

"You believed her?"

"No. I understood. There's a difference."

"What are you talking about?"

"I thought all this was your department."

"Mixing dreams and reality, yes," Rudy acknowledged with what could have been a wink, "But I have yet to adjust to your ability, and your unique take on the whole experience."

"She was with me in the reality phase with the monk and also when I defeated it with a dream."

"Then maybe she was real."

"Then maybe she is dead. I did kill her."

"Don't count on it."

"Then why couldn't I find her in any of the dreams I formed after that?"

"'The dreams I formed?'" Rudy repeated, "My, we are getting cocky, aren't we?" He stood angrily, left the screen. A soup commercial aired. He was back at his desk when the news came back on, rubbing his chin in a demonstrably pensive manner.

"Alex. You did last night what I practiced 500 years to achieve in the most rudimentary form. At this point I'm having trouble keeping up with what you did, how you did it, and why the hell you wanted to do it in the first place. You're a real puzzle, and you've confused me, and your own ability to recognize reality, enough to make me wonder what you are up to. Who knows? Maybe you did kill your wife again." He looked away, shamed perhaps by the cold candor he used when referring to what I had done to Cassie.

"I loved her more than anything," I said. Those were the only words I could summon.

"I know." After a moment of silence, Rudy leaned to me, "Can I come out now? It's a bit cramped in here."

"Come out of where?" I asked, feigning ignorance of Rudy's response, which I imagine helped him feel a little better about himself. As expected, he reached his right hand toward me until it touched, tapped, then slid through my TV screen. His hand waved comically about in my living room while Rudy smiled from the distant newsroom, separated by a thin wave of liquefied glass and a vast abyss of common sense. In spite of the absurdity of the image, or perhaps because of it, I clasped Rudy's hand without a thought and proceeded to pull him into my domain. I was looking at him through the bottom of a drinking glass until his head and shoulders popped through the twenty-inch picture tube. He was then able to assist my effort by grabbing the edges of the television's black plastic cabinet and vaulting through the screen. In a moment he was in the room with me, brushing off electric dust.

"Hell of a way to travel," he said, looking up at me, "I don't know how those TV guys do it every night."

"I think they only come into my room in a figurative sense, Rudy."

"Oh." Rudy said, "Alex. You look awful. You're so pale, like you just went fifteen rounds with the chair." I could see in his eyes that he knew I had. I nodded in affirmation anyway. He smiled broadly, folded his arms across his chest. How, I thought, could a guy this old be such a kid? Then his face reverted to a more typical reflection of his soul's relentless gravity. He regarded me for a few seconds, thoughtfully rubbing his chin in the same way he had when he was on TV.

"How did you do that?" he asked, "I didn't think it was possible to stay in the chair the full eight hours."

"I was inspired," I said. I also had no idea that I couldn't stay in the chair so long, or that it mattered, but I kept those thoughts to myself.

"Hmm. I suppose you were. Anyway, that's not why I'm here."

"Too bad, because it's certainly all that I'm concerned with."

"Perhaps I could reverse your priorities."

"That would be a neat trick," I said, absently offering him a drink by pointing to the bar in the corner. He nodded in acceptance. I poured some scotch into a clean glass and handed it to him without a word.

"You can still have Cassie."

I laughed, "She doesn't seem too available just now."

"Don't laugh like that, Alex. It makes me nervous. And God damn it, stop acting like you know all there is to know about this world you've blundered into. Ass-backwards."

"Excuse me," I said, dropping into my chair. What I did not mention was my incredulity at the fact that Rudy was one hundred and eighty degrees wrong about something. Not about the blundering, he was dead on there, but about my attitude. I decided that I would mull that anomaly later, myself. Rudy remained standing, above me. He looked serious, and also chagrined that I was showing little interest in his words. I understood that he wished to save the world from an evil dream-demon or something, and I could see that freeing billions from the cold shadow of unchecked evil was probably more important than my obsession with my twice-dead wife. I understood, but could not step away from the emotion. Cassie was gone. I made her that way, twice. I would accept it one day. "But not today," I said aloud. Rudy seemed to understand that bit of gibberish.

"No. No, not today. Probably not tomorrow, either, but there will be a time when you can reunite with Cassie."

That was it.

"Did you see what I did to her?" I shouted, spilling Rudy's drink as I sprang from my chair and grabbed his wrist. I was furious at him for continuing his carrot on a stick game with me, even after I had proven through my own actions that there was no room, or perhaps now even desire, for such hope. And yet he was able to rekindle my Frankensteinian needs with a word.

"Every second of it," Rudy whispered, his face inches from mine. Bottomless gray eyes grabbed mine, pulling them into the abyss of hated knowledge that they endured.

"Where is she?" I whispered back, through clenched teeth.

"Lost, for now. Safely but unhappily in the arms of our opponent."

"Her explosion was a trick?"

"No trick, but you can't die twice. I'll warrant she felt plenty of pain, though. No, the explosion was a concession to Freuzre, an admission of your lack of will. He capitalized on this and took your prized possession; your only real reason for continuing with me."

"That's not true," I honestly said, wondering for a flash why Rudy and his foe would concur on that fallacy.

"It was a prime selling point," he said.

"I will concede that."

"Anyway, what he has is, in a word, her spiritual essence. Okay, in three words. Which is why you haven't been able to make any dream contact with her. He's not harming her. He wouldn't know how to do that."

"You just said she was in pain."

"Freuzre leaves the causes of pain to other stimuli. There's never a short supply of that." I had no answer for that.

"What do I do?"

"Leave this world. Live primarily with your conscious in tune with the World. Live your dreams."

"Won't they lose power? My dreams, I mean, if I were to do that?"

"Of course not," Rudy said after a quiet moment. If I did not know that Rudy never lied, I would have sworn that he just did. Wrong, misguided, and lying, all in one conversation: I needed more scotch. I crossed back to the bar. Rudy followed me. I poured mine and refilled his. I looked for a bar napkin for his spillage, but gave up that impossible quest before entering into it.

"You want me to come with you, just like that?" I asked.

"Nothing is ever `just like that,' but yes."

"I would become like you, able to move between the whole spiritual enchilada and the regular earthly pieces too?"

"Perhaps in time, but at first you'll be too overwhelmed by everything in the World happening in your head at once to have much control over anything."

"Then why would I do it?"

"Because I need you."

"Sounds like you have more use for me here, well attached to terra firma. Or does the competition bother you?" He flinched at that bit of sarcasm, his fist clenching on his glass. His ice rattled. I paused to wonder where he got the ice, but he disrupted my query when he continued.

"Alex, please, I can't explain everything to you," he said quietly, suppressing an unidentifiable emotion.

"That was a joke, Rudy. And why not?"

"You're not ready yet."

"I seem to be ready to join you in Never-Never Land."

"That's different."

"Why?"

"Alex," Rudy said, slamming his glass down on the bar, "You're asking too many questions today, and I haven't got answers for you. I can understand the source of your inquisition, but that doesn't help. Just trust me."

"Fine. But let me think about what you're saying. Let me dream some more, too." That seemed to shake him. I had never seen Rudy shaken before, so I wasn't sure. If he was then, it was a landmark night indeed. I touched his shoulder before continuing in a lower tone, "Forgive me for noticing only now Rudy, but are you all right?"

"I'm fine. Just stress. This job is getting to me." That was strange. Nothing gets to Rudy. Except Freuzre, Max had said once. Rudy touched my forearm, looked me in the eyes again, and said:

"Listen, I've got to go now, things need attending to. We'll talk again. Please think hard about joining me."

"Can't you force me to join you?" I asked his back as he walked across the room. He turned his head and smiled. A real Rudy smile this time.

"Of course I can," he said. Then he opened a closet door and stepped inside.

Chapter Fourteen

Twenty-three seventy-five.

I held the invoice from the phone company for a few seconds longer than I had lingered over the other bills. I had to allow extra time for my chuckle at their unmatched audacity to pry unearned money from their customers. I owed almost 24 dollars for the use of a phone I hadn't touched in two months. The thing didn't ring once during the entire billing period. The bill, perhaps to justify the charges, was four pages long, and itemized. I tore it up and threw it down with the rest. I appreciated the bill, and its destruction, because it managed to break my somber mood at least for the length of time needed for its shreds to settle below me.

A small pool of paper had developed on the glass-smooth basement floor of Beaver Toys, ten feet below my dangling legs. It was the remains of my mail. Though all bills, catalogs, or pleas from charities, it still represented my last connection with the mundane world in which I once ignorantly yet placidly navigated. I felt it fitting to discard my mail with great ceremony into the last place where I enjoyed – well, had, anyway – physical contact with people who believed they existed in one agreed-upon concrete reality. In a moment of depth that struck while I was ripping apart the mortgage book, I tried to assume, or hope, that my exit from their world would somehow atone for the abrupt involuntary exit the employees of Beaver Toys had endured. Then I realized that my exit didn't involve death, or even much suffering, so I dismissed my heroics as patently unfair and returned to tossing the paperwork of my previous, useless, life into the remains of its final anchor.

I had suffered no trouble reaching my perch on the edge of the Beaver Toys foundation two hours earlier. The local constabulary had dutifully protected the empty hole with a tall barbed-wire fence, but metal twine alone cannot stop Wonder Wizard Alex Creaux and His Magic Escort. My ignorance of the source of the magic thrust upon me by Rudy and the World still prevailed, but it did not prevent me from constantly tinkering with its potential. This practice enabled some excellent refinements in my reality-bending skills. Like a race driver who knew nothing of internal combustion engines, I had learned to alter my environment like a pro while remaining clueless about the fundamentals of my new life, and position, in the World. And, like any good race driver, I had finally come to recognize, to believe, and to respect that the machine I operated was a thing that had potentially dangerous power, and that power was less an extension of me than I was a focus for it. I had come to terms with myself in understanding that I was not the god of my dreams, and certainly held no such position in reality. I just had a much better set of keys to the metaphysical strongbox protecting the secrets of both conditions than most people, especially the poor souls who were vaporized in my name weeks earlier.

One trick I had learned while tinkering with my innate skills was to create an ethereal cape of sorts. I dubbed it my cloak of invisibility, and, with some concentration, I could 'wear' it whenever I wished to pass unnoticed by my friends from the far dimensions. The freedom relaxed me, and the cloak was indeed handy because the need for that release from my friends had of late become a daily desire. Rudy had become too edgy, pushing his agenda by incessantly insisting that I leave home immediately. To me that meant that I must permanently abandon everything that was left of my old self, and I was not inclined toward letting go easily. Therefore I was not very good company for him, and he was a nuisance to me. I hadn't seen much of him in the last few intentionally dreamless weeks. During the short moments that our paths did cross, Rudy tried to brush off – or rather, take credit for – his absences. Business, he had said. Also, he would not help me locate Cassie, yet he was always happy to report that she was quite secure in her location even when I didn't ask. Though my failed forays to bring her back had given me twisted closure that dramatically reduced my desperation to have her, and increased my interest in letting her become a part of my past, I was still frustrated by Rudy's tease. For those practical reasons, and the uneasy feeling Rudy's uncharacteristic pressure gave me, I had decided that it was time to back slightly away from him. I was still on his side, of course, and ready for his fight, but I needed a pause from his Reader's Digest World. I needed to steep in useless, slow-moving simplicity for a while before caving in to his elastic rules.

I tore open the insurance bill before deciding that that was a part of my old life that did not need a good-bye. I dropped it without review. Not even eligible for the pile below, it vaporized in a satisfying cloud of hissing blue smoke before it hit the floor. I smiled again.

I raised my eyes to the totally normal, gloriously nondescript late afternoon sky, and realized that I had been seated on that ledge far longer than two hours. No matter, I thought; the time was not wasted, and where the hell else should I be?

Where else indeed? I finished the thought with a pang of guilt. I held my right hand open, palm down, in front of me and considered it absently. Hours earlier a corporeal part of me needed to return to the location of my old nothing job, to get an idea again of what I was two months earlier. Well I did, and was not impressed. Still, such a visit was an excellent vehicle for locking home the good and bad of what I was about to leave. It also served as a reminder of my true nature by highlighting my undeniable proximity to the mooing human herd. I hoped that obvious humility would help prevent me from pushing my magic games too far and making another Freuzre-like attempt at achieving godhood or something worse. The incorporeal side of me ached to continue contemplating the reasons why Rudy never opted for deity, but I was able to set that subject aside, on the grounds that I was there to escape him.

"Well, maybe not 'escape,'" I said aloud. Evade was a better word, and with almost as many letters. I kicked my heels to the tune of 'Yellow Rose of Texas' against the petrified foundation wall beneath me as I peered between my knees at the empty remains of the even emptier place that I once considered the center of my life. That center had shifted dramatically, separating me from this old world of pleasures as simple as manufactured toys. I had wanted to believe that I had separated myself from my old existence, but there was that hand, held out in front of me, pulsing warm blood, and still attached to me; to my body. No, I still was my old self. I just wasn't a part of the humanity around me anymore. I was on my own.

I knew that I did not break from civilization by myself. I couldn't have; too many details that I had not considered seemed to have been handled. Nobody investigated anything that publicly happened to me. No official curiosity arose concerning the coincidence of my neighbor's house erupting days before my place of business. They must have seen a correlation. If this were TV, I would have been pumped up with sodium Pentothal in a CIA dungeon somewhere. I could not avoid the impression that the authorities, and the casual observers whose ranks would include my family and old friends not employed by Beaver Toys, didn't care, or had forgotten to consult or concern me. Of course they could have thought that I was in the building with the rest of the crew when it went up. No, then I would be declared dead, my house up for sale, and relatives would be casting lots for my record collection. They had simply forgotten about me. I was not shaken by this loss. It was nice living in my own world for a while. The only albatross that remained was Cassie's lingering shadow.

With that I collected my thoughts, crumpled them into a tight ball and heaved them over the fence. The steady, cold wind that had been plaguing this locale for weeks would blow them back in time, but for the moment I smiled, picturing Nancy giving me notice of Fletcher's proximity. I should have cried at that thought. They were dead, all of them. Their demise came if not directly from my hand then from its existence. I assumed Freuzre had done the actual killing, but I was the target. If I had ignored Rudy's world and remained a neutral party, Nancy would be happily fretting her day away, still seeking my friendship. I probably could have clung to my old self, even after Rudy's house blew up.

"But you're not neutral," I said quietly, straining the words through a tightened throat, "You had no idea what was happening yet." Still...

I clamped my lips together, and struggled to purge the nonsense of Rudy's World again. My effort to crumple the past, present, and fears of the future into another tattered ball of newspaper drew blood from my clenched fists. As the plague of doubt, grief and misgivings faded once more into the wind, I relaxed. I was then happy to change the subject to a more concrete area by viewing, um, concrete. I scanned the huge open expanse of the basement, and managed to avoid the symbolism of the cross formed by the shape of the empty foundation. Instead, I pondered the splendid swimming pool the space would allow. I was considering my suggestion of just such a fixture at the next town council meeting when my mundane reverie was disturbed by the sharp screech of tires issued from a car that had stopped suddenly nearby. I could not see who it was, because the vehicle was hidden behind the six-foot hedge that had once formed the border of Beaver Toys' lawn. A door slammed, followed by a rapid exchange of muffled voices. Though I could not discern the dialogue, I was certain that these people were not lovers getting away from it all. Then again...

I stood to investigate, pleased by any distraction. I leaned around the edge of the still neatly trimmed hedge to see a New York City taxicab parked in front of the main gate.

"Fifty bucks?" A garishly dressed young woman cried. It was Mary. I could tell. Though her hair (now yellow), clothes, and makeup were different, Max's silhouette still flowed beneath the white trash trappings.

"Yeah, lady, that's right, and it's a cut rate. I said a hundred when we left." The driver, a grubby, standard middle-eastern cabbie type but with a Brooklyn accent, leaned aggressively against the far side of the hood. His stance was tense, ready to pounce. He probably would be willing to beat the fare out of her, especially after having to ride with her all the way from Manhattan.

"You said a `C-note,'" Mary snarled, "I only owe you ten bucks." The driver sighed, lifting his eyes and hands to heaven. I came around the bushes, passed through a convenient break in the fence, and began to stroll toward the cab. Mary spotted me long before I reached the gate. She tossed her half-smoked cigarette and waved frantically.

"Bob!" she shouted, "You're here!"

"Alex, Mary. It's Alex," I said when I reached the cab. Mary's tightly sprung stance betrayed her successfully suppressed urge to embrace me. She nodded dumbly, but still did not repeat my name.

"Listen *Bob*," the cabbie sighed dramatically, "The little lady owes me some money. I hope you can help out," he said 'hope' as he cracked his knuckles. I remembered that I had only ninety-six cents in my pocket, and even less in my bank account, but, on a hunch, I reached in anyway.

"I think I can," I said, whipping out a fresh one hundred dollar bill. I folded it twice and threw it to the hack. It wasn't a good toss, but the driver exhibited fine acrobatic skills as he dove for the bill, using the yellow car to break his fall. He unfolded it.

"Hey, this really is a C-note. Mister, I can't change this."

"I thought it was what you wanted."

The cabbie smiled broadly. "Need a ride anywhere, Mister?" he asked. He waved, blew a kiss to Mary, and pulled out, churning up a cloud of dust behind him. Mary screamed and chased after him, ruining his dramatic exit with acrid curses mixed with pleas to wait. The cab skidded to a stop, and idled while she caught up to it, her very high heels hampering her speedy progress on the loose gravel road. She reached for the passenger door handle, then suddenly yelped and jumped back, losing her balance. Before she could steady herself, a giant red canvas tote bag flew out the open passenger window and into her chest, sending her to the road spandex-ass first. Tires smoked again and the cab was irrevocably on its way. Mary had no more objections. I offered a hand, expecting her to indignantly slap it away. She took it. The motion of my lifting her to her feet inadvertently pulled us together, forcing our bodies to touch. We stood for a moment, our faces inches apart, regarding each other in silence. Then she frowned prettily and stepped back. We stood a second longer as if to reaffirm identities.

"What are you doing here?" we asked simultaneously. We repeated that three times before she gestured for me to speak first.

"I spent most of the last two years here," I said, nodding my head toward the ruin.

"You lived in a empty swimming pool?"

"No, I used to work in it. When it was a different sort of empty pool."

"What happened?" she asked.

"Fire. Big fire. Started in the puppet room."

"Oh. It was a puppet factory?"

"Close. It was called Beaver Toy Company."

"You made toys?" she chirped, "Like Santa's Elves? That's so cool!"

"Not quite. Other people made them. I wrote the instructions for putting them together."

"Really? If you ever told my dad that, you'd be a dead man."

"Lot of kids?"

"Eight."

"Sorry."

"You should be."

"Now what the hell are you doing here?" I asked, preempting her imminent reminiscences of broken toys, failed Christmases, and furious fathers.

"I don't know," she said. Her cheeks' natural color could just be seen as a hint of red under cakes of orange/brown makeup. I could tell that she realized where she was, or where she wasn't, but thought it wise to allow her to continue masking her confusion. She finished, holding both badly manicured hands in the air in front of her: "I only wanted to get out of the city for a few hours. It was an urge."

"Why here?" I repeated gently.

"It was the first address that popped into my mind," she said.

"1382 North Alabaster Boulevard, Tarrytown. I guess that could easily pop into anyone's head. You ever been here before? Who told you about it?"

"Nobody," she said, "I've never heard of any place outside of Yonkers, fer crissake." She was telling the truth.

"So this address just popped into your head?"

"I said it before I even knew it was out. I liked the sound of it, so I didn't change it. Good thing, too, huh? I didn't think I'd see you again."

"Nor I, you. So you just happened to take your first drive out of town to this place on the only day that I've been here since we met?"

"Hell of a coincidence, huh?" she said, oblivious to the forces influencing her.

"Mary, I have to ask: have you had any strange dreams lately?"

"That's a bizarre question, Bob! I really don't dream at all. But, now you ask, I do remember one I had a few days ago. You were in it."

"I was?" I said, trying to look surprised, "What did I do?"

"Not much. You were just another one of the people I stepped on."

"`Stepped on?'" I said.

"Yeah. There were millions of people, standing for as far as I could see, squeezed against each other like sardines. I had to step on you guys, see, because I was being chased--"

"By a black shadow?" I cut in.

"No. She wore black I guess, but this one was a woman, with flaming red hair. She looked familiar but I couldn't place her. She was screaming bloody murder at me."

"And she was chasing you?"

"She sure was. Funny, she didn't seem mad, just worried-like, shouting for me to stop. But I couldn't."
"Why not?"

"Cause of the heads I was running on. Turns out I was wearing spiked heels with sharpened spikes. Every time I slowed down my shoes dug into some poor sucker's head. They screamed real loud when that happened, too. It musta hurt them big time. So I didn't stop much. Anyway I noticed some people as I ran, and you were one of them."

"You recognized other people?" I asked.

"Yes and no. It was like I knew who they were, but they weren't quite themselves, so I couldn't name them. Except you."

"Except me?"

"Right. You were definitely you. Positive. Funny you were the only one, though."

"Funny," I said, hiding any sign that I understood what Mary's dream might imply. That would only confuse her, I assumed, or at least muddle her memory. I asked, "How did the dream end? Did the woman catch you? Did she tell you anything? What happened?"

"Louisa, my roommate's rat-dog, jumped on my face and woke me up. She does that a lot – the dog, not my roommate."

Fine, I thought, clenching my fists. The course was still worth following, though, so I said, "That's what brought you all the way out here? Me?"

"No such luck, Bob. I forgot all about that dream until right now."

"Sorry. I didn't mean to sound pretentious."

"Hey, no problem, whatever you were pretending to be," she said absently. I made a mental reminder to choose words containing fewer than three syllables when talking to Mary. She continued, "But I don't know what brought me out here at all. I'm sure it had nothing to do with you. This is all one of those coincidences."

"You don't believe this could have happened through the wishes of someone or something bigger than the both of us?" I asked. She laughed at that, and I did not blame her. It sounded ridiculous, like bad TV, though I was dead serious. What was happening to me? I chuckled politely.

"Only kidding," I said, "I'm sure this was all an accident." In a moment her laughter subsided, and we found ourselves mired in silence, each of us noting the self-consciousness welling in the other. In time Mary frowned, lifted her bare wrist as if to read a watch.

"It's getting late," she said, "I'd better start going home before it gets dark. I don't think I'll be able to get another cab around here. Any subways nearby?"

"That's nonsense, Mary. You'll come home with me. It's too late to find your way home now. I'll drive you back in the morning."

"No thanks. Really," she said apprehensively. Her sidelong glance said 'I hardly know you.'

"Don't worry about a thing, Mary. I've got extra rooms."

"I haven't got any of my things," she said, almost smiling. Apparently the hint of extra rooms went right over her head.

"My wife – she died a couple years ago – still has things you could use, or wear." Mary took a long, long look at me, straight into my eyes. Her unblinking gaze persisted for several minutes while something deep inside her assembled a judgment. I was momentarily enthralled by the power trapped within her eyes, mystified by their subtle betrayal of her green-eyed counterpart. Finally she closed them briefly, smiled slightly, and ran a hand through her stiff yellow tresses. The wonder switched off, and Mary returned.

"Well, maybe it will be all right," she sighed. Without a word from me, she started toward my car. I wondered if this wasn't all a game, then remembered Cleavus. The simple city girl and her morals made up everything that was this facet of Max/Mary. She was incapable of, or at least completely uninterested in, manipulating my thoughts or actions for some underhanded gain. Though she did have bouts of occasional accidental depth, Mary could not nurture even such a minimal evil. Without bearing any malice toward Max with the thought, I realized that Mary was pure. Not terribly bright, but pure. And still attractive: I admired her form once more when she stepped through the open door I held for her and into my car. She smiled shyly at my unconscious chivalry. I returned the smile politely, but my emotions were clouded. I had hoped that, if she realized that I wanted her around only to retrieve a message I assumed Max was trying to send me, Mary would heave a monumental sigh of relief. I thought it best to continue to keep my intentions to myself, though. Just in case. I shut her door, ran around to my open door, and stepped into the running car. We drove away, together, from Beaver Toys, my bills, and my past, for the very last time.

Chapter Fifteen

"Definitely."

"Well, all right, long as you're sure," Mary said, lifting herself off the sofa, "Night, then."

"Good night," I responded pleasantly, as if Mary were a long-time resident. My tone was necessary; I had just spent an hour convincing her that it was okay to sleep, alone, in my bedroom, and I needed to maintain the air of easy familiarity that she had at last accepted from me. Mary was obliged to submit, since mine was the only room with a bed, but some unnamed notion rooted either in prudence or fear compelled her to argue against my innocent hospitality. I assured her that I would rest in the spare room in the cellar, but I am not sure she ever believed that. Who sleeps in a cellar?

I was relieved upon her acquiescence, since I was growing anxious to begin my `rest' as soon as possible. When I was confident that Mary was safely asleep – a steady snore emanating from my bedroom less than five minutes after Mary said good night was evidence enough – I went to the kitchen, filled a squeaky clean tumbler with water, and wandered into my living room. I set the glass on a highly polished side table whose existence I had forgotten, careful to include a coaster in the mix. I sat back in my recliner, hands tucked behind my head. Okay, there isn't too much of a hurry to get back in the chair, I thought, I should allow myself one more serene look around. My cheeks ached slightly under the pressure of an unavoidable broad grin.

The living room was spotless, a dim reflection of the kitchen and dining rooms around it. Mary had been a whirlwind, fueling her cleaning vigor – and likely disgust at my woeful lack of domestic hygiene – with the unnecessary guilt of sharing my roof.

I assured her repeatedly that I did not mind, but restrained myself from halting her cleaning frenzy. I rationalized allowing her to continue working by deciding that her efforts helped her to feel better, more than words could. I knew in my heart that I was using her by capitalizing on her good intentions. Finally she settled long enough to catch the end of the Tonight Show with me. Now she was asleep, and I was free to pursue her counterpart to uncover what compelled Mary to unconsciously seek me.

I darkened the living room and kitchen, descended the cellar stairs, closing the door behind me. I no longer had to grope in the dark to find the Sound Room. The light usually came on before I was halfway to it. Occasionally it would fail to burn entirely; when I was in no mood to dream, or if I was coming down to do laundry.

I removed my shoes, socks and shirt before sitting down. Prudently, I left my pants on in case Mary had to wake me. I closed the door, sat in the chair. The lights dimmed, the red room left me.

Violet lightning flashed. I was on Macy's main floor, surrounded by a crowd of mannequins cheering their leader in the gilded balcony above us. A dressing dummy general orated, weaving feverishly to accentuate armless battle cries. None of the dummies noticed that the cold heavy downpour that made the makeup run right off the cosmetic counter salesgirls marred the general's speech. Feeling confined by the gyrating plastic about me, I turned around. I found myself strolling the hilly path that meandered through St. Anne's Cemetery. I wasn't surprised by the change in scenery, and I knew where I was even though my expertise hadn't advanced enough yet to know why I was there. I respectfully strode past the dark monolithic Guptil family tombs, climbed one small hill, and then made a left down the gravel path that led to Cassie's grave. There it was: third on the right after the ancient oak tree. She stood beside her clean, unadorned tombstone. I did not turn around.

Cassie's pale gown was gray morning mist that drifted seductively over her thin, still body. She said nothing. Her drawn, sorrowful face held no recognition. She may not have known that I was on the path. I didn't care. My previous resolutions forgotten, I ran to her, spread my arms and whipped them closed about her shoulders, ready to hoist her to the air and spin her around – carefully this time! – in joy. Instead of entering a warm embrace, I fell through her open arms. My face entered her passive visage. I encountered complete darkness for an instant before I emerged from a tuft of dark hair, hitting my face on the corner of her grave. I bounced back, rubbing my bruised right eye. I looked around with the good one, and coldly observed that I was alone in the cemetery. Golden shafts of morning sunlight cut through the mist that was dissipating near her grave. I understood grimly that Cassie was never there; specters don't count. My body shook with remorse. Through blurred vision I read the epitaph on her tombstone, which was written with flashing blue neon lights:

"The Frankfurter Sunrise rests not, wants all"

I laughed, picturing a hot dog dipped in a tumbler of tequila. An example of my concoction appeared, floating inches from my face. Enough of this, I thought, it's time now for something less obviously contrived. I started to turn, stopped to pluck the hot dog out of the glass, and then finished rotating around to face a new direction.

A flat horizon stretched in all directions. I was not back on the purple plain because yellow earth met featureless green sky to form the smooth crisp line that strangely intrigued me. That line, marred by only one dark object too distant to clearly see, seemed close enough to touch. So I did. I bent down, jammed my fingers under the sky and lifted the horizon. A brown hill appeared a few miles from where I stood, but it was a small, unimpressive little mound. Becoming slightly bored, but not ready to break from this sequence yet, I sought the dark object that marred the perfect horizon earlier. It surfaced a few points to my left, its blackness offering a pleasant break in the green and yellow monotony. By stepping toward it, I was able to discern its nature. Though still a hundred yards away, I could see that the object was a large, ancient fence post, nearly buried under the shadow of a giant black bird that perched on it. I jumped back reflexively, but then relaxed when I realized that this was not the monstrous raven I had encountered a lifetime of dreams ago. This specimen had a crown of rich red feathers above green eyes that glowed with unfettered energy. Delighted, I covered the hundred yards to it in a few steps. The creature had shrunk to the size of a normal crow when I was close enough to touch it. I reached out to pat its downy head, but it pecked at me before I could complete the gesture of friendship. Rather, it pecked at the long white satin cape I wore. I tried to deflect the pecks, then to walk away from the post, but the bird persisted its attack. It flew with me, evading my flailing arms, and continued to peck at the cape. I tried turning around, but I was still on the same yellow land, under the same bright sunless green sky, with the same redheaded bird pecking away at my cape. Finally I submitted to the niggling torture, and tore off my warm white fur covering. The garment burst into flames when it hit the yellow dirt, then disappeared.

"Thank you," the bird squawked. I recognized the song.

"No problem, Max" I said, "It is you, right Max?"

"Of course it's me! Who the hell else would let you turn her into a bird?"

"Why don't you be Max?"

"Hey, it's not my dream," She said, flapping her wings in what I imagined was an avian shrug. I concentrated for a moment on making her Max again, but failed. I had no trouble picturing what Max should look like, but the parameters of the current dream did not allow such a change. I was not alarmed; I had encountered this problem before. It seemed that in order to sustain a dream I had to let my unconscious reign in most of that dream's aspects. If my unconscious was not interested in my voluntary input, I could not change the dream. I had been making progress in communicating with my own mind, but there was still no perfect union between my two states of awareness. I shrugged like a human, held out my wrist as a platform for Max the bird, and said:

"Sorry. There's nothing I can do about it. In this dream, you're a bird."

"That's what I figured. Oh well, I'll have to quack and bear it." Max lighted on my wrist. She was heavy, but I chose not to insult her further and stoically supported her. Max looked at me expectantly, her little head cocked to one side.

"I think I got a message from you," I said.

"Yes. I haven't been able to get through to you, so I had to risk communicating with my counterpart. What's with the defense shield?"

"Oh, sorry about that. It certainly wasn't meant for you. Rudy was getting pushy, and I started to feel like he was watching me at all times, so I created a cloak of invisibility, if you will."

"The hell I will!" Max squawked, " I thought you died. I had to ask Rudy if you were still alive."

"He knew?"

"He knew. He said he still felt your presence but you weren't speaking just then."

"Well, that's about right."

"About right? Are you kidding me? Because of this `about right,' I had to almost die myself and risk the death of my--"

"Mary," I interjected.

"My counterpart," she finished coolly, and I had my first experience of a bird gesturing `don't you think I know that?'

"So anyway, what message did you need to convey?" I asked.

"I can't tell you."

Fine, I thought.

"Is it going to be a riddle, then?" I asked, aware of this practice. It was an annoying part of most of the fantasy books I had read, and was rapidly becoming intrinsic to the machinations of my new experiences.

"It's no riddle," I thought I heard passion twist her squawk, "It's the dream. It isn't right."

"What do you mean it isn't right? It's my dream; I make what is and isn't right. Well, one part or another of me does, anyway."

"I'm disappointed. I thought you learned the truth in your dreams long ago," Max the crow said. I agreed silently. Of course I understood that I didn't have full control, but I was sure that my unconscious would want her to speak. I didn't dare entertain the thought that something controlled my unconscious as well.

"Nobody controls your unconscious," Max said. I ignored the disturbing image of a crow reading my mind. She continued, "What I meant was that by now you know that other parts of the World might share in your dreams, if they so desired."

Oh.

"Sure," I said, averting my eyes, "I knew that. So, this thing you have to say is something you don't want someone to hear?"

"I don't know. I can't remember what it was."

"I can take care of that," I said haughtily.

"No!" Max chirped.

I ignored her and turned my thoughts inward. I forced my way into the nature of Max's place in my dream, concentrating on whatever force or personal objection might be interrupting her thoughts. I found nothing. I was actually not sure where to look. Though I knew it could be done, I had never before chosen this sort of investigation. I tried a different approach, feeling an odd, emotionally desperate need to hear the important message she had left behind.

"Just tell me what it is you had to tell me," I demanded, sounding like a father getting the truth about drugs from his kid.

"Alex," the bird panted, "Please. Don't do it this way. It hurts."

I had never heard a bird pant, but even that had no effect on my resolve. I ignored her plea by reasoning that she was simply under the influence of whatever was controlling her. Feeling power welling within me, I looked down at the pitiful little bird.

"Tell me what you must!" I shouted, peripherally seeing the horizon ripple at the force of my words. The crow jumped off my wrist in a flurry of feathers, mostly red. It tried to fly away, but could not. It eventually stopped flapping its wings and hung motionless in the air above my extended wrist.

"I can't," it cried, green eyes growing pale, "Alex, stop this, you're crushing me!"

I towered above the crow now, watched it flutter at my distant ankles. It had become a tiny startled black chicken between my stomping feet, physically subject to the relentless eddies of my power. I forgot why I was shaking the yellow ground, only that it was something I had to do in order to rid my universe of the trespasser who was stymieing Max.

"I am one of those intruders!" Max cried weakly from far, far below, her voice a whisper in the wind.

Those six faint nearly dissolute words woke me from the latest bout of my peculiar power madness. I reacted to them almost instinctively, freezing my actions, ending my artificial grandeur, and abandoning my contrived concentration. The dream stopped moving, almost like I had touched the pause button on my VCR. Max the crow and I were still on the empty yellow land under a nauseatingly green sky. I resumed normal size relative to her. The scene was silent, empty. The little bird was draped over my outstretched arm, limp and very still. Any emerald glow had vacated the battered bird's gaze. I shivered. Fearing that I had shut off the sophomoric show of force too late, I cleared my mind, with ease, of any interest in dreaming.

Without a perceived change of light or scenery I was again standing on the purple plain. Max, human, naked, and sweating, was lying on her side at my feet, crumpled in a tight ball. Her back heaved rapidly as her lungs strained to draw air. I fell to my knees behind her, tears fouling my vision. I gently touched her arm, her bare hip, the top of her head. Every part of her was wet, cold, and very wrong. I tried to beg her to come back to me, but my words were caught deep within my clenched throat. I fell beside her. I leaned my back against hers, perhaps for continued assurance that she was still alive without the burden of having to look at her, at what I had done. Again. We sat for what seemed like hours, though I knew in reality the chair would not let me sleep that long. In time color and warmth returned to her smooth skin, and she seemed to be breathing freely. So was I. I turned back to face her, though I remained seated, cross-legged, beside her. I slapped her wrist for a moment, thinking lamely that the gesture worked on television, so it could help here. I rested her head on my lap, draping some silk from the white robe I again wore over her shoulders and breasts. When her eyes finally opened, they focused on mine instantly and shimmered. Max smiled. I smiled. We both smiled, still unable to conjure words to explain our relief. Eventually we calmed enough where I felt we could break the happy silence.

"You're back," I said softly, my words trimmed by my bent throat.

"That I am," she said softly, without anger. After the initial relief, I had expected some real fireworks from Max, but she continued to lie placidly in my lap. I, however, was suddenly furious. I could almost feel my blood boiling in response to my repeated inability to maintain self-control. I had blindly basked in my newfound power at the expense of this perfect woman, the first person I could love since Cassie. I did not know where that thought came from, but it was true, and that it only compounded my guilt. I had almost killed her. What an interesting, but effective, way to attempt to make myself a part of her life! I succeeded in maintaining an outward calm, though, since there was no need to subject Max to my self-loathing.

"Max," I said, running a hand through her thick, soft hair, "What can I do to show you how sorry I am for what I did, or almost did?"

"Well, you can start by putting some clothes on us."

I looked down. Yes, we were both now quite naked. It took me a moment to get my eyes off her body, but finally I looked back into her pleased face.

"Funny. Those details are usually taken care of."

"I guess you had other things to think about."

"I guess so. You can't give yourself clothes?"

"How many times I gotta tell you? It's not my reality."

"Oh. Well, listen, you'll have to stand up so I can fit you."

"You're sure it's not just to get a better look?"

"Not entirely." We stood on the unchanging purple plain. I was dressed in my usual blue T-shirt and jeans before my legs were straight. She was not.

"Magnificent," I accidentally said aloud. She laughed, hands on hips, unashamed.

"You don't think Rudy keeps me around for my mind, do you?"

"I didn't think those things mattered in your world."

"Not as much, but remember: Rudy isn't completely part of my world. Now, enough of this T&A bullshit, Alex. Dress me!"

Reluctantly I pictured her briefly in a green silk gown that I thought I had seen some starlet wear at the Oscars a year earlier. She wore it instantly and, of course, it fit. I thought of a full-length mirror for her to admire herself. When it appeared beside her, she was not surprised. She twirled a few times in front of the mirror, apparently pleased with my choice. I could not keep my eyes off her. I knew now that what I felt was more than my hormonal reaction to her beauty. My inadvertent yet oddly deliberate attempt to kill her had opened something in me, something that had always been there. I put my hands on her arms. It felt right. She immediately wrapped them around my waist and pulled me in to a tight hug. We stayed that way for a long, glorious moment. Finally we parted. She sighed, looked about her at the emptiness.

"Nothing can touch us here?" she asked.

"You probably know better than I, but as far as I know, no. If I'm still dreaming, I have complete control here. If not, I share the place with all others like me."

"Met any others like you?"

"Only one so far."

"Then we're safe. I know Rudy would never hurt you." Wrong one, I thought.

"Good," I said, gesturing to the sofa on my left, "Then why don't we sit for a spell, and you can tell me what it is that all this fuss is about." We sat, huddled close on thick clean bearskins before the roaring fire in an old stone hearth a few feet away. It felt natural. Comfortable.

"I haven't felt this way in years," I said aloud.

"Quiet," she said, putting a finger to my lips, "Remember where I'm from, and that you still think Cassie lives." That slowed the juices.

"What do you mean, `think?'" I asked. I didn't pull away, but did stop stroking her smooth cheek at the mention of Cassie. "Of course she is alive. I talked to her."

"Yes. I know. I'm sorry I said it like that. I must be jealous. I take it back."

"Wait, don't take it back yet. Is that what you went to all this trouble to tell me?"

"I don't know."

"You what?"

"Don't know."

"Seriously?"

"Of course."

"Why?"

"Because you're not dreaming anymore. If you were dreaming then I could remember what I was supposed to tell you."

"But you couldn't tell me when I was dreaming--"

"Because some force would rather see me die first. No, not you. Get that horrible look off your face. And now I'm in your created world, powerless to remember anything except what I am, and what I feel right now. I'm not under the influence of the thing that I was supposed to tell you about, so it has been removed from me. Hell of an existence, huh?"

"Seriously. How could thought be removed from you?" I asked, exasperated. I wanted to get up and pace, but I did not want to break our wonderful contact.

"Well, not removed, exactly. When I'm with you when you dream, we share everything. In your dreams you are inadvertently part of the World," she pronounced the upper case, "But here with you, out of a dream, it's like I'm caught in your tight beam, and everything outside that beam is out of reach."

"So you can't tell me anything?"

"Only how I feel about you," she whispered. My heart leapt, then tugged conversely as I remembered that Cassie lived.

"And nothing else?" I tried to ask coolly, squeaking a bit.

"Nothing, though I had hoped that that bit would have been pretty important. The rest of my world is left outside your beam."

"Please. You know it is. I'm just a buffoon. Now, how do I widen this beam?"

"You become one with the World," she said. The pools forming in her eyes conveyed the toll drawn by her words.

"How do I do this?"

"I don't know, and if I did I probably would keep it to myself."

"Why?"

"Rather than that neat parlor trick, it could be your unique human sentience that is the real cloak protecting you from the evil of the World. Become one with all there is, and you may abandon your ability to combat that evil."

"Aren't I part of the World when I dream?"

"Part of it, yes, but not one with it. I am part of it also, as if I am always dreaming. I can't be `one' either, though this side of reality is a bit easier (and more fun) to move around in. Dreams are mobility, sure, but not unity. Even natives like me can get lost in the chaos of the World's thoughts sometimes. You've realized by now that Mary is my waking self. My unconscious is as unconscious as Mary's conscious. Don't make faces; it's true. We are separate, still joined by our, my, unconscious to make us the same person."

"How do you know this?"

"We full-time dreamers are more mobile, and curious than the nightly travelers; we have a knack for catching onto certain themes and rules. Plus, Rudy told me. He also said that Mary and I must never meet. You, however, have no separate waking self or dreaming self. That is where your power lies. That is what Rudy sees."

"And fears?" I asked, touching her cheek. She didn't answer that. Instead she regarded me carefully for a moment and took my hand. After a gossamer sigh, she spoke:

"I can't answer that, because I don't know what he wants from you. Except help. In the most desperate way."

"I don't know how to help him."

"And I can't tell you."

"Let me guess. I have to become one with the World to get all the answers?"

"Right."

"But in doing so I might lose all my earthly power, my spiritual independence?"

"I think so – I don't know. No one but Rudy has done it before."

"No one?"

"Yeah."

"What about Freuzre?"

"Oh, right. And Freuzre."

"What is Freuzre?"

"I can't – "

"Tell me that?"

"I am sorry."

"So I can't find out what you risked your and Mary's lives to tell me because my beam is too tight. And I can't widen that beam because I'd best not risk experiencing the World?"

"Right."

"So either way I lose?"

"Seems like it. Unless there was something in what I had to tell you that said you won't lose, but I – "

"Don't know what that could be," I finished with her. To fill the brief silence that followed, I studied Max's hand. It was soft, and unusually tan for a woman who had never been exposed to the sun. Her long, graceful fingers ended in unpolished, close-cropped nails. She did not need a manicure, or any other cosmetics, today. Finally I asked, "So what else about you fits in my beam?"

"Not a lot. Well, nothing important, anyway. Mostly a short history of how I came to know you. And love you." She squeezed my fingers but looked away, as if she feared that I would turn her back into a crow. I smiled at her misdirected fears, and got to my feet. I held that precious hand as I stood, lifting Max with me. A clear mountain lake shimmered on our left, and distant snow-capped Rockies pierced the dark blue sky. Birds chirped in the thick woods on the other three sides of us. A footpath, edged by tall grass that rustled in the warm breeze, circled the lake.

"Let's take a walk and you can tell me about it," I whispered in her ear, if only to feel her hair against my cheek. We started walking in the unchanging scenery.

"There isn't much to tell. Rudy is the instigator of it all, of course. A few years ago he recognized your talent and moved next door to you. I had already known him, and persuaded him to let me assist him. It wasn't hard; Rudy likes to keep pretty things around. I understood his mission, though I can't tell you what it is now, and I wanted to help. So I hung around.

"My first assignment was to keep an eye on you. I couldn't do anything, of course, since we're from different, um--"

"Dimensions?"

"What an excellent word! We'll go with it. Anyway, I could do nothing but watch. Now don't stop walking. I wasn't some two-bit voyeur with a camera trained on you 24/7 or anything. I just kept an eye on you, primarily during your dreams. But I sure did feel it big time when Cassie died. I think that was when Mary left home. But I never noticed any of the signs that Rudy told me to watch for."

"Signs?"

"Sorry," she said in a mock nasally voice, "Your beam is too tight in that area."

"Fine."

"I am sorry," she said, looking on the path for a pebble to kick. One appeared for her.

"I know," I said gently, "Go on." First she kicked the pebble. We followed it along the path to its resting place, and she kicked it again before speaking.

"I never saw any of Rudy's signs, but he kept insisting they had to be present. In fact, the only reason you are here today is because you got dragged in after the attack on his house. He decided you were ready, signs or no signs."

"I remember how furious you were at Fritz's when you heard that," I said. She bowed her head.

"I shared every feeling you had for years, Alex. I knew you, know you, like no one else. Not even Cassie," a tinge of arrogance surfaced, "I never wanted you `ready' for what Rudy faces on a daily basis."

"Freuzre?"

"I guess so, I can't completely remember. But I never wanted you ready. I never felt you were. I was furious at Rudy because I blamed him for bringing you in."

"Am I still not ready?"

"I don't know."

"Why do you love me?"

"To me that is a silly question but I have no answer for you." I stopped and turned to face her. I let Cassie slip my mind for a moment and pulled Max close to me. We could feel each other well through our clothes, but Max smiled when they dissolved to a fine mist and contact was unfettered. I completed the moment by kissing Max on the mouth, mixing my tongue, my pleasure, and my soul, with hers. I hadn't entertained such feelings in a very long time, but I was sure that everything was right, and something beyond magic was happening between us. This was real, and the intimacy was simply a confirming gesture. Unfortunately, I noticed an unwelcome change in the corner of my eye and forced myself to stop the long lingering kiss by gently pulling away from Max's lips. I looked over Max's shoulder and confirmed that the lake was opaque purple.

"Oh shit," I sighed.

"What?"

"I think my time in the chair is up. It's trying to wake me up."

"No," Max whispered urgently, "Don't go now."

"I can't believe it ran out so fast. Hold on, I can take you with me." I was sure I could, since she was all that remained solid. The images of the lake were gone. The purple plain was back, shifting violently to red as impure consciousness closed in. She pulled away from me, easily prying her hand from my grip, but seemed unable to step beyond my reach.

"Oh no you can't," she said, without fear this time, "My counterpart is in your house. Terrible things could happen."

"What?"

"I don't know! No one has ever had the chance to find out, so the warnings could be all talk. I don't want to be the first to test the theory, Alex." I could understand that. Purple was fading to red now, in a windless vortex around us.

"You have to let me go! Now!" she cried into the wind that should have been there. She still trusted me to do the right thing, but clearly she knew the instruction needed repeating. I understood, and knew that her faith was not wasted, but felt helpless upon realizing now the thin line on which my powers balanced. I had to let go. I pulled Max close for one last hug, had the uneasy feeling that she had less mass this time, then wordlessly let her go. She was smiling as she faded into the vortex. Max had sensed correctly that I wouldn't screw with her reality again. My chest ached when she vanished into the maelstrom of color. I settled back to what I felt was a reclining position and prepared to wake.

Chapter Sixteen

I assumed with multifaceted frustration that the mystic automatic machinery of the Sound Room had wrenched me from my glorious first intimacy with Max. When I opened my eyes, I was greeted not by the usual wall of soft red stuff, but by an extreme close-up of Mary. Max's counterpart was peering at me, her straight nose nearly rubbing mine. For a flash I thought Max had had a change of heart, and nature, and chose to follow me out, but conscious clarity quickly confirmed that this was definitely Mary. Her stricken expression shifted from concern to delight to a frown of consternation in about one second. She pulled her head back slightly, allowing me to see that she was perched on my abdomen, tightly wrapped in my Sunday-morning-coffee silk bathrobe. I could feel her hands near my throat, and what I assumed were her knees in my armpits. Her muscles were taught, indicating that she was about to or, I worried, already had begun to administer her version of CPR. Though I was angry at her interruption, I had to laugh. When I did, Mary reacted by squealing and jumping off my chest.

"I thought you were dead," she said breathlessly. She folded her arms, then unfolded them, then played with her yellow hair, then folded her arms again. I couldn't see them, but I imagined her feet were moving just as nervously based on the bobbing of her head.

"I've heard that before," I said. I swung my legs around to the floor to stand. In the process, I kicked Mary's ass firmly. She stumbled forward, chuckled politely. She thought it was an accident. The contact did seem to calm her, though, and it certainly made me feel better. The feelings, tastes, and touch of my last (pre-vortex) moment with Max still lingered, and I wanted to be furious that Mary had interrupted. Imagining her panic at my apparent death struggle helped stifle my anger, but I remained emotionally charged and pissed in general.

"Why," I asked, trying to stay calm despite my urge to scream, "Did you wake me up?"

"I'm sorry," she said, correctly interpreting my poorly masked tone, "Really. It's just that I couldn't get to sleep at all, so I went to see if you were having the same problem. And, I really did think you were dead after you didn't wake up right away."

"How considerate."

"Yeah. Well anyway, none of it was easy. I couldn't find you nowhere. I searched for hours," I thought about reminding her that I told her where I was going to sleep, but passed. She continued, "Finally I got up the guts to come down here. It's so dark. How can you stand it?"

"I think bright thoughts. How did you get in here?"

"Easy. After I fell down the stairs – you really ought to put in a light switch at the top – I bumped into the wall out there. I got scared and started feeling for the stairs again. Then I found this switch and the door slid open and the light came on. I thought you were dead, the way you didn't move at all, so I started giving you CPR."

"CPR?"

"Yeah, Cardio Pulmonary Resomething, just like on TV. And it worked, except that you were only asleep... sorry I woke you."

"No problem, now. What time is it?"

"Last I looked it was a little after four."

"Go back to bed," I said, "Feel free to wake me up at a human hour, okay?" I rolled back into the chair, faced the wall, and waited for Mary to quietly leave. After she did, I settled into a dreamless sleep (it seemed tacky, and perhaps risky for me to go after Max right away, so I pulled the "cloak" over me and got some real rest) until another alarm woke me much later in the morning. It took me a moment to recognize the odor of sizzling bacon through the open door of the Sound Room, but when I did, I was upstairs before my T-shirt was pulled down completely.

Mary was in the kitchen, wearing my red dress shirt and nothing else. Human foibles like a bad diet and lack of fitness prevented her from possessing Max's perfection of form, but dressed like she was, I saw how close she came. She turned to me and smiled from the stove, waves of delicious heat pouring over her long, wavy, and unrestrained auburn hair.

"Good morning," she said brightly. Apparently she had forgotten about her trip to the Sound Room earlier, which was fine with me. The good sleep, and the smell of breakfast, had done much to dissipate my anger. When I joined Mary at the stove I resisted, and was slightly surprised by, an involuntary urge to peck her on her cheek.

"It sure is," I said, stealing a slice of bacon. As I tossed the hot food about in my hands, I looked again at her hair.

"I thought it was yellow?"

"Yellow?" she asked, poking with her fork at the bacon in confusion before she followed my gaze to her hair. She absently touched it with long, slender, greasy fingers, and said, "Oh, my hair. Canary." Fine, codes again.

"Canary?"

"Yeah, that's the color I had in it, but I washed it out this morning. Back to my normal old brown. I hope you don't mind that I used your bathroom and stuff."

"Oh, no problem. The neighbors got pissed last time I sent a guest over there."

"They did?"

"Forget it. I sure appreciate this breakfast. I can't believe you walked all the way to the market to get the fixings." She blushed and stared at the sizzling bacon. I clasped the edge of the counter firmly.

"You didn't walk?" she shook her head, still avoiding my gaze.

"You called a cab?" I asked softly, hoping. She turned and looked at me with wide green eyes. No, she didn't take a cab. Her eyes were shiny now, polished by potential tears.

"My car?"

She nodded. A long, slow nod; like a child. I thought for a moment: What harm could she have done? The car can pretty much take care of itself these days, and nobody with a license could be a worse driver than me.

"Do you have a license?" She shook her head, looked back at the bacon, then at me, silently stating her case. I sighed.

"Car still in one piece?" I asked, putting a hand on her shoulder. She nodded again, briskly this time. Then she rested her warm cheek on my hand.

"Aren't you going to ask me how I like my eggs?" I asked amicably, rubbing her makeup-free cheek lightly with my thumb. It had the same porcelain smooth, soft texture as Max's. When she lifted her head to respond, I felt a mild loss. Her touch, and touching her, was comforting. I had to dismiss the feeling welling in me, though, because it could be sourced to one of too many disparate themes: Was it Mary? Was I looking to continue my moment with Max through Max's surrogate? Or was it because it had been so long since I had touched a woman, really? I did let my hand linger on her shoulder, though, just to let her know I wasn't backing off from sudden fear or embarrassment – I held a dim hope that she could catch that subtle a gesture.

"I guessed," she said too loudly, but happily, "Something told me you like them fried, over hard."

"That was a good guess," I said.

"I was right?" she asked, eyes wide again. Their glow screamed Max, but the cry was not enough to transform Mary's plain face.

"Sure were," I said, waiting for her to jump up in the air and shout `oh goody!' She didn't, but she did work the bacon more vigorously.

We sat down later to the first real breakfast I had had in months. It felt good. It was a welcome luxury to be waited on, even if Mary were here by no act of her own. We talked between bites. Breakfast talk, mostly: weather, sports, things that didn't interfere with enjoyment of good food. It was also a true relief to share something as earthy as a breakfast after a night of moving horizons and talking to crows. Simple reality was becoming vacation for me. When we had finished the hot food, and were prolonging the satisfaction the meal had given us with doughnuts and coffee, Mary quieted. She stared at the cream clouds drifting in her coffee mug for several minutes, ignoring the half of a jelly doughnut that rested, slightly squished, between her fingers. Without taking a sip of her carefully regarded drink, she raised her chin and looked directly into my eyes. Her expression was grave. I braced myself.

"Alex," she said, carefully setting the doughnut on the edge of her plate, "Why am I here?" I swallowed fast. I had hoped that Mary didn't consider such topics, but in my heart I had also known that the question would eventually surface. I knew the answer, of course. I had been preparing it since she walked though my front door the previous evening. After much rehearsal, I realized that there was no way to tell her the truth and still sound reasonable, or even sane. I responded with plan A, which was to simply evade the question.

"Shouldn't I be asking you that?" I asked.

"I may be a little dumb but I'm not stupid Alex. I don't even know you, but I keep remembering you, here. I've never been out of New York, but I knew where the convenient store was. I've never heard of this place but I have to be here. What's going on?"

"Do you always speak in paradoxes?"

"Give me a break."

"The truth?" I asked, slipping gracefully to plan B.

"Yeah. The truth. In words I can spell."

"Okay. It all has to do with my next-door neighbor, Rudy. Wait, he used to be my next-door neighbor. He hasn't been around much since his house blew up."

"Blew up?"

"Smithereens; really small smithereens. Look out that window. Yeah, the one that was too dirty to see through until you cleaned it yesterday, bless your heart. Anyway, Rudy for a century or so has been fighting a never-ending battle with an evil shadow who wants to destroy the earth...that's not fair. He really wants to save the world, but isn't very good at avatardom."

"Avatardom?" she asked, failing to restrain a giggle.

"Being an avatar: the art of being the embodiment, the concrete version, of the combined hopes and dreams of the world of human souls. So Rudy enlisted me, since he knew I possessed natural bidimensional talents that had taken him thousands of years to develop. But first (here's where you come in), he had to check me out, so he hired your ethereal counterpart, Max--"

"Ethereal counterpart?"

"The girl of your dreams."

"Hey! I'm not gay!"

"Not those dreams. Max takes care of business in dreamland while you are awake."

"Oh," she said, obviously feigning understanding. I went on without revision. There was no point to offer explanations; the tale was only going to get sillier.

"Max is you and you are Max, but never the twain shall meet, she thinks, so instead of calling you on the phone she gave you a little dreamtime nudge the other night. She was the redhead who was chasing you in your dream. She figured correctly that that nudge would send you my way, and that I would know from your presence alone that I needed to contact her somehow. So I did. I was with her all last night, you know."

"Last night?" she asked, looking toward the cellar door.

"Sure, but for a while there she was a crow."

"Like the bird?"

"Just like the bird. We chatted for a while, and things really picked up on the Purple Plain. Oh, that's my own flat in the dream world. Unfortunately, Max was unable to pass on the message she wanted to give me, and I haven't seen her since you woke me last night. At any rate that's why you are here."

Mary stared soberly at me for a few seconds, tears welling. Then, lips tight, her cheeks puffed a bit and her faced turned red. She held her composure for about three seconds before collapsing into a storm of laughter. Not, tinkling, polite giggles, but honest, raucous, snorting laughter. She punched the table then grabbed my arm as if to hold on. I smiled, barely retaining my somber expression. In time she steadied herself, rubbing doughnut crumbs on her cheeks as she wiped her eyes.

"That's rich!" she exclaimed, "I can't believe you thought all that up on the spur of the moment like that. I'm am so impressed!"

I tried to look hurt, but was relieved to get the expected results. She wasn't as dumb as I thought she was. Or, perhaps more relative to her nature, she wasn't as dumb as she was. That was something to consider later, I thought.

"Have you got a better explanation?" I asked with as much gravity as I could manage.

"Are you kidding? I could never top that story."

"Then there's no explanation at all. Shall we then blame coincidence for this lovely fate?"

"We shall," she said, sipping coffee with her pinky extended, "For now."

"Good," I said, happy to return to plan *A* by changing the subject when I asked, "How soon did you want to be driven back to the city?" While speaking, I stood with my dish in hand to bring it to the sink. She grabbed my wrist and snatched the dish.

"Not at least until I clean this kitchen," she said. I hadn't even realized that it was dirty, but I let her clean with a minimum of obligatory protest. She was pensive as she washed, her mood broken only when she had to chase me away with a wet dishrag during my attempts to help. As she wiped squeaking dishes, she asked over her shoulder, "When do you want me to leave?" I wanted to say never. She was wonderful, offering me a taste of companionship and domesticity that had been absent from my life for far too long, mixed with that constant hint of the presence of Max. I shook my head. Such thoughts were wrong, and unfair to this shadow of Max. I also pragmatically admitted that Mary's proximity kept Max away from me, assuming that I could actually bring the perfect dreamgirl across. Still...

"Are you kidding? Keep up this work and I'll keep you around indefinitely. What's your starting salary?'

"Thirty grand a year."

"No problem. I probably have it in my pocket right now."

"Seriously. Should I like, leave right now?"

"No. Stay a while. It feels like centuries since I had some real company. Are you in any hurry?'

"No. Got no job. I couldn't stand the creep at the theater. I was thinking of staying with my folks on the Island for a while again anyway, if they'll have me." I sensed from her wilted tone that they might not.

"Why don't you stay with me until we figure out why you're here? Assuming there is a reason, of course."

She thought about this for a moment, then looked up, "It's okay with you?"

"You know it."

"Maybe for a little while, then," she said carefully. She sounded relieved. I wondered if she was as lonely as I had been. I could imagine loneliness happening to a nice girl living where she did.

"Then it's done," I said, "What do you want to do now?"

"Soaps!"

"Haven't you done enough cleaning?"

"The ones on TV, silly. I have to see who's going to walk in on who at the worst possible moment today."

"Well have a good time," I said, still leery of the television. She nodded knowingly and went into the living room. In a moment I heard the TV. The voices were audible, but I could not hear conversation specifics. Mary understood I did not want to watch TV, but she didn't understand why. She thought I was a man, and soaps were uninteresting to me. I was glad she didn't ask. If I described Rudy stepping through the tube she may have laughed herself into a coma.

I looked around the spotless kitchen, still in awe at Mary's speedy handiwork. I noticed that she had stacked various books and magazines that were strewn throughout the kitchen earlier into a neat pile on the counter. She probably intended to bring them into the living room where they belonged, but didn't want to anger or confuse me further. I noticed one item in the middle of the pile, bound in cardboard and plastic, which did not seem to belong with the rest of the periodicals. Curious, I pulled it out, careful not to disturb her stack.

It was a photo album, representing one of the few attempts Cassie had made to convert the sideboard drawer packed with processed snapshots into a usable tool for reviewing our memories. In the album was a collection of photos taken during a visit to Disney World. Cassie, Rudy, and I made the trip about three years earlier. I brought the album back to the kitchen table and sat down to enjoy that fond memory once more.

It was strange to see Rudy standing on line for Space Mountain, just like any other Ugly American. He looked the same then, but was different. It was my attitude toward him that was different, helping me notice things I had overlooked before. He was in the picture with Cassie, arm in arm. Her thick brown hair, worn long and simply for that trip, was blowing madly in the wind on that blustery day. Every lock of Rudy's then shoulder length hair was in place. The camera betrayed the age in his gray eyes, though I had overlooked it the dozens of other times I perused the album. I turned the page to find Cassie and me hugging Minnie Mouse. I had never noticed that behind us, almost blurred out of focus, a redhead in black was waving to Rudy. I laughed quietly, and then looked for Max in the rest of the pictures. vShe showed up in only that one. I assumed that any more would have aroused my suspicions, and Rudy would have had stories to create.

Those were good days. Rudy was different, perhaps because he considered such mundane times with me a vacation. He may not have changed, but for the pressure he felt compelled to apply on me to abandon my links with terra firma. And he did so without supplying me with full truths, I thought, my mind drifting beyond the photos as I began to ruminate Rudy's challenge once more. I felt that I could not venture as far as Rudy wished into an existence that I knew nothing about. Indeed, his arguments, pleas, and examples were so vague that I could not even tell how far it was that he wanted me to go. I refocused on the album, determined to avoid this conflict for at least another afternoon. I changed the subject in my mind by turning another plastic page.

More of the same pictures: the three of us having a great time in Orlando. I never questioned Rudy coming alone with us. I figured he would have no problem once he got there. He did disappear every night, so I was satisfied with him. Cassie was not. She grilled him each morning as he walked through the wrong doors of the hotel to greet us for breakfast. He would boast about blond conquests. Occasionally he would joke about saving the world, which was talk that invariably angered Cassie. I had wondered if she were jealous of him. I tried to talk to her about it on several occasions after we returned home, but she had somehow forgotten every incident. Taking the hint each time, I forgot as well. In retrospect, I realized that Cassie probably never did forget. Her instincts about the true nature of people were amazing; perhaps she had Rudy's secret pegged as well, but kept it to herself in the name of her own reputation, or out of an unconscious fear. In either case, the suppression must have been difficult. I tried to dismiss my unruly line of thought by assuming that, if she really did have an inkling of Rudy's World, she would have shared it with me no matter how insane it sounded. Cassie was like that. Our relationship was like that. She probably simply felt something about Rudy that grated her pure soul, and it inexplicably angered her.

I turned the last page, closed the album, then opened it again and leafed through it quickly. The hard pages generated a breeze that tickled my forehead. I paused, rubbed my bristled chin. vSomething was missing, and it took the picture of me, Cassie, Max (I was sure), and Minnie to tell me what. Cassie. It was Cassie that was missing. Her images hadn't changed, but their impact on me had. Every other time I opened this album, my purpose was to look at the pictures of Cassie and mourn her absence. This time, though my thoughts certainly included her, I had omitted that pain, wasting little time on the normally staggering emotions that swept over me every time I was reminded in real terms that she was dead. I felt for a void, for something that would trigger deep sorrow. I even sat staring at the best picture of her in the album, taken after she had fallen asleep in our hotel room, and waited for tears to well. They did not come.

What was happening? I was at a loss. I tried to scramble explanations together: Rudy was filling my mind, Max was entering my life like a bat out of hell, and my world was expanding at too fast a rate to waste time wallowing in self-pity at my loss. Those explanations were all valid, yet wrong. Cassie was still alive, in some form; I was sure I believed that. Maybe that belief reduced my grief. That didn't make sense either, since my faith in such belief had never completely gelled (which was why Rudy could continue to tempt me with the possibility). I wondered for a moment if Cassie the person had been removed from me somehow. Her existence, as Rudy described it, did not fit into this Mary/Max, Cleavus/Clive dichotomy rule of the World. Mine didn't either, but I was told that I was unique. Perhaps my belief in her sustained existence actually was put temporarily on the back burner. I had been entertaining that thought for weeks, and did a fine job proving it with Max the night before, but my novel reaction to the photo album was the first sign of a real change.

I put the album down and rubbed my eyes. I wondered if I
really heard what I was thinking. I tried to steady my mind, to
undo some of the knots into which I had tied the strings of my
tortured logic. Wasn't Cassie the carrot originally held out to
tempt me onto this path? My belief in her being alive? Wasn't
that still important? I toyed with the thought that Max had
loosened my grip on that fantasy, but I do not forget that easily.
Yet, it was true. I was omitting traditional tears that moistened any
photo album carrying Cassie's image. Her impact on my self-
control had diminished. Though I was certain my love for Cassie
had not faded, I could not avoid the fact that I did kiss what
seemed to be a very real Max the night before while barely
acknowledging my dead wife's memory. But I did feel guilty, I
was sure. I shook my head, forcing the incongruities to find a
place in a darker recess of my rattled lobes. I knew how I felt
about Cassie, and she knew as well. I simply didn't feel as sorry
for myself anymore. But why was I so easy with Max?

"Enough," I said aloud to the album, "If I knew you were
going to be this much trouble I would have checked out the TV
Guide instead." I put the book back on the pile and walked into the
living room to see how my guest fared.

Mary was fine. The soaps had ended, and she was curled
up in front of an afternoon cartoon – *Powerpuff Girls*, I think. She
was sound asleep on the sofa under an old wool blanket that she
must have found while cleaning. She looked enviably
comfortable. She snored lightly. I let her be, turning off the TV so
the noisy supervillains wouldn't disturb her. And so Rudy wouldn't
appear in my living room dressed in tights and sporting a really big
head. I still was not ready for him.

The photo album had blanketed the passage of the
afternoon. I went out onto the back porch to enjoy what was left of
it. Leaning against the weathered rail, I absorbed the autumn
afternoon completely: the empty blue sky; the countless shades of
brown, red and yellow that blanketed the passing Hudson
Highlands as the trees prepared for winter; the long grass still
clinging to some summer green; the kids playing in the
construction next door. I held my face up to the rising wind,
enjoying its crisp touch. The more time I spent in Never-Never

land, the more I appreciated simple, concrete reality. Simple, yet blessed with infinite complication. My creations never began to house all those details. I gripped the rail hard against a sudden gust, appreciating the feel of its unpainted grain. I was sure that I could change the wood to jelly or steel by adjusting a few points in reality. I put those thoughts aside, enjoying rather the sense of its simple existence. Euphoria seeped through me, warming me in waves of visceral comfort. I felt like a 1960's flower child communing with the world around me. Details finally exhausted, I tried to absorb the whole porch picture at once. The mountains. The grass. The trees. The leaves. The stretch of dark storm clouds creeping up on the undulating horizon. I loved it all. Okay, not love, really, but complete appreciation, on a professional level. I had tried this kind of creation. I had thought I was successful. Now my back yard was showing me how little I had done. God may have created the world in seven days, but I could bet he spent the next hundred millennia working out the details. Like that perfect line of dark clouds. Who would have thought a moving front could contain such beauty? That solid ebony line that slowly became a crescent as it neared my house, and the contrasting azure sky. Beautiful.

The spell broke.

The rapture that held me in nature's embrace evaporated fully when the clouds broke ranks to encircle my house. Utter darkness closed in about me as the sky converged like a camera diaphragm. I rolled my eyes, said aloud amid a tired sigh:

"Here we go again."

Chapter Seventeen

My recognition of the artificial nature of what I had been admiring as natural nature surfaced too late for me to respond in ethereal kind to the encroaching storm. I doubted that any resistance I could muster would have carried real consequence: changing waking-world weather systems was dramatically out of my league. Besides, whoever had concocted this spell had done so swiftly. Even if I had more than rudimentary expertise in the reality-manipulation game, I was given no time to prevent my house from being snatched from its foundation by the swirling black tornado unique to the airspace above my yard. Of course, I could have been allotted weeks to fruitlessly seek a solution to the mess, but the excuse of a lack of opportunity to fail was comforting.

The house vibrated violently as its aged clapboard walls churned in collusion with the storm. It twisted free of its foundation with a sickening lurch. The loud pops of splitting beams and a disconcerting whine of rupturing plumbing filled the air. Once in thrall to the storm, the house began its ascent slowly, almost imperceptibly. It was fortunate for the Munchkins that Dorothy got bumped before her place launched out of Kansas. She otherwise might have hopped off the porch to safety, negating her opportunity to kill bad witches. I resisted the urge to jump myself, deciding that I would be wiser to stay aboard and find my Oz. My Yellow Brick Road may not have been consistently good to me, but I felt obliged to pace it. Even the unwilling steps I took, like clinging to the porch rail of a house any sane human would have abandoned, were probably worth the trouble. At least, that is what I told myself as I waited for forces beyond nature to fling my house into orbit. I had to. Rudy's World was so bereft of sense that I even toyed with the idea that the black storm was another of Max's attempts to get my attention. I dismissed that concept quickly, however. Not even Rudy would be so violent, and Max couldn't mess with the wind here at all. Or anywhere.

No, this was Freuzre's work, and I was already steeling my resolve to face him. My strength and experience were limited, I knew, but I could still feel pretty cocky about my chances. I had to believe I was unconsciously protecting myself already, since my house hadn't vaporized yet. I peered over the porch rail, down a hundred feet at the ground to see if my garage, originally attached to the house, had come with us. It had not. The shadow must have known about the secret weapon housed within. I sighed, already missing the novel security of the Escort. I backed from the edge of the porch, nauseated. The house's rotational speed was approaching that of the vortex, and it was being lifted higher into the perfect night above me. The total dark that engulfed the house forced my stomach to notice the movement before I could see it. The rotation was accelerating rapidly.

The variety of sickening thumps I heard told me that the centripetal forces generated by my house had caused its guts to swirl around inside with abandon. My furniture was sliding toward outside walls, pounding them with a staccato rhythm that was offset slightly by the house's off-center spin. If I concentrated, I could recognize different pieces of my old life shatter inside by their sound and where they hit. That occupied my time for about ten seconds, after which I was able to discern only the largest objects, like my bed and that Victorian china cabinet in the dining room as they slammed repeatedly, their sturdy frames reluctant to be splintered by such an alien power. I could have attempted to identify more objects as they crashed about, but I became more focused on reaffirming my white-knuckle grip on the porch rail. It was holding my weight with minimum complaint (and no frightening cracks of splintering wood), but I also wrapped my legs around the massive post by the back steps for insurance. If I were thinking clearly, I would have adjusted the density of that post to the consistency of steel and relaxed, but clarity was not welcome on this ride.

My short deliberation about attempting Worldly magic was rendered academic just before the ground below had vanished.

Had I attempted to adjust my surroundings, my concentration would have been broken quickly by a massive crash against the wall directly under the living room window behind me. That crash was followed by a long, shrill screech from Mary. Oh, shit, I thought, Mary! I had forgotten about her during the launch, or perhaps had unconsciously assumed that she would not be included in my adventure. I was vividly reminded of her existence when the window glass shattered and Mary sailed through the jagged opening, a ballistic blur of red shirt and pale white flesh. Her arms flailed wildly for a handhold. They found nothing but air, but she did have the sense or good luck to leave the tops of her feet wrapped around the windowsill, preventing a flight into the night. She continued to hang out the window just beyond my reach above me, perpendicular to the wall, face down.

Considering the environment into which she had found herself so violently thrust, Mary was relatively calm. She probably thought she was dreaming. Lucky girl, I thought. That impressive luck was manifested in her lack of even a scratch after passing through the windowpane. The steady fearful moans and occasional scream that burst from her signaled that she was not pleased by the experience, regardless of her interpretation. I lost track of facial expressions when the force of the spinning house gathered my shirt around her neck, covering her head. Aside from the affront to her modesty, this bunching of cotton around her head was probably beneficial to Mary's sanity. She was still clinging to the windowsill over which she had just flown by the tops of her feet, and the end of my tiny porch was closer to the house than her eyes. She would not have welcomed the sight of my former neighborhood spinning madly a thousand feet below her as it disappeared under a violent curtain of moving blackness.

Lacking confidence in Mary's tenuous grip, I decided that it was time to preempt disaster. I carefully unwrapped my leg from around the pole, and gasped when my legs lifted up and out from under me. Against my body's better judgment, I then released my left hand's grip on the rail and stretched it across to the window. I grabbed the sill inches from Mary, but I was too busy holding on to do anything about extricating her. Seeking a more stable position from which to rescue her, I swung my legs under me like a gymnast on the rings, and wedged my body beneath Mary's. I tried to plop down on the floor, but the spinning house forced me to push down to complete my descent to the porch floor with no help from gravity. The feeling of weightlessness was disconcerting at best, and proved truly dangerous when I lost my grip for a moment. I slid wildly in space, passing completely beneath Mary. I flung my hands above me and grabbed what I hoped was her knee. This slowed me enough to reestablish my right hand's grip on the rail, and my left on the sill. I set about lowering myself again, and was extremely grateful when my ass finally connected with hard wood. I sat still for a moment to nurse my ever-suffering resolve back to health.

The hair on the back of my head brushed Mary's smooth bare thighs as I settled into my 'safe' seated position on the porch floor. I gripped a spindle in the rail with my right hand, and pushed my left hand hard against the house. It may have been easier on my back muscles to face the other way, but I did not trust the rail, or the location of my head relative to Mary. The shirt still blinded her. I wished it would completely fall off. This was not to satisfy voyeuristic tendencies on my part, her exposure was complete already, but because the shirt's insular quality that I had recently admired had now become a problem. If her eyes weren't buried in red cloth, Mary would have noticed that she was nearly kissing the porch rail while her arms groped for a handhold above her, straight away from the house and nowhere near the rail. The red shirt had turned my relatively easy job of hanging on into a rescue attempt.

Five minutes had passed since she reentered my surreal world, and I feared I was already too late to prevent Mary from launching into oblivion. I knew I had to stop this; I had too many deaths on my hands, and, though I was not sure how the system worked yet, I feared that Mary's demise could include Max's. I did not want that either. Reminding myself that I had bent rivers, wrestled airplanes to the ground, and even created life – poorly, I asked myself how hard it could be to also be an action hero for a few seconds.

"Fuck it," I said, releasing my vise-like grip on the rail. I immediately began to move away from the porch, but halted my rise by jamming my left foot between two disturbingly loose spindles. I was getting good at it. Mary, however, was not, and if her feet lost their meager grip, she would be gone.

"Mary!" I tried shouting, "Just reach the other way. Grab the rail!" She did not respond to my frantic instructions. She should have been able to hear them over the roar of the storm; that she didn't, or that she was ignoring me, only enlarged the lump in my throat and intensified my efforts. An inch at a time, I reached my arms behind me and over Mary's shins. I planned to join my own hands and then use them like a hook to pull Mary down to `safety.' Before I could lock them together, an escaping brass lamp collided with my hands. I felt two or three fingers of my right hand crush on impact. I resisted the powerful urge to pull my flaming hand away when one of Mary's ankles let go under the new pressure. More objects flew out the window: books, pillows, a radio, and a six-pack of beer. Of course, each object found my smashed fingers. I screamed, yearned to retreat, but I could not back off. Mary was slipping, and I needed both hands around her to successfully pull her to the floor.

Following an ashtray and a work boot I hadn't seen in years, my large maple coffee table slammed against the window, effectively sealing the opening. I sighed with relief. Mary wailed in pain. The bare foot that had saved her moments ago was now sandwiched between the table and the sill. Though that also securely anchored Mary to the house, I thought it best to continue my rescue attempt. I grabbed my right wrist with my left hand, positioned them above Mary's knees and pulled down sharply. The effort required to draw Mary against the tremendous force of the house's spin was beyond my means, but not my will. Groaning wildly, tears streaming down my cheeks, I finally managed to bend Mary's legs, allowing her to fold up and join me on the floor. Throughout my rescue attempt I was able to ignore the pain by focusing on my concern for the single porch rail spindle that was now supporting the two of us.

Mary's head bumped the rail as she descended to me. Her flailing hands seized the opportunity, and the rail. I eased my grip. Her calves remained firmly attached to my chest. I looked at my hand. Big mistake. The sight of the two outside fingers billowing and turning purple only heightened the pain. For a moment I was fascinated by the specter of my blood dripping not down, but away from me, curving slightly against the spin as it neared Mary's covered face.

Mary, still moaning, seemed to notice the shirt wrapped around her head. Bravely allowing one hand to let go, she tore it off, and strained to look around her. Facing down and away from me, she struggled to turn over, but could only move her head. The rest of her was in full use keeping her attached to the porch, and me. Wide eyed, she shook her head and gasped in fear. She was trembling, and her skin had become ashen. Her mouth was open in a failed scream. She either didn't notice her nudity, or else didn't care. I assumed the latter, that she had her priorities, and did my best to avoid the appearance that I was staring. This was not easy, however, given that our current position had her about six inches from backing into my face.

I wanted to calm her down, but I had no soothing words that could alleviate the situation. If I did then I would have used them on myself. All I thought for countless spins was that I should have gathered Mary and jumped off when the chance existed.

"What the hell was I thinking?" I shouted to the wind, "I had no witches to kill!"

I realized that I had forgotten about Mary during the moment I could have escaped, but I like to believe that I would have remembered. I shook off those irrelevancies and struggled to overcome the pain and fear that threatened to defeat me by summoning the confidence I had felt at liftoff. I did not completely succeed, but I did manage to clear my head enough to remember that I might possess the innate ability to alter the current travel arrangements with a thought, rather than continued pointless and exhausting physical actions and reactions. This change of focus was punctuated by the fireplace poker that burst through the wall, inches from my head, helping me to become very interested in assessing the situation from a metaphysical point of view.

Though I chose at last to employ my unnatural talents to save the day, I knew that I had very little experience from which to work. I couldn't shake my fear that this was a real event – a house caught in a giant tornado might just do what we were doing, given the right circumstances. If that were true, then I was in unfamiliar territory. I had some success screwing with objects or events in the waking world, but those minor meddlings did not compare to adjusting natural forces whose magnitude was being clearly pounded into our souls. I looked at Mary, who had twisted herself around to sit at a crazy angle across my legs (her foot was still firmly sandwiched between table and sill), for inspiration.

And found it.

The light in my head did not switch on immediately. Before it did, I just looked at her. I noticed but was not, as I normally would have been, overcome by her fine, intimately close, and clinically exposed physical form. Her green eyes wide, Mary was stricken with silence. She may have been unable even to breath, with catatonic panic accompanying her acknowledgment that she was not caught in a particularly nasty dream. Her auburn hair was spread smooth like slightly parted curtains across her breasts, which were flattened into an improbable upward-pointing position. I may have been dishonorable in my extended, and certainly ill timed, survey of this subtly beautiful woman, but my perusal discovered the inconsistency that sent my mind back into positive motion. Her hair was spread smoothly over breasts that, even misshapen as they were, reminded me of Max's perfection.

"Smoothly?" I asked myself. That was impossible. The wind should have blown her hair into one solid knot, even if we were moving as fast as the tornado by now and felt no breeze. Then I was struck by an obvious detail: there never was any wind. Throughout the entire acceleration there was no wind. There was plenty of noise, and plenty of other forces acting upon us, but no wind. That should not have been the case. At first contact, the wind from the vortex should have knocked me right off the porch, and then sent the porch after me. I laughed loudly. This was not a natural occurrence. I knew while my house was still on the ground that the source of this crisis was not natural, but I did not guess that the whole storm was a creation. I had assumed that Freuzre had manipulated nature to create a targeted tornado, and that the tornado was real. I was wrong. If there was no wind, then there was no tornado. This entire event, the struggle, the broken bones, the fear and pain, was nothing more than a realized figment of a powerful and twisted imagination.

My laugh brought a new expression of panic to Mary's already contorted face. I would have attempted to console her, to tell her that it was not a laugh representing cast-off insanity. I would have told her that this enlightenment, based my interest in her features, said I could act under terms I understood against the force at the root of her terror. I would have attempted to say something, but I had neither the time or interest to do so. I decided that the necessity to cash in on this enlightenment before my house, my new friend, and my own flesh were obliterated overrode thoughtful conversation.

The initial adjustment to my newly flexible environment, simply picturing the house peacefully and securely attached to its foundation, failed. I knew that option was too obvious, that I had to convince the place to stop spinning using vigorously applied imagination, but I figured it was worth a shot. I was not deterred; there was still no wind, so there were no real natural forces to fight. I was going to win. Gaining confidence, I placed my hands on the straining floorboards of the porch. Every unattached item in the house was already plastered against an outer wall, so only the groans of stressed timbers and Mary threatened to slow my descent into complete concentration. I ignored them easily and set to work.

I touched the house. I wandered through its framework, feeling stress on this joist, studied cracks in that stud. I was one with it, joined on a lesser plane of elemental structure to which the red chair had introduced me. I tested my old home's integrity, and was not surprised to find very little strength left. Only the large central beam that spanned the first floor hinted surviving integrity, but it had been reduced to a straining wooden backbone ready to snap. I noticed that there was nothing below the beam. The cellar, and the Sound Room it harbored, was gone. Allowing no time for mourning, I left the beam and added my presence to the rest of the first floor, picturing its undulating century old wood as a great flat muscle. I imagined that muscle was still flexed tight after the house had executed an unending somersault off a heavenly diving board. I relaxed the floor, let it straighten, ease back to a static position. I felt woodwork chaffing against itself as the floor relaxed, encouraging the house's spin to decelerate. I sensed the roof flexing, cringed when it contacted the attic floor, and helped ease it back into position. I felt a dull pain as all the furniture fell to the edges of the floors as one. Then I felt a massive release of energy, as though the house were heaving a sigh. Then the house, we, were still. I exited its fibers slowly, backing out the way I came. I was sad to leave its structure. Its simple strength had served me well, and provided an easy to follow road map to recovery from the attack. Now I was obliged to wander back into the unknown, to weather surreal events beyond my imagination.

I surveyed our new, calm surroundings. Mary, still wide-eyed, no longer clutched the rail. She tenderly held her recently released foot in her hands, but was not looking at it. She was not looking at anything in particular. The house was still. The vortex silently spun around us, its wispy shadows in various degrees of blackness whipped by at an incredible speed, just inches from the edge of the porch. There was, of course, no wind. I stood, turned and looked into the house. Not much to see, other than a long thin pile of rubble lining the walls. I absently, and finally, wondered how I could see anything. The pure blackness all around us seemed to exist to preempt illumination, and there were no artificial lights left inside, much less electricity to fuel them. Even if the sun were still shining somewhere, the tornado prevented its penetration. To be sure, I took a gamble and leaned out over the rail and looked up, above the house. The shadows pecked at my forehead and hair as they raced by, but the storm was otherwise harmless. If it were a tornado, I reasoned, then its funnel might have been open to the sun far above, which would offer a natural explanation for the light. I saw no hole at the top, or even a hint of a funnel. Just speeding black shadows on shadows. I looked down to see that blackness had filled in below as well. Yet the house was awash in cool gray twilight.

Or was it?

I waved my hand in front of Mary's eyes. She did not acknowledge the gesture. Intrigued, I leaned in close to her face and inspected her pupils. They were enlarged to the point of nearly displacing her glassy emerald irises. The dilation implied that Mary's eyes were struggling to absorb light that wasn't there.

So. It was dark, completely dark, but I could somehow see. And, now that she was no longer spread over me, Mary might not have even known I was here. She may have assumed I went over the rail. One way to remedy that:

"Mary?" I said, touching her bare shoulder, "You all right?"
She cocked her head to her shoulder, and then grabbed my hand.
My good one, thank heaven.

"Alex?" she cried, "What the hell? What happened? Where
are we? Is this a dream?"

"It wasn't totally Hell's fault, I don't know, I don't know,
and no it isn't."

"Oh God. Oh God."

"You might want to invoke Rudy instead. He may be more
help in this case. Are you okay?"

"Don't know. Caught my foot. It feels in one piece though.
There's some blood, but I can't feel a cut. I felt like I was being
swallowed, but my foot didn't make it past the giant's teeth. Where
are we? Why is it so dark?" I heard the inflection of panic in her
voice. I was relieved that she couldn't see her surroundings.

"In a way, you have been swallowed. Remember that crazy
story I told you?"

"It wasn't so crazy?"

I shook my head, forgetting that she couldn't see me. She
sensed the movement, however, and bowed her head. She was
quiet for a few long moments. Finally she looked up, wide-eyed
again. This was the moment I feared; she would start screaming in
terror, her small mind blasted by the intensity flung at her. Her
face, which had been blank to this point in assumed darkness,
cracked into a broad grin. She laughed.

I could not believe the sound. My ears rang with relief.
Her laughter, like mine earlier, held no hysteria, and was not
accompanied by cackling or hair pulling. It was, well, laughter.
She seemed pleased. It subsided in a few seconds, but Mary's
composure had changed dramatically. She was still wide-eyed by
necessity, but the panic had left her. Color was returning to her
cheeks.

"Are you all right?" I asked, to be sure.

"Yeah, sure. No sense getting worked up over something I
know nothing about. Hell, it could still all be a nasty dream, huh?"

"That it could," I said, my voice far less steady than hers.
What she said sounded familiar. I continued, "Mary, you're
amazing."

"I could say the same for you. How about some lights around here? Can't see a damn thing."

"That can be taken care of, I think," I said, patting her head as I turned. She groped for my arm, found it. "Wait."

"What?"

"I got nothing on. You gotta find me something to wear before you come back with a flashlight."

"What makes you think you're naked?" I asked, realizing there was no need to look for a working flashlight in the rubble. My own acceptance of the impossibility of the situation made me forget myself. She rolled her eyes. I knew she was unaware that I could see her, but I also knew she probably would have rolled them anyway.

"I can tell," she said contritely.

"Couldn't it be fine silk you're feeling?"

"I was wearing your shirt."

"Was?" I asked, trying to sound angry.

"I must have lost it when I was trying not to be monster munchies. Sorry. Now, could you find a match or something? And another shirt."

With no further needling I thought about her sharing my light. Her eyes focused. She shook her head, and then looked around her. For a moment she forgot her modesty. When she remembered she blushed and tried to cover herself. vShe gasped when she felt the same silk gown in which I had dressed Max hours earlier. She released a cry of excitement and tried to stand to admire her clothes. Her damaged foot slowed her ascent, but she was able to steady herself on the rail and seemed to successfully ignore her pain.

"I could get to like these dream games of yours," she said, hugging me. I wondered just how removed from Max Mary really was while I held my bad hand out of harms way, felt it throb with the movement. I looked at it. Blood was dripping, at an oddly slow pace. I wished I could fix it, and Mary's ankle, like I did the house and her dress, but the image of my creations in the lagoon flashed in my head. I discarded the thought.

"It's not a game," I said, "But I am glad you're enjoying yourself. Sorry there's no mirror left for you to admire it."

"Sure there is, inside," she said, pointing into the window. Then she saw the rubble. "Whoa. What happened in there?"

"Same thing as out here. We were spinning like mad in this tornado, and the force drove everything out. That's how you went through the window."

"Is that what happened? It didn't feel like we were spinning. Not like the Roundup at Coney Island. It felt more like an elephant was sitting on my chest. Spinning?"

"Like a top. And if that table didn't catch you, you would be in the next world by now."

"Is that why my foot hurts?"

"Sure is. How is it?"

"It feels like that same elephant stepped on it, but I can stand up okay."

"Good."

"So where is this tornado?" she asked, leaning over the rail. I grabbed her with my good hand.

"Out there," I said, pulling her back to the wall, "Now let's go inside where it's a little safer."

"Aren't tornados real loud? I don't hear anything. Where's all the wind?"

"We must already be over the rainbow," I said, "Let's go inside and wait for this to not blow over."

Chapter Eighteen

I whistled softly when I spotted that familiar little red cross peaking through the scrambled debris that layered one side of my bathroom. It appeared that the first aid kit had survived the trip intact. I whistled again when I began digging through the rubble for it. How, I thought, could there be this much stuff in a bathroom? Granted I always was a sucker for shampoo commercials, but I had no idea that I had accumulated so many hair products.

"I'm a man, fer crissakes," I said to the sticky pile, "and on top of that, I don't even need to wash my hair anymore."

That figured, though. I should have tossed into the garbage and my past all those partially used bottles of shampoo, soft soap, and mouthwash yesterday when Mary was cleaning, I thought, exercising useless hindsight, it would have saved me a lot of trouble today. The array of fractured bottles had left an arguably appealing green and white pattern on the surface of everything. My shattered fingers provided enough incentive to ignore the goo while I extricated the kit. Once it was free and I had shaken off the larger chunks of sticky stuff, I set the kit on the sink, which, along with the toilet and tub, had not been torn from its original position. I called Mary in to use her two good hands to unlatch the kit. Its contents were still shrink-wrapped in their original packaging – until that day my injuries were normally treated with little more than a couple of paper towels and a lot of gin. The kit had been a gift from one of Cassie's less familiar sisters.

After I washed my hand under the faucet, a hellish experience in itself, I asked Mary to carefully dress my two battered fingers. I would worry about having them set another time. Since we were still in the stratosphere, or somewhere more mystical but just as remote, a trip to the hospital could not be included in our immediate agenda.

Mary tended to my wounded fingers with an easy expertise that betrayed her years of self- reliance. When she rewashed my hand, Mary didn't ask me about the source of the hot and cold water that flowed with excruciating pressure from the chrome tap. Even though I had no idea, I would have invited the question because it would have been fun to answer, and it would have showed that she was paying attention to her new environment instead of simply accepting it. That acceptance was beginning to give me shivers. Of course, those shakes could also have stemmed from my recent loss of blood.

"You do a good job," I said when she finished. I rotated my hand in an unnecessary inspection. My fingers still throbbed painfully, but they looked much better. I had also insisted that Mary wrap her ankle after she correctly denied me an attempt. The lacerations that had dredged the smooth top of her foot with two ugly, almost parallel purple and red gashes were far worse than she had reported when we were on the porch. The good news was, though there was plenty of blood shed, nothing appeared twisted or broken. Still, I was impressed that she had stoically kept her injury to herself until I insisted on examining it.

"Thanks. I try," She said. No you don't, I thought, but that only makes you more impressive.

"I should be thanking you, or apologizing" I said, "If I took you home last night, you would be safe right now. Look what I've gotten you into. And you don't even ask for an explanation. I'm surprised you're not throwing what's left of the dinnerware at me."

"Are you kidding? If I were `home' I'd either be with my parents or walking the streets looking for work. I'll take this over any of that. Besides, where else can I get such cool clothes for free?"

"But the danger I've put you in--"

"Be serious, Bob. I'm not totally stupid. I can see we're in for some nasty shit, but hell, you treat this `danger' like it's an everyday thing. If you can, I can." It was an everyday occurrence, I wanted to say, but that does not make it safe. I held my tongue, seeing no sense in fighting with her about it. I would rather have her calm for the landing – if we were ever to land. Mary continued, "I mean, shit, look at that hand.. Blood is still seeping through the wrapper. If that were me, I'd be screaming my ass off right now."

"Don't tempt me," I said, feeling that such a tirade from me was climbing my throat as she spoke. I had been holding back reliving screams of pain in the name of orderly calm, but my willpower was beginning to slip. Fortunately, such an embarrassing, unruly storm never broke. The moment that I decided, perhaps involuntarily, to allow myself some vocal wallowing, the house landed. It touched down, somewhere, with a gentle thud. Mary emitted a tiny "Oh!" then looked at me, wide-eyed:

"Are we there?" she whispered.

"Yes Dorothy, we are, wherever `there' might be."

"Bob, who's Dorothy?"

"Who's Bob?" I asked ruefully. I continued without waiting for an answer, "Now how about we go out and take a look at where 'there' is?" I got off the toilet and turned my puzzled houseguest around by moving her shoulders until they faced the open bathroom door. I imagined incorrectly that she was frightened, and prepared to gently guide her downstairs to the front door, but she was on her way cheerfully before I could find any consoling words. I realized that her hesitation came not from fear, but from her brain stuttering as it tried to work out the Bob/Dorothy conundrum I had laid upon her psyche. She must have dismissed the puzzle before she cleared the narrow threshold of the bathroom door. In spite of her injury, Mary reached the front door before I had descended half the stairs. When I reached the door it was still closed, with Mary working its brass knob vigorously. It was turning just fine, but the door remained shut tight. She saw me over her shoulder, smiled sheepishly, then stepped back and waited for me. Before I crossed to the door, I stopped at the front picture window for a look outside to determine that opening it really was the correct choice. I did not want to open the door if the action created a portal to a jungle full of voracious beasts or a desert with five-figure temperatures. The glance did not help: I saw myself in the window. I was pale and in general disrepair, but not a monster. I was also still inside. I tried a peek through a side window, and got the same curious result. The windows had become mirrors, reflecting all light from inside the house and allowing none to enter from outside. I couldn't change them, either. When I removed the light from inside the house, the windows did not betray anything outside. They simply became one with their respective wall. I sighed, brought back the light, and took the last step to the door. Mary had already brushed aside the requisite rubble with her good foot. I allowed a shake of my head and a confident smirk her way to help convince us both that I was still in charge. I expected, on many levels, the door to pop open for me with a gesture. Mary snorted when it stayed put without regard for my hand waving or stern stares. I tried the knob. It turned freely, but the door did not budge.

"Must have warped some while we were spinning," I said through clenched teeth as I threw my weight against the old wood. My violent attack did nothing to change the status of the door, but it did launch a volley of white-hot darts of pain through my hand. Switching sides made little difference, either to the door or the pain. Mary couldn't suppress a giggle at my sudden demotion from higher being to just another fool like her trapped in a bizarre wooden cage. I turned my head toward her, but she had adopted a pensive stance before my glowering gaze met her still dancing wide eyes.

"Uh huh," she said, fingers rubbing her chin. She waited for me to batter my shoulder against the oak door with a couple more futile impacts, then said, almost as an aside, "Didn't we leave the back door open when we came in?" She timed that observation so I would be mid-swing, unable to abort another useless ramming. I stayed against the door after I hit, stared at her blankly. She shrugged, trying to maintain a serious air.

"Mary," I asked, "Are you sure you're not pissed at me about something?"

"Course not," she said sincerely, her cheerful glow dimming slightly. I believed her.

"Fine," I said, "To the kitchen, then?"

"To the kitchen," she chimed, pointing an outstretched finger toward the kitchen as if she were marshaling troops. She led the way once more.

The kitchen door was indeed wide open, but, like the windows, all interior light (whose source I had become too

confident to wonder about) was reflected back into the house. I
hesitated in the middle of the kitchen, but Mary did not break her
stride until she reached the opening. It was not fear of the
unknown that made her hesitate; it was her reflection. She looked
herself over once, and then turned her head to me.

"Nice dress," she said casually, "And when did my eyes
turn green? It's kinda cool, but weird, you know? Okay, let's go
now." Without allowing me time to shout a warning, Mary
stepped through the doorway/mirror. It rippled like quicksilver
around her as she passed effortlessly through her own reflection.
Her dull silhouette remained for a few seconds. While it did, my
reflection filled the outline she had defined. I smiled, intrigued
that Mary was mirroring me, and that image reached beyond the
shimmer of our coalesced shapes that faded from the
doorway/mirror. I should have found her blind faith in me
startling, but I suspected that her confidence may have stemmed
from another, perhaps worthier source. That same source may also
have caused the change to her eyes that I had managed to not
notice. Emboldened by lack of choice, I unconsciously held my
breath and passed through the doorway.

Mary was leaning against the porch rail, looking out across
the purple plain. She was bent slightly at the waste, stretching the
green silk of her gown tightly across her body. I chided myself for
staring, but wondered absurdly if the trip had melted a few pounds
from her hips. She turned, smiling. Her eyes were indeed green. I
wondered briefly about their previous color, but could not
remember. Brown, maybe.

"Isn't it beautiful?" she asked, sweeping an arm like a game
show hostess to frame the smooth, seemingly prefabricated
horizon.

"I never thought about it that way, but yes, I suppose it is."

"Are you sure we're not dreaming?"

"Absolutely... Well, maybe not absolutely, but very
definitely. Why?"

"I've dreamed of that castle before."

"Castle?" I asked, scanning the empty plain, but seeing
only a vast purple swath of 'land' broken only by an equally
uniform white sky.

"Yeah. Oh, you can't see it from here. I guess we were meant to go out the front door. But if you lean over the rail a bit, you can see it. I was afraid to go around the house. That purple stuff don't look too firm."

"It's solid enough," I assured her, but opted first to lean over the rail myself without actually stepping onto the familiar surface. No sense leaping now, I thought. Then I wondered at Mary's easy familiarity with her surroundings, and from where she found the time needed for reconnaissance – I had passed through the silvered doorway seconds behind her. I dismissed any misgivings about time and space – why concern myself about subjects I would never fathom? – and leaned out to see what it was that she had spotted on the far side of my displaced house.

She was right. A dark gothic castle punctured the perfect horizon with an ominous obsidian presence. It resembled a castle that I had once seen enclosed within the trunk of Max's car. The medieval edifice loomed large in the distance, perched high upon spiny cliffs whose blackness was only slightly more complete than that of its own walls. Each of the countless spires that sprouted from its steeply pitched roofs seemed poised to poke through the Tupperware lid that I imagined was the sky. The uniform presentation of unreflective black evil architecture was broken by a dull red glow that pulsed softly in the oval maw that no doubt was the castle's gate. It was difficult to judge the size of the place from the safety of my porch, but I did not question its enormity. I glanced down, expecting to see Frodo Baggins peeking from behind my legs.

"Some place, huh?" Mary asked.

"Yeah. I know I've seen it before. Part of you has, too."

"I had a feeling," Mary said.

"You did? After all that laughter before, you're willing to accept this now?"

"Sure. It's easier than thinking I'm nuts." She hopped down the steps to the plain. "What'ya say we go investigate?" she asked. She tested the surface, bouncing on it a few times. She seemed satisfied with its integrity, but bounced a few more times just for fun. Then she gestured for me to come along and join her. The thought of a journey seemed to excite her or, more precisely, the novel experience made her happy.

"I don't see why not," I said, joining her. I paused to consider packing some vital items that we might want from the house, and then chuckled to myself. As I stepped onto the plain empty-handed, I silently wished for a dose of Mary's faith.

"Feels like Tupperware," Mary said, still trying to push a pump-clad foot through the hard, flexible surface. She stopped, studied the castle in the distance, squinting her eyes in an apparent attempt to convert them to binoculars.

"It looks like we're in for a long walk," Mary announced. She rubbed the belly of her dress, smiled wryly, and continued, "Unless you've got some other trick up your sleeve."

"You learn fast," I said with a wink. I grabbed Mary's hand and stepped in the direction of the castle. Instead of looking forward I kept my eye on her while I took the step. I wanted to witness her reaction to my awesome single stride that would draw us directly to the castle's main gate. After I finished the step, I was dismayed to see that Mary still had a blank, though expectant, expression. That was not the reaction I had anticipated.

I looked ahead, saw that we were not at the gate, and frowned. I could also feel the presence of my house, still right behind us. We weren't even one minor step closer to the castle. I was baffled, sure that the single pace should have worked. This was my plain; I knew its rules. Hell, I thought, I invented the damn thing. Yet we were still an arm's length from my back porch. Not interested in believing that other forces (like perhaps the one that had deposited the castle on the horizon) could be at work on my plain, I tried something simpler, like producing a mode of transportation from the ether. I tried and failed to conjure the Escort first. Then I looked for a generic car, then a bicycle. Nothing appeared. I could not even produce a skateboard. I returned to the original plan, but tried to move us in short leaps rather than one long one. That failed too. I was getting nervous. There was either something much more powerful than me on my plain, or I had somehow lost my power, or will, to change it. Maybe it wasn't my plain. I could feel sweat trickle down my forehead from the effort. Finally I released a painful grip in Mary's wrist and sighed. Mary was looking at me strangely as she rubbed her wrist. She wasn't frightened or angry, yet, just bemused. I decided to pause. I sat on my porch steps to mull a solution. Mary sat beside me, comfortably close. In time she stirred, playing with the soft white fabric that trimmed the hem of her dress.

"Something wrong?" She asked, gently nudging my arm with her elbow to get my attention.

"Yeah. Consider my sleeve bobbed."

"This means we walk?"

"This means we walk. Is your foot up to it?"

"Hardly notice it. Let's walk."

We walked.

For what was probably the first few hours – neither of us owned a watch, assuming one would even work on the plain – of our trek to the castle, we experienced the surreal impression that we were only half moving. My house shrank behind us as expected, becoming a dot on the flat horizon, but the castle's profile remained unchanged. I questioned the value of continuing to a place that was further away and far more gigantic than we had anticipated, or, worse, was moving away as we approached. I was also wary of losing sight of the house, my only familiar reference point in this strange world. That thought sparked a nervous pause in me that tingled my spine: though clearly alien to everyday life on earth, the purple plain had not been a strange place in the past. It was once uniquely mine, the soft cushion of my domain, and a jumping off point for my imagination. Now this plain of existence and creativity that I presumed I had brought into being had been usurped by someone else.

"How long do you think we've been walking?" Mary asked, her voice a hammer of sound that crushed the utter silence of the plain. We couldn't even hear our footsteps on the slightly resilient surface. Her sudden volume did not startle me, though; indeed, I was relieved to have my increasingly dark reverie broken by a pleasantly familiar nasal voice.

"It feels like hours, doesn't it? I don't know, probably half an hour, anyway. You tired?"

"No. You?"

"No. I should be, considering the shape I'm in."

"That's weird, huh?" she asked, and then giggled, saying something like `silly question' under her breath. My hands were in the pockets of my jeans. She casually tucked her wrist in the loop my arm formed. I didn't mind. She was becoming more like Max as each particle of the life she led in New York was slowly washed away by the sea of strangeness that now stretched before her.

"When will we be there?" she asked. If only she would start assimilating Max's smarts, I mused.

"Don't know," I answer flatly, trying not to be sarcastic, "That place doesn't seem to be getting any closer, does it?"

"Nope," she said, stopping. She turned around, shaded her eyes from a non-existent sun, squinted again, and said, "But your house keeps getting smaller. Pretty soon we might not be able to see it at all."

"My thoughts exactly," I said, surprising myself, "Do you think we should turn back?"

"Afraid we might get lost?"

"Damn straight."

"Doomed to wandering this plain in an endless quest for the castle, never tiring, never growing hungry? Just us, on this vast nothingness bridging the gap between home and castle?" She looked at me as she said this, smiling brightly.

"Where the hell did that thought come from?" I asked, taken aback.

"Don't know," she said, "It just appeared. All the words at once. Sort of like someone told it to me." She saw me suppress a grin, asked, "Does that mean we keep heading for the castle?"

"Sure, why not? We'll keep going as long as we can see the house. If we lose sight of it, we turn around and forget the castle. Deal?"

"Whatever you say. This is your show."

"I wouldn't be too sure of that," I said, distracted by a new event that was unfurling on the plain's distant/close horizon, out of Mary's line of sight but well within mine. There was a large group of blurred shadows flocking there. They quickly filled the empty purple expanse to our right, silently performing a chaotic dance cloaked in plasmatic darkness. I was too busy being awed by the distant display of perfectly unusual kinetic force to be frightened by the stereotypical symbols being presented, and their dance did not last long enough to allow the formation of real misgivings. With no warning or otherworldly overture, the shadows suddenly synchronized their movement until they had united into an opaque compression of darkness accompanied by an ear-shattering clap of thunder. Their unification caused a shape whose silhouette I feared that I recognized. Mary did, too; I heard her huff a gasp of awe that reflected my own.

The monster, which rose rapidly above the horizon as it approached us, and the castle, was a motorcycle. Not just any motorcycle, it was a customized Harley-Davidson bearing a leather-clad rider, and the duo boasted the physical displacement of an aircraft carrier. The sound blasting from exhaust pipes the size of houses was deafening. The motorcycle's sissy bar soared a hundred stories into the pale sky. The bike rumbled to a stop about a quarter mile away from us, and, to the relief of my already ringing ears, the helmeted rider shut off the mighty engine. His boot nearly hit us as he dismounted. I knew the identity of rider concealed behind the helmet's black visor. Mary did not, however, and I was obliged to dig my heels into the plain's pliant surface to prevent her from dragging me with her in a panic stricken retreat.

"It's alright, Mary!" I shouted over the rustling leather as the gargantuan rider squatted to get his head closer to us, "I know this guy."

"Well I don't want to know him. Especially if he has bad breath. The guy's bigger than Macy's!" She tugged some more.

"Who's dream did we say this was?" I asked into her ear.

"No dream. Real."

"Fine. Who's plain?"

"Yours. But don't tell him that," she stopped tugging. She calmed herself immediately, impressing me once more with her improbable ability to accept anything. She did stand more behind me than beside me, indicating that there was still some sanely timid humanity lurking in her malleable mind. The rider unfastened the zipper of his leather bomber jacket, a sound akin to an earthquake, revealing khaki coveralls. He doffed his helmet, smiled at us. Those perfect teeth resembled so many drive-in movie screens. He carefully lay down in front of us. The plain dented as much for him as it did us, relatively, so Mary and I found ourselves leaning against a steep purple hillside. He propped his head on a palm. The elbow that supported it was lost at the bottom of a slope fifty feet deep. I gathered myself, tried not to look impressed.

"Rudy," I shouted, sure he would never hear my tiny voice, "It's been a while."

"You don't have to shout, Alex," his six-foot voice said, "I'm right here. It's not my plain, so I wasn't quite sure what the scale was. Sorry if I startled you." The last sentence was directed, somehow, at Mary.

"Hey, no problem," she said tentatively from behind me. I felt her grip on my waist relax slightly.

"Alex," Rudy continued, "Where have you been? You've been hiding from me."

"Just looking for some privacy Rudy."

"That's a shame. I've needed your help lately. Freuzre's been working overtime. Have you read a newspaper lately? We're on the verge of a new world war. I'm having trouble curbing it."

"Don't try to make me feel guilty Rudy. I needed my own time to adapt. You were being too pushy."

"You got guts saying that to a thousand-foot man," Mary whispered. I smiled. She did not.

"Sorry Alex. I was in a hurry, I guess. Looks like you've been doing all right on your own."

"For someone who doesn't know dick about what he's doing?"

"I wouldn't have phrased it that way, but... On your way to find Cassie, are you?" I read the gleam in his eye. He hoped I was. Good. He had no ability to sense my changing mood. I decided to maintain his assumption, and quickly searched my meager repertoire for an earnest expression and longing tone.

"Sort of, I guess," I said lamely. He smiled. Damn, I thought, I keep forgetting how smart this big guy is, and how pathetic a liar I am. Rudy didn't push the issue, however. Instead, he gestured toward the castle with his free hand. The wind generated by his movement flattened us against the hillside.

"Sorry. Why'd you make that castle?" he asked.

"I didn't. It's just there."

He tried to look surprised, said, "You didn't create it? But Alex, this is your world. Is someone parked here illegally?"

"How the hell should I know?"

"There is that," he said. He rubbed his chin, sounding like a large fishing trawler being dragged across a pebbly beach, "Must be the Shadow that built the castle."

"The thought had occurred to me."

"Going to rescue Cassie, are you?" he asked again.

"If she's there," I responded with the most diligent inflection I could manage, "Do you know if she's there, Rudy?" He grinned, moved hundreds of tons of flesh as he shrugged casually. "Don't know," he said, "that's the Shadow's domain." That was not true. Rudy shared my inability to lie. He knew more about my purple plain than he wanted to divulge.

"Want to help me fight him?" I asked, knowing the answer, "He should be no match for you at that size. You're bigger than his castle."

"Sure it's not your castle?" Rudy asked, his forehead crinkled, "You should think about that.

"Whatever the case," he continued, "I have no power here. Believe it or not, I could step on you now, and you could shrug me off like an unwanted coat."

"You don't have to prove that, right?" Mary chimed.

"Don't worry, little lady. Alex, why did you bring her?"

"Not much choice, really. It was sort of a package deal."

"Do you have any idea what could happen?"

"Do you?" I asked. Rudy did not answer, though he did attempt a knowing frown. I stifled a laugh. The man's face couldn't produce a proper expression, even when it was the size of Rhode Island.

"Can you offer anything, Rudy?" I asked, my tone truly beseeching.

"Not here. Not while you still refuse to merge with the World."

"Gimme a break, Rudy."

"Fine, think what you want about the truth. I'm only here to help, you know."

"Then help."

"I can't."

"Why?"

"Guess."

"Tight beam?"

"What?"

"I'll try again. World?"

"World."

"Not yet, Rudy, not yet."

"Don't you still want Cassie back?"

"That line is getting old."

"What makes you think it is less true?"

"I know you, Rudy. At least I did when you were a much smaller person. I was blind to it at first, but I see now."

"See?" he grinned knowingly. He had mastered that expression.

"Clearly. You loved Cassie, Rudy," I said, trying as best I could to stare directly into his eyes. This was not easy because his platter-sized gray irises were a city block apart from each other. I continued, accidentally shouting again, "I dare say that you loved her as much as you did me, maybe a whole lot more. If you could have brought her to me, you would have."

"Did?" he asked nonchalantly, though his knowing grin had vanished.

"I assume."

"I'm hurt."

"Be hurt, then. You've changed, Rudy. You've--"

"Grown?" he asked, allowing a natural smile at Mary's covered-mouth guffaw.

"That too," I said, keeping a straight face, "No. It's more than that. I don't know. It seems that everything doesn't fit anymore. Ever since Fritz's."

"Ever since," he repeated. He dove into his own thoughts, his dark expression (the only other one at which he naturally excelled) loosening my knees, before he refocused on me. He gestured gigantically to Mary, "What about her? She seems like a nice girl. Are you going to risk her pretty neck? And Max's?" Rudy had shifted gears. I let him; this was a meaningful subject too.

"How?" I demanded, hands on hips, "I really need to know, Rudy. Tell me."

Rudy didn't answer for a moment. His face went blank. Not passive, which would have been his usual expression, but blank. Empty. In a moment he gathered himself, said, "I don't know."

The finality of Rudy's tone signaled the end of our conversation. He stood, got back on the bike in a single smooth motion that covered a quarter mile. When he shifted his weight off the plain, Mary and I were tossed six feet into the air. We landed safely, and tried not to make a show of our flight. I smiled: Mary's unwillingness to squeal – in fear or delight – in order not to impress Rudy indicated that even she had a few instincts about him. He turned its key, but before he pressed the starter button he faced me once more and spoke. This time his voice was in scale. It rained down from the heavens, showering me in pure volume. Each word made my body and the plain around me vibrate.

"I wish I had half your strength," the giant thundered. He tied his helmet to the sissy bar, waved, and said, "Good luck, dear Alex."

I tried to reciprocate his farewell with some deep words of my own, but he started the monster between his legs before I could form an interesting reply. The thunder from the coughing engine was probably just as well; I was sure anything I said in response would have been trite, and misinterpreted. The motorcycle's front tire lifted from the surface after Rudy popped the clutch. The impact from its return to the plain's surface knocked us off our feet again. We stayed on the ground to watch him ride away. He steered his mountainous machine away from the castle, but somehow still followed the same course on which he had arrived. He did not so much disappear over the horizon as fade into it. We lay still for a few minutes after he was gone, both of us left speechless by Rudy's visit. Once he was out of sight, our bravado dissolved, and we were overwhelmed by the sheer might of his presence. Mary was folded in my arms, waiting for me to make a move, to say something. My clogged throat prevented speech. Something more powerful than words had passed between Rudy and me, and I was too simple a soul to grasp what we had truly exchanged. In another minute Mary stirred. She looked up at me, eyes wide, alive.

"Let me guess: was that the guy from next door?" she asked.

"And then some."

"You're telling me,"

"Sorry I forgot to introduce you, Mary; I'm pretty awful about stuff like that."

"That's okay," she smiled, "I wouldn't have known what to say anyway." She stood, dragging me to my feet with her. For the first time since Rudy left, she looked over my shoulder. She drew her eyes quickly back to mine. Her expression had not changed, but something had. There was energy in her.

She asked, "Should we start heading for the castle again? Or did the big guy change your mind?" She wasn't being facetious; there was a depth to her question. Something in our exchange might have seemed like a warning to her. Perhaps he *was* warning me; his words, on the surface, were to that effect. I did not see them as such, or perhaps did not heed them. I wasn't sure. Whatever the case, I was at that point being pragmatic: My house was nearly out of sight in the distance. I was sure that another mile would obscure it completely.

"No, he hasn't changed my mind, but I am afraid we'll lose my house before we reach the castle, if we ever do get there, of course. But if you're game..."

"Oh," she said softly, her gaze wandering over my shoulder, "I'm game." Good, I thought, pleased. I needed her help in that decision. I would definitely have continued without her, but I did not want to risk losing her to this plain with, or because of, me. That was beyond my realm of responsibility.

"Well then," I said, turning back toward the distant castle as I spoke, "I guess we'll go on to the – " I was interrupted by a sharp break in my step. I had caught my foot on a worn gray granite slab, and could not bring my other leg forward before the inevitable tumble. Inertia from my turn sent me sprawling across a half dozen more of the ancient shallow steps.

"--The Castle?" Mary finished for me, feebly masking a grin. I tilted my head back and saw great black spires soaring upside down above me.

Chapter Nineteen

Our long ascent of the impossibly timeworn granite steps that were jammed in a straight incline against the side of the black cliff on which the castle loomed above offered me a new lesson in the incomplete, or at least incoherent, geography of my purple plain. My perspective of the plain had not changed at any point during our journey that took us high up an apparent mountainside. The distant purple horizon, and the relative position of the surface and sky, was exactly the same from our changing positions among the massive stones as it had been when we stood on the plain. I could not deflect an eerie feeling that the castle was coming down toward us, growing proportionately as it approached. I wondered if we weren't stationary, in spite of my senses' insistence that we were moving through space in sincerely nonrelative terms. The feeling was particularly disturbing because I should not have felt it in this place. The only feelings that I should have felt were those that I had already expected. I was confidant that that was one of the rules of my purple plain, though recent events were consistently thwarting my rules and, I feared, undermining my sanity with their very existence. I could feel myself parting further from the rational, intellectual core that was vital for survival on this plain with every unmoving step we took up the mountain. This is not good, I thought, but I could still not reason why.

"Three hundred steps and I'm still fresh," Mary was saying, brutally confirming my entire thought chain with a single innocent phrase, "Any way we can bring a piece of this place home with us?"

"Who said we're going home?" I snapped, disturbed as much by her interruption as her inadvertent corroboration of my observations.

"S'cuse me," she said, looking away. She was hurt, but unsure of what she had done to incur my wrath. I backpedaled my selfish introspection, and reminded myself where I was, and with whom, really, I was traveling. I stopped walking, if walking is the term that can be applied to leaping from one giant weathered stone slab to the next. Each leap was about two paces for me, in normal space, and my frequent missteps were compensated for by an energetic balancing act to avoid a painful landing on my bad hand. I should have realized myself that such exercise in the real world would have put me in a hospital. But I hadn't, and chose to snap at Mary for observing the obvious. I decided to remedy that mistake by saying:

"I'm sorry. This place makes me edgy. And we will get back, somehow. You can also believe that more than a piece of it will stay with you. I've been literally haunted by it."

"Haunted? That's a pretty strong word for this place, especially when we're heading for that lovely palace up there."

"You call that Frankenstein chalet pretty?"

"Some women call warts `beauty spots.' Let's give the place a chance."

"Why are you so strong?" I asked. I was not being sarcastic, either; her natural strength and ease humbled me.

"Don't know," she said as she reviewed, her hand inexplicably shading her eyes from a nonexistent sun, the long line of stones we had already traversed. "I thought the whole strength and bravery thing was your job." Mary turned to scan up the cliff face, but brought her hand down suddenly and clapped me on the back with it. She continued, "But enough talk, Bob. Let's go bang on that gate up there and tell them our car broke down." She stepped past me, forcing me to turn as she did.

Though I was sure we had only traversed about half the steps, the ancient stairway had ended. It landed on a wide ledge of smooth granite that formed the front porch of the black castle, which loomed cartoonishly huge a hundred yards away. Between the castle and us was a sheer rock wall that soared straight up at least fifty yards, broken only by the barred entrance to the castle. The wall formed a shallow horseshoe, with its open end abutting the cliff we had just ascended.

"You'll have to get on my shoulders to do it," I said. The dropped iron portcullis that barred our entry was over sixty feet tall, well in proportion with the edifice it protected. Its blue steel bars were less than a hand's breadth apart. I touched one. It was frigidly cold, and it was too thick for me to fully wrap my fingers around.

"You think there might be a window we could use around back?" Mary suggested in a deadpan tone, though her lips crinkled slightly at her joke. I smiled.

"Do you really want to go in there?" I asked, nodding toward the dim red glow of the distant courtyard.

"Please," Mary said with mock shock, "We've come this far, haven't we?"

"Hey, I had to ask, right? I can definitely see reasons to change our minds," I said. Seeing no change in her interest in proceeding, and certainly not interested in turning back myself, I took a long look at the portcullis, rubbing my chin in as thoughtful a manner as I could manage. After enough time had passed to offer the appearance of real perusal, I shook my head, and said, "Well, somehow I don't think they left the kitchen window open, even if we did have climbing gear to scale these mountains." She nodded in agreement.

"No back window, then," Mary said, "Want to try some more of your magic?"

"I can give it a shot, but I don't think it'll be effective," I said. I held back another sentence denoting my novitiate status in the World. I did not feel a need to share with Mary how little I knew about my `magic.' No sense ruining the image. Besides, I thought, sometimes my sophomoric mystical potshots had some serious, if occasionally unintentional, punch. My enthusiasm finally primed, I made a second, more attentive study of our surroundings.

I fondly recalled that in countless horror movies there existed a device whose discovery would provide us with entrée into the castle. This device was usually a hidden button or lever that, when triggered, would reveal a secret entrance, or signal unseen machinery to lift the gate. I assumed that, since the castle was a cinematic event in itself, the hidden switch scenario had to be viable. I then pushed a little further by attempting to convert

that assumption to reality. I even clamped my eyes closed for a
moment to better enact the spell. However, when I opened them
nothing had changed. We still faced the same uniformly smooth
walls and impenetrable gate. There were no magically revealed
hidden levers or knobs. I finally realized that there could be no
triggers anyway: this was my plain – a hidden trigger in a world
all my own would be accompanied by a billboard and a neon arrow
indicating the switch's exact position. Fighting disappointment, I
experimented with creating a few other, more mundane magical
routes past the gate, with imaginative variations that included
tunnels, ladders, and balloons, but nothing materialized. I began to
realize that I was consigned to create, or experience, nothing more
complex than the ancient, smooth granite floor embedded in oddly
fresh lumps of black rock. I began to wonder once more if I were
not a god of this plain after all. Perhaps I was a trespasser in
someone else's violet realm. I laughed, amused that someone else
might have used a purple plain as the symbolic junction of his
consciousness, his soul, and the World.

　　　When I took yet another survey of the tools apparently
available to me, I saw that nothing had changed. The shelf on
which we stood was as empty as ever, save for those few loose
boulders that had tumbled onto the landing recently or eons ago,
creating a shadow-free surrealistic backdrop to a very real evening-
gown-clad Mary, who had centered herself among the boulders.
The only exit was still the way we had entered. The top step was
visible, but the rest were lost to the steep mountainside. The
distant plain still seemed level with that first step, but I knew that
could not be. I was again careful not to taint my sanity by trying to
verify that personal truth. The rock walls arched around us,
angling together as they rose, leaving a circle of gray morning light
ten stories above us. The light entering through the notch for the
stairs was as white as ever. Funny, I thought, before discarding the
incongruity as unimportant in that neighborhood. What I did find
encouraging, though, was a distant memory of those walls being
perfectly vertical, forming no roof at all. Though I could not
confirm the memory, I was encouraged that there was still some
flux on the plain, even if it was not of my doing. I had to ask:

　　　"Mary, did these walls arch like this before? Or did they
go straight up?"

"Shit Bob," Mary said, eyes wide as she looked up, "I can't remember. But they're all curvy now, and everything looks so old, I bet that they always curved like this." She stared at me for a moment, probably reading my frustrated amusement at her answer, then continued, "Um, does a question like that mean that we might not be getting that big gate open with magic?"

"Sure does. Unless you've got some magic of your own to offer."

"I doubt that" Mary laughed.

"Don't," I replied softy. She heard me, but just shook her head. She acknowledged my subtle cue by initiating her own quick circuit of the landing. She strolled around its perimeter, touching the stone, tapping the smooth pillars of the portcullis' great arch. She finished her study, sighed, and sat on one of the boulders. She gracefully crossed her legs and ran a finger along one of her pumps. The beautiful woman I watched making such a simple yet perfectly feminine movement could have been Max. Mary's accelerating change of disposition was hurling new weight on my already struggling psyche. Instead of wasting time wondering what universe-rending damage I had done by bringing Mary into Max's world, I chose to focus my mind on more superficial problems, like whether to stay on the ledge or head back 'down' to the plain. Mary pulled her shoe off, examined it. She seemed puzzled.

"What?" I asked.

"They should be killing me," she said.

"Who should?"

"Not who. What." She tapped her foot, "Ever wear high heels?"

"Not since I tried to get out of the army."

"Well if you did, then you'd remember that they hurt if you have to stand for more than ten minutes."

"You hide the pain well," I said.

"What pain? That's what I'm saying. My feet should be so much pasta by now, but they feel fine."

"I really can't say I'm surprised."

"The point is, they should hurt. Your big friend should not have been that huge. The castle came to us. Magic is working here."

"There is no magic here, Mary. Just different rules."

"Fine. What say we follow those different rules then? Do your feet hurt?"

"No, but--"

"But nothing! You've got magic too. Sorry: you bend the rules too. That must mean you can do more."

"So can you."

"Maybe, but I don't know how."

"Does the top of your foot still hurt, where you clung to the window?"

"Shit yeah. But I think that's different," she looked at my hand. My feet were fine, but I was sure she could see my fingers throbbing. She continued, taking my good hand, "We got those in your house. It was different. You were fixing things there."

"No hands. I don't do bodies."

"That could be the only reason we're not fixed perfect. It's still a result of your magic, in a backward way. Trust the subtleties."

"Are you the same person I took to MacDonald's?"

"Yup. Now help yourself out here and try to come up with something. Really try this time. I have a feeling we had best not spend much more time here. The sky *is* different."

"So?"

"Alex! Come on!" she pleaded. Not Bob, Alex. I wanted to help her, but I was lost, and too proud to tell her. Lost as I was at Fritz's. I felt as helpless as a misplaced child at Macy's. In spite of my adventures, this was the first time I was completely on my own, without protection or the confidence that it was all just a dream. I remembered that Cassie would have led me out of this. She had an instinct for solutions, and I had always leaned on her for that. Even when I killed her. I paced about, shaking my head, waving my arms frantically. I tightened every muscle I could. I strained to wake up, to stop the nightmare. I squeezed my fingers until the pain drew tears from my eyes – that had to be better than pinching, I thought.

"Alex?" I heard Mary or Max in the distance, "What is it? What's happening?" she continued to shout at me, but in my frenzy of fear and frustration, I lost touch. I slammed about the black cage, trying to crumble the walls with my breath. I pounded my

broken fist against the portcullis, swearing vividly at each bar. I
was lost, baffled, terrified. Nothing was crumbling but me. I
laughed loudly at all the power that I thought I had. It was gone,
completely swamped by whatever it was that held this black keep
upon my plain. My plain!

"My feet are killing me!" I cried, "So are my knees, arms,
and everything else. And this damn hand is ready to explode!" I
was shouting at the wall, which was half an inch from my nose. I
couldn't turn. My childish faith in limitless power now absent had
led Mary/Max, an unsuspecting bystander, to her doom. I had
failed again, without ever even trying to cause harm. I simply
could not make the "magic" function here, where it had to. I could
feel the pain of my broken fingers through the veil of the plain, and
in spite of my expected natural ability to stop it. I continued to
pound the wall, seeing little. My cheeks were wet with tears.

Something gripped my arm, swung it and me about. I
could see nothing in the dim light. Suddenly I felt Mary tuck me
against her. She hugged me hard. I wriggled furiously at first,
unwilling to let myself touch, and potentially decay, her purity.
She was as strong as she was stubborn, though, and she held on
tight. Her embrace redirected the energy of my anguish, purging
waves of guilt and frustration from my quivering frame. In time I
could hear her soothing voice loosing meaningless words of
comfort into my ear. Her lips brushed my lobe in a very familiar
manner. I was calming.

As my vision cleared, she led me to a large rock, sat us
down. She stopped talking, and rocked me in silence for a while. I
don't know how long this went on, what I said, who I mentioned.
Guilt surfaced, Mary swept it away. Cassie. Beaver toys, Nancy.
Mary/Max. I don't know how much was vocalized, if any. I had
no control. No control.

Mary continued to hold me, let me relax. In time the
shaking subsided and all I could feel was Mary's warmth and my
burning hand. After another few minutes I was able to remove
myself from Mary's chest, where I had crumpled. I sat up. I
sighed deeply, shook my head. Mary held on to my shoulders, her
glossy green eyes focused on more than just my wet face. Why did
she care? I settled down more, became increasingly self-

conscious. I stood, folded my arms, and paced quietly. Mary stayed seated, watching, letting me be aimless.

"You all right?" she asked, having waited somehow for the moment I would be receptive to her query.

"Don't know," I responded, my voice still shaking. I sat with her again, and let her put her arm around me once more. My stomach was still swirling, but I was relaxing. I let her hold me again, this time more gracefully. In time I could feel my voice, and my nerves, returning to a level that I imagined must have been close to normal. I cleared my throat.

"What happened?" I asked.

"Shouldn't that be my line?"

"I suppose it should. Did I do anything real embarrassing?"

"You were too sincere for embarrassment. Besides, you gave me no time to think about it that way." Her face was inches from mine. So was Max's. I touched her neck with my good hand, drawing her to me. I put my salty lips against hers and kissed her. Long and slow. In time we parted. She looked away, smiling.

"So," she asked, her eyes ranging beyond the purple horizon, "What other emotions will we be experimenting with today?"

"That's it for now, I hope. Thank you, Mary."

"That's all right," she whispered, "There's really nothing I'd rather be doing." She turned and kissed me. The second kiss, her kiss, was as long and perfect as the first. Then she looked up and stood, pulling me to my feet. She said, "Now, I think we'd best get that gate open before the bird lands."

I shot a glance skyward. Sure enough, it was the black raven. The bad one. No red feathers this time. It was still far above us, obviously circling for a landing.

"Maybe it won't fit in the hole," Mary said.

"Don't count on it," I said, turning my attention to the gate. When I suddenly laughed raucously, I regained Mary's concerned attention. She reached for me, preparing to embrace me again.

"Well what do you know?" I said, pointing to the small, lighted button on the wall by the gate.

"It looks like a doorbell," Mary said, crossing with me to it. I poised a finger near it.

"Shall we?" I asked formally.

"We shall," Mary said, pushing my finger into the button. Though she was not looking up, her attention was still on the bird that we both knew was circling just above the hole in the ceiling.

With no hint of machinery, not a whisper of sound, the portcullis slid up into the arch. Its movement ceased when it was high enough for me to pass under without stooping. Pass under we did, too, seconds before the bird came to a silent landing behind us. It squawked rudely as it attempted, but failed, to join us as we passed under the gate. Easily three yards tall, it had no chance of fitting under the gate. I worried that it might downsize itself to fit through the opening, but that concern was abated when the gate closed just behind my heel. We were safe once more, somehow.

Mary and I turned to look at the bird. It was watching us as well, with black, intelligent eyes. It settled itself on a craggy black boulder in the center of the landing, and then lost interest in us as it went about grooming its long black feathers. Mary reached across and took my good hand in hers.

"Time to turn around?" she asked. Our backs were to the castle, so our ultimate goal was behind us in this mildly wild dreamland.

"Time," I said. We turned together, but Mary never let go of my hand.

What we expected to see, I wasn't sure, but I was confident that we would indeed see whatever we expected. Such hyperbolic logic conformed nicely to this place, this plainly surreal location that was simultaneously right out of my mind and perfectly alien. Whatever we saw, I knew would not be a surprise; I believed that nothing surprised me anymore. I suppose I was expecting that great cartoon hall in the Emerald City that Dorothy et al followed to see the Wizard. Well, Oz would certainly leave my mind this time. This time, I was caught off guard. Again.

"I don't believe this," I heard Mary say. I maintained silence, soaking up the vision.

We stood on a polished hardwood floor. A glass chandelier dangled inches above my head. Clean white walls soared a meager eight or nine feet on either side of us. Before us was a carpeted stairway with fourteen steps and a polished wooden banister. We were in the entry hall of a small and tidy townhouse. The painted wooden door behind us thudded shut, startling us from our silent reverie. Mary clutched my hand harder, leaned toward me.

"It looks like my parents' place on the Island."
"Seriously. But it's not hundred-foot doors and great halls, so we'd best not be too trusting."

"Do we look around or go home?"

"The way we came? The door might be smaller, but I'll bet that crow is still fully grown."

"Let's check the place out then," she said, "And why the hell are we whispering?"

"Don't know," I whispered, "Seems like the polite thing to do when you wander uninvited into someone's house."

I led her out of the vestibule and took a right, into the living room. It was a standard sort of living room, about twenty by twenty, with an arch in the back leading into the dining area. The windowless side wall featured a marble hearth, and a warm fire crackled within. A large picture window occupied the front wall. Outside, the sun was setting between two distant snowcapped mountains. An old Chrysler was parked on the quiet street beside a clean white sidewalk. Back inside an overstuffed couch with awful floral print upholstery dominated the area beneath the window. Seated casually on the couch, sipping tea, chatting, and as yet unaware of our presence, were Max and Cassie.

II

LUCIDITY

Chapter Twenty

"**B**ut I'm sure I hate tea," Mary mumbled. Hers were the first words that broke the two-minute exchange of silence we shared after Cassie and Max casually glanced toward the foyer and noticed Mary and myself standing stupefied in Max's entry hall, and perhaps also at the softened border of all of our realities. That gap in communication was centered more on our mutual inability to produce anything clever to say than it was on shock, or simple confusion fostered by the juxtaposition into which we all, with the possible exception of Cassie, had been tossed. Mary's tentative statement smashed the silence. Everybody laughed loudly and nervously, but ripples of relief were also evident in our heavily projected cheer.

"Hey," Max said above the din, pointing at Mary, "Isn't one of us supposed to explode about now?"

"Yeah, well *I'm* dead already," Cassie chimed merrily, touching an index finger to her head, and pulling an imaginary trigger.

"You're dead?" Mary said palm in the air, "Shit, I'm here twice, and my other me looks a shitload better than I do. And drinks *tea*. What is up with that?"

"Um," I interrupted loudly, "Can we worry about all this very important stuff later? We should settle down right now and figure out what the hell we're all doing here."

"Sounds good to me, Alex," Max said. She crossed her bare legs sensuously, rested her teacup on her knee, and nodded in a serious fashion to the others. When they quieted, and Cassie matched her pose, Max said, "Okay, you start. What are you doing here? Pulling a Rudy?" I looked around once more, my nerves tweaked by Max asking the question that should have been first to leave my quivering lips.

"What am I doing here?" I asked, still clinging to the cold comfort of incredulity, "This is my dream; not yours. Isn't it?"

"Well," Max said, smiling, "I can see we're off to a most excellent start. Who told you this was a dream, and why did you believe them?"

"I sort of told myself," I said, "It helps keep me from totally losing it."

"I hear you," Cassie said. She shifted her position on the sofa slightly, reminding me instantly of the thousand times she had done so before. I knew that in about three seconds she would speak the words she had really intended to use. She did, saying, "I imagine that all of us, except maybe for that nice young lady in my 1989 Christmas gown, can come up with outstanding explanations of where we are, who we are, and why we are here, so how about we start with her first. Is it Mary?"

"Yeah," Mary said. She stepped forward – we hadn't left the doorway since our arrival – to better introduce herself, but I instinctively thrust out an arm to hold her back. Max reacted as well, by somehow sinking deeper into the sofa cushions.

"Hold on there, Mary," Max said, "A good source tells me we are not allowed to come into contact, on any plain. It'll destroy us both."

"Funny," Mary said, scratching her head, "I don't feel too destroyed. In fact, I feel better than I have all day. Maybe that source of yours ain't so good. How about you, um..."

"Max," Max said, "It's Max, and I think you're right; the shit should have hit the fan by now, if what Rudy told me was true."

"Why don't you come into the room, Mary, and test her theory?" Cassie asked, her arms open in welcome. When her suggestion was met with a chorus of alarmed gasps and dropped jaws, she continued with a smirk, "Oh sorry, I forgot. I have nothing to lose in this. I can't be more dead, can I?"

"That I couldn't tell you," I said, "But I also wouldn't dismiss the concept. Max, I think Mary's right too, and I also think that, regardless of appearances, we're still on my plain. I don't know how that can happen, but, if it's true, then I do know

that I wouldn't let any harm come to you here." Another chorus
interrupted my speech, this time a simultaneous release of a guffaw
from Max, an hysterical giggle from Cassie, and a snort from
Mary. I paused, tried to look annoyed at their well-founded
cynicism, and continued:

"Fine. Okay, so I wouldn't do it on purpose. At any rate,
Mary and I are going to step into the room right now, and see what
happens. Anybody have an objection?"

"Nope," Max said.

"Come on in while the tea's still hot," Cassie said.

"Shit, I been lost since the house thing, no need to step
back now," Mary sighed, "Tea or no tea, Bob, we're payin' these
girls a visit." She hooked her arm around my still extended
forearm, converting me from guard to escort in one motion, and
walked with me into the tidy room. Cassie and Max stood, unsure
of how to greet us. Mary solved that problem by plopping
gracelessly into one of two wingback chairs that faced the sofa. I
took her cue and sat in the other. Max resumed her position on the
sofa, and Cassie followed, though she took a moment to pour us
each a cup of tea before sitting. I was curious about how she knew
to have four cups available, but I reserved that question for another
time; I was distracted. Cassie, and her typically loosely open
collar, entertained me as she leaned enticingly over the antique
coffee table while she poured. She always bent at the hip rather
than the knees, and I had missed spotting the cleavage-revealing
result of her lapse in etiquette. Max cleared her throat, startling me
back to sheepish attention.

"So anyway, Alex. What the hell are you doing in my
parlor?"

"This is yours?"

"Yes."

"Very nice."

"Is that a shock?"

"Maybe a little," I said.

"You're avoiding my question, aren't you," Max asked
pleasantly.

"Why yes, yes I am," I said, "And I'm sorry about that.
But I think my world has been stretched a smidgeon too far today

for me to invent fantastic answers that might entertain us over our tea and, um – ”

"Scones," Cassie said, passing me a hard beige lump of dough riddled with what I hoped were raisins, "A nasty habit I picked up after my death. My first one, that is." I felt the blood rushing past my ears in reaction to her thorny sarcasm, but I held my poise.

"Scones," I said, "I always wondered what they looked like. Anyway, Max, I guess I need to answer your question with two of my own: Where are we, and why are you having tea with my dead wife?"

"I guess that ranks higher than 'why are you tramping around with my material self?' on the scale of base questions," Max hissed. I sensed that I was not the most popular fellow in the room, and perhaps was in for a bumpy ride. I could not blame the women, though, since any pain that they had been enduring of late could be linked to me. I had hoped that the bliss shared by Max and me would have negated some discomfort, but memory can be precisely targeted when necessary. Max continued:

"But you're right. Clearly you deserve an explanation, or something, especially because you thought you were in a dream, or on your own intermediary (excuse me – purple) plain."

"Now wait a second," I started to say.

"Hold on there, Bob," Mary snapped, "Let's let Miss Gorgeous here explain shit to us. I think she's got the upper hand in the knowledge department today. And excellent taste in decorating, if I do say so. I'm still confused about the tea, though."

"Why thank you Mary," Max said brightly, careful to sip some more tea before continuing, "And thank you Alex for giving me a chance.

"First, me and Cassie. One of my assignments from Rudy was to keep tabs on her, especially after the second time you bumped the poor girl off. So I started hanging out with her, um, current incarnation I guess you'd call it. We got to be friends, and Cassie eventually moved into my place. It's much easier to watch her this way, and Rudy didn't seem to mind my interpretation of the word 'surveillance.' At least, he never had anything negative to say about it. Come to think of it, the man never had anything at all to say about it. Cassie, do you think he doesn't know you're here?"

"I know I'm here, so he knows I'm here," Cassie said, her easy smile gone, head bowed, "There isn't a chance in any hell I've visited recently that Rudy has lost track of me. I can't say why I know, but it is true."

"Oh," Max said, "And, wow, by the way. This brings me neatly to Rudy. Alex, we have a real problem, I think."

"Wait," I said, looking around demonstrably, "Can't Rudy hear what you're saying right now? I don't think my shield covers all this."

"Your shield barely covers you," Max hummed, checking her nails, "Of course Rudy can hear us, if he felt like listening. Since our trouble is the opposite of this, you probably have nothing to worry about. See, Rudy seems to have ceased listening to anything, or anybody. He appears when he pleases, and still acts like a god when he's around, but he seems totally ignorant of where we've been or what we've been doing. He hasn't asked for a report on you, or Cassie, in weeks."

"So, he's changing?" I asked. Mary abruptly cleared her throat.

"Changing from what?" she asked impatiently, "What was he before? Better or worse?"

"Damn good questions Mary," I said, smacking her knee with my palm and embarrassing and confusing myself on several levels at once. Touching Mary in front of my dead wife and my new love (of whom Mary was now a slightly larger reflection), while Mary was wearing a dress for which I apparently had some fond but consciously forgotten memories opened far too many doors for humiliation's easy entry, and dared to permanently shred my tattered psyche. I quickly wrapped both hands around my teacup and sipped some of the hot green tea it contained. I stared at the shimmering liquid and opted to speak casually and hope that no one noticed my gaffe or guilt, though I was sure that everyone had:

"Maybe we should back up a little bit. Max. Is there anything you can tell us about Rudy, and his history, that might help out here? Last time we talked about this you were a bit short on explanations."

"Yes I was, wasn't I?" Max said, blushing slightly, "All right, I'll give you the *Readers Digest* version of the Life and Times Of Rudy – help me out here, Alex, what's his latest last name?"

"Frisset."

"Frisset. Okay. Bizarre choice, but I can work with it. Anyway, the life of Rudy Frisset started about 11 centuries ago somewhere north of what is now Italy. Rudy was never really clear as to where and when precisely he started life. He also never mentioned parents or any other family, so don't ask.

"Rudy was a mystic who stumbled on the potent power of his own dreams at a very early age. Apparently he spent time as a boy in a remote monastery whose occupants were into a variety of prayer and introspection of which the pope at the time probably would not have approved. Those monks taught Rudy about dreams and their direct relation to what is really going on in the world. Rudy was dazzled by the scope and potential of the worlds of consciousness he explored, and decided – yes, decided – at the ripe old age of about 14 that the future of humanity was in his hands. So, he made some sacrifices, did some studying, and immersed himself body and soul into the World, as he calls it. He was able to stop his physical aging fairly easily, which was important because it took him far longer than he had anticipated to figure out how to baby-sit reality.

"About a century ago, things finally started coming together for Rudy, and his loyal opposition. The gloves came off, and both sides frantically tried to outdo the other in their good and bad deeds. Think about it. The last century endured two world wars, the age of dictators, unprecedented famine, overpopulation, and general degradation of the human condition, but it also enjoyed a doubling of human life expectancy (in the western world anyway), the development of technologies that would have been termed sorcery in any other century of human history, the planet-wide triumph of democracy (well, almost), and the fact that nuclear weapons were only used twice – *by the good guys*. Rudy and Freuzre, as you call him Alex, were really duking it out over the last 100 years. They both feel that they've made great progress, but they both know that their true goal – unifying the souls of all people into one World modeled to reflect each of their respective visions – has not been met. Which brings us to now."

I put down my empty teacup, and reviewed the rest of Max's audience. Cassie appeared almost disinterested, but was politely nodding. Mary hovered at the edge of her seat, every visible muscle tense. I knew Mary now, and understood that this tension was not excitement or fear but a marrow-deep effort to suppress another bout of manic laughter. I could not blame her. I looked back at Max, who maintained the masque of a true storyteller: grimly earnest, with just a hint of excitement. She too was leaning forward, her face less than the length of her slender forearm from mine. I leaned back to give her some air.

"That's a hell of a story, Max," I said.

"Yes," she replied flatly, "Yes it is."

"And you heard it where?"

"Why," she said, her perfect lips stretching in an involuntary grin, "Everything I've told you comes directly from the source."

"That would be Rudy, no doubt?"

"No doubt."

There was a brief silence as Mary and I sorted out our responses to the tale. My first reaction was that it all made sense; especially in light of the adventures we had endured over the last few months. But something wasn't right. I felt it, and Mary was about to start rapturously singing her doubts. Cassie broke the silence by politely clearing her throat. We all looked at her. She took Max's hand, looked into her eyes.

"Okay, Max," She said softly, "That was a great story. Can we hear the truth now?"

"The truth?" Max said, trying to appear flabbergasted.

"You mean that tale wasn't true?" Mary snorted, hands to her cheeks, "My heavens!"

"Max?" I asked.

"What? I gave you Rudy's history, just like he wants you to hear it. Verbatim. Now you're questioning me? Please!" Max sat back forcefully, either in a show of indignant pain, or perhaps just to do something physical to keep her façade from breaking down. Had there been any in the room, emancipated dust would have burst from the sofa from her impact.

"Oh, don't get all hissy," I said, joining Max's game, "I know you owe Rudy a lot, and that you feel obliged to tell his story as he recited it to you. But if there's more, you ought to share."

"If there's more," Mary said, "I might have to leave the room."

"Oh, so you think I haven't told you everything?" Max asked, her voice quivering slightly, "That I've left something out?"

"I wouldn't say you left it out intentionally, Max. It might have been an unconscious omission brought on by your intense loyalty to Rudy." Max jumped to her feet, balling her fists. Her face was tightened into an expression of fury, but her eyes could not conceal her amusement. I stood too, and assumed a classic pugilistic pose with the grimmest expression I could muster.

"Okay," Cassie said, head in her hands, "This is getting silly. Max, you know you left something out."

"I did?" she asked, "Like what?"

"Like the truth?"

"Oh, yeah," Max shouted, slapping her forehead with the palms of both her open hands, "The truth! You're right; I might as well take the initiative now and resign from Rudy's gang now, while he's not in the room to vaporize me."

"Us," Mary corrected.

"Us. Anyway, sit down, Alex, there is indeed a bit that I left out. And you can stay Mary – it gets a lot less funny." I sat, sipped some more tea from my refilled cup. Mary sat back, folded her arms tightly against her belly as though to better display breasts that seemed smaller though better defined than before, and waited. Cassie began repairing a loose thread she discovered on the arm of the sofa. Max sat forward, and spoke softly, conspiratorially:

"The truth. Okay, here you go: the truth.

"The single aspect of his story that rings with any truth is that Rudy really did stop aging – mentally, and at about twelve. Because of this, his judgment, opinion, and respect of others are minimal. So, when he loosed me upon the World, his childish arrogance prevented any notion to rise in him that I would see beyond his projected vision of the World, and his own history. Since he thought he made rather than met me, I can understand his error. Well, in the course of building the skills I required to watch you and mind Cassie I did see beyond his prefabricated, infantile horizons." She drew a breath, took another sip of tea, and paused. Mary and I waited, feigning indifference while Max worked unnecessary drama into her story. She continued, speaking as if she were talking about an errant neighbor who was having an affair. Later I would realize that, in a sense, she was.

"Rudy is not 1,100 years old. No one is. He's about 45, I think. He was born in Mahwah, New Jersey, and grew up in the 'burbs far away from anything even remotely religious. From what I can glean about his childhood years he was fairly but not unusually bright. He was a loner, more than a little lazy, and he was bored, bored, bored.

"Rudy apparently took his boredom very seriously, and he longed for a solution. He sought a new life that would provide him with everything he lacked: excitement, interesting times, an easy life with huge rewards requiring little input and no work, and maybe some sex. Since he grew up in the '70's – the 1970's, for those of us who lost track, there was a lot of material available that promised such things. His imagination enlivened, he bought everything he could find that offered rewards without sweat. He devoured New Age pseudo-occult books, meditation tapes, tested those insane machines with lights or magnets that are supposed to change your aura and cosmic awareness, and he even took a couple of weekend retreats with the Hindu guru du jour. Somehow he was able to sift through all the schlock and remain a true believer in a potential life fueled by powers beyond those of mortal men. In his singular desire to succeed, he finally made a connection.

"I doubt that even Rudy remembers what book he was reading, what machines were plugged in, or what drugs he was on. All he remembers is that one day he stopped sleeping through his dreams. He became fully conscious in the midst of a dream, still asleep but aware of his state, and primed with the generally vapid knowledge of a thousand volumes of magical mystical mojo. He used that knowledge as a lever to help him lift the veil of his dreams and witness their creation. It all goes downhill from there."

Max stopped speaking. She dramatically sipped her tea while she waited for a response from us. We were listening intently, because the story Max told breathed with the truth. We wanted her to continue, to finish the antithesis of Rudy's heroic mythology.

"So?" I asked, "What does this mean, this downhill?"

"Oh, you know. He started having delusions of grandeur before he was old enough to drive, and these delusions were only amplified when he started 'creating' reality in his dreams. None of it was easy for him, not like it is with you Alex (and spare me your dopey face!). It was a real struggle, more work than he had planned, but his successes impressed the hell out of him. In time, as he mastered the navigation of the dream realm, the place he soon saw as his own, he began to believe that he could do anything.

"This attitude, if left untempered, can definitely snowball, especially in light of all the positive reinforcement he was receiving. And, in Rudy, snowball it did. He came to think that he could do anything, at any time, to or for anybody. He thought this even though about the only mundane reality he ever twisted on his own was that car, and his ability to shuffle effortlessly around the world. He did finally manage to be able to live an exciting life without real effort, and he may even have had some sex (there's that face again – not with me, Alex!), but he discovered quickly that that wasn't enough for him. He wanted more."

"Let me guess," I said, "He wanted to save the world."

"You got it. He decided that he should use his powers to rescue the sad misguided peoples of earth from their own misdeeds. Since he really didn't have enough imagination or raw ambition to change things on his own, he decided that he should be earth's champion, and sought out the evil that pervaded its cultures."

"Freuzre?"

"Freuzre. He was known simply as the shadow for years; I guess Rudy decided a name would better appease you. The timely arrival of the shadow gave Rudy an excuse to do almost anything he wanted to do, all in the name of fighting evil. Everything was moving along fine; Rudy had lots to do, misfits like Clive and me were gainfully employed, and, honestly, the world didn't give a crap what we did. Then you arrived."

"Me?" I asked, pointing innocently to my chest. Please God, I prayed silently, don't let all this be caused by my unconscious actions.

"Yeah, you. Rudy spotted you immediately. Well, even that might give him too much credit. What really happened was you began appearing in his dreams. You didn't even know it yet (you would have been a teenager when he noticed you), but you were having a nasty effect on his dreams at a couple of levels. The first level was that you were simply there, interfering accidentally with his clever games. The second, and really the clincher in this saga, was that you were naturally doing all the mystical things Rudy wished to do. You were shifting among dimensions, adjusting reality, and proving all his theories about reality manipulation right in front of him – and you didn't even know! Rudy was pissed. He immediately drew up (yes, he actually wrote it down) a long-term plan to bring you into his fold and control your power. He basically moved in next-door and waited, priming the pump by establishing a friendship with you. His opportunity arrived when Cassie accidentally offed herself – sorry, girl – and your grief completely lowered whatever unconscious guards you had raised. He still wasn't making much progress until Freuzre nuked his house and you crossed the bridge into the World on your own. Right after that all hell broke loose, like your toy place getting waxed, and Rudy's 'rounds' actually working. I think this happened because Rudy, through your example, could finally understand how to translate his wishes, his dreams, into physical action."

"That's why you were so angry at Fritz's?" I asked.

"I guess so. I knew by then that what he was doing was wrong, and I sensed that you might be empowering him, and maybe Freuzre, somehow. I still didn't believe it yet, and I certainly knew I couldn't voice my concerns to Rudy. All that I could do was complain. His tactics, like using Cassie as a carrot, were starting to piss me off big time, too. But what could I do?"

"And that brings us to my becoming aware of all of this," I said, rubbing my eyes, "The truth is far more impressive than his official cover story."

"But not nearly as fun," Mary said, "I got just one question, Max: How the hell did you find all this out? Yer telling us stuff that Rudy would never admit to, even if he knew it."

"Good point," Cassie said, still focused on that loose thread.

"Um," Max said, scratching her forehead, "That's the thing. Rudy doesn't know most of this story, if any. At this point, I'd bet that he truly believes that he's been around in one form or another for a millennium. Therefore he certainly couldn't have told me, even if I ever summed the courage to ask – which I didn't. I seem to just know this stuff…"

"Oh come on!" Mary snapped, "That's bullshit. Now tell us really, or we won't believe you anymore." I appreciated her acting as conscience by asking her counterpart the question, but I was sure at that point that Max's story was without error. I folded my arms and waited for Max's justification anyway. Maybe her defense would reveal something.

"Sorry my Mary, but it's true. I just seem to know. I mean, I can back up a lot of the recent stuff because I was there, but the earlier events and attitudes are things that I just know. How? Please don't beat me up for this, but I think the shadow – Freuzre – told me."

"Whoa," I said, "I didn't see that coming. The shadow told you?"

"Yeah, somehow."

"But you can't remember talking to him?"

"Talk? I've pretty much only seen him in those most excellent dreams of yours, and you know how much talking was going on then."

"Then why do you think he told you?"

"I don't think," Max said, looking askance at Cassie, who still bowed her head, "I know."

"How?" I insisted. Mary suddenly stood and held out her palm to my face.

"Okay Bob, that's it. She told you the truth about your buddy, and I can tell she was totally righteous about it. Now cut her some slack and drop the fourth degree."

"Third," Max corrected.

"Shut up girl, I'm helping you here. Anyway Bob, I think you got enough jerky to chew fer now." She grabbed Max's wrist (nobody was annihilated, though I did wince), yanked the smaller woman to her feet, and continued "Besides, I want Max to give me a tour of this place before your dream ends or you start us off on some new adventure and we gotta leave. C'mon Max."

"I'm with you," Max said as Mary dragged her across the room. She did not have much choice, from my perspective. She called over her shoulder to me, "I didn't have anything else to say anyway. You guys coming or what?"

"I guess so," I said, agreeing that I had heard enough for now, and happy to have a change of subject so I could avoid dealing with the facts thrust upon me for a while longer. I stood and mimicked my earlier involuntary promenade of Mary by holding out an elbow to Cassie. She graciously took it and walked with me behind the nearly matched set of high-energy redheads who cavorted three paces before us. She walked easily, but something had clouded her mood.

"What's the matter?" I whispered before we caught up to Mary and Max.

"Nothing," She whispered back. I knew that tone all too well, and dropped the subject.

Max was leading Mary up the stairs. She pointed to the door at the top.

"That's your bedroom, isn't it?" Mary asked.

"Uh huh."

"Why did I know that?"

"I don't know, and I'm not sure I care. Go on in, so you can tell me what you think about how your other half lives." Mary hesitated, either in fear or perhaps to increase the drama, until we had joined her on the landing. Then she entered Max's bedroom. We followed her in, watched her twirl around the gray room that sported an army cot, a steamer trunk, and no windows. At least it's clean, I thought. Cassie and I glanced at each other and shrugged in unison at Mary's pleasure. Our confusion was negated quickly.

"My God, Max, I cannot believe what you have done with this room! The bedspread, the drapes, even that psycho orange dresser from the '60's are all exactly the kind of things I would have done! This is so cool!"

"Oh," Max said, "You have no idea how that makes me feel, Mary Mary."

Mary stopped her spinning, and ceased moving her hands in curious jerky motions that I deduced represented her touching the intriguing objects she found in the room. She faced Max, held both her hands, and looked down those two or three inches of extra altitude she enjoyed into Max's eyes. Four fiery green eyes blazed in close quarters for a few seconds, bringing us all into a sudden state of almost transcendental euphoria that was gone as quickly as it struck. Then Mary spoke softly:

"Oh," she said, "I think I do."

"Yeah," Max said, "You do." She stared for another three seconds, then shook her head and pulled Mary close, until their bodies touched in a few enticing places.

"Do you want to see the rest of the house?" she asked breathlessly.

"Shit yeah!" Mary responded. Giggling madly, they plowed between Cassie and me and ran from the room, heading down the hall, away from the stairs, to explore. We dutifully followed. The next room was as gray and meaningless to us as the first had been, but Mary and Max spent ten minutes excitedly discussing an extensive library. Though I was intrigued that Mary could even pronounce the word, much less be interested in a library, I was feeling displaced by the tour. I looked at Cassie. She had adopted that familiar tense posture that told me that she too was uncomfortable, and probably a bit bored. She still smiled and nodded, though, making sure that her background contribution was positive during this important moment for Mary/Max. I however, was not as sensitive as my dead wife.

When Mary/Max skittered like schoolgirls on helium to the next room, I grabbed Cassie's wrist and pulled her with me through a random door across the hall that they had not yet opened.

Chapter Twenty-One

I stepped lightly on a patch of neatly trimmed lawn with Cassie by my side. The soft grass slithered between my bare toes, pleasantly tickling them with each drop of a foot. There would not be many of those, though, because the lawn we traversed was less than ten by thirty feet in dimension, and it had to allow space for the trees, a babbling fountain, and flowers that populated the compact arboretum. Space was limited because the garden we were enjoying was perched atop the western tower of the Brooklyn Bridge.

Lower Manhattan loomed majestically behind us, dazzling in the noonday sun. Cassie stepped to the edge of the garden, resting her hands on the cold, waist-high wrought iron fence that framed the garden and locked the East River and New York harbor behind its closely spaced bars. She leaned out in an effort to be closer to the skyline, mindless that she risked a puncture of her stomach by the fence's sharp pickets. She stared west for a few seconds, shook her head slowly, and said:

"You got it wrong, Alex."

"Wrong? What do you mean? It's New York, just like I pictured it; skyscrapers and everything."

"That's very good, Stevie, but you forgot the biggest buildings in the lot. I know they were an eyesore, but Rudy's going to rank you among the amateurs if he catches you leaving out the World Trade Center."

"Oh," I said, not sure how to proceed. Our backdrop was correct – I haughtily assumed it was real, but Cassie's death predated the low point in the history of human interaction that brought down the World Trade Center. I thought quickly, debating whether an explanation of the towers' destruction would clarify, confuse, or simply allow the opportunity to cast a new chunk of blame upon Freuzre. I decided, in less than three seconds, to duck the issue. I touched her shoulder, coaxing her look at me.

"What do you mean?" I asked.

"What I mean is that you left out the twin towers!"

"You sure?" I asked, turning her back toward New Jersey. In her eyes, the towers again dominated the lower Manhattan skyline. Damn, I thought, I wish I could've done that two years ago. Cassie nodded.

"Oh," Cassie shrugged, "Nice trick. Never mind."

"I won't. You remember any of this?" I asked, sweeping my hand over the city.

"Remember? How could I forget? My God, sometimes I think we have a memory stashed on every block of that island. Remember the time you made me walk all the way from Grand Central to the Battery, and then back to Macy's?"

"How could I forget? I thought I had killed you then, too. Sorry about that."

"It's all right," She said. She turned her attention, and her words, to some other aspect of the city, the U.N. I think, but I did not hear her. I was still rolling her response to the previous conversation repeatedly across my mind, struggling to embrace or preferably deny its significance. We had discussed that long, romantic, exhausting walk a thousand times since we experienced it more than a decade earlier. Whenever we did, we might vary the descriptions, or order of events, but without fail I would conclude the discussion with the phrase, "Sorry about that," to which Cassie consistently responded, "No problem, just be glad you learned about subways on the next trip." The exchange was a ritual forged on the intimacy and strength of our shared history. My stomach churned violently, voicing its displeasure at Cassie's gaff. I had to agree with my gastronomic misgivings, but still chose to dismiss her omission. She was, I reasoned, dead. I had to allow her some room for forgetfulness. With effort, I refocused on her narrative:

"– until it rained. Then we had dinner at that excellent Italian place in the Village. Remember it?"

"Luigi's. On Fourth," I said. How could I forget?

"Yeah," she smiled, "That was it." I decided, against the wishes of my former self, to test her once more. We had frequented that restaurant because the pasta was excellent and the wine was affordable. On our initial visit we were seated at a table with three place settings. The waiter, who spoke about as many words of English, assumed throughout our meal that we were waiting for another party. He brought the place setting a menu, water, a glass of wine (which I drank gratefully), and even a cup of espresso at the end of the evening. Cassie and I enjoyed the error immensely, and were happy for the vaunted company of the unseen guest. Whenever we returned to the restaurant, we insisted that our table include a third place setting. We even named the spectral guest at our table Oscar. The memory represented a defining moment in our life together. In life the mere mention of Fourth Street elicited a giggle from one of us, or perhaps a moment of silence for our good friend Oscar. I swallowed, looked out toward Greenwich Village, and said:

"Yeah. I miss Oscar."

"Who?" Cassie asked, her response squeezing my stomach like a ripe grape again. I bleakly wondered if this ill-informed doppelganger gracing my presence perhaps was not Cassie. I almost laughed aloud at the contradictory thought. Of course she isn't, you idiot, I thought. Cassie, the woman I loved, married, and lived with for a decade, was dead, consigned years ago to memory. The construct that fidgeted and chatted less than a tender touch away from me was excellent, even invigorating, but it was not Cassie. I sighed, resigned myself to simultaneously accept this fact and continue playing the game that the very real aspect of the woman at my side presented. There was a point to her presence. I was just missing it.

"Never mind," I said pleasantly, waving my hand to dispel her follow-up. I continued, "We should get back to current crises anyway." I paused, waited for her to take one last long look at the skyline before turning her back to it. Then I said, "So, now that we have Max's short history of the life and times of Rudy out on the table, how would you like to take a moment and give me *your Reader's Digest* version of his story?"

"I really don't have anything to add," she said, carefully examining her fingers while fighting an urge to revisit the panorama behind her, "All my memories of Rudy happened with you around, so you should know everything I do."

"Okay then. How about you just tell me what's been happening with you over the last few months? Maybe we can find Rudy in there somewhere. And don't worry about what you say; nobody but me can hear you."

"Sure," she said brightly, "I can do that." She sat on the ornate stone fence (I would have sworn it was wrought iron when we entered the park), modestly fixed her gauzy pink sundress around her pale thighs, and closed her eyes. She projected an expression of concentration that I recognized with a leaping heart as purely her own. I wrestled my emotions to the rear guard of my racing mind, and struggled to maintain some objectivity as I waited for the suddenly accurate avatar of my dead wife to spill dark truths about my best friend. It wasn't easy. After a few pensive sighs, Cassie looked up at me, snatching the full attention of my narrowly suppressed emotions with a familiar flutter of unpainted eyelids over her soft brown eyes, which had been moistened by the confused anguish that coursed through her ethereal veins.

"Okay," she sighed, "Maybe I can't. Rudy, his past, my past, our past, have all mixed into a really, really weird blur. It's like my life, or I guess my afterlife, has been tied in giant knots too complex for me to unravel. I feel that I'm not supposed to even try. It's also real scary." Her last colloquialism was a phrase she released whenever she was trying to tell me that her situation had transcended her ability to cope. I sat on the wall beside her. I swallowed a gasp of exclamation that the granite was downy soft and quite comfortable, and put my arm around Cassie. Her shoulders melted into my grasp, like they always had. No, I thought, this was not going to be easy, but it was necessary.

"Don't worry, babe," I said, "You have to expect that Rudy, Freuzre, or whoever the hell set you on this path will have laid some pretty serious roadblocks to protect the truth. vJust relax, and tell me what you can. Tell me, even if what you say sounds wrong to you, or like it was a thing planted into your thoughts. Maybe, after you get something out, we can clear things up for both of us." Cassie smiled. I knew this, even though I was speaking through her thick hair to the back of her head. There was a certain ease of tension in her shoulders that betrayed the grin that I knew was crossing her lips. I relaxed, and remained silent while she returned to the assembly of her tale. Eventually she sat up and twisted around to take in another view of Manhattan. She spoke while her eyes reviewed the chaotic glory depicted in stone, steel, and glass.

"My life over the last few weeks, or hours, or centuries (trust me when I tell you I have no concept of how long I've been here) has been less of a life than it has been a collection of moments. Most of those moments involved you, and the variously sweet and shitty stuff you did to me. But if I sit very still and wait patiently for a knot or two to loosen, I can remember a few other moments that were shoved aside by your radiance. They're extremely vague, like dreams that flash by while I'm in the shower, but I think they involved Rudy." She stopped. I waited for her to assemble a few more thoughts, but I realized by the renewed tension in her shoulders that she had nothing left to say. I gave those soft shoulders a slight squeeze.

"Can you remember anything about those moments with Rudy?" I asked softly.

"Not really. I already told you that I couldn't touch upon anything that makes sense."

"I know, but tell me what you can anyway. Try to do so even if what you find is difficult, or nonsensical. It might matter."

She looked at me, patted my hand.

"It's okay, doll," she whispered, "I know how important this is. I'll try."

"Cool," I said, and waited silently for her to speak. While I did, I absorbed the serenity of the scenery we had placed ourselves within. Our spectacular position atop the bridge was complemented by the warmest of breezes blowing cleanly from the north (rather than New Jersey), the warm sun, and the near silence that our altitude afforded us. Were it not for the drama that drove our conversation, and the bizarre notion that I shared the exchange with a piece of my past, I would have been perfectly euphoric in this surreal techno-pastoral setting. Cassie stirred, disturbing my reverie.

"What I remember about Rudy," she said without preamble, "Is a whole series of positive moments in time and space. Assuming I'm still allowed to make the trade, I can't for the life of me put those moments together in a way that you, or I, would understand. I guess the best way to say it is that every memory of Rudy that I have is intimate." I bristled, and she pulled away slightly. She placed her hand on my knee and continued:

"Don't worry. I don't mean intimate like that. I don't think Rudy brought me back from the dead for his use as a private sex toy. No, the intimacy was subtler. I can't remember any specific situations – you know, concrete moments – when I was with Rudy, and God knows I don't remember him saying anything at all to me, specifically, since I was alive. What I do remember is a whole sea of instants. It's almost like my memory has been sprinkled with Rudy's essence. Like wherever I've been, so has he. None of this is making sense, is it?"

"Not really," I confirmed. I took her hand from my knee, locked her long fingers between my own. Though I savored the depth and warmth of the archetypical connection, I could not avoid noticing how much larger Cassie's hands were than Max's. I set the oddity aside, and finished my thought, "But in a way it does. So what you're really saying is that, though you can't remember ever spending a moment with him, your past is filled with Rudy's presence?"

"Um, yeah," Cassie said, sounding almost relieved, "You really could put it like that. That was excellent! How did you do that?"

"I haven't a clue. So is there anything else? What about things that don't involve Rudy?"

"Oh," she laughed, "That's a hell of a lot easier. Like I keep saying, my memories of your intrusions in my afterlife are clear as a bell."

"Gosh, that's just wonderful," I said drolly.

"Isn't it? Beyond that, my life seems to be no more than just a lot of waiting in my house for the next thing to happen. Since I have no real concept of time I couldn't tell you how much of it I spent between adventures. And it doesn't matter anyway, since it was spent doing nothing but sitting around knitting or watching TV and wishing for a window to open."

"You had TV?"

"Only reruns, of course."

"Of course."

"But the set was always on. I never could find a remote, or even a switch on the TV."

"Wow," I said, "That could really suck."

"Tell me about it."

"And no windows?"

"Nope. Just gray walls with awful still-life oil paintings. Like a Holiday Inn."

"Or like the rushed creation of a guy who needed a place to put you."

"Or that. Sure. But the odd thing is that while I'm there it's much less painful than when I remember being there, as though there is some sort of complacency spell about the place.

"And that is my whole post-death history. As best as I can remember it."

"And what a history," I said, "I should also mention that you don't, or didn't knit pre-death, either."

"No?"

"No."

"I had a feeling about that. I never could figure out what the hell I was making. Well, at least it's a new skill. Maybe I can use it someday."

"That's positive," I said, acknowledging her sarcasm with a squeeze of my fingers, "Now, I have just one last question, and you don't have to answer it if you can't."

"Shoot."

"As you look back over everything you can remember at once, and you think about what Max told us, and what I've been saying about Rudy, how do you feel, intuitively, about him, and about me joining him?"

"Intuitively? I'd say stay the hell away from him and his master plan. Far away. And you know what? From the depths of my soul, if I still have one, I think I would have told you that when I was alive."

"That tells me a lot," I said, "And I think that puts us both in the same light regarding Rudy."

"Yeah. A dim, shadow-casting light that is best left switched off."

"Yeah," I said, cleanly missing the hint she had inadvertently hurled at me, "This is all getting way to deep for me, and I'm not totally sure how strong my anti-Rudy shield is out here in the open. How about we head back to Max's place?"

"Sounds fine to me. Though I would have welcomed another trip to FAO Schwartz."

"Maybe later." Without unlocking our fingers, I set my feet on top of the wall and stood, gently pulling Cassie up until she was beside me, and turned us both around. Gently. We stood on the hard brick ledge for a moment, basking in our eagle's view of the greatest city in the world, and then I stepped off the Brooklyn Bridge into the warm afternoon sky. In spite of our apparent altitude, and my outwardly suicidal regard for the position, Cassie moved in unison with me, without question or tension. As the weight came off our back feet, separating us from the bridge-top garden and the security of thousands of tons of masonry and steel, Cassie pulled slightly closer to me.

She was not motivated to move closer by fear. Instead, she nuzzled close to offer me a peck on the cheek. Once planted, she pulled away, her eyes cast down either in embarrassment or in mixed admiration and respect for the East River flowing thirty stories below our splayed bare toes. Her intimate gesture rendered me misty-eyed, which threw a mild obstacle at my attempt to bring a doorway into being less than one step away (two steps would, even in my reality-warping environment, have been one too many). I blinked through sudden emotion to confirm that an ornate iron door hung, slightly ajar, in space just below and in front of us. I was thrilled to remember the slightly ajar part. When our toes, now wrapped in Nikes and red pumps, safely crossed the threshold and landed on the hard granite that lined the darkened vestibule beyond the door, I looked at Cassie. She was just visible in the orange twilight glow that filtered through the rusty screen door that slapped shut behind us, and she was still smiling.

"What was that for?" I asked, now that it was safe to do so.

"What was what for?"

"You know. The kiss you just gave me."

"Just? My God, that felt like a lifetime ago!"

"It was only a step."

"Helluva step. I think we're in Kansas, Alex. Why are we in Kansas?" I glanced casually back through the screen door, acknowledged the sea of Midwestern wheat that lapped against the brown front lawn of the strange house we had entered. I was careful not to turn fully around to take that glance – it was time to regroup at Max's, and I didn't want to wander aimlessly through dreamland trying to locate her address.

"It does look like Kansas, doesn't it? Maybe Nebraska. I have no idea what we're doing here, or who abandoned the farm. I guess I was paying too much attention to forward and not enough to what was behind me, and space just got a little away from me."

"Cool!" she chirped. I had to smile at her natural, familiar, enthusiasm, but I was careful to augment that smile quickly with a clearly contrived look of consternation.

"You're avoiding my question," I said.

"What question was that?" she asked merrily.

"You know for a dead person you have way too much fun. You also know exactly what question."

"Of course I do. I just want you to ask me again."

"Fine. Why did you kiss me?"

"Oh, that," she said softly. She took my other hand, faced me at arms' length in the dying afternoon sunlight, and looked directly into my eyes. "I wanted to thank you," she said.

"Thank me?" I asked, hoping my voice didn't squeak, "For what?"

"You know what."

"I do?"

"Yeah, you do," she said, releasing one hand and turning toward the faded wooden vestibule, indicating that my inquisition was over. And it was, because I did know. Her kiss was her way of thanking me for not torturing her to death again with my powerfully misguided passion. She was right to thank me, especially because it reminded me that I had not even thought of trying to morph her into anything that she wasn't already, or to drag her into some more concrete version of my personal reality. I had let her be herself, in her own place in the world, without even thinking about it. I was very pleased with that thought, and the ramifications I could infer from it. For a moment I almost felt like a responsible adult. Then I remembered that we were standing in a whitewashed vestibule in Kansas, or Nebraska, that used to be granite and floating above the lower east side of Manhattan. I refocused. I slid my hand from her fingers to her upper arm without ever letting go – I was not sure, but maintaining touch could be important – and looked deeper into the vestibule.

"Yeah, I do," I said, "And we're both welcome, I think. Now let's get the hell back to Max's before the hair twins miss us."

"Any idea how we do that?" she asked without a hint of irony or concern.

"I'm guessing we walk through this house and look for a sign."

"Like 'Max's Place?'" Cassie giggled.

"A lit doorbell button would be just fine, I think." I moved us through the worn wooden hallway, deeper into the old, abandoned farmhouse through which we had found ourselves trespassing. Before the orange light from the open front door had waned, we found a heavy steel door in the left wall, under the stairs, that could not have been part of the house's original architecture. I nodded toward it. Cassie took the initiative without hesitation and twisted the unlocked chrome latch. The door opened easily, and we stepped through it into a long door-lined hallway with awful brown carpeting that would have fit neatly into any modern motel in the country.

"Well," I said, listening to the fire door slam shut behind us, "I guess this is a good sign. I'm guessing that our next turn is through one of these doors; we just have to find the right one."

"Yeah. I'll bet the wrong door would be very bad in a place like this."

"Embarrassing, anyway. I'm hoping that my cloak is still keeping us incognito."

"Oh, yeah. I keep forgetting about that cloak; I guess I'm glad you don't."

"I can't. It's not allowed."

"Why don't we try that door? The one up ahead on the right there."

"Why?" I asked. The door appeared as nondescript as any of the others in the hall.

"Um, how about because it has two knockers?"

We both laughed loudly, and opened the unlocked door with the innocence that accompanies righteous certainty. Max and Mary, both dressed in loose black satin pajamas, spun around as we entered Max's front hall, startled by our continued laughter.

They quickly concealed their involuntary joyful yelps with tight lips and fists on hips.

"Where the hell have you been?" Max snarled.

"Yeah," Mary said, "Where the hell? We were taking a tour of this awesome place, and then you guys just vanished. Don't ever do that to us again, man!" I was afraid one of them might strike me in anger, or overplayed jest, and their sincerity confused me.

"What's the problem?" I asked, "we've only been gone about five minutes."

"Five minutes!" they cried in unison, "Try five days!"

"Damn," I said, "I have got to get better at that whole time and space thing."

Chapter Twenty-Two

"Shouldn't you be cooking or something?" I asked Max from my perch atop her kitchen counter. As they had been for hours, she and Mary were babbling happily and in unnerving detail about the history of Mary's surprisingly expansive and adventurous love life. She apparently wasn't 'easy,' as I had already suspected, but the grain of Max's soul that had managed to hold fast to her physical form had made her an exciting catch once a suitor got past her simple exterior. Their sharing, fascinating in its early stages, had met its limit of exposure to my attention, and I was uncomfortable. I was being selfish, I knew, but I had convinced myself that they were wasting precious time. I also had nowhere to hide from their dialogue. It was time to make a polite, or even rude, interruption to damn the brook. After I spoke, they faced me in unison. Their wide green eyes were still wet from the tale of Mary's last boyfriend, Stu (she called him Mr. Pid).

"What do you mean?" Max asked.

"Well," I said, hopping off the counter, my landing on her white ceramic tile floor cushioned by the Nikes I acquired during my excursion with Cassie, "This is a kitchen, isn't it? The place where food is prepared?"

"It's also the place where good friends and family *always* gather to have their most meaningful discussions," Mary said, "Didn't you know that?"

"Nope."

"Shit Alex, you're getting less bright every minute," Mary said with a wink. Yeah, I thought, and my wits are funneling into your rapidly improving brain. I wondered briefly if such transference were possible, but then dismissed the fear. Besides, if anyone were depositing cranial functions into Mary, it would have been Max. And Mary knew she was changing, and seemed to be enjoying the concept.

"Besides," Max added, "I'm not very hungry. Are you?"

"No. But that wasn't the point. We're in your kitchen. Kitchens are where you cook. Why do people always meet in the kitchen, even when they're not even thinking about food?"

"How brave of you to broach the subject in a roomful of women," Cassie chuckled from her seat at the 1950's era chrome dinette, "And you should know why anyway, since I can vaguely remember half your family jamming into the kitchen for every gathering, regardless of where the buffet was set up."

"That doesn't count. The wine and beer were always in the kitchen. My family had priorities."

"And a severe streak of laziness," Cassie finished. I didn't argue, but was intrigued that Rudy had buried such an odd tidbit into her current memory. He probably thought it would be a clever lure if Cassie could reminisce about such unusual items.

"There is that," Max said, "But there are many other excellent reasons to gather in kitchens. For instance, they are always warm, well lit, blessed with lots of handy flat surfaces, and usually bereft of amenities like comfy couches that distract people from their conversations."

"Sure," Mary said, "I mean, I don't think I ever saw the inside of my parents' kitchen, but I did always see them get put to good use in the movies. They used them for settling arguments, fixing TV's, planning invasions, ending or beginning marriages, deciding what to do with feeble family members – "

"Okay, Mary" Max said gently, "Enough said. Really. But she makes a good point, Alex. Her examples are excellent, too, especially the one about planning invasions. Isn't that what we're supposed to be doing here?" She plopped down on a kitchen chair, seductively nesting its vinyl back between her bare legs. Her position forced her black leather skirt to hitch further up her already generously exposed smooth slender thighs. I smiled, and raised one finger.

"Now there," I said with a heavy dose of macho bravado, "There is a reason for being in the kitchen. We are planning an invasion of sorts, aren't we?"

"Oh?" Cassie asked, nodding toward Max but looking at me through slightly slit eyes.

"Of Rudy, you dirty-minded ghost you," Mary said, smacking Cassie and me on the shoulders simultaneously.

"Yeah," I said, "What she said. An invasion of Rudy's empire."

"An insurrection, more like," Max corrected, interested, "But there does need to be a plan, doesn't there?"

"Absolutely. Especially because Rudy's probably got our lives – and after-lives, as it were," Cassie rolled her eyes at my reference, " – planned out for the next few decades in exacting detail."

"Not mine!" Mary interjected.

"That's an excellent point," I responded directly to her, "And I would bet we can cash in on that oversight by Rudy somehow. But for now we need a starting point. In order to derail Rudy's intentions, or even infiltrate them, we've got to assemble some tools."

"Tools?" Max asked, unable to mask her dejection, "What the hell is a tool that would help us just communicate with Rudy, much less infiltrate his schemes?

"I mean, the man is shifting through realities so quickly and with such random abandon that not even his erstwhile allies, like me and you, can track him. I probably know him better than all of us, and I couldn't imagine what we could use to find him. And again, that has to happen before we can find out about him."

"That's a good, if depressing, point, too," I said, "But there has to be something. Something simple, that one of us already can access, that maybe Rudy has forgotten about. It also has to be a thing I – we – can understand how to use."

"Like that big red chair in your basement?" Mary asked. We all just looked at her. She looked back, raised her palms and said, "What?"

"Does it shock you that she would state the obvious, when the rest of us high-minded brain surgeons are looking around for more subtle tools, perhaps in a feebly guarded attempt to stave off the inevitable?" Max asked me, arms folded tightly across her chest in a kind of glowing defiance.

"I can see that you two are destined to be a real asset to our struggle," I said drolly. Max took a deep breath, eyes blazing. It was time to hold up my hands.

"I meant that in the nicest of ways," I said hurriedly. Max relaxed slightly, forcing back a smile that I was able to retrieve when I touched her elbow lightly and said, "And, tools or not, I wouldn't know where to begin without both of you at my side. Sides. I mean that."

"Yeah, sure," Mary said, "So now that you might have a tool, what's your plan?"

"That I couldn't tell you. What I'd really like is to get back to the real world, assuming there still is one, and try to figure out exactly what Freuzre and Rudy are fighting about, or at least which poor souls they are using and abusing to wage their imaginary apocalypse."

"Let's hope it's still imaginary."

"Why do we care if someone imagines apple cow lips?" Mary asked.

"Alex," Cassie said, " I agree with Max. You should be very careful about what you term imaginary. Things you dismiss as unreal might just rear up and bite you in the ass after you arrogantly pass them by." She was right, I knew, but I felt compelled to concoct a patronizing response that would thoroughly conceal my deep-seated confusion. I sat in the vacant chair beside her, took her hand, looked for my reflection in her eyes.

"Don't worry about that, Cassie," I said softly, carefully holding her gaze while I spoke, "Rudy's taken me on enough tours of his meddlings with reality that I'm inclined to believe he's got his hand in far more than he probably does, not less. I'll be careful."

"Oh, please," Max said, pinching her nose with her thumb and index fingers, "Let's get back on the subject here before my legs stink from wading in the bullshit. Plan or no, I agree that it is a good idea for you to get back to concrete stuff. This place we're in now can be pretty damn insular."

"But it's a nice kind of insulation, Max," Mary said, "I could stay longer, I'm sure. I haven't got much to go back to anyway."

"Just the rest of my life," Max said sharply. Mary recoiled slightly, growled, but no fur flew. That subject no doubt had endured some recent discussion between Max and Mary. I saw their pause as my cue to return us to the subject.

"At any rate," I said, "I think I do need to get back. I don't suppose any of you know an easy way to do that?"

"Hey," Max said, "You're the superhero in this flick. I'm just the trusty badass sidekick. What do I know about the rules?"

"In other words, since you always get dragged into whatever space you occupy by me or Rudy, you never had opportunity or need to learn how to navigate."

"Couldn't of said it better myself," Max agreed.

I looked at Cassie. She retracted the hand that I was unconsciously still holding.

"Don't look at me, Alex. I'm dead."

"As many times as you say that, it still isn't funny," I said. I turned to Mary, said, "How about you? You've been showering me with surprises since we met, have you got one now?"

"Nope. Not this time. Hell, it were me I'd probably just do something real dumb like head back the way I came." I shook my head, Cassie laughed and Max released a quiet "ah hah." Mary looked around at us nervously. "Now what?" she asked.

"And the showers continue," I said, "For lack of a better choice, and a multi-dimensional road map, that's probably our best bet."

"You just wish you were bright enough to think of something that obvious on your own," Max sang.

"You got that," I admitted, "But going back might not be so easy."

"You got us to the Brooklyn Bridge," Cassie mentioned.

"Yeah, but that wasn't real. I think." I hoped it wasn't since I had neglected to remove the World Trade Center before we left.

"It sure felt real," Cassie observed, "So does this."

"So do I," Max added, "Don't I?" She wriggled for me just a little, eliciting a quiet giggle from Mary and a sigh from Cassie. I felt my blood begin to rush in wholly inappropriate directions.

"Okay okay, I get your points. *All* of them. On some level everything is real; I should know that by now. But reality comes in degrees, or pieces, and those pieces don't always get along as well as you guys do. We must comprehend those pieces before we can navigate between them. And right now we're in a place none of us understands that is off the compass from where we want to be."

"So?" Mary asked, "You keep saying that you just have to think about a thing or a place and then there it is in front of you. Why not just do that again? Why are you making this so hard? You afraid of something?"

I sighed, sincerely. Mary was correct again. I was still trying to complicate the situation, perhaps in an effort to prolong my stay in this safe happy enclave that nestled so distantly from the turmoil into which I knew I had to dip us all. Well, I thought, slapping my leg loudly, that was the sort of selfish concept I could grasp and, therefore, work with by doing no more than moving quickly away from it. I abruptly stood, signaling Max and Cassie to do the same. Mary was already on her feet near the door.

"All righty then," I said, rubbing my hands together, "Enough with complicating things. Let's just get off our asses and go see about saving the world!"

"It's about friggin' time," Max said, jumping to her feet, "Let's go."

"Yeah, let's," Mary added. Then she put a finger to her chin, "But, um, where are we going?"

"Home," I said with an honest confidence that surprised me.

"How do we get there?"

"You might have me there, Mary, but I figure we should take your advice and start by retracing our steps. Maybe I can conjure up my purple plain and, from there, figure out a way to wake up."

"We're not going to be spinning around in any more houses, are we?" Mary asked softly, rubbing the top of her foot with her the bare toes of the other.

"God I hope not," I said, "But I'll do my best to avoid anything dangerous. I can't offer any guarantees, though. And, if that chair's been destroyed, I'm not sure about anything, including getting off the plain."

"That's encouraging," Max said, "Don't look at me like that Alex! We're still with you."

"Yeah," Mary added, "We don't trust you for shit, but we both have a feeling that you'll lead us in the right direction. Even if you don't mean to."

"Thanks, I think," I said. I rubbed my hands together once more, and said, "Okay, then. Let's go. I don't think we need to pack or anything. We'll pick up what we need as we go."

"Just try to keep us all dressed this time," Max said sharply.

"Like I said, no guarantees. Don't worry; I'll try. Let's go then." I turned and left the kitchen immediately, walking steadily through Max's apartment until I reached her entry hall, which appeared exactly as it had the other two times I was in it. I put my hand on the doorknob, and turned to review the troops. Max and Mary were crowded against me, visibly steeling themselves for the inevitable blast or other calamity that would accompany my opening the door. Cassie stood, hands in her pockets, across the vestibule, still framed by the doorway to Max's kitchen.

"Cassie," I said, "Aren't you coming?" I knew the answer, but waited for her reply anyway.

"No," she said.

"Why the hell not?" Mary asked. Max remained silent. She was patiently shifting her gaze between the doorknob and me I had yet to turn.

"Because I'm dead," she said solemnly.

"So?" Mary asked, probably guessing that Cassie was again speaking lightly about her condition.

"Mary," Cassie said gently, "I mean it. I'm really dead. I don't even know if I'm real, if I exist."

"That's just stupid. You're standing right in front of me!"

"And where exactly is 'right in front of' you?" Cassie asked, with either a lump or a bit of anger rattling her words. Mary didn't answer; she was beginning to understand. Max, in whose unreal home we all still stood, kept her counsel. I, however, felt a sudden need to offer some rationale for taking Cassie with us.

"Sure," I said, "You're dead. I know it. I watched you die. It's all true. But truth has been getting a major overhaul lately, especially from my perspective. Maybe you're more real than you think. Maybe Rudy's more powerful than you think. And maybe, just maybe, he implanted the thought that you can't come back into your head, like he did when he convinced Max that she could never meet Mary."

"Maybe, Alex." Cassie said, "And maybe the only thing keeping me aware is my presence in your dreams. Don't try to force me out of them." A tear had formed in the corner of her eye, but it was unnecessary. I understood. However, I knew that one more thing needed to be said. I released the doorknob, crossed to Cassie. I took both of her hands in mine, and looked into her misty brown eyes whose lids were swung wide open as to absorb every detail that they could before we left.

"Cassie," I said so only she could hear, "What if the only reason you exist is because we're here? Maybe you need to come with us, just to continue being."

She looked away, swallowed deeply, but did not break my grasp. She looked back at me, smiled weakly, and said, "Then I'll stop being, won't I? That certainly wouldn't be a novelty for me, now would it? It might not even be permanent. But going home with you, back among the mud that my corpse is rotting in right now, would be wrong. Trust me Alex. I know it. And I know you do too."

"But Cassie," I protested through her fingers.

"But nothing, mister," Cassie said, holding her warm and very soft hand over my mouth, "I don't want to hear anymore. You know I'm right. Now leave me behind like you have to, and get this noble mission rolling before we all start believing that you're just a big staller." I smiled at the familiar reference, paused for a second to reset my rubbery knees, and nodded. I removed her hand from my mouth

"Okay, okay," I said, placing it carefully by her side, "I get it." I turned back to Max and Mary, who still attended the door. While my back was turned, they had changed their clothes. Each had donned matching faded jeans, heavy denim shirts and hiking boots. I released Cassie's other hand, touched her cheek and said:

"It's been great to see you again, my love."

"Yes, it has," she said, her eyes still wide as she took my hand from her face, caressed it, "It really has. And maybe you will again. But Alex, please remember that I'm dead. Please."

"I think I can do that now. It seems like an ass-backward concept, what with me standing here talking to such a warm,

living, human version of you, but I think I can," I said. I paused,
then added with a wink:

"Don't ever tell Rudy that."

"I wouldn't dream of it," she said, smiling, "Just be sure
that you don't. He can be tricky. Now get the hell out of here."

"Okay."

"Oh, Alex," Cassie said, almost under her breath, "There is
one other thing."

"What?" I asked.

"Take very good care of these girls. She loves you more
than you can imagine."

"Now that's just weird coming from you," I whispered
back, "And I don't just mean grammatically. Don't worry, though,
I will." I turned from her, crossed back to the door, and touched
the knob again.

"So," Max said, "I guess this means she's staying behind?"

"Yup," I said.

"Wow," Mary said, "Remind me never to take you with me
to buy a car."

"Bye, Cassie," Max shouted too loudly back to my dead
wife, "We'll see you again real soon."

"I hope so," Cassie said, "If you can, look for me at my
place. I don't think I'll be able to stay here without you."

"Will do," Max said. Then she grabbed my elbow with
vein-bursting force and said, "Okay boss, let's get moving."

Without another word to her, or to Cassie, I turned the
polished brass knob. While I turned it, I also turned my mind
away from all but two thoughts: the simplicity of the purple plain,
and waking up.

Before the knob was fully turned, Max's house was gone.
Everything was gone: the castle, Cassie, the bird, my ruined
house. Nothing remained except my fully clothed comrades, the
purple plain, and me.

"Well," I said softly, "So far so good."

"Yay," Mary said, "Now what?"

"Another damn good question, Mary. And, having given
the situation as much thought as ever – "

"Meaning none," Max interrupted.

"As ever," I repeated, "I guess the next step is to just wake up."

"Sounds simple enough," Max said, trying to build my confidence.

"Yup. Trouble is, my house may be gone, so I'm not real sure where this waking up thing is going to happen."

"Hey," Mary said, "We're dressed. Wherever you bring us to will be just fine. Right partner?"

"Wherever!" Max said with more cheer than sarcasm, "Just do it now, Alex, before you lose your nerve. And try not to think about oceans or deserts."

"Fine," I said. I took one each of their hands in mine, and closed my eyes. I tried to picture being awake, and laughed instead at my inane attempt to envision such an abstraction. Finding humor must have been enough to relax me, to help me change my environment, because when I opened my eyes the world around me was black.

I felt my heart rate climb in excitement. I was in blackness, but it was a familiar void. And it was not empty. I still held Max and Mary's hands, and could hear their breath cut the silence. I could also still tell which was Max, by her grip, and which was Mary, by her calluses, and that ability to differentiate them in the dark oddly encouraged me. On an elated hunch, I looked straight ahead and, for effect, said, "Lights."

Crimson brightness instantly surrounded us. Max and Mary both jerked their bodies in surprise at their new positions right beside me, indeed against me, on the red chair, whose impossible cushions made it difficult for them to know they were reclining until they saw their orientation.

"We're back," I said proudly, "And it looks like home, too." And how do I work this magic? I asked myself silently.

"So you think your house is still there, um, here?" Mary asked, her lips deliciously close to my neck as she spoke. That was too much; I crunched my abdomen, and leaned on my elbows after my shoulders were elevated a few safe inches above the cushion.

"The Sound Room is," I said, "And that's a most excellent sign. Maybe our adventure was just a dream."

"How's your hand?" Mary asked.

"Like new," I said, realizing suddenly that I had long forgotten our injuries, even when Mary rubbed her ankle earlier. Yet she had remembered. What had I done to her?

"Another excellent sign," Max said, "How's about we all get up now and find out for ourselves? Not that this isn't quite the cozy spot."

"That it is," I said. I laid my hand on Max's thigh and gave her a heavy shove. She flew off the chair with a screech, landed on the soft floor without a thud. When her head reappeared from below, she glared at me. Mary was in hysterics.

"What the hell was that for?" she yelled.

"You're closest to the door. Someone had to get up first."

"You could have asked!"

"What fun is that? And speaking of hot and heavy, Max, I think you've been putting on weight."

"That's it!" Max said. She grabbed my wrist and hurled me off the chair. I flew through the air and hit the padded wall harmlessly while Mary just continued laughing, clutching her sides. Max made a motion to grab her as well, but Mary anticipated the move and dodged her, leaping to her feet. She wiped a tear from her eye.

"God, this is all so much fun," she said, "Especially when nobody's getting killed."

"Let's hope it stays fun, then," I said, "And now let's hope really hard that it all was just a dream and the rest of my home sweet home is above us." The door to the Sound Room had opened, and I led Max/Mary out through the well-lit basement. That the electricity was on was an excellent sign, I surmised. I pulled them to the basement stairs, which had somehow remained dark. That figures, I thought, resolving once more to someday install a light above the permanently darkened stairwell. I took the steps two at a time, holding my hand in front of me so that I could feel the kitchen door before I slammed into it. I never felt the door. Instead, I sailed at full throttle through the gap in the cellar ceiling made by the stairwell, and swept into the open moonless night that ranged freely above my basement. I skidded to a stop on a small landing created by the few floorboards that had remained behind after the rest of my house had begun its trip to Oz. Max and Mary slammed into me, nearly knocking us all off the landing and back into the empty basement, which was now a darker square of unpleasant blackness below us.

"What the hell?" Max asked.

"You got it," I said, "It looks like Hell did win, after all."

"Shit," Mary said, "This sucks."

"Yes, it does."

"But at least your garage is still there," Mary said hopefully.

That it was. I could see it silhouetted in the dim light offered by a distant streetlight. I felt a primal wave of emotion surge from the frontiers of my consciousness, threatening to bury me under a shattering sense of violation and righteous anger. I curbed the natural reaction before it ever fully emerged by deciding that I could not allow my mind to be clouded by selfish bawling and that I had perhaps been done with my house and the life it represented anyway. That rationale failed miserably, but I avoided a petty breakdown by holding my attention on the garage.

It was the only thing left intact on my property, aside from the Sound Room that loomed monolithically in the shadows below us. The rest was a disturbing reproduction of the elimination of my former neighbor's house. I felt briefly proud, like I had been admitted to an elite club of sorts, but that pride was immediately washed away by the guilt of my memory of others, like my coworkers at Beaver Toys, who were briefly admitted against their will to the same club. That sobered me, eliminated all other mundane feelings that accompanied the revelation that my house's flight was not a dream. Wary that my focus was drifting inward again, I returned my attention to the garage.

"Yes," I said to Mary, less than five seconds after she spoke, "It's there. I wonder if the car still is."

"Probably not," Mary said, "Look at all the yellow tape. Yer garage looks like a freakin' giant yellow Christmas present. The cops've been here big time, and, if they were here, they probably towed your car. You know how they love towing cars."

"That they do," I said smugly, "But they may have had a problem with mine. Let's see if it's still there."

"Okay," Max said, "How?"

"Not the way I would have done it two months ago, that's for damn sure," I said. My tone drew a snort from Mary.

"You better hold on sister," she said, "I heard him talk like that before, and we're in for a ride."

"Not this time, Mary," I said, "I'm getting good at this metaphysical shit." Adopting the same attitude toward my surroundings that I would have held on the purple plain, I pictured the three of us standing in the garage near the car. I took one each of Max/Mary's hands again, and closed my eyes. I felt nothing, except the confidence that I could do this magic, and opened my eyes.

We were in the garage.

"Ho!" Max gasped. She squeezed my hand tightly, pulled me close to her and hissed, "You should know to warn a girl before you do something like that! Jesus!"

"Sorry ladies," I said, "Last time I warned, nothing happened, so I figured I would surprise you and also prevent your doubts from clouding my concentration again."

"Dude," Mary said, "We will not doubt you again. I promise." In spite of her admonition, I believed that Mary had not been surprised or shocked by the sudden position shift. She continued to treat her exposure to these preternatural experiences as though she was watching them in a theater.

"Mary," I said, "Could I borrow a cup of your psyche? I sure could use it."

"Huh?"

"Never mind."

I checked the Escort. It was indeed parked where I had left it, though the ransacked appearance of the garage and opened large door hinted that someone, probably the police, had attempted to move it. The failure of the authorities to complicate my life further caused my chest to swell in unnatural pride. I was not aware that I was reacting that way until I noticed Max looking at me with a puzzled expression.

"Okay, Alex," she said, still holding my hand, still wonderfully close, "Your battle tank is still here, and so you can still call yourself a man. Even if it s just a Ford."

"Ha ha," I said. Then I released their hands and turned to face Max and Mary, with my back to the car.

"Okay," I said, folding my arms, "Now that we know what assets are available to us..."

"Assets?" Mary asked, rubbing her rump thoughtfully.

"Yeah, the invulnerable car, and that very poorly decorated base of dream operations in what used to be Alex's basement," Max said, ticking the items off on her fingers and making it clear that she used only two.

"Oh," Mary laughed, "I thought we were talking about money or something, um, else. Never mind."

"I won't," I said, "Anyway, we have our tools. And, all model types and red fluff considered, they are good tools. We just have to figure out how to use them to best ascertain where Rudy is and what he is doing."

"So," Max said, "In other words, here we are, once more on the brink, with no idea where to jump, whether to jump, or even where we'll land."

"Yup," I said, "Here's where my pathetic lack of experience in, well, pretty much anything that matters prevents me from turning us all into James Bond types who always find themselves one step ahead of the bad guys. I know we need a plan, some clever way of rooting out Rudy's intentions and then doing something to stop him, or at least slow him down. But I could use a clue to get me started." The statement was rhetorical, but Max and Mary both stood silently for a few minutes, pensive. Eventually Mary looked up, shrugged, and said:

"Why don't you just call Rudy up and deal with him?"

Now that, I thought, was an excellent clue. I hugged Mary, kissed her on the mouth (eliciting a half-hearted "hey!" from Max), and slapped them both on the ass.

"That'll do it Mary. We have a plan."

Chapter Twenty-Three

"Are you sure this is going to work?" Mary asked from her position beside me on the red chair. I could feel her nervous tension stiffen her body, which touched mine at several points, but her most significant signal came from her hand, which was firmly clamped to my forearm.

"Oh come on, Mary," Max said calmly from my right side, "You know it'll be fine. Alex is a veteran at this shit now."

"Yeah, a veteran," Mary repeated dully, "But I been with him on a trip through his shit. It can really hurt."

"Not this time, Mary. We're just taking a short hop to familiar territory. I can do this. Trust me."

"Do it, Mary," Max said, "Trust him." I appreciated Max's steady-voiced support enough to avoid asking her why she gripped my other arm with a vigor that exceeded Mary's. I also knew that she might be more nervous about my intentions than she was about my ethereal navigation, and I definitely did not wish to discuss those misgivings with her. My confidence was shaky enough already; I did not need to defend missing goals to further confound it.

"Fine," Mary said, "Just don't come bitchin' to me if he drags us up a tornado hole."

"Lights off," I said loudly. My excess volume was technically unnecessary, but it, and the lights that obeyed my voice, did serve to quiet my lieutenants. The Sound Room was immediately black and silent, save for a startled stereophonic gasp from Max and Mary. I realized that even their reactions were silent, and I was less hearing them than I was feeling shudders of anxiety course through their bodies simultaneously.

In spite of my house evaporating around it, Rudy's dreaming chamber still worked to perfection. He was thorough in his generosity, I thought. I closed my eyes, reaffirmed Max/Mary's grip, and pictured the purple plain. I was careful to envision my base for imagination empty save for the three of us, fully clothed. I opened my eyes.

The first thing I saw was not the reassuring flat horizon of my plain, but a pair of wide green eyes hovering inches beyond my nose. I reflexively jerked my head backwards, but the motion was stopped in mid-swing when my skull struck another object with a sickening thud. I saw stars orbiting Max/Mary's (I couldn't tell which) smiling face in front of me. I stayed conscious though, because any opportunity for passing out was negated by the sharp jab of a fist into the small of my back.

"Ow!" I heard one of them shout from behind me. I gathered my wits and pushed the amused woman in front of me away so that I could better review my surroundings. I was seated on the purple plain, propped in that position with my legs stretched straight before me. My backrest was losing its resilience, and I had to lean forward to maintain my seated position. This was because one of the women, Max I think, had relinquished her position against, and supporting, my back. She had taken to her feet and was coming around to join Mary, who knelt beside my legs, her hand resting casually on my denim-clad thigh. Mary waited for Max to join her in my field of vision, and then gave her a slight nudge with her elbow, as if to confirm that it was okay to speak to me. And speak to me Max did.

"Alex," she snarled, "Where the fuck have you been?"

"What do you mean?" I asked, grabbing my knees and pulling them close. Max softened after she noted that I was not primed with another useless explanation, but that only reduced her tone from pure aggression to just plain pissed off.

"What do you think I mean?" she snapped, "We've only been sitting around here on this freaking soft ceramic tile planet of yours for about a week now, waiting for you to fucking wake up."

"A week?" I asked, incredulous. I rubbed my eyes.

"Maybe longer," Mary said pleasantly, "It's hard to tell without night." She couldn't hide her relief in my consciousness as effectively as could her counterpart.

"Yeah," Max said, "Mary made me stop guessing what time it was a day or two ago."

"A day or two?" I repeated, "A week? But I just closed my eyes and opened them."

"The ones on your face, maybe," Mary said, "But our eyes popped open way, way before them, and all we could do was sit around here waiting for you to wake up. We were afraid even to stop touching you."

"See, now, *that* I don't see as a totally bad thing," I said lightly. Max growled, and Mary actually tossed her a furrowed-brow glare that unmistakably bore stifling instructions. Max turned away.

"Yeah, well maybe the touching wasn't so bad for the first forever, but eventually we just got totally bored, and maybe a little cramped. We been working shifts holding you up, because Max all of a sudden got scared that if you stayed laying down you might think you're asleep, and wake up back in the chair without us." Good call, I thought.

"Yeah, and you thank me with a head-butte. Nice guy!"

"Sorry about that, Max," I said, careful not to blame Mary, "But I really do feel like only a couple of seconds have passed since I turned off the lights in the Sound Room."

"Yeah well, you've got to do some homework on that whole space and time thing before it fucks you up big time."

"Tell me about it," I said, "I'm sorry, really, but keep in mind that I am new to reality bending. I'll try to include time as an ingredient in my next spell, but I have to admit that it's almost impossible to remember that something that has seemed so natural, and expected, all my life has become its most artificial aspect. In other words, remembering there's no such thing as time ain't easy. Just be happy we were all dressed the whole time. Now help me to my feet." Before the last sentence was out four slender hands grabbed my wrists and hauled me into the air, nearly removing my arms from their sockets.

"Um, thanks, I think," I said, unconsciously brushing non-existent dust from my clothes as I gathered myself. I looked around more conclusively, relieved to see that we were on the purple plain, with no foreign additives like the castle, the bird, or oversized bikers in our midst. At least something worked. I noticed with a mild thrill that Max and Mary were still holding my wrists. Then I remembered that they were unwilling to let go for practical and not romantic reasons. I carefully slid their iron grips down to my fingers for the equally unromantic purpose of returning blood flow to my arms. These women were strong, tireless, and had been very frightened. They did not fight me. We three stood silently for a few minutes, studying the distant or perhaps near horizon that denoted the placement of the great white Tupperware lid that served as my sky. Once I was sure that we had all settled our nerves, and were again a team united in love and in some cases shared DNA, I spoke again.

"So," I said, squeezing the identical hands I held with equally tender force, "You guys didn't happen to come up with that plan while I was sleeping, did you?"

"Plan?" Max asked, "Oh yeah, we almost forgot because it's been so long. You're supposed to be saving the world. We sure hope the world is waiting for you." I, too, hoped that the world exercised patience if I was indeed destined to come to its rescue, but I was too proud to share that thought with Max/Mary.

"No, Bob," Mary said solemnly, "No plan. And it sure wasn't for trying. We just don't know anything."

"Attagirl Mary," Max said, "Way to make us sound good."

"But you really don't know anything." I confirmed somberly, knowing that they would understand my meaning without being insulted.

"How could we? I'm a freaking dream, and Mary here is just, well – "

"A freak?" Mary finished, "Freaking stupid?"

"I was thinking more along the lines of insular, but, since you're me, I guess I can be honest. So, yeah, Alex, I don't exist in reality and Mary's a hopeless dolt. How, when, and where exactly were we supposed to come up with your plan?"

I smiled, unable to contain the pleasure of being exposed to the vivacious personality that Max/Mary had inadvertently assembled. I was also unable to hide my relief that they were able to continue solving my problems for me, and to this I spoke:

"I think you just did," I said, pulling them both a subtle inch closer to me. I was not sure whether it was because the two women were nearly physically identical (Mary was still slightly taller and heavier), or that they had independently helped to change my life in the most positive of ways, but I was beginning to lose all interest in concealing the fact that Max/Mary had taken full possession of a portion of my soul which I had thought dried up years ago. Max/Mary barely noticed my slight tug, and certainly overlooked my silent convulsion of love, but they did grow confused by my conclusion.

"Huh?" They asked simultaneously.

"I said I think you two might have done more planning than you think."

"How so?" they asked together again.

"Okay, one at a time from now on. That's just getting too weird. Alternate your responses or something, just to be fair. What I meant was that you guys, who, unbeknownst to me, are the only true tools that I have to work with – "

"Thanks," Max interrupted sardonically.

"It's a good thing, really," I said, "And had I noticed it before we left my place, or even Max's for that matter, I might have saved us all a shitload of time."

"And misery," Max added.

"And misery. Sorry about that. Anyway, had I realized earlier the kind of contributions you guys could be making to my cause, I would probably have left Max's place by myself."

"Why's that?" Mary asked on cue. Max was already nodding.

"Why? Because I should have had the good sense to recognize my blessings, my assets. I should have left you two in your own elements. Especially now that Mary you both know about Max and that there might be more to life than your next meal."

"Yeah, I guess," Mary said, "But so what?"

"What? Why, 'what' is that I should have sent each of you away by now, so you can act as my sensors."

"You want us to be your spies?" Mary asked. "Shit, Bob, I barely know English. How am I going to be a Russian?"

"It's okay, Mary," Max said, "I think I know where he's going with this. Alex has already established that he is almost helpless in the dream world – "

"Thanks," it was my turn to say.

"No problem. And we've seen his exposure to the physical world has been guarded at best."

"Thanks again."

"No problem again. But I'm a veritable dream world sprite, and Mary, whether you like it or not, your connection to the mundane is near perfect, and your sanity is at a level that can handle constant communication with me (you're welcome). I think what Alex realized during his days of meditation at our expense – "

"I swear I really didn't grasp the whole time thing," I interjected.

"Yeah, yeah," Max said, rolling her eyes, "You had no idea. You're a god, a hopelessly ignorant god. Anyway, Mary, Alex thinks we could give him perspectives on Rudy's movements that are beyond his own ability."

"He does? You do? Why?"

"Don't ask why, Mary," I said, "Just believe her. It's true. I'm only sorry that I couldn't think of it before."

"But Bob," Mary said, "Intelligence and me are two words that never got along real well."

"That," Max said, resting her other hand on top of mine, "And the fact that I might not exist without you." I considered saying "nonsense" to both statements, because I instinctively knew they were each untrue, but I bit my tongue when I saw the water gather in Max's eyes. Regardless of her history with Rudy, and myself, she still believed that her existence as a thinking entity was at the pleasure of my, or Rudy's, indulgence. Instead of arguing, or offering another incorrect patronizing speech, I just shook my head and sighed.

"Oh, Max," I said, gently tugging my hand, with both of hers in tow, to her eyes to wipe her tears, "You are more real than I could ever be. Don't ever question that, no matter what tripe Rudy feeds you. You're real, and now you're eternal because of our love. No. Don't question me, or argue, or look for any goddamn loopholes. It's true. Out of his own ignorance Rudy set you up to fear meeting Mary, but I think your meeting, buildup and all, was the best thing for you both. Now you both know there's more, and, one day, you'll both grow enormously from that knowledge. Don't ask me how, but I do know it. And I know this, too: be confident that you're alive now, and you will only become more so."

There was a long pause. Max's perfect face relaxed and clenched in a rapid rotation of love and confusion. Her respectful silence implied that I had led her to understand that she was important, both to the world and to me, and that I loved her. Mary, sadly, was more removed from the moment we shared.

"Max," she said, poking Max's flat belly with her free hand, "I think he thinks you're fat. Or else that you're going to be." Max saw me bow my head, and then she laughed loudly. She threw her arms around me, which also pulled Mary in close to us. I did not mind; indeed, Mary's close proximity to our intimacy seemed correct enough to naturally ignore. Max kissed me long and with enormous energy while Mary just hugged us both. I didn't mind that, either. In time Max backed her face from mine just enough to allow Mary's to enter her field of vision.

"Mary," she said rapidly, "You no doubt understood more of that lame speech than I did, but you know what? I think 'Ol Alex/Bob here is trying to say he loves us both, and that we're going to stay strong whether he's around or not, and whether he likes it or not."

"Really?" Mary asked, excited. I had the sudden sinking feeling that I had missed a meeting, but I was glad to know that my feelings were understood, or at least acknowledged.

"Close enough," I stammered, still reeling from the effects of our kiss. Then I pulled them apart, so I could turn my head comfortably between each of them. I fought off the disturbing feeling that I was talking to the same person twice, and continued:

"So can I get a promise from each of you that you'll do what I say now, and not worry any more about all that other crap?"

"Promise!" they said in unison. Mary held up two fingers to cement the deal.

"Good. Here, then, is the plan. Max, Mary, you're both going home. Not my home; we've been there. You're each going to return to your own homes."

"Oh joy," Mary said.

"That's the plan?" Max mumbled, "Can I take back my kiss now?"

"I know that's not the most exciting assignment on the board, but it is the best way that you can help me. Max: go back to your place, both your apartment and your position at Rudy's side, if he'll still have you. Mary, go back to reality, which is a place you alone among us can still see and understand without prejudice. Both of you watch and wait."

"What about you?"

"Like Mary said. I'm going to give Rudy a call."

"All by yourself?"

"At first, yes. I think it's the only way."

"Well then you're only an asshole."

"Maybe, Max. But it's how I have to do this. Now both of you promise that you'll go quietly, and that you'll keep those gorgeous eyes open." Max and Mary considered each other silently for a moment, and then looked back at me in unison.

"Okay," Max said, "You win. We're in."

"Yeah," Mary added, "Even if I got no idea what I'm looking for. I'm just a dolt, you know."

"Oh please!" Max snarled playfully, "You know what I meant."

"Sure she did," I said, "And Mary, don't worry about what you're looking for."

"He's right," Max said, "You need to be more worried about how to get home in the first place."

"Good point," Mary said. I let go of their hands and put an arm around each of their waists. I turned us around as a unit and started walking.

"That will go a little easier this time," I said firmly.

"And will this time take less time too?" Mary asked. Max laughed. So did I.

"Yes. I promise. And not only because I'm in a hurry to get all this behind us so we can be together again, either. For instance Mary, you're just going to wake up."

"Where?" She asked.

"Hopefully in the chair. When you do, get out of my basement and find your way back to your life. There'll probably be some money in the car's glove compartment. Don't take the car this time, okay? Just the money; I might need the car. Don't get all huffy, now; I know you can do it."

"Then what?"

"Then go home – I suggest you reunite with your parents, and that you don't go to your lonely hovel in the city – and watch.

Keep an eye on the news, on the attitudes of people around you, and maybe watch for anything unusual in your environment, like yellow skies and pink water. And, most of all, wait for one of us to contact you."

"I can do that," Mary said, smiling, "Yeah, you know I think I can do that." I could feel her confidence, and I knew she understood that I had no intention of abandoning her to her old world.

"That's good. Now, do you two have any good-byes to make before I send you on your separate ways?" I asked. The question was moot, because the two counterparts of the same amazing woman were already locked in a tearful, wordless embrace. They held each other, with Max still careful to continue touching my wrist, for about thirty minutes. To me this seemed excessive after the first five minutes, but I was not inclined to try to break them up. They had sacrificed enough time for me; I could spare them half an hour. Also, I was aware that they might have been exchanging more than just affection. A force far deeper and closer to their shared soul may have been energizing their embrace, and I did not wish to disturb that cosmic osmosis.

Eventually their grip on each other loosened, and they pushed apart until they had an arm's length between them. I wondered what they saw as they regarded each other one last time. My eyes saw the same woman twice, but I wondered if my own perceptions had gone awry. Mary (I knew it was Mary because of her position, and her question) looked at me and asked:

"So now what?"

"Now you wake up." I had barely released the thought before Mary faded, without a single cry of pain, to nothing. Max and I were left alone on the purple plain, silently clenching each other's hand.

"So," she asked eventually, "She's going to be okay?"

"Seriously, Max" I asked, looking into her eyes, "Are you asking me or telling me?"

She smiled broadly, said, "You know. I was right about one thing."

"What was that?"

"You are a pompous asshole."

"Hey!" I said, "You never said pompous."

"Yeah, well I never meant it either," She said as she pulled me into a tight hug. She spoke from my chest after a long moment of nestling: "Do I need to go home now too?"

"Yes," I said to the billowing red flames of her thick hair, "And you can't know how sorry I am to say so."

"Yeah I can," she said. She pulled away so she could look into my eyes, and said, "Just remember that I'll be keeping an eye on you. That's my job, you know."

"Was your job, but I'm looking forward to being watched. In the meantime, go home, rest, and, if you see Rudy -- "

"He'll see me."

"Fine. When Rudy sees you, tell him I'm looking for him, but say nothing else."

"Like how I feel about you?" she asked. That felt good.

"Especially that," I smiled. I turned her by her shoulders, pointing her away from me, and said, "And here's you. Goodbye, Max. We'll meet again soon. I promise."

"You sure you don't want to come in?' she asked.

"I do, but I can't. I would never leave."

"I know," she said. Before I could stop her, and not assuming that I would have, Max turned back to me and stood on her toes to kiss me. She held my mouth against hers for a very long time, our tongues working together with a familiarity that belied our brief intimate time together. Eventually we parted and, without a word, Max opened the picket fence in front of her and ran the twenty paces to her front door. When she reached it she turned, waved, and said:

"Kick his ass, Bob!" Then she, and her townhouse door, was gone. Though I was alone on my purple plain, I could only feel that, for the first time in years, I was no longer alone. I wished I had had that feeling while Max/Mary were still standing in front of me. They would have appreciated the sentiment. I shook my head vigorously, deciding that I should stop wasting time wondering about my decisions and get this thing done.

A pay phone appeared before me. I picked up the receiver and held it to my ear. I heard nothing, not even a dial tone. Then I put it back on its hook, accompanying its click home with a mild curse. I had forgotten to remove my Anti-Rudy Cloak. I did so immediately by pulling a white silk cape off of my shoulders and tossing it to the ground. It burst into flame when it landed, then disappeared. Confident that I was now fully prepared to meet Rudy, and perhaps less vulnerable to his influence and hopefully his power than I was in the past, I fished a quarter from the pocket of my jeans. I picked up the receiver again, dropped the coin into the phone, and waited. I could hear the phone ringing on the other end, but after a dozen rings I knew that Rudy was not going to pick up.

"Okay," I said, "I guess you have caller ID. Well, so much for the easy way."

I replaced the receiver, checked the change bin for my quarter (it wasn't there) and then turned around. I was reaching for the passenger door handle of Rudy's Porsche before it came fully into view. The door opened for me, and I stepped into his car. It was empty, and the steering wheel was missing. I looked through the windshield and saw that the car appeared to be parked on my street on a leafy fall afternoon. I could see the rest of the neighborhood, but the angle was wrong to check Rudy's lot, which was behind me. I couldn't see my own house either, because I would have had to look through the passenger window for that, and only the purple plain was visible through it.

I noticed that the key was in the ignition. Curious, I gave it a turn. The engine turned over a couple of times before the weak battery was exhausted. Rudy's Porsche was, for the first time in my memory, dead. And back in front of his house. Apparently I needed to follow a less obvious route to connect with Rudy. I left the car, walked a few paces from it, and stared out across the welcome emptiness of my plain. I rubbed my smooth chin, wondering if the abandoned car was a symbol of sorts, left by Rudy to indicate that he had chosen a new vehicle for his travels and work. Work, I thought; work that had become more like mayhem. With that last thought still firmly lodged in my throat I turned again. I nearly lost my footing on the steeply inclined cobblestone street.

"Might as well start at the beginning," I said aloud, my words sounding like German when they bounced back to me off a nearby alpine building across the vacant narrow street. I looked to my right as I strolled down the hill, fearful both that I might miss the intended address, and that I would find it. After completing a few more paces past rustic storefronts still slumbering in the predawn light, I found the address. Fritz's, however, was still absent.

Someone had tied a rope at about waist level between Fritz's neighbors and parallel to the sidewalk. It suggested that passersby avoid the empty lot that was all that remained of Fritz's. The thick old length of coarse hemp was an extremely minimal marker, considering all of the good people who burned in the tavern uncounted weeks earlier, but perhaps in its simplicity was truth – there could be no bronze plaque at this spot, no billboard, or even one of those piles of flowers Americans are wont to drop at the scene of preventable death. No, this disaster was best left unexplained, and avoided. The lightly sagging barrier reminded me of the equally simple fence erected around the site of Beaver Toys. Both served well to gently keep people out, and to persuade them to ignore, or forget, a special hell that befell their neighbors and not them. Ultimately the hemp line and the dusty dead lot it protected offered me no clues as to the whereabouts of Rudy, so I turned myself around with perhaps too much energy, because I wound up standing on the moon.

Well, not the moon, exactly, but more a cartoon artist's rendition of the cheesy version. Dangling loosely from the bottom tip of the moon's crescent was Max's car. Since there was only a small amount of real estate to cover, I was at the 1950's monument to automotive excess in a couple of bouncy Apollo astronaut moon-man steps. The car's trunk lid had broken off, and the space was empty save for a few pounds of crumbly blue cheese. I saw that this vehicle was also missing its steering wheel, as well as the left front seat. The rest of the car had thoroughly rusted, as if it had been left hanging on the moon for eons. I avoided wondering how it could have rusted in space by taking a deep breath of fresh air. Frustrated, I kicked the rear chrome bumper, dislodging the car from its perch, and leaving it to fall screaming woefully into the distant Sun. I munched on a handful of cheese while I surveyed the two dimensional solar system and pondered my next move. In time I smiled, dusted any cheese scraps from my hands, and hopped off the moon.

I fell through space as fast as I could imagine, and burst into the Earth's atmosphere in an awesomely obvious ball of flame. I plummeted toward the ocean, slowing my pace so that I could both see where I was headed, and be seen by anyone who knew to look. I passed the cliff I dove off so long ago to rescue a fair maiden from a plummeting plane. I did not, as I had hoped, pass any birds.

I dove headfirst into the cold ocean, then swam to the surface and grabbed onto the empty fuselage of the downed Cessna. I climbed aboard, noticed three indents in its soft tattered surface before my weight forced the tiny plane underwater. I stepped off the plane before it submerged and onto the stoop that fronted the sky diner. I refrained from tugging open the tinted glass door, however, because I decided inexplicably that this was not a place where I wanted to actually encounter Rudy. I peeked inside, though, and didn't see him, or anyone else, anyway. I moved down a couple of the diner's front steps, which descended briefly toward the majestic young mountain range far below. I put my hands to my face to form an impromptu megaphone.

"Rudy!" I shouted as loud as I could to the roof of the world, "I know you're out there somewhere, and if you won't meet my on my terms, then I'll find you for sure anyway! Why not make this easy, and come out come out, wherever you are?" I waited for my plea to finish echoing "All ye all ye out's in free," unanswered, off the distant mountains. It seemed to take hours. I was reclining on the bottom concrete step, my feet swinging in empty air where parking lot should have been, and thinking about my next move when I noticed that my voice had at last been completely replaced by the cold arctic wind. I was careful to keep only my immediate plans at the surface of my thoughts, fearful that the thoughts I really wanted to have, primarily of Max, would twist the world around me in a direction that might put her in danger.

"Why don't you just wake up," a familiar voice spoke eloquently from behind me, "And seek our good friend on more familiar turf?"

Startled, I spun around, nearly knocking myself off the edge of the diner. Clive grabbed my flailing wrist and pulled me ashore.

"Sorry Alex," he said with a grin, "I only allow one toss from this establishment per month."

"Clive," I said, converting his grip to a handshake that I assumed he would appreciate, "What the hell are you doing here?"

"That, unfortunately, is more your domain to answer than mine. I am simply here."

"That helps," I said. Then I brightened, and continued, "Could your presence mean that you have a message from Rudy? I have been looking for him."

"So I, and most of central Asia, have heard. My presence could very well mean what you say, Alex, but unfortunately Rudy left nothing in my scope of experience today to remind me what that message might be."

"Nothing at all?"

"Not a wit."

"But, aren't you with Rudy a lot?"

"Almost all of the time, since Maxine has gone missing."

"Gone missing, huh?" I said quietly. He nodded, knowingly. I wondered if Clive was an ally or an enemy to my haphazard struggle, or neither. I pushed a little further when I continued, "So you've been with him constantly, as far as you can tell, but right now you have no idea where he is, how long he's been gone, or when he will be needing your services again?"

"That is it, Alex!" Clive said, smiling broadly and clapping me on the back, "You've got it exactly."

"So what you're really telling me is that Rudy is totally not in this realm."

"Yes, now we have returned to the beginning of our conversation."

"So we have," I said, "Only one of us just got a little brighter."

"If that is you, Alex, then I am delighted to have been enlightening. I think I should leave you now. The restaurant seems to be losing its coherency."

"So it is," I observed as I extricated my foot from where it had sunk, ankle deep, into the filmy concrete step, "That probably means something too. Damn I wish I'd paid more attention in psych class."

"Don't worry," Clive said as he climbed the steps to the front door, "You are far more impressive a being than any of us, *any*, choose to admit. Stick to your natural abilities and powerful emotions, and you'll be fine. Rudy, I'm sure, would say nothing more."

"I'm sure," I said, "You take it easy, Clive. I'll bet we'll meet again soon."

"Goodbye, Alex," Clive said passively. Then he disappeared behind the glass of the closing door. When it clicked shut I dropped my eyelids. When I raised them I was back on my plain.

"Okay, Rudy, I shouted to the blank purple landscape, "I can play hide and seek just as well as the next guy (as long as the next guy is totally blind and drunk); Clive has confirmed that I've been wasting my time in the dream world, and suggested that you're screwing around on the physical plain. I should have thought of that, but you know me: lazy to the last. Well, I'm pulling up my boots and heading on in. Ready or not, here I come." There was no echo this time.

Chapter Twenty-Four

When light redefined the Sound Room I was still alone. Before awareness had fully set in, I realized that my latest awakening was significant. Something about it was different; a major parameter had changed.

When I sat up I noticed that I was not suffering the global disorientation that usually accompanied acknowledgment that I had left the realm of power and limitless freedom that was my dreams to revisit the purgatory of the mundane world, to be governed again by the cold unflinching laws of physics. The sad confusion was absent because I knew that with this reentry I hadn't entirely left the dreams behind. I now had the confidence and close alliances necessary to maintain my sense of purpose, and focus, without concern for losing my sanity. Magic could work well for me in the mundane, if I avoided being awkward, confused, or ever surprised by the miracles wrought.

"Now all I need is to find my damn neighbor," I said aloud. I rubbed my eyes, and confirmed by sniffing my armpits that my clothes – faded jeans and a blue polo shirt – were fresh enough to wear in public. I chuckled at my involuntary inspection, wondering when, considering my confusion with time, was the last time I had done laundry, or even washed. Ah, well, I thought, habits are habits. I reviewed the familiar soft red walls of the Sound Room, taking my time in order to postpone just a little longer the next phase of my search for Rudy.

Since the obvious gesture of calling him directly had failed, and a tour of our shared dream world barely offered a hint of his existence, I assumed that Rudy had either forgotten about me, thanks to the miracle of my cloak of invisibility (and yes, I do chuckle each time I invoke the title), he was efficiently avoiding me for unknown reasons, or he was simply too busy doing battle with Freuzre to make himself available to me. I reasoned that the latter explanation held more veracity, especially if Rudy had gotten wind of my waning interest in joining his cause. He may also have been annoyed that I had stolen Max from him, I thought proudly, and that I had allowed her to unite with Mary without incident. None of that mattered: petty rationale or brief moments of pride had been eclipsed by my newfound sense of purpose. Though normally I would have accepted Rudy's chronic absence as a bit of luck portending less for me to deal with, I now felt a true need to find him. I wanted, for reasons honestly beyond my understanding, to define his interest in me, his place in the world, and his true intentions. I smiled at my thoughts, which were akin to dictating a mission statement for the CEO of a psychotic ward, but I did not care. Something substantial was finally lurking just beyond my reach, I knew it, and I actually possessed both the interest and means necessary to pursue it. I felt good.

I felt a little less good when I passed through the Sound Room door and into bright afternoon sunshine that poured unnaturally through the open ceiling above me. It whitewashed my basement in cheerful unwanted light. I swept away the debilitating feeling of violation with the rough bristles of purpose, and strode evenly to the stairs. I stopped at their base, remembering that they did not go anywhere. Instead of simply thinking myself to my garage, I walked on the floor of my basement toward the concrete steps that once served as the outside entrance to my house's basement. I crossed the smooth surface easily, my Ice Capades routine on Rudy's basement floor a distant memory, and climbed from my foundation with genuine indifference. I maintained that neutral stance when I noticed Joe and Lois Croft, who lived across the street, staring from their front porch in awe at my unlikely exit from my ruined house. I didn't offer a friendly wave. I just traversed my overgrown lawn and stepped through the back door of my yellow-bandaged garage. On the way I noticed that Rudy's house had been fully rebuilt, and appeared to be occupied by new residents. I am amazed by the speed with which people fill in the empty spaces around them in their drive to restore normalcy. I wondered if the only thing keeping humanity from seeping back into my yard was proof of

my demise. Now the fire sale of my property would be put off
even longer, or else the Crofts were in for a serious ethical
dilemma.

The Escort was prepared for my arrival, as expected. Its
engine was quietly idling, and the driver's side door hung open. I
got in without ceremony and backed out of the garage. In a matter
of minutes I was speeding south on Route Nine, headed for
Manhattan. That island was not my destination, I knew.

"Then where?" I said aloud. I had lamely hoped that the
car would magically know how to take me directly to Rudy, but
that was not happening. I was obliged to find him myself. In order
to fend off easy indecision inspired by my well-founded fear of
choosing the wrong path, I decided immediately that I should
begin the search for Rudy in the most obvious spot in the world.
That spot, I surmised, had to be in the Middle East, the area I was
sure Rudy would have labeled the epicenter of the world's strife – I
was sure he had never been to a Wal-Mart. I of course had also
never been to Jerusalem, but I had been raised Catholic, and had
seen enough of it on television to recognize it spread out below me
after I had crested a low hill just south of Ossining.

"Nice town," I said.

"Gorgeous," I heard from behind me, followed by a
surprised and familiar squeal. Startled, I skidded the car to a stop
on the desert road, nearly absorbing the rear end of a crowded tour
bus that then rushed past us, horn blaring. The force of the sudden
deceleration pulled Mary headfirst into the front of my car. Her
head flashed past me in a blaze of red before it landed solidly in
the passenger seat foot well. Her left thigh, thankfully clothed in
Capri pants this time, rested against my cheek. The rest of her legs
kicked in the air over the back seat in which she had been hiding.

"Mary!" I shouted, grabbing her legs to help her right
herself in the front passenger seat, "What the hell are you doing
here? I thought I told you to go home!"

"Yeah well I was gonna go home," Mary said to her lap,
"But after I woke up in your chair all alone and all I started to get a
little nervous and, well, I guess I just froze. I don't think I have a
home anymore, in Manhattan or on the Island; at least not one I'd
want to turn up suddenly at. So I hid in your car while I waited. It
let me in, so I figured that was a good sign, plus it seemed like the

safest place to be, because you got a lotta strange kids wandering your neighborhood."

"Tell me about it. So why didn't you tell me you were back there?"

"Why didn't you see me?" she asked, and then smiled, "I mean Jeez, it's just an Escort. All you had to do was turn your head a little bit."

"Point taken," I said, "But I must have been gone for days. You spent all that time in the car?"

"I got out to pee now and then. You got nice neighbors, by the way." My anger vanished. I thought I had recognized Mary's outfit as the one Marsha Olson wore all summer the previous year. I started the car moving toward Jerusalem again, and touched Mary's knee. Her inner strength must have diminished when magic, Max, and I no longer surrounded her. I forgave her temerity, or disinterest, in returning to the struggle that was her life. Though I still thought I needed her to be a lookout for me, I accepted that the glory to which she had been exposed might have made it fundamentally impossible for Mary to complete her assignment.

"Okay then," I said, "I guess you're with me for now."

"Cool! What're we doing?"

"Looking for Rudy to find out what he's doing, and then maybe try to stop him."

"From doing what?"

"I don't know yet."

"Oh. Will finding him be dangerous?"

"I sure hope not. Why do you ask?"

"I don't know. Just curious, I guess. Do you know where he is?"

"I think so. I had about given up, but then I had a sudden hunch, right out of the blue, that he would be where the most trouble is. So I headed here."

"There's trouble in Las Vegas?" Mary asked, surveying the desert city we rapidly approached, "I always thought that was a pretty neutral town."

"Las Vegas is. That's Jerusalem down there."

"Oh. That's different," Mary said pointedly, ignoring her geography skills, "Jerusalem's been a pretty nasty place for years. Ever since Godspell."

"Ever since," I agreed without humor. She was, after all, correct.

"So Bob," she said, scanning the city with her hand perpendicular to her forehead, though no glare had dared corrupt the Escort's windshield in weeks, "You got any kind of clue about where you might find Rudy in that mess?" Although we were still several miles away from its impoverished perimeter, we could see that Jerusalem was a very busy city. I sighed.

"Not a clue," I said, "I'm hoping that Rudy'll announce himself somehow."

"Yeah, that'd be nice. Maybe he'll be on another really huge motorcycle?"

"Let's look for something more subtle," I said. A ten-story Harley would have been most welcome. Like chaotic nature rising against my novitiate ability to twist reality, the crowded streets we approached seemed to rumble in the humidity's haze, ominously indicating that Mary and I were on the verge of becoming seriously lost. Mary, however, was innately incapable of being captured, deer-eyed, by the awe of the exotic location we approached. Instead, she pointed to a plume of black smoke that had been rising above the center of the ancient city since we had first crested the dented horizon.

"How about that black smoke over there?" she asked, her husky voice devoid of sarcasm, "Is that subtle?"

"Why yes," I said, rolling my eyes at the obvious discovery that I had overlooked, "Yes, that might be just what we're looking for. Do me a favor and turn on the radio. Let's see if there's anything being said about the smoke."

"Radio? Won't that be in the wrong language?" Mary hardly finished the question before she slapped her forehead with an open palm, and said, "Oh. Duh. They're all going to be in English, aren't they?"

"To us," I confirmed confidently. My assertion was vindicated when, after much fumbling with the radio's controls, Mary tuned in a news station that was reporting the story unfolding beneath the growing column of smoke. Apparently a bomb had been detonated in a shopping mall, obliterating a department store and the plaza it faced. The announcer had broken away from the variety show he was hosting to cover the carnage. He didn't know yet how many people had died, but the authorities were estimating in four digits. This bomb was huge, the announcer said, vastly more powerful than anything that the Palestinians had attempted in the past. The announcer breathlessly concluded that a blast of its proportion would redefine the conflict between Israel and the Palestinians, perhaps finally fomenting an all-out war. As he spoke, his tone wavered between unmasked terror and sincere confusion. This kind of attack by a Palestinian suicide bomber was foolhardy, selfish, and more damaging to both sides than any other single event in their tumultuous history. I shook my head slowly, said, "That was easy," and pointed the car toward the smoke.

When we passed through a massive ancient gate on the eastern side of the city, a gate whose stones were laid centuries before Rudy imagined he was born, we were immediately engulfed in the realized drama of the attack's aftermath. We were still at least a mile from the blast, but the streets were already crowded with people whose action ranged from rubbernecking curiosity to outright panic. Almost everyone was moving, mostly on foot and mostly toward us and away from the site of the blast. The only vehicles in motion were military. Trucks and armored personnel carriers, laden with angry soldiers, crossed our path or whizzed by us frequently. None tried to stop us until we reached the roadblock that had been set up about a half mile from the source of the billowing smoke that now filled the sky, blocking the high sun.

Two armored personnel carriers had been splayed across the street to block access to the still hidden scene of destruction. I observed that the space between them was wide enough to accommodate my Escort. I slowed the car, which had to that point only been moving at little more than a fast walking pace. We approached the roadblock. The soldiers manning it unshouldered their rifles and moved toward me.

"This should be fun," I said.

"Can't you use the force on them or something?" Mary asked, her quivering voice betraying her apprehension.

"Nope," I said, "I left Dagoba long before I could learn about Jedi mind control."

"Then how about we don't stop? This is a pretty tough car, you know."

"Now that is a good idea," I said, choosing not to tell Mary that I had already decided to thread my car between the parked armor.

We waved to the soldiers as we passed them, responding to their adamant shouts and leveled rifles with vapid smiles and shrugs of confusion. I hoped that this, coupled with the car's New York license plates, would convince the soldiers that we were just stupid Americans inadvertently placing themselves in harm's way, and we were not worth the effort of pursuit. I was wrong. Automatic weapon fire rained on the back of the car, and I saw one of the APC's jolt into motion in my mirror. Two more cars, a motorcycle, and a helicopter soon joined them.

"I guess jumping roadblocks is a pretty big deal in this burg," Mary observed.

"I guess."

The chase meandered through the narrow crowded streets at a slow pace. My horn and our pursuers' machine guns worked well to part the crowd before we contacted any bodies, but I still was unable to exceed twenty miles per hour for fear of bumping into the more cynical, or deaf, Israelis who held their ground until my front bumper was inches from their shins. Our path did remain clear, and we soon could see the flames from the burning store creeping around the edges of distant buildings. I expected a frontal assault at any moment, and was wondering why I had chosen to investigate the aftermath at the possible expense of Mary's life – and mine – when I noticed that our pursuers no longer filled my mirror, and that bullets had ceased their ineffective pounding of my rear window. The helicopter veered off and headed into the dusty sky.

"Hey," Mary said, "They gave up. Like they lost interest. Now why do you suppose they would do that?"

"I don't know," I said, "Why don't we ask him?"

"Who?" Mary said, looking at me. I lifted a finger off the wheel to point at a figure leaning against a lamppost on the next corner. His back was to the mayhem unfolding on the next block. His tan khakis and red bowling shirt were clean, his smile was fresh, and his thumb was out, as if he were a student looking for a lift to Cambridge, and not a wanton reality manipulator possibly responsible for the death that had formed his backdrop.

"Him," I said.

"Why?" she said. Then she recognized Rudy, sighed, and said, "Oh. Him."

"Yup. How about we give my old friend a ride?"

"Sure. It'll be nice to meet him at a normal size, too."

"Yeah, nice."

When we drew to within a few yards of Rudy, Mary's mood suddenly swung south. She gasped and grabbed my wrist with a force that nearly spun the steering wheel. I slowed the car to avoid jumping onto the crowded sidewalk, but held back my censure to Mary because she was already speaking.

"Bob, no," She said, her voice a panicked whisper, "We can't pick him up."

"Why the hell not?" I asked. I tried to sound defensive, but I did want to hear her warning. Mary/Max's instincts had already proven themselves formidable.

"This guy's bad, Bob," Mary said frantically, clutching my arm tightly, "We can't trust him."

"Alex, Mary, *Alex*," I said calmly, "Yes, I know we can't trust him, not yet, anyway. But we have to talk to him, if only to get a bead on Freuzre's activity."

"But *Alex*," Mary said sternly, pointing at the smoke, "I got this feeling that Rudy, he's the guy who brought that shit down. That freezer guy isn't even in town, I'll bet." I stopped the car about twenty yards from Rudy, who hadn't moved, or even acknowledged our approach. I turned to Mary. Her eyes were wide, her lips parted and stretched tight over clenched perfect white teeth that were once brown from years of smoking. She was sincerely shaken, breathing fast, and seemed ready to bolt from the car. I took my left hand from the wheel and gently laid it across her wrist.

"Mary," I said, "You may be right this time, but we have to pick him up."

"Why?"

"To get to the truth. Rudy is the only one who knows. Besides, he can probably do less harm to us here in the car with us than he can from a safe distance outside it, right?"

"I guess that's true," Mary said, her grip easing slightly.

"Good. Let's pick him up now before the authorities get interested in us again."

"Okay," Mary said. She looked in my eyes once, smiled, and then climbed into the back seat with surprising grace to make room for Rudy. I started the car moving again, pulled to another stop against the curb on which Rudy stood. He took no notice of us until I unlatched the passenger door from the inside and gestured for him to enter. Then he did a mild double take, acting surprised to see us, and fell into the car with enthusiasm. He slammed the door and I turned the car around. We left the city unmolested, and I drove toward the distant brown hills from which we had come. Rudy was silent for a while, no doubt waiting for me to start the conversation. I knew what my first words would be, though, so I withheld them. In time he decided to break the silence.

"Alex," he said, taking no notice of Mary, "Though I do appreciate your picking me up, I must ask why you came to Jerusalem, right at this moment."

"Why do you think?" I said, my eyes fixed on the dusty asphalt unwinding before me, "Did you do that?" My question was accompanied by a gesture toward the mirror, which was dark due to the spreading cloud over Jerusalem.

"Yes, I did," Rudy said without hesitation. I could feel Mary's feet lifting the springs of my seat, just to let me know that she was right.

"What the hell for?" I demanded, still concentrating my senses on the changing road while my intellect was rattled by Rudy's easy admission.

"Alex," Rudy said calmly, making no effort to conceal his patronizing tone, "I had to, and I can't easily explain why."

"How about you give it a shot? There must have been some clear reason to bump off a thousand people."

"More like two," Rudy mumbled, betraying for the first time a hint of anguish at what he had done. He continued more vocally, "Fine. I allowed this terrorist attack to succeed to the fullest expectations of the madman who ignited the truck bomb. Let's call it an attempt to thwart a far more destructive plan that Freuzre had in mind. The reaction by the civilized world to this attack will be speedy and without parity. It will also preempt plots by the bad guys to use weapons of mass destruction simply by raising the world's interest in the folks who want to deploy them."

"So you kill 2,000 people to prevent Freuzre from convincing someone like the Iraqis from lobbing a couple of nukes at Jerusalem?"

"Or any other large city on the globe. Yes, that's exactly why I let this happen."

"'Let?'" I asked, incredulous, "How about 'encouraged,' or 'caused?'"

"Those would work too."

"And this all is completely sane and rational to you?"

"Of course, and it should seem the same way to you," Rudy said, his tone one of dismissal. He was going to change the subject. I didn't mind; I wanted to continue discussing the bombing, and was insulted by Rudy's trivialization of the tragedy he induced, but I knew that I still had to play his game to best understand his motives. He turned toward me, still taking no notice of Mary, who was leaning forward in a tense crouch, her face inches from the front seatbacks. Rudy continued:

"But enough about this depressing big time shit," he said brightly, "How the hell have you been, Alex? If I knew that you could, I'd say that you've actually been avoiding me these last few weeks. What have you been up to?" He finished his question with a casual glance toward Mary. She whipped back into her seat.

"I've, we've, been fine, Rudy," I said tersely, "We've just been keeping to ourselves lately, because things have been getting a little out of hand, perhaps even a little beyond our understanding."

"'We've' been fine?" Rudy asked, shaking his head, "Who's we? Or are you just using the royal 'we' due to your newfound power?"

"All right, that's it," I said, stopping the car. I could feel an almost viscous anger well up inside me, tightening my throat and causing my hands to shake. I was confused by the influx of strong emotion, since Rudy was still operating within character. I would wonder later if his presence, and not his words, was the source of my anger, or if it was something, or someone else, but for the moment everything was aimed at Rudy. It needed to be. But I also

needed to be calm. I sighed heavily, turned to Rudy, and hung my
arm over his seatback. When I did, Mary held my hand lightly.
That helped steady me when I continued, "You've successfully
pulled my strings after just a few seconds, and you wonder why
I've been steering clear of your bullshit?"

"Is that what it is?" Rudy asked, placid, "Bullshit? Have
my loyal lieutenant and her idiot twin cowering in your back seat
completely buried you in their petty, ignorant blankets of fear?"

"Maybe they have," I said, not so placid, "And maybe I've
been weaving some blankets of my own without their help. I can
tell you this, though: these women haven't been playing games
with me. It wasn't they who dangled carrots like impossible power
and Cassie before me, sans explanation or follow-up."

"I think you're saying that I haven't been totally honest
with you," Rudy said, rubbing his forehead, "When was it that I
wasn't totally honest?"

"No," I said, "You've always been brutally honest with me,
Rudy. That's not your problem. Your problem lies in these games
that you play, that you think must be played. These games get a
kazillion people killed, and you don't care. They blow up my
house, my employer, and now thousands of innocents, and you
don't care. They twist my life into a bizarre pretzel, leave my dead
wife fluttering in the wind as a permanent lure, and you don't
care."

"What makes you think I don't care?" Rudy rumbled. The
power of his voice made my windshield rattle, and Mary gasp.

"Because I know you, Rudy. I've seen you care. I've seen
you react to the damage Freuzre causes. I saw you at Fritz's.
You're a great and powerful man, Rudy, you can care." Rudy did
not respond. Instead he stared straight ahead, silent, eyes open and
bereft of emotion or water. Having played poker with him a
hundred times, I could spot his tells easily: he was planning. I
reminded myself to whom I was talking, but opted to continue
acting without thinking. That was the only way that I could beat
Rudy in poker, and it seemed to be my only reliable action now. I
turned around to Mary, squeezed her hand. She did not have to
look at me, because I don't think her eyes left me since Rudy had
acknowledged her presence. She was waiting for instructions,
waiting for an excuse to leave. I gave her one.

"Mary," I said with an even voice, "It's time for you to get out."

"Huh?" Mary asked. She was confused, but her eyes brightened involuntarily at the prospect of getting away from Rudy. I missed the innocent abandon she enjoyed when she had assumed this was all a dream. I half hoped that she would wake up in her own bed the next morning, relieved that it was indeed all unreal.

"It's time for you to get out; of the car. Go home. Or go to a nice hotel. Get some sleep. Your purse is on the floor. It's full of cash and functional credit cards, I'm sure. Go home, or find yourself a new one, and I'll come back around as soon as I can."

"You're leaving me?" she asked, her plaintive tone real, but not powerful enough to quell her relief.

"Only for now. Rudy and I have some business to take care of."

"We do?" Rudy asked.

"We do. Now let Mary out, and please be sure to get back in after you do."

"No problem," Rudy said. He exited the car without a word, and even flipped the bucket seat forward to ease Mary's egress.

"How the hell am I supposed to get home?" Mary whispered, "I don't even know where Jerusalem is!"

"Don't worry about it," I said, "You'll do just fine."

"But," Mary said, pointing out the window. Then she sighed, rolled her eyes, and said, "Oh. You know I'll never get used to this."

"Me neither," I smiled. I pulled her toward me, gave her a peck on the cheek, and said, "Now you take good care of yourself, Mary Mary. And keep those pretty green eyes open for me." She flashed a glance in my mirror before protesting the eye color, and nodded. Then she held her head very close to mine, looked right in my eyes, and said:

"Alex, I want you to be careful. If you get yourself killed, you know Max and I will hunt you down wherever you are and kill you."

"Only you can make a sentence like that work, Mary. Don't worry. I'll be as careful as I can be. Now get out before

Rudy gets tired of waiting and we have to go looking for him all over again."

"Okay," Mary said. She suddenly thrust her head forward that last few inches and stole a long, passionate kiss from me. When we parted she hit the side of my head with her open palm and said, "You be careful. Too many of us have fallen in love with you to lose you to the devil here. Okay?"

"Okay. I promise."

"Good," she said, not smiling. She picked the Gucci bag up from the floor at her feet, stared at it in awe for an immeasurable instant, and then left the car without glance at Rudy. She crossed Times Square, walking quickly in a direction away from the ratty movie theater in front of which we were parked. Rudy got back in the car, shut the door. He was wearing leather pants a matching jacket over his white T-shirt.

"Nice girl," Rudy said.

"And packed with wisdom."

"I'm sure. What now?"

"Gee Rudy, are you actually allowing a ball to fall in my court?"

"Alex, how many times must I say that you're worth it?"

"Oh, please," I said before entering the near trance of concentration necessary to travel anywhere successfully, with the possible exception of New York. Rudy remained silent as well, allowing me without sarcasm or advice to conjure my next move. I carefully avoided thinking, or attempting to invoke power that I knew I could not control, and instead focused on repositioning us in a place where our upcoming conversation would affect as few innocent souls as possible. While I cruised a morning-sun splashed Broadway, I raced through my memory for an arena that would keep Rudy, or Freuzre, should he join us, from causing damage to innocents. I thanked myself for wasting all that time in front of the tube watching the Discovery Channel, and made a right turn off Broadway.

"So where are we going?" Rudy asked conversationally. He seemed his old pleasant self, outwardly interested in nothing at all, and content with all things exposed to him.

"South," I said curtly, unwilling to even think of our destination, much less tell Rudy.

"Okay," Rudy said slowly, "South is good." He produced a pair of Ray Bans from his breast pocket, flipped them open with a flourish and set them on his nose. I ignored the gesture.

We fell into silence while I concentrated on images I had seen only on TV, and in National Geographic Magazine. I followed the West Side Highway north to the George Washington Bridge, waited patiently in gridlocked traffic that I was sure I could circumvent with a little reality twist. Rudy must have hated my reticence, but he kept any objections to himself. We eventually reached the bridge, and traffic speed picked up once the freedom of New Jersey and its very wide turnpike beckoned. We never reached the Garden State, however. The mighty steel of the George Washington Bridge had faded to dusty rope before we were halfway across the Hudson River. A disturbing rattle of loose boards replaced the steady rhythm of asphalt and expansion joints under the tires. I risked a glance out my side window to admire the dry arroyo over which we passed, then looked ahead to be sure we exited the narrow ramshackle bridge, lost a century ago to southern Chile history, safely.

We did, and then we drove for a few more miles across an empty, flat gray desert devoid of any memorable features or discernable life. When the terrain was identical for as far as I could see in all directions, I stopped the car. I knew Rudy was looking at me, so I was careful to look left while I got out of my car. I stood outside the Escort for about five minutes, waiting for Rudy. I was patient, and happy to have a moment to admire the vista that I had represented through my own effort and logic. It was an amazingly empty place, reminiscent of my Purple Plain, with two glaring exceptions. First, it was not purple, but gloriously colored in every shade of gray, white, and blue imaginable, and second, because I could not avoid the one notion I knew must not enter my awareness: that this plain lacked the magical potential with which my purple plain seethed. The familiar creek of the Escort's passenger door announced Rudy's movement into my arena. I did not turn around. I heard Rudy's footsteps in the sand, a sound he probably had to add to his repertoire for my benefit, but still did not acknowledge him. When he was standing beside me, scanning the empty horizon broken only by distant mountains, I did not look his way. I knew now how easy it was to be enthralled and weakened by Rudy, so I did not look. I needed every watt of energy available to me for the next phase of a plan that I had yet to even consider, so I did not look. In time Rudy shuffled his feet, cracked his knuckles, and spoke softly:

"So now what?"

"Now?" I said, turning to him and looking directly into his ageless gray eyes, "Now we talk."

Chapter Twenty-Five

The warm breeze was unruffled by the sudden departure of my Escort. I was shaken, but I suppressed the wave of anxiety that struck when I knew that my car was suddenly and simply not there. Understanding and accepting its absence was not an impossible task, since I was the one who had willed it. Removing the car was actually easier to do than making the decision to do it: it was my last link to the mundane world, my first affirmation of power in it, and its removal from Rudy's shadow was a necessary sacrifice. I had to show Rudy that I was on my own in this, with no handy armor or escape vehicles nearby. It was a trust issue, and I hoped Rudy understood.

"Nice touch," Rudy said, breaking the silence that defined the long, brooding pause ironically created by my announcement of our need to communicate. He dropped his Ray Bans into a breast pocket and strolled across the space my car had occupied. I avoided the fear that he would bump into it, revealing that the car was not actually gone but just invisible, by swallowing hard and pushing the image from my mind. I was still sure that merely thinking such things might make them real. Rudy sighed slowly, and then thrust his hands deep in his pockets to form his upper body into a sort of shrug.

"I can't say why, but this place – we're in Chile, aren't we? I thought so – this place reminds me of that trip the three of us made to Jones Beach a few years ago. Remember?"

"Yeah, I remember. There were a few more people around there, though. Listen Rudy – "

"I thought you would. Do you remember that you didn't want to go? Some nonsense about the crowds, the drive, the wet ocean, or all three?"

"All three, I'd imagine" I said, letting him play his hand.

"I'm sure. And you were right. The traffic was a nightmare in both directions, there wasn't an unoccupied square yard on the beach, and the water, which you spent half the day cavorting in, was indeed wet."

"And cold," I confirmed. What's your point, Rudy?"

"No point. Just a memory. A good one, I think. Cassie shined that day, didn't she?"

"She did use a lot of suntan oil."

"You know what I mean, Alex. And you know what else? It meant something. There we were, surrounded by the thing you profess to hate most in life, a gigantic herd of human cattle lolling in its own laziness on the shores of a semi-clean ocean, and you were happy."

"I was, wasn't I? If I wasn't, would you have blown them up too?"

"If I had to," Rudy said softly, eyes dead on mine, "I would have."

"And that doesn't bother you?"

"Should it? Haven't I already proven to you, and you to yourself, that we are so much more than the gooey sacks in which we choose to spend a shallow century on the physical plain?"

"No, Rudy, you haven't. And neither have I," I held his gaze, and let the words flow from me without thinking about them first:

"Who the hell are you to mess with the decisions of 2,000 souls? If they choose to live, or die, then they do, on their own time. We can't realign people's destinies, or shatter their dreams, no matter how mundane, just because we can!"

"Even if we're right?" Rudy asked.

"Even then."

"Even if their dreams, ambitions, and aspirations suck?"

"Especially then."

"Dude," Rudy said, shaking his head, "You got it bad."

"I got what bad?" I could feel the tips of my fingers tingling.

"Humanity. Think about it. You've been given access to the World, to perfect freedom and creativity, to permanent contact with your soul and the souls of others, and all you worry about is the dust from which you came."

"And the dust of others, which I have no right to churn," I said. Rudy ignored the interjection, and continued:

"You're obsessed with your roots, Alex. Hell, you're still driving a Ford, for Christ's sake. If you just made the attempt to break away, to become that to which you aspire, you would see that a few shattered physical lives don't amount to much."

"Mary was right. You are a monster."

"Only from her water-borne perspective. In reality, I'm a hero. A savior."

"A demon."

"Oh," Rudy said, absently cracking his knuckles, "Is this where we part ways philosophically, and the conflict ensues?"

"That already happened, *dude,*" I said, stepping back a few feet, "Your ego was just too damn thick to notice."

"Oh, I am hurt, Alex," Rudy said, "Not by your words, but by your sheer idiocy. You have a natural talent that can reshape the world – "

"In your image?"

"Perhaps. But you have it, the talent. And you're too much the simpering human to do anything about it."

"That," I said, "Was the nicest thing you've said so far," I said, "I'm happy to consort with these confused, often stiflingly stupid people because, in truth, I'm one of them. And so are you."

"Am I?" Rudy said, raising an eyebrow. For him, that was practically a shout. I tensed, preparing for the onslaught, but he had more to say: "Am I really? Maybe once, ten centuries back, I still clung to my status as a card-carrying prisoner of the planet. That was a long time ago. A very long time."

"Please," I said with honest distaste, "I know, *really*, how long it's been." Rudy reacted to my words by abruptly stepping forward and parking his face a few inches from mine. My horizon became Rudy's bottomless gray eyes framed by ageless crow's feet and nothing more. Feeling my spine and knees giving way to primal fear that only a god could summon, I strained physically to hold my position. Rudy stared into my eyes as if he were mapping my retinas, and then he spoke in a hoarse whisper that I had never before heard emanate from him:

"Do you? Do you really know? Or do you only know what those stooges, *my stooges,* told you? Think about it."

"No need," I whispered back with difficulty, "I believe them." To my relief Rudy strode away from my words and turned his back to me. I could enjoy the respite from terror for only an instant, though, because he vented his frustration with a long preternatural scream that rolled off the distant mountains and rattled my fillings. When it subsided I continued, for the sake of my own skin and to maintain my projected bravado, by saying, "What? Does that bother you? Why would it? Surely the sincerity of your own pawns must be a reflection of your own power, your own perfect success. Right?"

"Yeah sure," Rudy said, looking down, "Right. Assuming that you're not overestimating the power of my own will."

"Or your servants' *free* will," I finished for him. I did not expect my glib response to deliver much meaning to Rudy, but somehow it did. He visibly folded into himself for several seconds, his eyes closed, his normally elusive emotions completely obscured. I decided to interpret his reaction as a momentary lapse of humanity, and stepped toward him. When I had closed the distance between us to an arm's length I stopped, and laid my left hand on his left shoulder. I concealed my right hand, which was balled in a tight fist, behind my back. Rudy did not respond to my touch, but I knew he was there, with me on all the necessary levels, so I asked the question:

"Rudy, tell me," I said to the back of his head, "Is there an end to all of this? Your battle with Freuzre, your 'use' of Cassie, your endless attempts to recruit me into your army, your complete disregard for the people you and Freuzre have vaporized. Will you close the door on it all, and leave us 'prisoners' to our own often misguided fortune?"

His reply was very long in coming, but after several minutes Rudy twitched slightly and his lips parted with a tiny fleshy click. Then he spoke, softly, without opening his eyes:

"Alex, Alex, Alex. What on God's green earth are you asking me? And with such sincerity, too! Who do you get your information from? Max? Clive? *Cassie*? Whoever's been supplying it is extremely confused. Trust me." He opened his eyes and spun to face me. He was the old Rudy, littered with sincerity and depth. He continued:

"No. Really. Trust me. Me. Not them. Centuries of caring about this complicated, duplicitous world have led me to this spot, this moment with you. Not my ego, or ill-gotten power, or even the will of Freuzre; just hard work and compassion. I mean it. No matter what they tell you, I am in this for them all. For you, too. I will grant that I'm truly frustrated, and maybe slightly humiliated, by the fact that you can play my game without even reading the rulebook, much less showing up for practice. But in the end I recognize the value of your innate talents, and beg you once more to join me in my struggle to get the World spinning at its proper speed once more."

"Your struggle?" I asked, wondering if he had processed that thought in German.

"Excuse my usage. It's not just mine. It's ours, theirs, everyone's who suffers for good. Freuzre has us all by the short hairs, and we need your help in curbing his evil plans. I need you. Cassie needs you."

"What about Max?" I asked, risking his discovery of my love for her. I quickly added more, to better help him overlook my syrupy tone, "And Cassie doesn't need shit. She's dead, and she has been in that irreparable condition for three years."

"Liar!" Rudy shouted, his cry a peel of echoing thunder. Whoa, I thought, now where did that come from? No matter: if high volume was a tell betraying Rudy's pain from raw nerves I had exposed and pinched, then all the better for me. Rudy began to pace, taking a half dozen strides to my right before turning around and marking a dozen in the other direction. He repeated the drill exactly, retracing his footprints, while he spoke in an enraged staccato, never once looking at me:

"Cassie is not dead! I know that, and so do you. I have shown her to you, and you personally have forced her to stand before you, in the flesh. Hell, you even killed her again once, or so I hear, and still she wandered back into the fold. She won't die, Alex. Not as long as I want her around."

"Don't you mean as long as 'you' want her around?" I asked, catching his gaff. My comment didn't help his mood. I noticed black clouds forming on the horizon. My clenched fist tingled again.

"You know what I mean," he said. I did, but kept it to myself. Rudy finally looked at me before he continued, "Alex, I have to ask you one more time. Please, give it some real thought this time, not another empty dismissal. Join me in the fight. Become one with the World. Abandon the dirt of the mundane. Look to the big picture. Do it, and I'll give you Cassie."

"You'll give me Cassie?" I asked, tense, "Is she yours to give?"

"Of course."

"And you would really lose her to me again?" I asked. Rudy stopped pacing. He faced me, his eyes possibly wet.

"What?"

"Rudy. You hide your love for my dead wife about as well as you prop up your sincerity whenever you deliver your 'join me in the World' spiel. Sometimes I think you want her more than I ever did. And sometimes I wonder about that oven."

"Alex, I – "

"Never mind," I said, noting his confusion, "And please stop asking me to join you. I might have it all wrong, but I finally do have it. I know what to do, and who to avoid. I know that my power, my soul, is sourced in the dirt you so despise. And I know, for certain, that Cassie is dead. And that you can never have her." Ouch. Rudy moved back to my face, and began speaking in a paced monotone, as if softly reciting sentences he had been rehearsing for years:

"Have her? Is that all you think that I want? To have some frigid bitch who would barely give me the time of day while she breathed wasted air? No. I wanted more, so much more. I worked for centuries, dedicating lifetimes to mindless meditation while I perfected my craft. I gave up everything to have the power to change, to create, to help the ungrateful herds of humanity hopelessly indisposed to folly, hatred, and destruction. Everything. I sacrificed it all. I have never been in love, never been married, and never fathered children. I couldn't, because I had purpose. I had to focus every fiber of my being on becoming one with the World. They all needed me. Humanity was a disease spreading across the face of the earth, unwary of its own power and ultimate fate. I knew, centuries ago, that I could form that disastrous destiny into something good. So what happens when at last I make my final push, achieve my status at the right hand of all there is?

"You happen. You were born to the World. Shit, you were flipping me in your dreams like a McDonalds hamburger before you could talk. It was almost like God Himself placed you squarely in my path, just to mock my efforts. But I knew I had to stay on that path, my path, so carefully formed that it begged my tread. I decided years ago that you must exist for a reason. Your easy control of reality, your effortless contact with your soul, must be a tool meant to augment my struggle. And it did, too, until you started to wake up from the dream.

"Remember Fritz's? Remember all those bodies? They were my friends, those bodies, or as close to friends as my path would allow. I sacrificed them for you, simply because I raised my profile by speaking to you personally. You think your friends, as you now consider them, at Beaver Toys would be dead today if you hadn't joined me sooner? Well, old friend, they wouldn't be, because they only died to take your mind off the useless crap for which you believed you were living."

"Rudy," I interrupted, my voice shaking in time with my reeling mind, "Tell me you didn't – "

"Oh, I did," He said, his monotone unflinching, "I did. And I must admit it smarted. What else could I do? Your perfect connection with the World was required, you wouldn't come on your own, so I simply tried to coax you with a little patriotic fervor."

"You heartless bastard," I whispered, my fear overwhelmed by fury that Rudy had allowed Nancy to die in order to sustain an argument.

"Yeah," He said, "Maybe. But it was for a good cause."

"A good cause?" I shouted, "You idiot! Has your psychosis clouded your vision so completely? The 'cause' was the continued flotation of your own self-esteem! Nothing more. You needed to win my allegiance so you could still be the best. You took Cassie from me, you son of a bitch, you killed hundreds to make me unemployed, but you still couldn't overshadow me. And I never knew! What an asshole I was for ever even speaking to you!"

"Maybe," Rudy repeated calmly, still two inches from my face and disregarding the spittle my words had spattered on his, "Maybe you're right. I never quite saw it that way; I probably never will. But maybe you're wrong, and maybe I am a power for good."

"For good," I sighed, "I wish you would stop using that phrase before you completely melt its meaning into a cliché of empty permanence. For good. Tell me again why you obliterated that mall in Jerusalem."

"You know what I said," he obliged, "I had to up the stakes in Freuzre's endless conflicts. The cattle needed to stampede now, thus preventing the greater slaughter that was promised if they continued mindlessly chewing their cuds in the paddock."

"Nice analogy; or, rather, a nice recitation of a tired old comparison," I said, "Are you sure you didn't toast that mall because you knew it would get my attention?" Rudy stepped back. I could feel the air crackling around him as its fundamental atoms rattled under the influence of his power. I swallowed, wondered if I had taken the conversation too far, but held my gaze firmly on him and waited for a reply.

It never came, at least not in the form of words. Without warning, Rudy shifted to attack mode. He grimly tilted his head and the ground split open beneath me. I stepped back a pace, in time to see a bottomless crevasse form in the desert floor. When the ripping ceased, Rudy stood on the far side of the tiny canyon, about five feet from my position at its near edge, and the crack stretched to the horizon in both directions. Rudy pointed to the crack, then to me, his eyes as cold as ever.

"Now that," I laughed, truly amused, "Is about as cliché as you could get. You're daring me to cross your line in the sand, aren't you? How insufferably human!" Rudy failed to fall prey to my insult, but he did betray a flash of shock when the desert surface returned to its original featureless condition. He rested his hands on his hips, smiled, and said:

"Then that's it, then."

"I guess so," I said, resisting a powerful urge to close my eyes.

"Good-bye, Alex," He said with a flutter in his tone that I would always believe signified love. For a blessed instant I hoped that he had had an epiphany of human goodness, and was taking his leave of me to sort out what he had done. But then I heard the train whistle.

I looked down and saw that my feet were bolted firmly to two railroad ties. The parallel steel rails that crossed those ties were singing. I looked to my left and saw nothing but empty desert. I looked forward, and saw Rudy passively looking to his left. So, I slowly swung my head to my right, and saw the freight train approaching. I couldn't see the whole train, since the track was straight and the front of the engine concealed the tonnage it pulled, but I knew that there was at least a mile of steel behind it. Not that it mattered. The first few inches would normally do the trick. I looked back at Rudy. He stepped out of harm's way and folded his arms. I turned my attention to the approaching steel. The train was a few hundred yards away, its air horn blaring. Then I smiled at Rudy.

"Please," I shouted over the din of the approaching train, "Could you at least try to be subtle?" Without removing my eyes from his, I lifted my right foot when the fierce volume and vibration of the locomotive indicated it was just a few ties away. Never doubting, I lowered my foot onto the tiny model train that was passing on plastic tracks beneath it, crushing it. The toy disappeared on contact.

"Subtle?" Rudy said, inspecting his fingernails, "Yeah, I can do that."

I was gasping for air before I realized that Rudy had swung again. Nothing had changed around us, except that my lungs were empty. I was in a vacuum. Okay, I thought as my chest heaved painfully for absent oxygen, that's pretty subtle. But such a tactic could only work on those whose existence was founded only in the physical world. After my initial instinctive reaction passed, I reminded myself that my sustenance drew power from sources other than earth-bound molecules. I ignored the vacuum, breathed deeply, and obviously for Rudy's edification, and then decided that it was time to test my own imagination, time to take the offensive.

A giant raven, with a fifty-foot wingspan, swooped in low over Rudy's head. He ignored it splendidly, but could not ignore the half-ton of guano the bird dumped on his head as it flew by.

Rudy parted the sticky gray stuff from his face, and actually smiled through the scum.

"How symbolic of you, Alex," he said as his face and body returned to their usual cleanly form, "But you gotta hurt more than my feelings."

"I know, I know," I said, "How's this?" Before the question was out, two mammoth claws dug deeply into Rudy's shoulders and hoisted him into the air.

"That's much better," Rudy shouted to me from high overhead. The bird continued to rise with him until both disappeared from my sight. The sky was clear for a moment before I spotted a black Lear Jet, its nose painted yellow, finishing its approach to the desert floor about a mile away. It landed gracefully, and then taxied over to my position. Its passenger door swung open, and Rudy stepped out, flanked by two half-naked, buxom, blonde, and drunken stewardesses. That is a telling image, I thought. He kissed them both, then stepped off the plane. It vanished behind him as he crossed to within a few feet of me.

"Much better," he said. Then he waved a hand, and finished the flourish by pointing casually toward a cloud of dust that had formed on the horizon. "Now we play for real," he said, smiling broadly.

The rare show of teeth by Rudy was nearly enough to deplete my interest in what roiled those acres of sand. Only nearly: my racing heart realigned my senses. I thought as quickly as I could but could muster only one parry before the dust had begun to envelop me. In the instant before I moved, I could see clearly into the gritty haze, and was relieved that I had decided to shift my position rather than face the nightmare Rudy offered. Or, nightmares – Rudy had opted to be literal with this attack, sending a thousands-strong herd of dead horses to do his bidding. They represented every stage of decay, from recently dead bloody monsters to bleached skeletons. None had riders, but all had backlit red eyes focused upon me. I saw all of these details in a flash, and then, as planned, the horses, and Rudy, were a mile away from me. After I stepped aside the stampede vanished, leaving the tiny figure of Rudy in the distance.

Alone on the empty desert, Rudy appeared vulnerable, but I could glean no comfort from the image, especially because he immediately became life-sized, and just a few feet away. Rudy was back, and I felt that I hadn't moved at all. In fact, I had a queasy feeling that he had scrolled the land beneath me, in its entirety, to bring me back to him.

"Unsettling, isn't it?" Rudy asked. Then he was gone. I imagined that he did not want to get wet.

Neither did I, and my brain raced to conjure a painless retreat from the ten story tall wall of water that was closing on me from all sides. Shifting my position in reality (I tried everything from a few yards to a small church in Connecticut I oddly remembered) no longer worked. Rudy must have had a counter to that maneuver in place. I tried flying, like in a dream, but either my concentration was failing me, or Rudy's anti-Alex-position-shift spell worked in all directions.

"Come on Rudy," I screamed, "I'm not bright enough for this!" But then, seconds before the water crashed down on me with the wallop that only a few million tons of liquid muscle collapsing, iris-like, from each of 360 degrees onto one point can make, I had a bizarre thought. With the thought, a tidy pair of stainless steel elevator doors appeared in front of me. They slid open with a pleasant ding that I was surprised to be able to hear above the roar of the approaching seas. I stepped inside, turned, and pushed the only button on the panel. It had no label, and I had no choice except to trust it. The elevator dinged again, and the doors slid closed. Okay, I thought, I may not be bright enough for this test, but something is definitely keeping me healthy here.

An eye-rolling Musak rendition of "Dream a Little Dream," plastic wood, and pale white light comprised my universe for about a minute. I felt no motion, but for obvious reasons I assumed that the elevator had done its job. I was at the point of wondering when the doors would open again when, of course, they did. I stepped out, my mechanical savior was gone, and Rudy and I were back on the plain where we started.

"Nice work," he said, arms folded, legs wide, "But don't expect that elevator to be in service any more today."

"It'll work if I want it to work?" I said. The words were supposed to emerge rippling with defiance, but they instead spewed forth as a question. Ah, well, I thought, there goes my credibility. I was flustered not only by the magnitude of Rudy's initial thrusts, but also by his new costume. It was all black, with leather pants, a leather vest, and a black silk shirt open to the waist with billowing sleeves comprising enough wispy silky fabric to clothe a small town. I had to comment:

"Nice outfit. You dancing on Star Search, or just going to a Stevie Nicks concert?" I winced slightly, expecting a very physical response to my sarcasm. There were no giant hammers from hell, or hungry dragons, or even those nasty agents from The Matrix.

"Ha ha," was all I got. Rudy had remained calm. Then he rubbed his new goatee with one hand, displaying an inch-long pinky nail that sported a chrome manicure. I had insulted his wizard outfit, and I sensed that he would not humbly let my arrogance slide. My mind was blank, my skinny repertoire of tricks ran thin, so I simply waited for him to move again. Instead he spoke, "Alex. I'm going to try one last time. You're my best friend, and I owe you that. You have the potential to change the world, for good. But you can only do so by my side. Join me, please." His visage returned to the form of my next-door neighbor, with perhaps a little Vaseline on my lens. I didn't bite.

"Or?" I asked.

"Or," Rudy smiled, his face returning to the Typical Wizard format he had established moments earlier, "I sadly will need to erase you from my World before you do anymore inadvertent harm to my plans."

"Tough choice," I said, hands on hips, voice cracking, and knees rebelling, "But I guess you'd best find a really big pencil." Oh, real bright, I thought, give the man ideas. I strained my peripheral vision to spot a giant inverted #2 without taking my eyes off the ersatz wizard before me. Rudy just sighed, shook his head, and turned his disco back to me.

"Okay then," he said, "Can't say I didn't try. Goodbye Alex. It was more than entertaining knowing you."

I braced myself, my mind racing to prepare defenses to all the attacks I already knew that Rudy could muster. I had very little knowledge or experience, but my confidence in my connection to whatever astral forces flexed the universe's muscles was nearly without bounds. I would be ready for his fire, his vacuum, his tornados, and even multiple nuclear weapons if he chose to toss them. I heard a distant seismic tremor to my right. I wouldn't take my eyes off Rudy, though. I was sure he was the real threat. He helped me by turning to face me, teeth aglow, pointing toward the sound to my right, and then vanishing. Released, I turned to prepare for the next round.

"Well Rudy," I said out loud, "Your imagination is borderline useless, but at least the delivery is always awesome." I was going to whistle, but chivalry prevented me. Chivalry, and the fact that I did not want to offend the 300-foot-tall woman that was approaching me from under the low afternoon sun.

The woman was, of course, Cassie. She was nude, save for a filmy sarong that hung loosely from her slender hips. It did not cover much of her anatomy as it flapped gently in the desert breeze, but it probably comprised enough material to house a circus. Her skin was oiled, her breasts shimmered as they shook with each gargantuan step, and her legs simply dominated the scene. It was Cassie, all right, just the way I remember her from that vacation in Barbados. I think she was about 25 then, and at the peak of her beauty. Oh, Rudy, I thought, this attack is a greater betrayal to your nature than it is a monster to mine.

I had a serious problem kneading any apprehension initially, because the vision restored more warm feelings, and heated blood, than it did worry me. That changed when Cassie was within a few hundred yards of me and reminded me of the scale of her presence. I could also see then that she took no notice of me, or anything else in her environment. I guessed that this was not the Cassie I had left in Dreamland, but merely a projection, albeit a really big projection, of a particularly lewd memory that Rudy had stored in his broken mind. I wondered what a projection could do to me, especially if it could not see me. Big as she was, I was still fairly certain that I could avoid Cassie simply by stepping out of the way. Then the unexpected happened.

Cassie stopped moving about fifty yards away from me. She unwrapped the sarong, snapped it once in the breeze with a sound akin to a child bursting a balloon inside my ear, and then laid it out like a towel on the desert floor, and on me. Before I could react, I was engulfed in tons of bright fabric woven with threads as thick as my wrist. A couple of those threads caught my shoulder and back, striking like hammer blows. I was thrown to my knees. The sarong settled around me, stirring a choking cloud of dust as it rumbled to the desert floor. The distance between the weave was enough for me to wriggle through, so I avoided being pinned by the giant scarf. What I would not avoid, however, was the approach of Cassie's naked buttocks. She was sitting down, just like she had that day on the beach. I was still in too much awe of the imagery to muster real fear, but a part of me knew that I would be crushed in a very real way if that particular part of Cassie's anatomy landed on the ground and I did nothing but watch like a slack-jawed adolescent.

So I moved, in the only direction that I could. I dove for the crease between Cassie's thighs just before she landed with an earth-rending crash all about me. I was temporarily safe, a few feet from her crotch, surrounded by rippling thighs, and quite pleased that Cassie had shaved that day. I was also glad that Rudy's voyeurism was simply visual, and that he hadn't subjected me to magnified scents as well. Very glad, given my current position. That position, though more pleasant than I think Rudy had intended, was also still fraught with danger. Cassie had to merely shift her weight and I would be crushed like a crab. No, not a crab, I corrected, a bug. God, I thought, this situation is twisting me big time.

With that admission I snapped my fingers in a minor expression of eureka. Hell, that was it, I realized. Twisted is as twisted does. I hoped that Rudy was as accurate as I believed he would be with his giant Cassie doll, and headed for her clitoris like a marine at Iwo Jima. I was there in three steps, and stood in silent awe for a moment. I could easily fit between the slightly pouting lips, and had to resist an embarrassing urge to try. Instead, I reminded myself that one vaginal fart and I was through, finished paying my respects to the magnificence before me, and put my right hand on the huge pink ridge. I knew just the spot, and I had a revolting feeling that Rudy did, too (though his experience was from a distance). I placed my left hand on top of the right, and pushed against it with all my might.

Instantly, Cassie leaped to her feet in a rush of sand, sarong, and acres of oily flesh. Her squeal was familiar even in its titanic amplification. I ran like hell. While running, I looked behind me to be reassured that Cassie was moving off in search of a less invasive spot, and also perhaps just to look. In a moment she was gone, and I was alone on the plain. I spun around a few times in the fading sunlight, looking for Rudy.

"You're a sick, sick man, Rudy," I shouted to the distant mountains, "But if that's the best you can offer, then keep it coming. I'm ready."

A voluminous white cloud appeared above me. It split vertically, like great vaporous curtains parting, and a blinding white light flashed down on me from the opening that resulted. A cartoon image of a typical bearded-old-man God peeked from behind the clouds. It spoke with the requisite booming voice:

"Ready? You cannot even grasp the concept."

"Oh, God," I shouted, "That's pretty fucking trite, Rudy. And you'd better be careful about Who you're mimicking there; you don't want to piss off the wrong folks."

"The wrong folks are already angered," the God caricature boomed, "And their anger will be avenged by your death."

"Bring it on, big fella," I shouted, my words once more sounding like a question.

"Fine," God said. Then He, and the cloud He rode in on, disappeared. I was alone again. I took the moment to steady my breathing, relax a bit, and to attempt to prepare my mind for its next defense. If the show so far was all Rudy could produce, I knew I had a chance. He might have the experience and the will necessary to produce more scary weapons than I could, but I sensed that he lacked my natural power. I did wished I had a better ability to tap that power, but I hoped that my current grasp of it might be enough to hold off Rudy until he was fatigued enough to allow me to subdue him.

"Or not," I concluded sullenly upon spotting Rudy's latest thrust. It was a mountain, or rather a two or three-mile wide segment of the range that formed the distant eastern border of the plain. Rudy had split the land around it, releasing the animated mountain from its roots. It was moving toward me at a rate that had to approach the speed of sound, because initially I couldn't hear it. When I did, I wished I hadn't. The sound, only a harbinger of its more substantial source, was by itself overwhelming. It shattered my thoughts and threatened my physical ability to summon a defense. When the foothills of the moving mountain were close enough to display their boulder-toothed bluffs, I found myself thinking that it might not have been so bad to be crushed between Cassie's thighs.

Chapter Twenty-Six

"This is your best shot?" Lara Croft shouted from her position at the co-pilot's seat of Edgar Rice Burroughs's Iron Mole, "I can't even steer this thing!" Since Lara was a computer animation inexplicably lending me a hand, I was talking to myself when I replied:

"Hey, I was under a little pressure."

"Yeah, well, we're about to be under a whole mountain's worth of pressure. Let's hope this Victorian beast works like it did in the movie." I shared her concern, but had to do more than hold out hope for success. It was my confidence in my connection to reality that was keeping me afloat, or preventing my burial, and that confidence needed to be at a pinnacle in a few seconds. After that, a few billion tons of rock would be testing my 'connection,' and my resolve.

"Edwardian beast, I think, but never fear," I said with mock British reserve, "Fire up the reactors, and we'll simply tunnel through that exaggerated molehill as it passes over."

"Roger. This thing has reactors?"

"Hell, I don't know. Just get that corkscrew thing out front spinning, and we'll be fine."

"Oh. Roger."

Lara got it spinning by reaching her cartoon hands above her to turn a series of valves and flip some toggles that were attached to the ceiling. A loud mechanical noise began to compete with the din of the approaching mountain. I could see from the movie footage displayed in the iron-framed video monitor at my side that the machine was functioning. Its conical screw began spinning with proper cliffhanger timing by reaching operating speed with the mountain's foothills only yards away. When we dove into those small hills – we didn't actually dive: we were stationary and the mountain was moving past us – I dared to flirt with the conclusion that my half-witted last-instant solution might work.

"Nice to know you're flirting with something around here," Lara sighed.

I had no time to retort that my shyness extended even to computer graphics before the mountain proper reached the Iron Mole. In a few seconds that were stretched into hours by the magnitude of the event, the mountain rolled over us, and squashed the ancient burrowing machine like a bug.

And not a like crab at all, I thought without humor as I was tossed about the shattering cockpit. A steel bulkhead broke from its riveted seam and slammed without mercy on my leg. Pinned to the deck by the displaced wall, I closed my eyes in animalistic defeat and prepared myself for the oblivion that would accompany my ultimate pulverization.

In time the cacophony faded, and the only sound I sensed was a curious electrical crackle, augmented by what I was sure was plaster falling from a short height. Guessing that dead people hear loftier notes than those upon admission to the Great Beyond, I reopened my eyes and looked around. Lara had been deleted, but the interior of the Iron Mole was secure, aside from my bulkhead and a few random sparks. Then I smiled, remembering that the hero of those old movies never died in the first reel.

"No," I said aloud, perhaps to the broken bulkhead, "They just get hurt real bad so they can be extra heroic in the second reel." I finished by shouting loud enough to override the spreading pain, "And why all this steel? I thought these sets were plywood!"

After the series of visceral sensations that accompanied my relief at not being dead, my acknowledgement of the real pain that accompanied my crushed leg, and the sheer idiocy of picking an ancient science fiction movie as source material toward fending off Rudy the Dream Wizard and His Trained Mountain, Spike, I remembered who I was, where I was, and that I had proven to possess the power to mostly deflect wandering mountains. I boldly sought to reenter the fray before that mindset seeped once more from my battered psyche.

I was not prepared to mount an offensive yet, but I could extricate myself from the current mess with relative ease. Cued more by my confident resolve than direct instruction, the steel sheeting melted coolly, spreading like quicksilver around me and gently releasing its heavy grip on my leg. The bulkhead disappeared, along with the rest of the movie props, into the low stone cave that the broken Iron Mole once occupied. The incandescent light from the Mole's cabin had faded with it, but I was able to 'see' well enough in the dark, in the same manner that I had in my house during the trip to Oz. The pain in my leg did not disappear but, still reluctant to meddle with the course of nature, I avoided magically repairing the break. Odd, I thought, that I would do that to myself, but did not think twice about animating countless yards of earth, which is what I did next. I asked the dirt and stone to step out of the way in an even pattern above my position. In seconds I was presented with a hemispherical dent in the cave. When I moved, the dent grew more pronounced. When I dragged myself a few feet, the dent became a tunnel. That brief attempt at movement confirmed that I was not going far without help. I needed a tool, a mobile partner that would move with my thoughts without dissolving with scene changes. In essence, I needed something real that could support me and transport me with just a bump of manipulation.

There was a very loud bang a few feet away from me, followed by a gravelly swoosh and the stink of sulfur. I turned my head toward the sound, and then shook it. A wheelchair, apparently crafted from the stone of the mountain, rested, still smoking, half a pace away.

"Duh," I said. I dragged myself into the chair, and pushed a large green button on the armrest labeled 'GO.' And I went, at great speed, through a tunnel that dug itself as I accelerated through the rock. I wished that I could enjoy the rush of this impossibly novel experience, but I knew who was waiting for me outside the mountain. I also knew that, though I had natural strength that consistently parried Rudy's thrusts, he had experience that could, and no doubt would, wear me down. I was in trouble. I didn't have the mental wherewithal, yet, to conjure and defend at the same time. Rudy was strong enough to keep me from *thinking* of any holds with which to bind him. So, I thought, I can't exactly go home to mother, I'm committed to this course.

I raced the wheelchair through the last few feet of mountain, and into open air. It landed neatly on the same Chilean desert floor. I did not reduce my speed. Instead, I accelerated toward Rudy. He was seated beside a kidney-shaped pool about a mile away, under an umbrella, with a frozen margarita in his hand. Though I expected him to be sporting a Hawaiian shirt, he still wore his evil wizard outfit. I approached to within fifty feet of his pool. Close enough, I cautiously circled the wheelchair around him, tracing a large circle in the desert floor with my stone wheels. Rudy continued sipping his drink while expressing a casual interest in my return. He nodded slightly, and spoke.

"Very impressive," he said between sips. He spoke softly, but I could hear him perfectly in spite of my distance, speed, and the crunch of my wheels in the sand. He continued, "Ready for round two?"

Fuck me, I thought, that was just one round. I hoped ours was not a heavyweight bout.

"You're an asshole, Rudy," I said. I decided that I needed some distance, and instantly Rudy was again a mile away. I stopped the chair. Rudy remained where he was, silhouetted by the mountain he had just dropped on me. What, I thought, could he possibly do for an encore?

In answer, the shapes behind Rudy shifted until the mountain was gone. We were still surrounded by gray dusty desert, but the sky was black, the horizon was oddly bent, and the Earth was rising above it, just behind Rudy's umbrella.

"Oh," I said, assuming that he couldn't hear me through vacuum, but mindless of the fact that there was no air to breathe (been there, done that), "Well you're still an asshole." Rudy had apparently expected a different, more terrified, reaction from me, because he did not change the scene again or offer a new threat. This opened a door for me to take an initiative. It also allowed me a few calm seconds to recognize a previous tactical error on my part: I had been scouring my memory for options, weapons, and escapes, and then sought to manipulate *reality* with those meager thoughts and precious little knowledge. I had no chance to grab and twist enough of my physical surroundings to spar equally with

Rudy. I was half sure that he had planted that seed of despair in me, but there was little I could do about that. Except treat this battle like a dream. Or a nightmare.

"And what do I do in a nightmare?" I asked aloud again. Rudy's head tilted slightly, in anticipation of my rhetorical answer. Shit, I thought, he could hear me: ah well, no matter – might as well finish my sentence for him, "I walk away."

I immediately turned 180 degrees about, and rolled the wheelchair forward. The moon was gone, and I was falling through space, high above the earth. Its surface was approaching at incredible speed, the details of landmasses, clouds, and oceans growing as I watched. I had no fear of this – it was my dream now, reality or not, and I would follow it through. I plummeted further, faster, until I saw the east coast of the United States approaching. Might as well go home, I thought as I nudged the chair toward New York. Manhattan took shape below me. I deftly swooped the wheelchair in a tight arc, leveling off at about one thousand feet above the skyline. I steered north, looking for familiar territory. Originally it hadn't made sense to stick to places I knew, because all I could picture were Beaver Toys sized holes scattered about the Westchester County landscape. Now the choice of venue, my home field, was glaringly obvious. That Chilean plain was a bad idea. Sure it was safe, but I needed to be surrounded by the archetypes of my life to properly fight Rudy. And fight him I would.

I was feeling genuinely superior by the time I crossed the East River. A crushing rush of abject terror immediately deflated that swollen pride when I spotted a giant baseball catcher's mitt hovering above Yankee Stadium. It was directly in my path, and far too close to maneuver around. I shaved most of my speed before impact, but not enough; I could hear bones snapping throughout my body when my speed was reduced to zero by the massive piece of athletic equipment. The wheelchair, which was stopped by my body, sandwiched me against the glove's open palm. I could hear Rudy's voice in the clouds.

"Didn't your mother ever tell you not to run away from your nightmares?" it boomed.

"Fuck you, Rudy," I gasped, but I doubt he heard me, since my face was pressed firmly against the thick but surprisingly supple sweet spot in the catcher's mitt. There was a response, however, because I suddenly lifted away from the brown leather surface through no effort of my own. I watched the mitt shrink beneath me for several seconds before I realized that I was not rising. I was falling, away from the mitt, toward terra very firma. Okay, back to work, I thought, and I set aside the pain and primal fear to return, easily, to my nightmare scenario. I determined that I should risk another one-eighty. This move might buy me some time to gather my wits, and limbs, to face my true nightmare, Rudy, before the fifteenth round.

I rolled over, careful to ignore the pain that struck my right ribcage with the motion. The turn had no effect beyond clarifying my descent. I was still accelerating toward the same section of the Bronx. I oriented myself with the approaching ground, which appeared as though someone had toggled a 'zoom' function behind my eyes. I sought to remember the feeling of acceptance that I had enjoyed long ago at the end of my long descent from the dream diner. Another zoom frame revealed that I was falling toward a church on a lush hillside, surrounded by an old cemetery. An appropriate target choice by Rudy, I thought. It was still too far away to tell, but I was sure that one of the graves was freshly dug, empty, and would act as bull's-eye for my fall.

With its next fade, I gave some welcome seconds of thought to the zoom function. Because of it, the churchyard did not rise to greet me steadily. Rather, the scene maintained stable dimensions for a few seconds before shimmering slightly and, with the next click of the zoom, appearing closer. This doesn't happen in the real world, I thought gleefully, I could certainly accept that. I was able to set aside the waves of pain flowing through my body by filling my mind with the image of my inevitable landing in the empty grave that I could see directly below me. I would land, yes, but not before converting the grave's floor from hard dirt to a long fluffy tunnel that would gently turn me around and open onto a happy and as yet unimagined place filled with the weapons of destruction that would most menace Rudy, or at least remove a sizable chunk from his ethereal hide before he finished pounding me into submission.

The grave enveloped me with the last zoom, but I entered it without concern. That sentiment survived until I was a foot or two above the grave floor. Then a flash of terror zipped through me when I sensed that my tunnel had not formed. The fear quickly dissipated when I did not land in the grave, or anywhere else *I* had imagined. Instead, I found myself sitting on a stool at Harry's Pub, in perfect health and zero pain, sipping from a freshly poured pint of Guinness. The transition was unsettling, but I did not question it in light of the alternative fate I had expected during the last foot of my fall.

The beer helped me through the sudden scene change. Incapable of denying my priorities, I swallowed the mouthful of cold soothing liquid before I surveyed my new surroundings. I was seated at the polished old bar, on the wooden stool that I usually chose during countless visits through the years. Harry's was a cozy little place, nestled on the main street of an otherwise forgettable hillside town along the Hudson River. Their food was overpriced but decent, there was an endless supply of unshelled roasted peanuts available, and the Guinness was on tap, so Harry's was usually my first choice. I heard a rock ballad from the 1970's, sung by Kansas, playing in the jukebox. Rudy, with his signature bottle of Budweiser cupped in his hands and sporting the Hawaiian shirt I had expected earlier, was seated on the stool beside me. The only details he had omitted were other patrons and a bartender. We were alone in the small taproom. Otherwise, Rudy had done a fine job flipping the reality switch; the Harry's status quo was complete. I studied his image in the mirror behind the bar while Rudy examined mine. Neither of us chose to look directly at the other but, once our eyes met behind the mirror, neither of us dared break the lock. I casually took another sip of beer. I let it sit on my tongue for a few seconds before I swallowed.

"So," I said to the mirror, "You going to kill me in Harry's?

"Alex," Rudy replied, "If I wanted to kill you, you'd be dead by now. Materializing a golf ball in your heart would do it, and you would have no way to guard against it."

"Until now," I said. I had already realized that one formidable weapon in my arsenal was my instinctive ability to throw up defenses against Rudy's attacks, but this talent was activated only if the possibility of the attack existed in my mind. I would never have imagined that Rudy could commit such a subtle, evil attack, but the fact that he mentioned it highlighted my ignorance. I continued, "What then? You're beating me to a pulp for kicks?"

"You don't seem any pulpier than normal right now, Alex," Rudy said. I saw him lift his hand, as if he was going to place it on my right shoulder, but he dropped it back to the bar.

"Guess I learned how to duck."

"Or something. I don't want to hurt you."

"Then why the hell are you working so hard at just that? Somewhere, outside this bar, is another version, the real version, of my body, and last time I checked there wasn't much left of it."

"And this was *my* fault," Rudy said. I imagined that he released the phrase as a sardonic question, but it struck my ears as a confession. I chose to work with the meaning I imagined, rather than what I heard. At that moment I was too angry to feel sorry for Rudy.

"Yeah," I said to the tan foam on my beer, "Yeah, it was your fault. All of it. Now I'm asking again, and no doubt for the last time, why are you playing this game with me?"

"I'm not sure. I've been trying to figure that one out myself. About the best I can manage is that I am not hurting you. You're hurting you."

"Oh please, Rudy. That even *sounds* lame. And desperate."

"On whose part?"

"Then why did you stop? Why are we at Harry's? And what happened to all my broken bits? I sure hope I'm not bleeding to death in the Bronx right now."

"I stopped," Rudy said, touching the tips of his fingers as he ticked off his answers, "Because I know we can still talk. We're at Harry's because we've had some of our best conversations here; I figured the atmosphere, and a couple of beers, might soften us both. All your broken bits are still with you and as broken as ever; you've just chosen to ignore them for the moment. And no, as far as I can tell you're not bleeding to death anywhere." His words and tone, both meant to console me, failed. Though I was relieved that I was not dead yet, I knew that Rudy was still exercising his penchant for evasiveness. I finished my beer, slammed the glass on the table, and turned to face Rudy. He didn't flinch at my sudden movement, or remove his eyes from the mirror.

"That's all a real comfort, Rudy," I said, allowing the rant that had been spooling for days to unravel unabated, while it could, from my temporarily healthy chest, "I'm truly honored that you've opted to take a moment from your inadvertent annihilation of me to further discuss the depth of our true friendship.

"Who the hell do you think you're talking to? Yeah, I might be new at all this shit, and I may not be able to recognize this Freuzre, or his threats, but I sure as hell can tell when I'm getting shit on by my friends. And this is one of those times. I mean, first you're doing everything you can to nurture this cursed talent of mine, telling me I'm a natural. Then you're telling me I can only do the stuff I've already been doing if I join your 'World.' Then, probably because I found a way to keep you out of my shorts, you start killing people to get my attention. Then you start killing me! And now, no doubt, you're going to ask me once more to join you, which of course will guarantee that everything will be just perfect!" I could have continued, but I felt my clarity slipping, so instead I took a deep gulp from my refilled glass. Rudy may or may not have heard my speech. I could not discern his reaction because his eyes were locked on their own reflection in the mirror. His face was a slab of granite, and he absently sipped his beer throughout my rant. He was in the midst of one sip when I finished, and he carefully set his beer down and wiped nonexistent foam from his upper lip. Then he pivoted on his stool, turning toward me bodily. He regarded me directly for a moment before he spoke.

"Alex, what am I going to do with you?" he asked with such dripping sympathy that I expected him to reach for my hand, "I've tried so many times to tell you, show you, even physically give you the truth in the form of my dream chamber and your moments, however wasted, with Cassie. And what do I get for my effort? You hide from me. You chat about me behind my back. You screw around with Max and, God help us all, Mary. You ignore my warnings, and my promises. Basically, you've betrayed me, Alex."

"Oh, please," I said. And I meant it.

"Okay," Rudy smiled, "I'll cut the melodrama. But I did offer you something very large, and you did shy away from it. So, I'm going to run the brass ring past your horse one more time whether you like it or not:

"Join me. Unite with me, in the World, so that we can fight Freuzre together with weapons that he cannot repel." Rudy looked deeply into my eyes, rooting around in them for loose strands of my soul on which to cling. His plea was sincere, as was his wish for me to join him. I knew all this, but I wanted only to ask another question, and I decided that this shared moment of emotional lucidity might finally elicit a plausible answer from him.

"Rudy. Once and for all, who is Freuzre?" I asked. I could almost feel Rudy's gaze backing out of my eyes empty-handed. He dropped his lids, patted his pockets and pulled out a cigarette. Unaware that he does not smoke, Rudy tossed the cigarette's unfiltered tip into his mouth, lit the other end with a chromium Zippo that had appeared, in his hand, and opened his eyes.

"Alex. Once and for all, and for real, on so many levels, Freuzre is all that is wrong with the World. He's less a 'who' than he is a 'what' – a force whose only purpose is to dissolve the natural communal affinity shared by the souls of this planet until we have all reverted to the mindless, survival oriented, instinct-driven animals from which we came. He may not even be sentiently aware of the damage he is causing. Where is he from? For whom is he an agent? That I couldn't tell you. I've pondered those questions myself for centuries, and I've decided that Freuzre could be anything from an instrument of a defensive and frightened Mother Nature to a schizophrenic soul who shares your innate ability, but not your humanity."

"That's beautiful, Rudy," I said. I paused to enjoy one last long draft of beer, and continued, "Well stated, and no doubt worthy of posting on many a cult's web site. Unfortunately, I don't believe you." This time I dove into his eyes, in fruitless search of anything at all, before I continued, "And, if I can't believe you, then it would be wrong for me to join you in your World or in your fight with Freuzre. And, it would be right for me to continue doing all I can to stop you from wantonly killing or otherwise messing with people's reality just to make a point."

"I see. So you won't be joining me?"

"Nope."

"And you're going to continue fighting me?"

"Yup."

"Even though it will kill you?"

"Yes," I said, projecting the word with dignified volume that I wasn't aware I possessed.

"Fine then," Rudy said. He hopped down from his stool, rubbed his hands together, offered me his trademark deep, unhappy smile, and said, "Bye, Alex."

The bar was gone, I landed with a mighty thud on my back in the empty grave, and everything hurt again.

For a moment I lay still, watching the clouds cross the dirt-lined blue rectangle above me. They were fluffy, white, and were moving at that accelerated pace so often portrayed by cinematographers in search of a vehicle with which to portray time's inevitable passage. Then an unshaven old man with a filthy painter's cap and a shovel leaned into the bright blue frame, shook his head, and disappeared. Shortly after, I heard a familiar scrape that chilled what was left of my bones, and I saw the shovel break once more into my placid sky. This time it carried a load of loose dirt. It flipped over, and the dirt landed without compassion on my weakened chest. I cried out, but the old man could not hear me. Another shovel full of dirt fell into the grave, covering my face. I turned my head, spat moist grit from my mouth, coughed a bit, hoisted my shoulders up until I could rest on my elbows, and smiled.

I was at ease, in spite of the alarum of raw nerve endings firing chaotically throughout my body, and in spite of the dirt that continued to rain down about me. I was at ease because I finally, after all the questions, the examples, the waiting, the explanations from Max et al, had an answer to my fundamental question about Rudy. I still could not fully understand how I came to this conclusion, but I could understand that I was correct. I knew joining him was wrong. Dying was a better option, yes, but other choices still existed. Somewhere.

With dirt still raining on my head, I sat and stretched as if getting out of bed, looked up at the blue sky, the racing clouds, drank in their simple beauty in a way that I never had before, and said, "Back to work, then."

Assuming that burying me alive would seem facile to my adversary, I waited for something new to happen as my grave slowly filled in around me. My patience began to give way to panic when the dirt had reached the level of my shoulders. And dirt is a deceptively heavy material, so that weight was as physically pressing as it was psychologically disturbing. I belatedly tried flailing my arms a bit, but they didn't have the strength to work without the aid of my useless, and buried, legs. When the dirt reached my eyes, and I was spitting the stuff out of my mouth to maintain a hole for breathing, I noticed how like swimming that effort was. With the notice came knowledge, and I relaxed. I pulled my arms easily through viscous dirt, clasped my hands behind my head, remembered lazy childhood summer afternoons spent lying in my father's pool, just floating and staring at the clouds. I was not surprised that my legs rose until they were level with the rest of me, and I was suspended above the closing grave. When the fresh dirt was flush with the surrounding cemetery lawn, I was mildly disappointed because I knew this comfortable reprieve would cease upon my exit from the grave.

I was right. I emerged from the grave in a seated position. The dirt became hard-packed ground as soon as I was clear of it, as expected. There were thirteen mourners gathered in a semicircle beside my gravesite. My attendees consisted of a dozen people, evenly mixed between men and women, no children. All twelve wore black, and none wore faces. The thirteenth mourner was Rudy, who was back in his wizard outfit, which seemed appropriate for the occasion. He held an open bible in his left hand, and was tossing bright red roses on my grave, at my feet. Each rose contained a tiny version of Cassie or Max within its closed flower, and the little women were screaming as the buds chewed them voraciously. Though the image was disturbing, I wasn't concerned. I concluded that, since there were so many separate images of Cassie and Max being eaten, the tiny tortured women were not real. I shook my head at Rudy, but he hadn't taken notice of me. He seemed more interested in finishing the ceremony. When he pronounced his final solemn 'amen,' the flowers were quiet, and the mourners had wandered off, he pointed

at me. His eyes were clouded with tears, but at that moment I
assumed those tears were part of his show.

"Alex Creaux, you had your chance," he shouted, his voice
a stereotypical echoing god-boom, "Now I need to get you out of
my way before you are corrupted by Freuzre!"

"Oh," I laughed, "Is that where you're passing the guilt?
Nice."

"Alex Creaux!" Rudy shouted again. His goatee had
stretched into a long white beard to better complement his wizardly
ensemble. He held his hands high and wide, forming a familiar
'I'm collecting the power of the cosmos' pose that Rudy must have
adopted from watching Star Trek reruns. Not inclined to ignore an
overt hint, I crawled behind a nearby gravestone before I heard the
thunder rolling in. The sky had blackened behind Rudy, and two
jagged blue lightning bolts struck the gravesite where I had been
sitting.

"Oh, Rudy, this is too much," I sighed. Can't you be a
little more original?"

"How about this?" I heard him whisper in my ear, though
he was nowhere near me.

"What?"

"Turn around."

I did, and just in time. The front bumper of a speeding
tractor-trailer was just a few yards from me. I slithered
awkwardly, and painfully, off the busy highway on which Rudy
had deposited me. The semi's driver didn't even honk his horn as
the massive vehicle sped past my new position in the grassy
highway meridian.

"Okay," I said to the air, "That was better." I closed my
eyes, struggling to keep my lungs inflated while also wishing for
nothing other than to pass out.

"Thanks," his voice tapped against the inside of my
throbbing skull, "But you should keep those eyes open – closing
them will make this too easy."

There was no need to ask him what was too easy. I simply
opened my eyes, and spotted the red and vastly oversized moon
that rested on a low hill under a clear twilight country sky. At first
glance it reminded me again of childhood, when the occasional
rising summer moon was blood red and so dominated the horizon

that we thought it had settled on the crest of a nearby hill. Because we were certain that we could hit the moon while it hovered at such close range, we would throw rocks at it. A second glance revealed that this red moon fulfilled the childhood fantasy. It was physically on that hill, and had begun to roll down it toward me. Blood splashed from the great glowing orb's liquid surface as it accelerated. I could not run from it, and I lacked imagination enough to form a new conveyance. Apparently one of the Rules for Fighting Rudy was that no conjuration could be used twice, so a wheelchair or elevator was not available. No vehicle would have helped anyway, because I did not have time to climb aboard. Fear or the bloody orb itself did not consume me, however. When the moon had approached to a point where it filled most of my field of vision, I realized the obvious. I scrambled to the shoulder of the empty old asphalt road to which the scene of my imminent demise had shifted, and found a handful of pebbles.

"I hope I'm not too late," I said as I side-armed the pebbles at the moon. I swore softly at my insincerity as I scraped up another handful of pebbles. When am I going to learn, I asked myself before releasing the next handful and shouting, "No. I *know* I'm not too late!"

A small red rubber playground ball bounced harmlessly over my head, and down the deserted rural lane until it disappeared around a bend. I laughed, delighted that I had managed to dodge two more of Rudy's attacks. To that point I had assumed that he was playing with me; that he could, as he said, have erased me with a thought, but I began to wonder if perhaps I possessed a defensive edge that he could not overcome. I had hoped to cling to that thought, but discovered with my next attempt at movement that it wasn't going to matter. My body was battered, inside and out. I could do little more physically than wince in pain and cough up multi-colored fluid from my lungs. I may have had an advantage over him, but I had wasted that advantage by not jumping out of his way often enough, and by too easily assuming that he had the upper hand in the reality department. In truth, I was still doing it. I wondered once more if he hadn't somehow planted that thought in my head.

"Alex," I heard Rudy somewhere nearby, outside my head and with his conventional voice, "Get up."

"You're kidding, right?" I asked, managing to turn my head toward Rudy. He was standing behind me, dressed in faded jeans and a denim shirt. The beard was gone. The old concern was back.

"Nope." I felt pressure under my armpits as Rudy hoisted me to my feet. He spoke conspiratorially into my ear, "You have to be standing up for this. Here, lean on this bar."

A polished wooden railing appeared in front of my hands. Rudy gently set them on the smooth, worn surface. He backed away after he knew I was reasonably steady. I felt quite taken by the railing. It was warm, thick, and strong. Its support was firm and guaranteed. I found myself examining and appreciating its grain, the thickness of the varnish, the color of the wood. It could have been cherry, or mahogany. My rapidly numbing mind had chosen to focus its remaining resources on this shock of good wood. My attention toward it was complete enough that I did not hear the sharp rap of two other chunks of wood slamming together until at least the third or fourth blow. Then I heard my name, I think.

"Alex Creaux!"

I did hear my name, I thought, now who the hell would be calling me, prying me from the comfort of this railing? Who else?, some other, cynical part of my brain responded. I pried my attention from the wood and looked up. I was in a courtroom. I didn't recognize the place, but it was a standard small-town setup, with lots of natural wood, but minimal open space. Behind me and above me was the gallery, and, though I saw none of them, it was teeming with hushed but deeply concerned observers. I could feel their energy. I hoped, but doubted, that they were on my side in the case that Rudy, at the table to my left and dressed in a three-piece pinstriped suit, was about to present. I followed the sound of the gavel to the raised bench. Rudy sat there as well, officious in his black robe. A pince-nez perched cosmetically, and woefully incorrectly, near the tip of his nose.

"Alex Creaux," Judge Rudy shouted again, "Having been found guilty by a jury of your peers for crimes against humanity, deity, and your own misbegotten soul, I hereby decree your sentence." I glanced to my right, at the jury box. It was filled with a dozen copies of Rudy in all manner of male and female garb. All of him were dutifully solemn, and none had the courage to look in my eyes. I fought through the haze, gasped for a breath of air, and heaved out some words:

"Rudy – Your honor, I mean," I said, "How can you find me guilty when there hasn't even been a trial yet?" I could hear a rustling behind me as a hundred familiar voices simultaneously shared shocked whispers about my insolence.

"Objection!" Prosecutor Rudy shouted, thumbs in his vest, "This trial is complete, Your Honor. You said so yourself. The defendant said so himself!"

"I did?" I asked meekly. The gallery burst into laughter. I recognized the laughter, and did not need to turn to know that everyone in the gallery was me. Judge Rudy slammed his gavel repeatedly to quell the crowd. In time they settled into a tolerable murmur, and he continued.

"Objection sustained. Now shut up Alex, you had your chance." I shut up. I understood.

"Anyway," Judge Rudy said in a singsong, auspicious manner, "Having been found guilty of the aforementioned and heinous crimes, the State of the World sentences you, Alex Creaux, to take one step backward!" The gallery went into hysterics, the jury solemnly bowed their heads, and the prosecutor thrust a fist into the air. A step back was apparently a very bad thing, though my only immediate problem with the sentence was abandoning the security of my railing.

"Do I have to?" I asked. Judge Rudy's cold gray eyes pooled at my words. The gavel slipped from his limp fingers as he raised his hand to his chin. He brought up his other hand as well. Both of them seemed to shake slightly as he rubbed his eyes and face for a few seconds. A part of me – a very small part of me – felt sorry for him. Then he rested his chin in his palms and looked at me. He nodded slowly.

"What do you think, Alex?" he asked in the voice that was honestly his, and it did quiver slightly.

"I have to?"

"Take your damned step," Prosecutor Rudy said in his god voice. This Rudy was now garbed in his wizard costume. He turned away from me.

"Fine," I said. I drew a deep breath, held my spine as straight as I could, and released my comforting grip on the railing. Pain ripped through my leg as my weight settled on its separated bones. I was unable or uninterested in imagining myself as lighter, or perhaps inflated with helium. I had forgotten all about my 'powers,' as though this moment was encased in a real, normal, dream. Or bathed in inexorable reality. I edged my bad leg behind me first, hoping my good leg would support me until it was far enough behind me to be considered a step. I struggled to maintain consciousness. It was very important for me to take my step with dignity, rather than have my unconscious or lifeless body dragged backward a single pace.

Judge Rudy was still looking away, though the jury stood and watched with quiet respect. Prosecutor Rudy was playing his Game Boy, and, though I could not see to confirm it, I believed that the folks in the gallery had gone home. I pushed my mangled leg a little further. I winced when I anticipated again settling my weight onto it so that I could quickly move my good leg under me.

There was no need. My bad leg didn't hit the floor. When I fell I did not hit the floor either. There was no floor. I turned my head in time to see the nature of my sentence. Rudy had set an abyss behind my table – it had already swallowed the gallery – that, being a standard abyss, had no bottom. Like his original line in the sand, it was no more than a crack, with perhaps fifty feet of air between its sheer walls. I looked back, and up, at Rudy. He was standing at the edge of his creation, dressed in his jeans and cotton shirt. His faced was buried in his hands. He seemed to be sobbing violently. I really didn't care. I didn't care much about anything. I was falling. I knew that, because I had agreed to take the step, to accept my sentence. There was nothing I could do. No more tricks; I was to fall, permanently. Rudy's spell had enveloped me completely. He had won. Man, I thought, this really sucks.

My windless, soundless, motionless decent continued for a few miles, or hours, or days – I did not know – before my mindset began to shift away from hopeless submission. Perhaps I was bored, and craved a change of subject. Also, since there was no apparent gravity in freefall, the torture of my nerve endings by my injuries was more tolerable. I tried to fill the void by thinking about an escape from my fate. I questioned whether Rudy really had sealed all my exits with the impenetrable logic of his rules. I imagined stopping, sprouting wings, donning a parachute, being somewhere else, turning into a vapor, the rungs of a ladder, and I even whistled for my car. Nothing worked. I wondered if nothing worked because I was sure that nothing would work. Perhaps in another month or so I could change my mind, assuming that there was time in this dark empty place. If there was no time, then I supposed that I never could refine my thinking.

The single exception to my loss, the scintilla of hope to which I clung, was my discovery that, try as I might, I could not resign myself to my fate. It was wrong for me to be falling, Rudy was wrong to have sentenced me to this abyss and summarily removing me from the Freuzre drama, and, above all, I knew it was wrong that I had been torn from my new and as yet immature relationship with Max. I could offer myself no rationale for this feeling, but I felt it was true. And the truth that the feeling pushed inexorably to the surface of my consciousness was simple: I was not yet done. A warm wave of hope splashed over me, helping me to imagine that there was a bottom to the abyss. That meant to me that the abyss was not an abyss, and that Rudy's spell might indeed wear off. He hadn't won yet.

"So," I said aloud, "Why am I still falling?"

In answer, I felt a change in the darkness around me. A kind of warm electricity was wandering the darkness with me, occasionally nudging me with a charge that I found agreeable, even familiar. I tried to move a bit, to follow the charge around, but I was still unable to change my position. My immobility was inconsequential shortly, because the sensation soon filled all the silent space around me. I still could not define the feeling that was tickling my soul with a tender ethereal feather in a manner that filled my eyes with water. I was awash in its warmth, its good will, and its unconditional support. I smiled, knowing that I was having an epiphany on two levels. First, I was feeling, actually being touched by, the power of love. Second, that this abyss, this sentence, was a feeble prison for such power.

Before another thought could enter my mind, the former abyss was bathed in soft yellow light. I turned my head slightly, looked behind and, finally, below me. A portal, in the form of an old wooden interior door with worn white paint, had opened directly beneath me. I turned my head back, and waited.

In a few seconds – and I could tell they were seconds – I passed backward through the threshold of the open door. I landed heavily in Max's open arms. She slammed the door shut with her foot.

The world righted itself, and I could feel a firm floor under my feet. Max's arms were around me, and her body was pressed tightly against my back. I felt it all, and it combined nicely with the deep sense of relief and love that had already revived my tattered mind. Then gravity, and everything else, kicked in. The pain only swept through me for a second before my moment in Max's physical and emotional grip, and my consciousness, faded to black.

Chapter Twenty-Seven

Wandering whispers of gentle light danced beyond my closed eyelids. While I pondered what mysterious force, what spectral Jackson Pollock or Henri Matisse could project such intriguingly random yet subtly complete patterns of light against the thin membranes that stood sentry to the doorways to my soul, a tiny grain of sensibility from somewhere in the back of my brain crawled forward through the thick morass of pain and recent denigrating experience that had tinged the gray matter it traversed a moribund shade of wet garden slate. That grain, that spot, that iota of personal energy, eventually found its way to my eyelids and there shared its simple power. My eyes fluttered open.

Oh, I thought, it's a fire. How nice.

I was lying on a firm modern couch, my battered body covered in green woolen blankets that served to keep me warm and to consolidate my pain into a single gentle, and wholly tolerable, metronomic throb. I knew that the couch was modern because it was far too large, too littered with clumsy pillows, and too paternal in the manner with which it supported me, like the contemporary polyester behemoth that I had liberated from my living room over two years ago. A few feet away from me, across a polished hardwood floor protected by a tattered red throw rug, roared a three-log fire. It was secured in an old stone fireplace whose slate hearth encroached nearly two feet into the room. The hearth must have been warm, because Cassie rested her feet on it while she knitted in an antique rocker by the fire. She noticed my scan, and smiled brightly. She dropped her knitting to her lap, and waited. She must have been expecting me to speak. So I did.

"Where am I?" I asked. Cassie laughed. The unassuming, slightly singsong tone and easy cadence of her expressed amusement delivered more warmth to me than the fire could ever manage. I had always loved Cassie's honest laugh. I welcomed its role as the first human sound I heard after my narrow escape from Rudy's deadly ministries. She shook her head slowly and said:

"You come back from the fight of your life, survive a joust with a god, and the best you can come up with is 'where am I?' That is just so Alex."

"Sorry. I am still me. I guess that's a good thing today. But I did have to ask, because for a second I thought I was home, you were alive, and the last few years of my life were just a dream. Then I remembered that we never had a fireplace. After that I got a wakeup call from all the broken stuff in my body. So, I figured I wasn't home, not really. Are you going to tell me?"

"What?"

"Where I am?"

"You're home."

"Weren't you listening?"

"Not *your* home, silly. *My* home," Cassie hummed. She resumed knitting. I remembered that Cassie did not care to know how to knit when she was alive. That was odd, I thought, that she pursued a hobby in death that she had successfully evaded in life.

"You have a house?"

"Of sorts. I'm not sure how I got here, or why, but it's nice enough, and warm." Cassie liked a warm house.

"How did I get here?"

"Oh, that's much easier. Max dropped you off with me."

"She knows where you 'live' too?"

"Well duh. She dropped you off, didn't she?"

"Good point. Where is she now?"

"That I couldn't tell you. Probably off helping some other poor schmuck who's too stupid or clumsy to get out of his own way."

"Thanks," I said. I tried to sit up, but the raw nerves that tended three or four shattered ribs in my chest dictated otherwise. I gasped in pain and reclined slowly to my previous position squarely on my back. Cassie jumped to her feet in response to my discomfort. She knelt by the couch, and gently laid her hand over mine.

"Listen," she said quietly while stroking my fingers, "You have to keep still for a while. Max dropped you off with me because she figured you would be safe here. She's pretty sure that Rudy thinks you're dead – real dead, not my kind of dead. Plus, he doesn't know where I live. So, she asked me to keep you out of trouble, and off Rudy's radar, while you heal."

"Why?" I was going to ask something from my heart, like 'why would either of you do this for me?' but instead I finished with, "Why would Rudy not know where you live? He must have set the place up for you."

"I would have thought so too. Of course I never had the opportunity to ask him myself – he doesn't talk to me much, but Max thinks that he never made this place. At least not on purpose."

"He built you a house by accident?"

"It's not really a house, but you'll see that later, when you're a little better. And yes, Max believes that Rudy doesn't truly think I exist at all. He did such a great job recreating my image for you – "

"Or for him," I interrupted knowingly. Cassie smiled and touched the tip of her nose with an extended index finger.

"Or maybe for him," she said, "In any case, he made me so well (and I do appreciate that) that my image came with all the trimmings, even some details that might not have occurred to him."

"So your house, and you, is a serendipitous byproduct of a crazed unconscious mind?"

"Yeah. That makes it all sound so small, but I guess you could say that."

"Did Max tell you why I'm here?"

"She said Rudy kicked the living shit out of you."

"She would. And he did. So you know I've been through a lot?"

"Yup."

"Then could we maybe take a break from discussing the metaphysical aspects of your existence, at least until I can sit up?"

"Sure," she smiled brightly, then leaned forward and kissed my forehead, "But you asked me." She stood, and returned to her rocker by the fire. When her needles started clicking again, I was compelled to ask one more question:

"So why are you knitting?"

"I haven't a clue. Now go back to sleep and heal."

I did.

At least I assumed I slept, because when I opened my eyes again I was lying in a large four-posted bed under a small mountain of white down comforters. Cassie sat in an overstuffed armchair beside the bed, reading an old hardbound book. The change of scene was the primary hint that I had been asleep, though I had no memory of dreams or near conscious moments to lend a dimension of time to my nap. I suppose it made sense that, while a guest in Cassie's dream world abode, I would not experience any dreams; that would simply be too far beyond my ability to cope logically.

A secondary sign of time's passage was that I felt much better. The fires that had raged almost randomly throughout my body had diminished to the point where I had to move in order to be singed by their aching embers. So, of course, I moved, testing the new sensation. I took a deep breath. The effort still hurt, but I no longer felt my lungs shredding as they expanded. I sat up. That motion was still painful too, especially among my damaged ribs, but I could successfully raise my head off the pillow. Cassie tended to me immediately by jamming pillows behind my neck and head to cushion my inevitable collapse. She was visibly agitated that I had either waked, moved, or both.

"Alex," she sighed, "What are you doing? Lie still. You'll have plenty of time to get up later, when the effort doesn't rip you apart."

"Yes doctor," I mumbled through a wince as I settled into the wonderfully soft pillows. I looked around the plain bedroom. Its gray walls were broken only by a closed set of heavy green drapes that spanned the wall I faced from floor to ceiling. It was a nice room, and a very comfortable bed, and I felt again like I was at home. But I was not. I turned my head toward Cassie, who was in her chair again. She pulled an afghan over her legs, picked up her copy of *A Tale of Two Cities* from the nightstand, found her place and began reading without noticing that she held its ornately filigreed antique cover upside-down. The attractive image of Cassie settling into serene luxury triggered an unexpected yearning in me for Max's company. Cassie noticed me looking at her, and smiled. I smiled back.

"So how are you feeling, Alex?" she asked with real sincerity.

"A helluva lot better than I did last time we spoke. When was that, anyway?"

"I couldn't imagine. It must have been a while, though, because your bruises look much better than they did before."

"Who's been taking care of me?" I asked, puzzled that the thought to ask such a question occurred to me.

"I guess I have," she said.

"You've been feeding me?"

"Nope."

"Giving me medicine?"

"Uh uh."

"Bathing me?"

"Unfortunately, no," the sudden blush that swept her soft cheeks delightfully contrasted the high Victorian lace collar in which they nestled.

"Then what have you been doing?"

"I guess I don't know," she said brightly, "But it feels like it's helping."

"Well," I said, running a quick inventory of my needs, "I do feel a lot better, I'm not hungry, and I'll be damned if I've ever smelled this good, so you must have done something right."

"Oh, thank heaven," she said, "Because you know they never tell me anything around here. All I know is that you should keep on trying to get some sleep. It helps a lot. So why don't you close those pretty eyes and try to sleep again, so I can finish my book?"

"Fair enough," I said, "But you ought to have it facing right side up when you read – you might get a headache otherwise."

"Oh, you!" Cassie laughed as she snapped the book closed and leaned forward to attend me again, mindless of the observation that had prompted the humor. She yanked free the two pillows that she had only seconds earlier stuffed behind my head, allowing them to fall to the hardwood floor with a thick cotton rustle. My head tumbled to the remaining pillow with a commensurate firing of my few thousand remaining raw nerves, but I didn't mind. I was safe, I was healing, and I was going back to sleep.

I opened my eyes again to identify an odd metallic sound, a scraping of metal against stone backed by a constant sharp click. I was seated on an ancient high-backed wooden bench, in what appeared to be my kitchen. My elbows rested on a sturdy oak table, its dark surface heavily distressed from years of service. Across from me was a matching, empty, bench, completing a tasteful antique breakfast booth that I had never owned. I was nude but I was not embarrassed or cold. Like in a dream, I thought. Very unlike a dream were the splashes of violet and red that marked recent injuries to virtually any part of my body that I examined. I turned toward the sound, and shook my head slightly when I spotted Cassie, in dark jeans and a red flannel shirt, sharpening a large kitchen knife on an old, foot-operated grindstone. She noticed me looking at her, stopped grinding, and smiled.

"Oh, good," she said, tossing the knife into a nearby open drawer, and wiping her hands with a rag as she stood, "You're sitting up." She left her wheel and slid onto the other bench. She folded her hands and set them on the table. She smiled, patiently waiting for me to continue the exchange.

"So I am," I acknowledged, "But I don't remember even waking up."

"Me neither. Are you feeling better?"

"Matter of fact, I am. I feel like I should be asking for a cup of coffee in this sort of room, but for some reason I don't want any."

"That's good because we don't have any. No food either."

"No problem. I'm not hungry," I answered her truthfully. I was not disturbed by the absurdity of our conversation, and sensed no need for confusion.

"Good," Cassie said, "Then why don't we get the hell out of the kitchen? You ready for a tour?"

"That would require standing up?"

"Uh huh."

"Then," I said, swinging my legs out of the booth and standing carefully, "I may be."

"Wonderful," Cassie said, "But how about I give you a little support anyway?" She hooked her arm around my waist and held about half my weight as we took our first step out of the kitchen. I appreciated her strength, because my legs were either painfully stiff or still a few weeks away from resuming their ambulatory duties.

We hobbled down a narrow hallway, stepping carefully across plain green scatter rugs and between beige walls. I remembered that Cassie's tastes ran polar to the décor in her new home; apparently Rudy did not. She would have festooned this hall with colors: in the wallpaper, the rugs, and specially chosen artwork, all to hide the drab windowless space to which she had been committed. I wanted to consider this detail, because it seemed an important piece to the puzzle that was Cassie, but it was quickly stricken from my mind by a sudden onslaught of pain from my leg and ribs.

"I think," I gasped in failed nonchalance, "We have to end the tour for now, even though I didn't see any other rooms."

"That's no problem," Cassie said with concern. I felt her arm tighten around me until she was probably supporting my entire weight.

"Damn, Cassie," I said as she turned me around, "Have you been working out?"

"Not a bit," she said cheerily, "I guess death wears nicely on me."

"I guess. I sure hope life starts having a little respect for me soon. This is getting annoying."

"I hear you. But you are a lot better. Trust me. Just a little more rest may be all that you need."

The living room, the one with the cheery fireplace, was now at the end of the hallway where the kitchen should have been. I didn't question the anomaly while Cassie led/carried me into the room – the couch, even though I once thought it awful, was more tempting than that wooden bench would have been anyway. I let Cassie lower me onto it, and then relaxed while she covered me with blankets. She took her position in the rocker by the fire and picked up her knitting project from a basket near the hearth. Whatever she was knitting was about as complete and unidentifiable as it had been the last time that I saw her working on it. I was relieved to notice that the pain was no longer intense enough to relieve me of consciousness at its own will, but I was exhausted by my short trip down the misguided hall. I chose to contentedly and wordlessly watch Cassie knit while I drifted off to sleep to the sound of the crackling fire.

When my eyes next fluttered open, I felt as though I were truly waking from a long sound sleep. I still did not remember any dreams, but I felt that I had naturally rested. I raised my arms in an automatic morning stretch, and then flinched when I remembered how much such a movement would have hurt me during previous waking moments. With a little testing, I discovered that this time there was no pain associated with the movement. I felt good for the first time in recent memory. I sat up in the four-posted bed, checked my surroundings with real interest for the first time.

Cassie was at her station beside my bed, still reading that Dickens book upside-down. She lifted her head at my movement, and smiled.

"Well good morning, sleepyhead," she said in a motherly manner.

"Have I been sleeping long? It feels like I got a good twelve hours."

"I don't have a clue."

"Really? You don't have a clock?"

"Not even a window to catch the sunrises," she answered wistfully.

"That sucks."

"The sunrise thing or that time is not here? Because I agree with the first, but I kind of like the second. It makes the days go by faster, if that makes any sense."

"Not a wit," I said. She smiled to acknowledge my jibe. I swung my legs out of bed, grabbed the red flannel robe that hung on one of the bed's posts, covered my pale but bruise-free naked body and stood. My feet did not land on the floor, but rather inside a pair of soft leather slippers. I tested the fit of the robe, wiggled my healthy toes in the slippers, and said, "You know, I could get used to this kind of luxury."

"Nope. You couldn't."

"Why not?"

"Because you're not dead?"

"Oh," I said, "I think I'll take that as a complement. I also think I'll change the subject. Do you mind if I stroll around a bit, maybe stretch some of these old bones that seem to be working again?"

"Not at all. Explore to your heart's content."

"Thanks. Care to join me?"

"No. I'm fine here. And I think I already know where everything is."

"Okay then. Bye." Since it seemed to be the way she wanted it, I left the bedroom through its only exit without further comment. The heavy oak door, which raised my eyebrow because all the doors in my house were cheap hollow-cores, closed behind me with an ominous click after I cleared its threshold and stepped into the blue-carpeted hall. I deflected a wave of panic by turning around and quickly reopening the door to be reassured by an unchanged image of Cassie in her chair studiously reading her inverted book. Satisfied, I turned again, pulled the door closed with my own power, and began an easy, pain-free stroll down the hall.

Each padded step was a release. Though I didn't share my disquiet with her, I had become wary of my cycle of sleep and waking, always under the companionship, or guard, of my dead wife. The hazy nature of the experience, and the continued presence of Cassie, was leading me to believe that I had died or was dying, and that I was trapped in a Purgatory either of my, Rudy's, or Cassie's making. Such thoughts, and the unhappy conclusions to which I would no doubt jump slightly after they did, had not completely entered my mind yet, and the act of moving through space of my own volition and sinuous locomotion was an effective tool toward belaying them.

Aside from the carpeting and the numbingly dull green paint on its walls, the hallway was an exact match of the passageway that once wove the upstairs rooms of my own now obliterated house. Before turning right into what should have been the guest bedroom (cleanest room in the house, Cassie always said), I took note once more that the place was a near match, and any variance was consistently duller than reality. I accepted the subdued translation and filed away any misgivings about it before my hand finished turning the, yes, dull brass knob of the guest bedroom door. I opened it, stuck my head in tentatively before entering – architectural surprises and assorted vortexes had taken their toll on my special confidence lately.

"It's okay," Cassie said from her reclined position on the nicely made queen-sized guest bed. She wore white satin pants and a pink fuzzy turtleneck sweater, and was playing with a glass snow globe as she lounged on the bed. I couldn't quite see the figurine among the glitter floating in the globe, but it may have been an archetypical wizard. Figures, I thought. Cassie continued, "You can come in, it's totally safe." So I did.

"Are you in every room?" I asked.

"No," Cassie answered, furrowing her lovely ivory brow, "I'm in this room. What do you mean?"

"Never mind. What are you doing?"

"Playing," she responded absently. I left her to it, and made a quick scan of the room. It was indeed our former guest bedroom, sans windows (or even curtains) and closet. The mission dresser was there, as was the huge mirror we lugged home from New Hampshire one happy summer. So were the end tables. Unfortunately, the dresser and tables had no drawers, and the mirror failed to reflect. I walked over to where the window should have been, and tapped on the wall. It rattled like my knuckle had contacted a pane of glass.

"This is too weird," I muttered.

"Huh?" Cassie said.

"Nothing. So how come you didn't keep me in here to get better, instead of the other bedroom?"

"What do you mean? This is where you stayed."

"Okay."

"You don't believe me, I can tell," she said. Then she scratched her index finger against her left temple and finished wryly, "Maybe it was all the bumps on your head that made you forget."

"That could be," I said. I snapped my fingers as though a light bulb had just ignited over my head, and continued, "I got it! Howsabout I go back out, and come back in and we start all over?"

"That'd be cool, I guess," she said, puzzled. I immediately spun on my heel, exited the room, and stepped into the hall without letting go of the doorknob. The instant I heard the latch click home, I turned to face the closed door. Without releasing my grip, I reopened the door. With this twist of the brass knob I felt no panic, and sought no reassurance; I was curious. I pushed the door open to reveal a bright, windowless kitchen that vaguely resembled our own. I leaned into the room, but kept my feet on the hall carpet. Cassie, dressed in a sleeveless tan sundress and nothing else, was perched upon one of the metal barstools that we had used to the point of their own destruction several years ago. It appeared that she was mixing a batch of brownies, but the material in her steel bowl, though brown, did not otherwise resemble food. Her face became pleasantly animated when she caught me watching her.

"Oh, there you are!" she said, "I was wondering when you would turn up again. Have you finished your exploration?"

"Um, nope," was all I could get out before I reflexively shut the door and opened it again. Cassie was reading a National Geographic magazine in our TV room. She peeked over the top of it, smiled, and was probably going to say something but I slammed the door before she could. I held it closed, leaned my head on it, and sighed.

"Okay," I said aloud, but not with volume that I expected Cassie to hear, "I think I get it now. Cassie, you tried to tell me weeks ago, but I wouldn't listen. You're part of the décor in this place." I was profoundly disappointed by my observation, and equally confident in its veracity. I walked away from the door, slowly wandering the short first floor hallway without wondering how I got downstairs. I felt bereaved again as I approached the door that would have led to my book-lined and habitually ignored study. Though I had been asleep during most of my stay with her, I had come to enjoy Cassie's company, or perhaps her presence. I knew she wasn't the woman I had loved, lost, and through Rudy believed for a moment that I could regain. But she had still been a three-dimensional personality who had dropped everything to help me. Now I understood that Cassie was as rudimentary as the slightly incorrect decorations adorning this windowless abode. She was real, I was sure, but her reality did not stretch beyond the blinders of her maker. She turned at the sound of my entry from

her position at the open rolltop desk. She was paying bills. I
played along.

"Oh, sorry," I said brightly, "Didn't mean to disturb you."

"S'okay," she said, leaning away from her work and
stretching, "I could use a break."

"No, I wouldn't have it," I said, "I'll just go back to my
tour."

"Okay," she said, "If that's what you want. I'm real glad to
see you up and about though. And you're wearing pants and a
shirt again too. Very encouraging."

"Thanks," I said, pulling my head from the doorway and
closing it gently. I let go of the knob, feeling oddly inflated by her
observance of my improved health. I did not wonder when I had
changed out of my bathrobe and slippers into street clothes.

"How can a mannequin be glad?" I asked aloud. I resolved
to shelf my misgivings about Cassie's nature. Instead I would
appreciate her presence, in whatever room or guise, and leave it at
that. Regardless of where she came from, even if it was at Rudy's
hand, there was still something good that seeped through her
ethereal pores. Hell, I thought, there's still plenty of good locked
up in Rudy, too. Maybe she was trying to remind me of that. Or, I
considered with a shudder, perhaps Cassie and this place were my
creation, and not Rudy's. If that were the case, I would need to
make a more substantial effort to abandon my current thoughts. I
worried that any acknowledgement that I had created something as
wonderful as Cassie might bring about her destruction. I did not
understand my logic, but, from experience, I trusted it. Rudy, me,
or God himself; I didn't care. Cassie and this place existed, and I
would leave it at that.

I continued my meander through the strange house for
possibly several days. Sleep and hunger had apparently joined
time in their continued absence from the equation of my existence
in this place. Each doorway yielded the same results: one room
that was a mildly inferior copy of an original from my house, and
one extremely accurate version of Cassie. Rudy clearly spent more
time admiring my wife than he did my house. After I had
completed about a dozen circuits of both floors, never
encountering quite the same room, but always the same, if
rebooted Cassie, I grew fatigued. Happily, this fatigue was drawn

from boredom rather than pain; my healing wounds were barely evident. I supposed that the hours, days, or weeks that I had spent in this pleasant prison had served their purpose, and it was time for me to move on.

Without consulting any of the Cassies, I began to work on an exit from her home. I stood at the base of the stairs and faced the wall where the front door should have been for several hours, I think, but I could not coax my door into forming. The place was well sealed. I wondered briefly if it was sealed to enclose or to protect me. Us. Not that it mattered, I thought as I regarded the blank wall that did not lead outside for the hundredth time. It was the same. My hand still smarted from my recent attempt to punch through it. I even tried chipping through the paint. The walls, unfortunately, were made of something other than plaster and wood, probably something other than material. I wondered if there was anything, at all, on the other side of them. I turned from the wall, leaned on it, and urged myself to calm down. I had no real call for anxiety: Rudy had yet to create a situation without an escape, and I wasn't bright enough to completely entrap myself. I absently surveyed the hall. I noticed that Rudy had done a better job replicating it than he had the other rooms. That made sense, and helped confirm in my still wary mind that Rudy was truly the house's creator. That was because he had spent most of his time in that hall, waiting for me. The colors were right, if slightly faded from the bright reds and blues that Cassie had used against my wishes, and the furniture was perfect, down to the antique telephone that rested neatly on the "gossip bench" we picked up at a garage sale once, and refinished together.

"Oh for God's sake!" I shouted, smacking my forehead with an open palm. I strode across the foyer to the bench and picked up the phone. It had no wires, but I put the handset to my ear anyway. There was a dial tone. "I am such an ass," I said, "How many weeks? Oh well, I guess I had to wait until I was ready."

I dialed 629-6279 and waited. The phone at the other end rang once before a familiar female voice answered with a nervous "Hello?"

"Hey," I said, "You can come pick me up now."

Chapter Twenty-Eight

The single electric 'ding,' universally translated to 'going up,' was identical to the announcement of an arriving elevator at the former Beaver Toys building. The familiar ringing tone invited a harsh flash of unwanted nostalgia, but it did not surprise me. Cassie's abode may have been a Rudy construct, but its exit, for whose imminent materialization the bell was harbinger, was my device. The parameters of that exit, whether consciously wished for or not, were drawn from my expectations.

Polished steel double doors appeared in the wall where my house's front entrance should have been. They opened too slowly for Max, who was dressed in new skintight jeans, a red velvet halter-top, and four-inch platform shoes – an ensemble that could no doubt trace its origins to Mary's closet. She tried to exit the elevator before its doors had separated enough to accommodate her slim body. She shook her head, commented under her breath about uselessly slow machines, and pushed the doors aside with fury. When they whipped apart with a metallic clang, Max left her arms outstretched and stepped toward me. I immediately wrapped my arms around her, and then held her tightly for a few minutes. The proximity and warmth of her body solidified her presence in my mind, and in my soul. I hadn't felt this complete when touching another person in years, if at all. And it was not because she had pulled me out of the abyss – well not that abyss, anyway. It was because she was who I needed, on all levels. I had sensed that earlier, even dared to know it as a possible truth, but, in this first moment of contact after our long separation, I finally understood it. I briefly wondered if Max did, and I knew I would never care to ask.

"Easy big boy," she said to my chest, "It's not like you haven't seen me for months."

"Yes it is."

"That's sweet, but I just dropped you off three days ago. I must say I am amazed again. Given the shape you were in when I left here, I wouldn't have imagined that you would summon me so quickly."

"I guess I'm a fast healer."

Max broke the embrace, took a step back without letting go of my hands, and thoroughly scanned me from feet to hair. She seemed to be reviewing me for more than medical data. I liked that.

"Damn," she said, "I guess you are."

"It's really only been three days?"

"Give or take an hour. Maybe time works a little differently in the Cassie zone?"

"A lot differently. Still, I would have appreciated a visit. I also would have liked a minute to thank you for catching my sorry ass. I'd still be falling if it weren't for you."

"Who says you're not?" she asked, then squeezed my hands when she felt me grow tense, "Just kidding. But I don't think you really would have appreciated me coming by. You know the rules: I don't come to you of my own volition. Hell, I don't go anywhere of my own volition. You gotta summon me. The only other way I know of to get here is on the coattails of your buddy Rudy, and I'm sure neither of us would have wished for that just now."

"I'm sure," I agreed solemnly before turning us back to the subject, "So, I didn't want to see you for all those weeks, um, days? That seems odd."

"Maybe you wanted time alone to work Cassie," Max said playfully. Then she allowed her bright green eyes to wander over my shoulder.

"So where is she?" she asked, letting go of my left hand and dragging me along by my right as she marched down the hall shouting, "Cassie! Where the hell are you?" I pulled back on Max's hand and slowed her progress.

"Don't bother," I said, "She doesn't seem to like the hallways. Let's duck into a room."

"Which one?"

"Doesn't matter."

"Huh?"

"I thought you've been here before."

"I have, and on my other visits she usually was waiting for me at the front door. Now there's not even one of those. Aside from last time, when I brought you up to your bedroom, I'm sure I've never been in any of the rooms; just this front hall. Weird."

"Weird it is. Maybe Rudy's spirit-harboring rules have changed in the last few weeks. Days. Or maybe it's just different for you when he does the summoning; the front hall was the only spot in my house that he got mostly right, so I could see his involvement centering there. You know what? Never mind any of this bullshit. Just walk through that door right there; the one that may or may not lead to a kitchen." Max shrugged and led me through the door at the end of the hall. When she pushed it open I worried that the Cassie spell may have worn off with Max's arrival. I hoped not, because, doppelganger or not, I wanted to thank Cassie for literally being there for me throughout my oblong convalescence.

We were not disappointed. The room we entered was a kitchen whose details were, for a change, remarkably true to the original, give or take a cabinet. Cassie sat at the counter near the sink. She was dressed in a loose gray sweatsuit, her brown hair was knotted behind her head, and she was laboriously passing a marble rolling pin over a sheet of empty waxed paper. She acknowledged my entry with a tired nod, but then stopped working when she noticed that Max accompanied me. She wiped her clean hands with a dishtowel, and forced a smile. That smile shook me more than the elevator bell had. Why would a fake Cassie have emotions that require masking? No matter, I thought, as I stepped into the kitchen and embraced Cassie. I understood why she was reluctant to be pleased by Max's arrival, because it both foretold her immediate future and clarified her condition. She knew I was leaving, and she knew that to me she was a memory, and that Max was my present. I held her for an extra moment, to wordlessly assure her how deeply I valued that memory. Cassie softened slightly in my arms, offering me a hint that she understood my sentiment. I did not, again, care to try to imagine why I would want to convince a construct of anything.

"Man," I heard Max groan from behind me, "Crack a few of a guy's bones and he turns into a hug fiend." I smiled, but not at Max's joke. The hug I shared with Cassie felt familiar and completely normal. I reduced the lump that had gathered in my throat by wondering how Rudy had learned about this detail, or if perhaps my own invention had somehow seeped into the mix. I also registered the profoundly different emotions I encountered when holding Cassie, any Cassie, instead of Max. The tandem hugs helped to define my feelings, or my decisions about what to feel, for each of these women.

"No matter," I said aloud, separating myself from Cassie, "I have to go now."

"You do?" Cassie asked, eyes wet, "But didn't you just get here?"

"I'm beginning to wonder about that myself. You might not remember, but I want to thank you for all the help you gave me, for bringing me back to health."

"I did that? You were sick?"

"Yes. Yes you did, and yes I was. Thank you."

"But I didn't do anything."

"You know," I said, "You're probably right about that. Still, whatever it was you weren't doing really helped, because I'm totally healed now, both inside and out."

"Well," Cassie said, blushing lightly, "You're welcome then." She looked past me to Max, who took the gesture as a cue to move forward and take one of Cassie's hands.

"Hi Max," Cassie said, "Are you here to visit, or just to take Alex away from me?" I knew what she meant.

"Oh Cassie," Max said pleasantly, "You make me sound like a monster when you ask like that. Of course I would love to stay and visit for a while, but Alex has some pressing business waiting for him."

"You'll both come back, won't you?" Cassie asked with Victorian sweetness, "I do so enjoy your company."

"Sure," Max said, kissing Cassie on her cheek, "Or maybe we'll have you visit us. Either way don't you worry; we won't leave you alone for long. Alex, we should go."

"Okay," I said, smiling at Cassie, "We're out of here, then. Cassie, you take care of yourself, and I'm sure I'll see you again."

"Meeting repeatedly does seem to be our fate, doesn't it?" she asked with one thin eyebrow raised high on her smooth forehead, prodding me to wonder again how much this image of a woman I once loved really knew.

"It sure does," I said. I would have said more, but that damned Beaver Toys elevator bell, augmented by Max's sharp tug on my elbow, interrupted my parting speech.

"What's the rush?" I whispered as we turned toward the opening elevator that had appeared where our sliding glass door to the back porch should have been.

"Sorry," Max said, "I didn't know I was hurrying. I guess I'm anxious, and more than a little worried about leaving a healthy Alex within spell-casting distance of his dead wife."

"Nice," I said drolly, "Didn't that dead wife tell you I'm a changed man?"

"Nope. But I'm sure you are, my love," Max said with a wink. She knows too! I could feel my heart scream, but didn't dare amplify its declaration with useless words. Max continued, "Now push the button for our floor and let's go. This Musak is making me crazy." I was going to ask which floor, but when I turned to the panel and saw that there was only one button to push, I held my tongue and jabbed the unmarked button with my thumb. It glowed orange from my touch, the doors slid closed on a homey image of Cassie in a floor-length velvet robe waving to us from our bedroom, and the Musak got louder. An instrumental version of "The Look of Love" was playing over unseen speakers.

"I don't know," I said, "This music's not so bad."

"Oh, please."

"You're just not open-minded, that's all. So how long is this ride, anyway?" I noticed that the car had never started moving, "Not that I mind, of course, I've developed quite the affinity for one-button elevators."

"I'm sure you have, but I'll bet this'll be pretty quick," Max said, her optimism a poor mask for her visible impatience. She stood with her arms folded, staring at the closed doors, effectively negating the moment of hot intimacy I had anticipated we would share once we were alone. I wanted to ask what was agitating her before we reached our destination, but the doors swung open with that same singsong single ding before I could.

Max stepped out of the elevator and into the glass vestibule of the diner in the sky. I followed her, my back leg clearing the elevator's steel threshold an instant before its form dissolved into the opaque picture windows that had preceded it.

"Was that what you were worried about?" I asked quietly as I followed her through the glass doors that opened on the diner's main salon, "Getting stuck in our ride?"

"Maybe," Max said to the air in front of us, "I don't know. It could have been that, or something else; I hadn't even realized I was nervous. You hungry?"

"I don't think I've touched food in a month. I could probably eat."

"Good," Max smiled, taking my hand, "Let's sit down then. I'll bet we've got a mountain of things to discuss."

"We do, I'm sure. But don't say mountain here, okay?"

"Ha ha," Max said. I could feel myself melting as she relaxed. Then she pointed across the crowded dining room toward those giant, crystal clear, easily traversed windows, and said, "Oh, there he is. Clive!"

Clive, seated at a booth, *that* booth, beside the panorama, heard her shout above the din of the other patrons. He gestured pleasantly for us to join him. We wove through the randomly scattered tables of diners, all human but unfamiliar, and all feasting merrily from plates heaping with shredded pages of dictionaries. No doubt the OED, I thought, noting the smart formal attire adorning everyone.

We arrived at Clive's booth, and Max slid onto the red vinyl bench across from him without hesitation. I, however, found reason for pause, and for snatching a wooden chair out from under an obese woman draped in acres of blue taffeta who was gorging on R's at a nearby table. The woman hit the floor with a gaseous slap, but nodded her approval at my theft with gentility, and without pausing her mastication of fine printed pages. I set the chair at the end of the table, as far from the window as possible, and sat. Clive shook his head.

"I understand the hint, Alex, but you need not worry. There will be no theatrics, or unintended exits, today."

"That's good to know," I said, "But just the same, this seat is fine."

"Alex," Max said, "You are the most powerful chickenshit I have ever encountered."

"And she has waded through many a pile of fowl feces in her time," Clive added.

"I'm just being careful," I said, hands in the air, "Please bear with me. So, can we eat soon?"

"Certainly," Clive said, "I will summon a waiter." He fished a banana from the inside pocket of his tailored linen suit, and tossed it to the floor. An orangutan in a tuxedo appeared to hand out menus. I opened mine. Its pages were blank.

"I guess I'll have the chicken," I told the hairy waiter. The orangutan bared his teeth and nodded, and then looked at Max, who ordered the same. Clive asked a few questions about the specials, and then ordered something French. The waiter retrieved our useless menus and waddled toward the kitchen.

"Anyway," Max said, "You probably can trust Clive as well, or even more, than you can me. Unlike me, Clive and Rudy never, um – "

"Reached a consensus," Clive finished, "It's true Alex. Though I do value the experiences the man has offered me, I simply never warmed to Rudy. This is particularly valid now that I am aware that he has consistently misled me in his unnecessary effort to dissuade me from meeting that lout of a corporeal shell with whom I share my eternal soul."

"Fair enough," I said, symbolically leaning across the table and clasping Clive's hand. His grip was weak, and he clung to my four fingers rather than my palm. I let go without passing visible judgment, and smiled uneasily. Though I trusted the sincerity of his current pledge, I still doubted Clive's ultimate allegiance. I should have questioned him further, to confirm that he had actually grown cold to Rudy, but I had no interest in stirring new drama. Clive could wait, or even be totally ignored, I decided; the rest could not. Feeling another distracting train of thought accelerating toward me, I glanced out the window seeking reorientation.

I found it. The diner was still suspended over the roof of the world, but the magnificent sky had darkened since my last visit. Its timeless twilight demeanor was still present, but it had seemingly been tinged with blood. I chose to accept the symbol, and, with that acceptance, to rejoin the fray.

"So Max," I said, "How is Mary? Any news?"

"She's fine, and of course there is."

"Could you maybe expand on that?"

"Oh, Alex," Max said, leaning forward with delight, visibly struggling to hold back a flood of words that she had been damming for days, "You could never understand what bringing Mary to me has done for me, her; us. The doors that have already opened since we met are taking me places, and to experiences, that I was sure I could never encounter."

"So basically you're happy to know Mary?" I said. Max laughed.

"You know it. And you do, don't you? But it's not all good, Alex. Mary is my open line to reality, and most of the time I can't believe the shit she shows me. Through all these years with Rudy I never once caught a real glimpse of the morass of despair, fear, and stupidity our souls must navigate every day. I knew it all was there, intellectually, but to actually see how it feels to be helpless – my God, it was a bloody epiphany!"

"So basically you're happy to know Mary?" I asked again. Max laughed again.

"Yeah," she said, "I am. In spite of all that miserable truth, I am."

The arrival of the entrees forced us to politely pause our conversation while the dapper primate wrestled a live chicken to submission before me, and then dropped a juicy cordon bleu in front of Max and what could have been veal Marsala at Clive's place. My companions dug right in to their meals, taking no notice of the fat white bird squatting passively on my plate. Ah, well, I thought, I wasn't hungry anyway; maybe next week. I set the chicken on the floor by my feet, patted its feathery behind and sent it on its way. Then I refocused my attention on Max, whose cheek was puffed with a great wad of gourmet food.

"So Max, were you or Mary able to glean any useful tidbits about dear Rudy through your euphoria of unification?"

"Of course," Max mumbled through her full mouth. Rolling her eyes, she finished chewing before she spoke again, "Mary's been keeping an excellent vigil, even reading newspapers, and she can report everything she sees to me whenever she dreams. I have no idea how, but it works. Pretty cool, huh?"

"Cool," I said, rotating my wrist to encourage her to continue, "What has she heard?"

"Well, Mr-All-Business-Who-Couldn't-Care-Less-About-His-Main-Squeeze's-Triumphs, she's heard quite a bit. Rudy got right to it after he finished with you down south, apparently. He and Freuzre must have some tight deadlines, because Mary's reported that to her it looks like chaos is erupting everywhere. By the way, Mary says that Chile has been closed to the public; a whole country – can you believe it?"

"Um, yes, I can. So Mary said that, about the chaos?"

"Well, no, she said that the news is totally fucked up and everybody's totally scared shitless, but I knew what she meant. Anyway, she says it's getting worse by the minute: the world's leaders are all confused and disorganized, everybody on the planet seems to be having the same two Armageddon dreams – one positive and one negative, but both littered with world-rending biblical symbolism that's scaring the shit out of everyone, especially Hindu and Muslim clerics – and the talking heads on TV aren't arguing anymore."

"That's bad," I said, picking a bit of Max's food from her plate with my fingers. She let me take it, as though it was something I did all the time. I liked that. I didn't like the chicken, which tasted like warm wet socks. After I discretely removed the chicken from my mouth and dropped it into the waiter's open palm, I continued, "Before you go on, tell me something: did Mary have these dreams? Maybe there's something in them we can key on."

"Nope. Odd, huh? She only read about them, but they've been universally described as either lots of death and destruction at the hand of hordes of evil creatures, or lots of death and destruction at the hand of endless ranks of angels. Nobody seems to remember any specific details, or at least they haven't reported on them, but everyone is truly confused."

"I can't blame them. Rudy and Freuzre certainly can't be credited for their originality. They should have known that half the world would have no idea what they were talking about, and the rest would just freak out."

"Seriously. But that was only primer for the pump; Rudy's 'rounds' must be having a solid effect on the physical world too. I initially figured that Mary was just mistaken, this being the first time she ever picked up a newspaper. But when I asked her to relay some headlines to me, like the one where the entire Chinese occupying army ran screaming en masse from Tibet, on foot, looking over their shoulders for dragons, I understood that she was spotting some serious weirdness."

"That was a headline?"

"Mostly. Point is, I got the impression that things on the physical plain really are a mess and, though Mary had no way to confirm, they sure did smack of Rudy." Max continued with her outline of bizarre world events, but I stopped listening. Max/Mary's report was confirmation of what I had expected to hear; details were unimportant to me. News items like a worldwide cessation of all aggressive activity on Tuesday, followed Wednesday morning by a mustering of angry armies on scores undisputed borders, did not surprise me. Though important in their own context, and in the pain and confusion they generated, to me it was all old news, rends in the fabric of reality that I had already endured. I was pleased that Max/Mary supplied the information they had, and, more so, that they were supplying it to me and not Rudy. But their thread was just a thread, a detail in a tapestry woven from bent dreams and psychotic interpretations of history that was about to be spread across the land, smothering it uniquely. The thought shifted my attention inadvertently to Clive. I glanced at him.

"You hear anything from your counterpart, Clive?"

"I fear not, Alex," Clive said, *after* finishing his petite forkful of food and taking a dainty sip of blue wine, "I do not enjoy Max's intimacy with my earthly, and quite earthy, alter ego."

"Would you like to?" I asked, rubbing my hands together.

"Please no," Clive said, recoiling slightly, "And for that I promise never to toss you through a window."

"Enough said," I nodded. And it was enough, because it helped answer a question that had been swimming just beneath the surface of my thoughts. Max had been unconsciously agitated – if a creature *of* the unconscious can *have* an unconscious, of course – since our reunion. The nature of Rudy and Freuzre's corruption of the worldwide psyche explained her misgivings, and her need to rush me from Cassie's place. Yet Clive was totally calm, sincerely disinterested in the fate of his counterpart, and therefore himself. I wondered about that, briefly, before allowing the question to sink again, rejoining the rest of the niggling details whose definite import my mind was simply too small to consciously absorb.

I absently wiped my hands with the cloth napkin that I did not need on my lap, and decided without much thought that lunch was over. I desired to stay and chat with Max for hours, days, even years, but it was time to abandon easy pleasure and immerse myself once more in Rudy's chilly pool of global manipulation. I rested a hand on Max's wrist, cleared my throat and addressed my lieutenants in a manner reserved by field officers who choose to lead from the front ranks:

"That's it, then. The fabric of the physical world is being shredded by my historically and spiritually challenged ex neighbor, and I have this undodgeable feeling that I might be the only one who can do something about him."

"Alex, please," Max interrupted, taking my hand "We've hardly told you anything yet. You need more information, more preparation."

"It's okay, Max," I said softly, "I'm not going lie down in front of another one of Rudy's steamrollers. I learned that lesson. No, when next Rudy and I meet, we'll be playing by my rules. I hope. I have no idea what those rules are yet, but I do know that I'd best figure them out and jot them down quickly before Rudy realizes that I'm not quite dead yet.

"But I do know that time is extremely short. If all this happened in the last three days, Freuzre must have stepped up his schedule, or Rudy has struck out on his own to terrify his unruly masses into submission. Either way, the psychic noise those two are passing out will wear thin pretty fast. Part of the human condition is an innate ability to get used to anything."

"You'll vouch for that," Max said without humor.

"Yeah, I suppose I would," I said, "Anyway, the people will incorporate the dreams and psychotic behavior into their daily grind almost instantly. It's easier that way. To make the more permanent impact that they both desire, Rudy and Freuzre will feel compelled to invade life on earth in a much more final manner soon. I have no idea what they'll do, but it will be done."

"Well said. What will you do now?" Clive asked.

"I'm going home, to familiar turf."

"Haven't you already been there?"

"Yes, but I'm better informed now. I think."

"My heart shivers at your confidence," Max said. Her sarcasm failed to mask her concern.

"Yeah, mine too. Don't worry, I'll be more careful this time, and I won't lose sight of my goal to stop Freuzre, and then convince Rudy that his crusade is over."

"That's a tall freaking order," Max said.

"Tell me about it."

"And you've no concept of a plan, or even a source for establishing one?" Clive asked.

"Nope," I said, and I wouldn't tell you if I did, I thought, feeling oddly empowered by my suspicions.

"You a re truly valorous," Max said. She easily pulled my chair close to her bench so that she could rest her head on my shoulder.

"No, I'm an idiot."

"Here here," Max said, raising her glass of white wine. She did not sip it, choosing to hold her position against me as long as possible.

"On that note," I said, "I'm out of here." I signaled to the nearest waiter for our check. He responded by eating it, and I saluted the generous gesture. I again shook Clive's flaccid fist. After pausing a moment to enjoy the soft bouquet of her hair, I kissed the top of Max's head and stood. Max sighed sullenly, but slipped back to her position in the booth without rising from it.

"I'm going home to find out first hand what's happening down there," I continued, "And maybe in the process a direction for action will materialize. In the meantime, I'd appreciate it if you two would keep on paying attention, stay clear of Rudy should he resurface, and, above all, stay alive."

"You too," Max said, looking up at me.

"I'll try," I said, running my fingers through her thick red hair, "I'll try."

I turned away from Max once more, successful this time only because I knew, *knew*, that our parting was temporary and only physical. Without looking back I waded through the noisy diners alone, and left through the front doors. Though I felt that my poise telegraphed purpose and solid direction, I wondered silently just what the hell I was going to do, and how I was going to get away with doing it before Rudy tossed me down another bottomless well.

Chapter Twenty-Nine

Two days after my heroic exit from the diner, I was meekly piloting my Escort west along Interstate 80 somewhere in Iowa. At least I was confident it was Iowa: it is difficult to remember where you are when you are perfectly incapable of being lost. I was suspicious of my location when I passed Altoona, but I still wasn't sure of the state I was traversing until I saw a sign for Des Moines. I took the first available off-ramp, assuming that the Des Moines metro area would be as good as any to find a comfy room with a TV.

After circling the globe a couple of times in the last day, I had to smile at the odd choice of Iowa as my final destination. The logic, that it was best to stand still in a place where I had never been before in order to stay under Rudy's radar, was sound, but I wondered at how this locale had randomly emerged from the vast gamut of places to which I had never been. Ultimately I did not care; Iowa was a nice state, even if no one other than national political aspirants or diehard *M*A*S*H* fans would ever choose to visit there.

My search for signs of Rudy, though invigorating in a tourist-from-hell sort of way, had yielded no results. I had browsed the surface of every continent, including a brief slide through Antarctica after boldly assuming that Rudy may have created his own little paradise where no other human would tread. I abandoned that silly assumption after I extricated myself from my fifth barren ice shelf. Rudy loved humans, and would be truly out of character to settle in total isolation. But he was also not where humans thrived in Europe, Asia, Australia, or North America. I could not find him in Africa or South America, where he might have been helping those humans who don't thrive so well, but there was no evidence of change beyond the flustered reports posted by a group of geologists and cartographers in Chile.

My searches were limited to the viewing range of my eyes in whatever spot the Escort toured. Those eyes are extremely untrained in the ways of subtle manipulation, so Rudy could have been present and constructing his artificial Armageddon in any environment through which I passed, and I would never have been the wiser. I required about a dozen stops in every locale I could imagine before I accepted that my quest had been doomed for failure from its start. Cocky as I may have grown in my dual-worldly nature, and in my survival of Rudy's held punches, I simply did not have the wherewithal to properly track the man's movements. I decided that the best thing to was to find a room, watch some CNN, and get on the Internet. I would enlist journalists, whose job it was to unearth megalomaniacs with global ambition, to find Rudy. Of course I did not regret my ill-conceived physical search. How often does a suburban stooge like me have an opportunity to see the world from behind the steering wheel of his own car? I had acres of fun touring all the places where Rudy was not, meeting people, polar bears, and penguins who had no idea who he was, who I was, or that there was a rest of the world that mattered. I decided that I would make that enlightening and entertaining trip several more times, but I would do so only after the Rudy issue was resolved so that I would not be preoccupied.

"Sure could use a way to resolve that damn issue," I said aloud from my position in heavy traffic that shuffled slowly along a four-lane swath of straight asphalt that was littered with fast food restaurants, strip malls, and Wal-Mart. And God help me I pulled onto the meandering vehicular tributary that directed the endless flow of rolling steel into Wal-Mart's vast parking lot.

I had to stop at the giant discounter that often succeeded in its obsession to homogenize small town America and define the purchasing process for all of society. I needed a computer with which to connect to the worldwide web, and the generic retail behemoth that squatted monolithically in countless erstwhile empty fields across the nation was the easiest source for locating a decent, albeit not excellent, laptop computer.

After completing several circuits of the packed lot I found an available spot in which to park the Escort. I chuckled at the notion that I could flit through time and space with little more than a thought, but it was still nearly impossible to park at a Wal-Mart. I considered leaving my invulnerable vehicle in the fire lane directly outside the main entrance, but I knew that would be wrong, as would creating a handicap sticker and parking in one of the fifty empty spots reserved for the few needy people who required the advantage. So I waited, lurked, and eventually tagged a space near the door anyway, between two mammoth sport-utes. I climbed out of the car, stretched a bit, gathered some more resolve, and took those painful steps between the electric doors and past the inevitable cheerful greeter. But, when I was inside the giant store, surrounded by the requisite crowd of shopper-zombies, a strange thing happened: I didn't mind being there.

It was most likely the knowledge that I could leave, instantly, whenever I wanted to do so, mixed with the fact I was there to successfully purchase a computer in spite of my lack of money, or even a wallet, but the milling crowd itself had raised my spirits as well. For years I had hated that crowd. They filled the store, at any hour, and seemed to wander mindlessly through the endless aisles, looking for things they didn't need but might be able to afford. I was routinely angry that so many of my fellow sentients could so easily succumb to their herding instinct, so happily abandon individuality and hygiene. But now, with my new perspective and respect for the depth of all minds, coupled with the Max/Mary example of the duality of intelligence, I valued these people, even the ones who would not look in front of themselves as they pushed their laden carts down the crowded aisles. My fellow shoppers, what they were doing, and whatever they touched, were real. I hadn't made them up, manipulated their worlds, or even let them know I exist. Neither, I was sure, had Rudy. They were pure humanity, safely ensconced in one of the most powerful institutions known to nature for curbing the individual. I felt good while I myself wandered aimlessly, ostensibly searching for the electronics department. Eventually I spotted a distant wall of TV sets that were tuned in concert to the same rerun of Seinfeld. I strolled in their general direction, sure that computers would be placed somewhere near TV's even at Wal-Mart.

I passed a cluttered cashwrap manned by two thin young men in blue smocks. Fully engrossed in a heated discussion of

Lara Croft's true nature, they didn't notice me browsing the rows
of what appeared to me were identical laptops displayed on shelves
across from the cashwrap. When I picked one up at random (the
most efficient way for me to choose a computer) and carried it to
the gadget-infested glass case that separated the youths from me
and set it down, they stifled their conversation and stared at me
with slack jaws and glazed semi-open eyes.

"Does this one connect to the Internet?" I asked.

"Dude," the taller one said, scratching his nose while he
spoke – at least he didn't pick it, I thought – "You can't do that."

"Can you show me one that does connect?"

"It'll get you on line. They all do that."

"Then what can't I do?"

"That," the youth said, pointing at me. Well, I thought, this
is going about as well as I had expected. I thought for a moment,
trying to step onto the correct playing field. In a few seconds I
decided I had it.

"Oh," I said, "I know it's a display, but you must have
some in boxes."

"No, not that," the other one said, examining the computer,
"You can't bring it over here."

"Wrong department? It says electronics on your badge,
Ed."

"No, no," the tall one, Josh, said, waving his hands, "You
can buy it, and we're the right place, but they're tied down."

"With steel cables," Ed added, "And bolts."

Oops. I smiled sheepishly, realizing I had let my will
handle things unconsciously again. I must get a handle on that
some day, I thought. I shrugged:

"This one wasn't," I offered.

"That is too weird," they said in unison, which also caused
them to share a glance and giggle.

"I guess," I said, "So it will connect me to the Internet,
right?"

"Dude, of course it will," Ed said patronizingly, turning the
computer toward him to confirm that I hadn't broken anything
when I ripped it off the wall, "Like I told you, they all do that."

"Oh," I said, "I knew that. So it doesn't need any software,
or anything extra? I just have to plug a phone line to it and go?"

"You got it dude," Ed said, though he did double-check with a quick glance at the plastic description card beneath the space the laptop once occupied, "Just plug it in with the wire that comes with it."

"Cool," I said, reaching into my pocket, "How much?"

"Just one moment, sir," Josh said, graduating me from 'dude' to 'sir' when he saw my hand enter my pocket. Josh turned to his cash register, punched about fifty keys, and looked up.

"Would you like a service contract for that?"

"Why? Is it going to break?"

"No, but we offer one. You know, just in case. It lasts a year and only costs $49.95."

"No," I said, choosing to avoid the debate, "I won't be needing one."

"Your choice," Josh said knowingly, "That makes it come to $1,346.67."

"I'll take it," I said, "But could you grab me one in a box?"

"Absolutely, sir," Ed said. He disappeared while Josh worked a few dozen more keys.

"How will you be paying for that, sir?" he asked.

"Cash okay?"

After at least three seconds of the inevitable blank stare that follows such a question – necessary while his mind checked dusty files for the meaning of the word 'cash' – Josh shrugged and said, "Sure. I guess." I pulled my hand out of my pocket and laid a neat pile of 27 fifty-dollar bills on the counter. Josh just stared at it. When Ed came back with a cardboard box a dozen times the size of the computer it contained, he set it down and stared at the cash too.

"Everything okay?" I asked.

"Uh, yeah, sure," Josh said, picking up the money. He counted it slowly, trying not to make it too obvious that he was checking for counterfeit bills.

"Do you need a department manager to okay that or something?" I asked.

"That's me," Josh said without looking up, "I'm the manager."

"Oh good," I said, biting my tongue before I congratulated him on reaching a position of authority before exiting puberty.

Josh finished counting, tapped a few more keys. The register opened. He carefully placed the fifties under the cash drawer before he counted out my change and handed it to me with my receipt.

"You need a bag for that, sir?" Ed asked numbly. I wanted to believe that he was still dumbfounded by the event, but couldn't avoid the conclusion that he was simply numb.

"Sure," I said, if only to be entertained by his immediate search for a suitably large bag and then, after he found one, his two-minute effort to get the box into it. Finally, fully bagged and receipted, I pulled my purchase off the counter. The boys thanked me robotically, and I them, and then I turned. Before I took my first step away from the counter, I abruptly about-faced, lifted my free index finger, and said:

"And you know, Lara Croft can't drive an Iron Mole for shit." When their jaws slackened a bit more I smiled.

"Sorry," I said, "That needed to be said. Bye."

As I made my way back through the store I found myself wondering if there was anything else I needed, like toothpaste or trash bags, to purchase before I left. I was not sure if the impulse to make more purchases, or just look for more stuff, was sourced in the fact that it was there, my disinterest in ever returning, or perhaps some deeply instinctual desire to do what everyone else in the place was doing. Wal-Mart may have profitably tapped into the primordial hunter-gatherer and herding instincts that still lurked beneath the consciousness of its unwitting patrons.

"I'd best get out of here before I start getting fat," I said aloud, drawing a glare from a rotund woman who was towing her obese, crying, child away from the toy section. As I exited I waved goodbye to the greeter, dutifully confusing the old fellow. I walked to my car and threw the computer into the back seat of the Escort. I quickly shed the inadvertent spike of camaraderie for my fellow denim-clad lemmings I was enjoying when I surveyed the war zone of narcissism and displaced fury that is any given Wal-Mart parking lot. After much maneuvering, a half dozen wrong turns and three long pauses while my fellow shoppers remembered what to do at a stop sign, I found myself back in heavy traffic on that main strip. While I absently scanned the horizon for a hotel I wondered where the hell all these people came from, and where they were going. I carried that thought whenever I was on a crowded road, but it seemed more meaningful out there in the heartland. In the movies these places were always empty. I set aside the thought trail when I spotted a familiar green and yellow sign, with a "Congratulations Bill and Sophie," written in black plastic letters on a small marquis beneath it. I pulled out of traffic and into the driveway of the Holiday Inn. There, where empty parking spaces were numerous, I was allowed to double-park in front of the office. So I did. I entered the office's lobby and earned a strange look from the chubby young woman working the registration counter when I asked about vacancies.

"Um, yes," she mumbled, "We got plenty of rooms."

"Do they have cable?"

"Sir please, this is a Holiday Inn. Of course we have cable."

"Sorry," I asked, stifling a snicker at her company pride, "How about a way for me to hook my computer to the Internet?"

"Sir," she said, visibly trying not to roll her eyes, "All you gotta do is unplug the phone wire and plug yours in. Now what credit card will you be putting this on, sir?"

Understanding that cash rarely works in this situation, I produced an American Express platinum card from my bottomless pocket, and watched carefully as she swiped it in her machine and awaited approval. Now this, I thought, is a true test of my talents. I tried not to think about the transaction, beyond confirming to myself repeatedly that it would obviously work. And, seconds later, I spotted the approval code on her little blue readout. Okay, I thought, this new life has definitely got its perks. When I completed the blank registration card she slid over greasy black Formica to me, I was careful to glance at both the name on the credit card – Albert Croft, go figure – and the Escort's license plate to be sure everything matched.

"Ah," I said aloud as I wrote, "So many details in life to keep track of."

"Tell me about it," the woman sighed as she turned to get my key. She handed it, and a paper diagram of the motel with my room circled on it, tried to smile, and said, "You'll be staying in room 217. To get there you just drive halfway around back, park by the door, go up the stairs that are just inside, and turn right. It'll be just near the end of the hall on the left. And have a pleasant stay."

"Why thank you," I said, "I think I just might do that." I turned away, noticing her plastic smile vaporizing before it cleared my peripheral view. She probably thought I was being sarcastic, I thought. I guessed it was fortunate that I didn't tease her about giving directions in a motel with no more than fifty numbered rooms. I returned to my car, moved it to a space near the specified door, which wasn't locked, and found my room. I was uneasy about checking into a room without baggage, but that feeling only heightened the novelty of the moment. Besides, I was carrying the laptop, still in its box, so at least I offered the appearance of propriety.

The room, my room, was the same as any of 100,000 mid-range rooms in the country: two stiff but big beds, sturdy furniture, brass lamps with white shades, cheesy art, a noisy HVAC unit under the window, and that strange dusty/disinfectant smell that someone must be bottling for the hotel chains. I found that endearing, especially because I wasn't worrying about costs, or theft, or how my house was faring without me. The freedom from its mundane requirements seemed to make the material world more interesting. The cookie-cutter hospitality I was enjoying was a vacation from the surreal chaos to which I had been subjected in my current existence.

I made a trip to the ice machine down the hall and filled the plastic bucket I had found in my room. I bought, with the change from the computer purchase, two candy bars and potato chips from a nearby vending machine. Yes, I knew that I could have simply uncovered the bucket and ice would have been there, and I still wasn't hungry or thirsty, but these tasks had to be done in order to fully distend the flesh of my vacation. I returned to my room, popped the paper lid off one of the glasses that sat inverted in a plastic tray centered on the maple-stained and glass-protected desk, filled it with ice. I got some water from the sink that sat outside the bathroom, tested it with a sip – it was drinkable, though heavily softened. I grabbed the remote off the TV set, hopped onto a bed with my water and snacks, fluffed a couple of pillows, switched on the TV, and set to work.

I surfed the channels until I found a headline news station, and watched. I was hoping for inspiration for my next move. I still had no plan, or even a notion of one. Every moment of my search for Rudy had been consumed with a palpable fear of actually encountering him while I remained helpless and without direction. Maybe, I thought as I bit the end off my Snickers bar, that was why I couldn't find him. The news, or the Internet if the TV failed me, would probably reveal some pattern that I had overlooked, something that I wasn't prepared to see, having been removed from current events for the better part of a year. I let the headlines run full cycle, finishing the candy bar and munching most of the chips during my vigil, but nothing seemed very different in the world. The same partisan politics, the same weather, the same celebrities, or variants of them, getting into trouble, and the same stock market insanity ruled the reports.

"Maybe Mary was pulling Max's leg?" I asked aloud, amused by the image the statement had dropped into my mind. Max/Mary could have been confused, I reasoned, because it was the first time that Mary had ever really viewed the news. Her first exposure to the media, which was designed for far more jaded souls, might have been a shock regardless of the reported information. Then I remembered that nobody misinterprets stories about Chinese soldiers running from dragons, and watched more; there had to be something different.

A couple of new wars were brewing in South America and Asia, but neither seemed to be drawn from anything more than the history that defined the countries involved. I noticed that there was no news about the Middle East, which was a major hotspot the last time I cared. I realized that I would not get far with the headline station's signature general delivery, so I switched to CNN. That move did not help, though, because a member of the British royal family had died, and CNN was providing full coverage of the funeral, and nothing else.

"Why?" I asked aloud.

I followed the headline ticker that ran beneath the shots of a coffin traveling the streets of London, but they offered little variation from the headline news channel. I also acknowledged again that there was still not a word spoken, or written, about the Middle East. I decided to fire up the computer.

I removed it from its carton, lifted the lid, and yelped with glee at the latest example of my ability to mess with reality: the computer came to full, usable life immediately, with the words "WELCOME ALEX" spanning the large flat screen in a bright green oversized font. A single icon in the shape of a bulls-eye floated below the greeting. I removed the phone cord from the wall, located a short length of patch cord in a small plastic bag taped to one of the chunks of Styrofoam that filled most of the computer's box, and connected the computer to the phone system.

Before I did anything else, I took a brief hotel break. I gathered the pillows from the other bed and stacked them on mine. When satisfied that all had as much fluff as the foam would allow, I snuggled into them. Then I chewed my last candy bar, sipped my water and surfed the dozen available non-news channels for an hour or so. The mind-numbing inactivity mixed well with the moderately comfortable pillows, and I felt myself relax to a point where my greatest dilemma was whether or not I felt like dragging myself off the bed to refill my water glass. I was in middle class heaven. In time I sighed deeply, shook my head, and sat up straight against the pillows. I decided to return to the task at hand I abandoned completely to the pleasures of doing absolutely nothing. I muted the TV set, set the laptop where it belonged, on my lap, and double-clicked on the bulls-eye.

A browser appeared on the screen. It was not a branded browser, because I had trouble using all of them. Instead, it was a simple screen with two blank fields. The first field was labeled "topic," the second was called "subject." I entered the word "world" in the topic field, and "news" in the subject field, and hit the return key. A series of news sites began appearing on the screen: CNN, MSN, Slate, Salon, several major newspapers. Each remained on the screen until I had thoroughly scanned it, and then faded to be replaced by another.

"This is so cool," I said, "If I could patent it, I'd be rich."

I was soon agitated that one subject was consistently absent from the websites. I returned to the original search page, and typed "Middle East" into the topic field and hit the return key. I failed to get a single hit. Maybe, I thought hopefully, there's some new politically correct rule that precludes the use of the term. On that hunch I entered every Mideast term I could remember, one at a time, into the topic field. I tried Israel, Palestine, Jordan, Saudi Arabia, Iran, Iraq, Hamas, Jerusalem, Arafat, Syria, Arab, Saddam Hussein, and about fifty others. All yielded nothing. When I tried Egypt, a thousand hits were noted, and I got similar results with Turkey, Greece, and Serbia. Information about everything between them was unavailable. I found plenty of links when I entered "mosque," or "Hebrew," but any reference to their Middle Eastern roots was universally omitted.

"Shit," I said, slapping my thigh, "Even I never thought about the Middle East until now!" Though my physical search had covered every corner of the globe, I had ignored the most likely place on its surface where trouble, and no doubt Freuzre or Rudy, thrived. I had also forgotten, until that moment, the signature explosion in Jerusalem that was my first fitful step on this difficult path. I slammed the laptop's lid closed, unplugged the phone line, and ran from the room with the computer under my arm. My vacation in the wonderful reality of hard beds, TV, and Wal-Mart had concluded. I took the stairs two at a time, left the hotel and dove through the open door into my Escort.

I drove for miles on route 80, almost reaching Illinois before I firmly established that nothing around me was changing. I apparently was not going directly to the Middle East via my usual mystical transportation system. Every place I imagined there yielded no change in my orientation on the planet. Fine, I thought, then I will find another way.

In minutes I was driving on the Van Wycke expressway on Long Island, following the signs to the Kennedy International Airport terminals. When I arrived, I noticed that El Al's terminal was gone. I parked in a loading zone in front of the American Airlines terminal. Inside, I walked directly to an available ticket agent (I would definitely be a rich man, I thought), and asked for a ticket to Jerusalem.

"Excuse me?" the agent, a tall man with an arresting if insincere smile and a very high tuft of blond hair, said.

"Jerusalem," I repeated, drumming my fingers on the counter, "Are there any flights available today?"

"Is there a major destination that this place, Jerusalem, is near, sir?" The agent asked hopefully. Oh, my.

"Sure. How about Damascus?"

"Where's that?"

"Near Jerusalem. Syria."

"Is Syria a country?"

"Maybe not. How about Saudi Arabia?"

"Sir, are you playing with me? I have other customers, you know."

"Actually, you don't. But thanks anyway. I think you've answered my question." I left the airport in the Escort, and, to solidify my suspicions, I repeated the same exercise at Dulles, Logan, and Heathrow airports. There were no flights to any place that I remembered being in the Middle East, and the history of the place seemed to have been erased from the minds of every baffled person I asked. On a hunch I parked in front of the New York Public Library on Fifth Avenue, and ran into the reference room. I found a terminal, and tried searching for Middle Eastern books.

"Well now, that's odd," I said when my search yielded tens of thousands of references to all things Middle East, from geography to history to culture to Jesus Christ and Mohammed themselves. Apparently Freuzre did not read books, or had very little faith in popular interest in them. What I did not find, consistently, were any references in periodicals that were less than a week old. I left the library, got back into the Escort. While I sat quietly for a minute, idly watching a traffic cop issue me a parking ticket, I let my mind slowly review the revelations I had encountered in the last hour. I was not immediately aware when it recognized my mission for me, and kindled new resolve for action. I rejoined my senses moments later, and knew that I had to go to the Middle East physically, on foot if necessary. Regardless of my continued ignorance of its specific nature, and that I had no plan to follow once I arrived there, my mission was in that forgotten region. I started the car moving, and struggled to remember what Greece looked like this time of year – or at all, for that matter.

Chapter Thirty

The rising winter sun transformed the tight hillside jumble of ancient, random and worn white homes into a dazzling orange and red wall of human history. It was a beautiful sight, a beautiful town. I only wished I knew what town it was. The novelty of being perfectly lost had grown perfectly tedious.

"Before I patent this, I'd best come up with a built-in GPS," I mumbled. I had tried producing a GPS unit from the ether, and did pull several black boxes with gray screens and many tiny buttons from my glove compartment. Unfortunately I couldn't imagine how the global positioning system works and looks, so the boxes did little more than make endearing beeps and offer a decent version of Tetris. I wondered if Rudy had ever taken the time to learn the mechanics of navigation. Probably. Hell, I thought, even celestial navigation would have worked a couple of hours ago. A compass I had – I had equipped the car with one years before my evolution into a font of hapless power, but a sextant, which I could produce, required knowledge, which I could not produce. I considered making a second visit to that Wal-Mart in Des Moines to purchase a GPS set, but I feared that time was too limited to backtrack.

"So I know which way is north, at least," I said. I slowed the car's already mild pace to a crawl. The coastal town I had almost randomly encountered was small, but it probably catered to tourists at some level, and tourists always demand information. I decided to spend a few precious minutes to find a repository of information – a souvenir stand or even a well-stocked smoke shop would do – in the hopes of pinpointing my location and guarantee that my next step was in the correct direction.

I drove around wonderfully winding narrow streets, dodging fruit vendors and early morning commuters walking to work. After a few listless circuits of the town, I spotted a modern building on the crest of a low bluff with several floors and all of its windows that had to be a hotel. I turned off the narrow street when I found an unmarked gate that opened onto a freshly paved asphalt lane. The long tree-lined drive ended in a brick paved circle that abutted the backside of the glistening white building I had seen from afar. I looked for a sign, and eventually found a brass plaque beside the main entrance that read "Princess" in Greek. Good, I thought, these guys should have maps in their gift shop.

I bravely exited the Escort (my interest in leaving my tank was directly proportional to my proximity to the Middle East and Freuzre) and wandered through the unattended ornate lobby to the gift shop. Since dawn had just emerged, the shop was closed. I could not wait for an employee, so I strolled directly through the locked glass door. Nobody noticed me browsing the store's extensive line of maps, and eventually I located a chart that covered the entire Adriatic and eastern Mediterranean coastline, including a decent map of the Middle East. It was refreshing to note once again that the recent history sweep of that region was not universal. Although, I thought darkly, it was the only copy. I shook my head and prepared to leave. While I scanned the cashwrap for a business card or letterhead that would betray the name of my locale, I noticed a GPS device behind the counter.

"Well now, that's a bit of luck," I said, and walked behind the cashwrap. The cabinet was, of course, unlocked. I removed the device, irrationally checked for batteries, and then rummaged through the shelves beneath the counter until I found its box and operating instructions. It wasn't priced, so I left twenty U.S. fifties in the spot it had occupied, locked the cabinet, and went back to the Escort. I did not wish to risk the odd chance that Rudy had some ethereal feelers released in the area, so I made sure nobody noticed my presence at the hotel. I knew that if Rudy could detect my presence through the experiences of random Greeks, he would have little difficulty spotting an anomaly like a GPS device transforming into a thousand dollars in the retailer's subsequent reaction, but I still had to be careful. I had no idea how much information my 'cloak' concealed.

I drove off the hotel's property, and stopped immediately in case I accidentally switched towns before consulting the general map of Greece that I had purchased. The business card I did not purchase said that the Princess Hotel was a premium residence located in a town known as Thessaloniki. I was sure I had never heard of the place, but its name was strangely familiar. It did sound biblical, so it was probably buried somewhere in my Catholic unconscious. Who knows? My mind may have offered some subliminal travel assistance when I was searching it for a point as far east as possible. I quickly found Thessaloniki on the chart, and was relieved to see that I had had the good sense to imagine myself in the northeastern corner of the country, making the ground journey to Jerusalem slightly shorter. I still had much more of this country yet to traverse, plus passage through Turkey, Syria, and Lebanon before I gained Israeli sand, er, soil. The map I held only showed Turkey as a gray shadow, but it was a big gray shadow. I was in for a very long ride, through countries that no doubt did not possess the interstate highway system to which I was accustomed.

"I am sure I don't have time for this," I said.

I considered teaching the Escort to fly, but then worried that Rudy might easily spot my progress through the sky and wonder what I was doing. Or just swat me like a bug. I also thought I should steer clear of Freuzre, though instinct insisted that I only had to avoid Rudy's flyswatters. No, I decided, I would have to stay low. I began to drive east, away from the water. At first I enjoyed the ride, admiring the ancient countryside sliced neatly by the old mountain road. I was moving at about 100 M.P.H., (that must have freaked out the natives; this wasn't Italy), but, after an hour of driving I spotted a sign that said I was approaching a town called Kavala, which the map confirmed was still well within Greece. I was amazed at how quickly I had been spoiled by the ease of simply *being* somewhere. I drove on, becoming more frustrated with each mountain corner I had to maneuver around at high speed. It was fun, but the joy of this ride was dissipating rapidly, and the trip was going to consume many hours, or days, in spite of my speed. I sighed and decided to live with the delay unless I suddenly imagined a more efficient option. Besides, the road had rejoined the sea, and the views were spectacular. I tried to enjoy them, determined to bolster my patience. It wasn't working. I drove faster, increasing the car's speed well beyond the speedometer needle's range to what felt like 150 m.p.h.

I almost lost the car on one corner, feeling the two right wheels drift into empty air as I quickly pointed the car in the right direction. I brazenly admired my skill, ignoring the fact that it wasn't driving prowess that held half the car in the air while I corrected an error. Any normal car would have been under water by now.

That thought was all I needed.

"Oh, my God in Heaven!" I shouted, slamming the wheel. I was approaching another sharp turn. Instead of worrying about negotiating it, I floored the accelerator and held the wheel straight. The Escort dutifully whipped forward to the best speed I could imagine. We cleared the low guardrail and flew in an impressive arc off the mountain and toward the Aegean far below. I remembered that little yellow flying sub from *Voyage To The Bottom Of The Sea* and urged the Escort to mimic my memory. It did, crashing into the clear blue water at very high speed, and then settling on the sea floor with a dusty thud. The back left wheel landed on a boulder.

"Okay," I said, "That's a bit too accurate." I turned the wheel, stepped on the gas, and the car began to move through the water at a decent clip. In a few minutes I regained my ability to be lost. Though the concept of traveling underwater was sound, and I had proven the Escort and my imagination were up to the task, I realized quickly that it was not practical. Beside the fact that I couldn't get my new GPS set to work in the depths, my discomfort in navigating through the murky alien world substantially slowed my progress. I never did like to know what I was swimming with.

"But straight is a good idea," I said to my reflection in the windshield, "Maybe I'm just too low."

I turned us back to the surface, where we floated a few hundred yards off the stern of an old trawler manned by a vociferously amazed crew. I waved to them like a fellow seafarer should, and then turned on the GPS. After I deciphered, with the help of the manual in its box, the machine's readouts, I compared them to the chart, which I had opened and spread across the passenger seat. I noted that I could simply head southeastish to the Mediterranean, make an easy left after Rhodes, and then straight on to Israel. Piece of cake, I thought, and I'll hold the car to a few feet above the water for the journey's duration. It would be flying, I conceded, but the spectacle of a flying Escort would be much harder to register if I skimmed the sea's surface. That way I could travel almost unseen in that desired straight line with all the speed I could imagine, provided I was careful to avoid fishing boats and islands. I ran the course through my head once more, then beeped the horn and stepped on the accelerator. The Escort leapt to life, lifting about three feet off the water and immediately accelerating to a couple of hundred miles per hour. The exhilaration of the conveyance filled me, pushing aside any mortification that was still drifting in my veins for thinking in so few dimensions earlier when I had assumed that my only option was to drive over land. As I swept away from the trawler I wondered if its crew would share what they saw with their families or enter some sort of pact of silence to preserve an image of sanity among them.

I convinced the Escort to risk discovery by increasing its altitude to about one hundred feet after I demasted a small sailboat that had entered my field of vision too late to be avoided. I hoped that the Escort's diminutive size, speed, and unlikely route through mundane space would compensate for the higher altitude, and still prevent us from being seen by Freuzre or Rudy. This was assuming, of course, that they were looking; Rudy probably still thought I was falling in an abyss, and Freuzre hadn't reared his shadowy visage in months. Though I continued a struggle to maintain the Bad Guy's importance, I occasionally had the strange sensation that the memories of my encounters with Freuzre were fabrications, like dreams.

"Yeah, like dreams," I said, "That no doubt flags him for non-existence. Along with Max, Cassie, Clive, and most of my life for the last few months." I decided that I must establish a new lexicon of reality before my mind left me completely. I supposed that whizzing along at about mach three in an old Ford Escort was as good a place as any for broaching the subject. Unfortunately, the changing scenery interrupted my reverie. A large landmass was approaching, which the GPS confirmed to be Crete. I made my shallow left turn and headed due east for Israel.

The water below was clear of islands, and I hadn't seen a surface vessel of any kind since the sailboat mishap, so I reduced my altitude slightly and relaxed my attention enough to turn on the radio. I set the controls to seek all FM stations. It stopped several times, but only on stations playing music, without commercials or commentary. There did not seem to be any news stations on the air that day. Odd, I started to think, but the mainland that was rising rapidly ahead of me distracted my thoughts. I reduced my speed to that which a normal fast boat might make, and dipped the Escort's tires in the water. If anyone looked out from the shore that was still a few miles off, we would have appeared to be no more than a small boat making good time and throwing a substantial wake. No one looked, however. I considered ducking under the surface, but navigating in the alien environment still made me nervous, even that close to shore.

I made landfall on a deserted rocky beach. While I quickly traversed it, I absently wondered why a beach would be empty so late in the morning of a warm and cloudless day. I turned right onto an asphalt road that hugged the coastline. My curiosity was tempered with relief that I did not have to explain to anyone why an old Ford driven by an American happened to wade ashore. I parked the car, but resisted the urge to step outside and stretch while I got my bearings. According to the plan, Jerusalem should have been perpendicular to the beach, about 40 miles inland. The GPS indicated otherwise.

I had landed over 100 miles north of my intended destination, in Lebanon. The machine, and the map from the hotel, agreed that I was just outside a place the map listed as Al 'Abda, though there was not much of a town present, aside from the group of buildings surrounding a scaffold-laden old fortress on a hill above me. And there seemed to be no people around it either, save for a group of homeless types near the fortress wall. Fine, I thought, my sense of direction is as good as ever. I allowed myself to assume that I had erred, and had drifted off course in spite of the fact that the course, and the car's direction, were laid by my unconscious connection to reality, and probably should not have been able to be wrong. If I had thought that through, the coming events would have drained a little less blood from my soul.

I sighed, restarted the car, and headed south, on the only road in sight. In a short time I began seeing signs for Tripoli. Whistling the theme from the Green Berets, I drove into the large port town, excited by my opportunity to see a little history, and to wander among throngs of people who had never heard of Wal-Mart. Within a few blocks of truly old buildings I discovered that my idle wish was only half fulfilled. The place breathed age, but suffered a severe paucity of population.

Like the ancient fort that met my arrival, there were a few people wandering the streets, their heads hooded and bowed, but not the crowds I had expected. Indeed, mine was the only vehicle on the wide main boulevard whose fresh tar ran like a straight petrified river through the heart of the old town. I stopped near a group of people seated on the stoop of a government building. I hazarded to roll down my window.

"Excuse me," I said into the hot dry air, knowing that I would be understood, "Could one of you tell me where everyone is? Did I come on a holiday?"

Only one of the half dozen locals who I was sure heard me, a young woman with wide black eyes, bothered to react to my query. The rest held their heads lower. One left, shuffling backward, as though fearful of turning away from me. Uh, oh, I thought. The young woman continued to stare.

"Miss?" I asked gently, "Can you help me?"

"No one can," was all she said before pulling her gray shawl tightly over her head and walking away. She presented her back to me without pause. Shaken, I rolled my window back up, and took a long look at the town. Shit, I thought, something very bad happened in this place. I couldn't identify any signs of Rudy's meddling; his overt actions in the past were far more pointed than generally scaring people off the streets. I wondered if this would fall into Freuzre's tactics, or if another more mundane crisis had erupted that I did not know about. Sensing that there were no answers in that solemn place, I decided to press on to Jerusalem. Perhaps, especially if I hazarded to exit the Escort, along the way I could glean some more descriptive answers from the locals about the unusual peace from which they appeared to be suffering.

I drove south on the same road that had brought me into Tripoli. I had left the Green Beret theme behind, along with my tourist's curiosity, and accelerated grimly to the static of my radio's constant search for nonexistent stations. I had to check my speed as I maneuvered past a broken stream of refugees walking north on the highway. They were as dejected in appearance as the lost souls in Tripoli, and each seemed to be walking alone. Also, unlike refugee footage I was accustomed to viewing on the news, none of these people carried any possessions. There were no exceptions; every person I passed walked with his or her dirty bare hands at their sides. I stopped the car several times, asking for information, help, directions, the address of the nearest McDonalds, whatever else I could think of, but these people could not even afford me words of warning. They just walked north, alone. When I reached the outskirts of Beirut the stream had dissipated to a trickle, but I passed enough groups to notice one more oddity about these refuges: there were no children among them. A numb sensation swept over me, perhaps in preparation for the shock that awaited me farther south. I barely acknowledged Beirut when I drove through it, aside from observing that it was completely devoid of all life, even plants and animals, and that the buildings were perfect. Everything was clean, as if built yesterday, with no signs of wear, bullet holes, or the random stains of life. Beirut had become an image of a city. I wondered if I could knock down the facades just by touching them, but did not dare exit the preternaturally safe confines of the Escort.

I left Beirut as quickly as possible. There were no refugees traveling south from the city and, after a few miles of lifeless empty desert, no refugees at all. It was easy to see why: the further south I traveled, the less there was. Of anything. Initially I imagined that I had somehow accidentally transported myself back to the Chilean plain, but a consultation with the GPS set confirmed that I was exactly where I thought I was.

"But why should I believe the machine?" I asked the windshield, "Because it's right, God damn it," I answered. I slapped the steering wheel with palm-stinging angry force. I was too late again. My trip was going to end very badly.

In time the road itself vanished, and the horizon flattened to an empty gray streak wallowing under a hazy blue afternoon sky. There was nothing, in any direction. I was beginning to identify a theme in the nothingness that was typical in all my encounters with

Rudy. I did not know what it meant, but emptiness trailed him like the spreading wake of a coal barge motoring across a glass smooth river. Maybe, I thought, Rudy's just not bright enough to imagine productive solutions to the Freuzre problem anymore, and now all he can do is erase reality, cleansing any environment that the Shadow may have sullied.

"Oh, that's too harsh," I said. I consulted the GPS once more. It seemed to be working – Rudy was probably just enough of a Luddite to forget about satellites – and gave me the direction and distance to Jerusalem. Smothered in false hope, I stomped on the accelerator and rocketed the car straight across the flat, dry, dust-free expanse until the GPS confirmed that I had reached the point where Jerusalem once was. I stopped, stepped out of the car and into the heavy dry heat with a map of the Middle East in my hand.

"Holy shit," I said. Assuming that Rudy and Freuzre operated with a certain symmetry, I produced a pencil from the ether and drew a circle around Jerusalem, with Turkey (since I knew Lebanon was effected) as a center for the outside border. The circle encompassed all of the Middle East, including Cairo and Baghdad. I would not have been surprised if the entire Arabian Peninsula, plus Iran and Afghanistan, could have had similar circles drawn around them. Rudy, in just the manner that he had promised, had solved the Mideast problem.

"Now," I shouted to the heavens, as if they were listening, "Who's he going to clean up next?" With surprising calm, I sat on my hood and gave it some thought. I had lost all my paranoia, even letting the 'cloak' drop while I considered what Rudy would consider the next hot spot. He seems to have a problem with Moslems, I thought, so maybe he's working on them. It was a simplistic, stereotypical assumption on my part, but my reads on Rudy had been fairly accurate lately, so I chose to pursue the obvious. I had read once that there were more Moslems in Southeast Asia than in the Middle East, so my, and I hoped Rudy's, next stop should probably be to the east. I got back into the car, reclasped my cloak, and thought very hard about things Indonesian.

My world shifted immediately from plain gray to complex urban. The bright sun and blues sky were gone. I was surrounded by a city, a new city, but a crowded city, its concrete towers sullied and weakened at an early age by the relentless pressure of dense humanity. Then I noticed the wind. It whistled between the buildings, laden with dust and ocean mist, with a force that panicked the natives, who voiced their terror in a manner that did not require magical translation. I stepped back, figuratively, attempting to take a longer, more global view of the wind that whipped the frightened citizens of Jakarta.

That wind was round. Too round. I could follow its shape by watching tossed flotsam range among the towers of the downtown section of the crowded nation's capital. The circular motion the blown debris followed was a little too perfect, a little too centered on a particular pair of office towers that dominated the block just beyond our position. The wind was the clue, the sign that this was not a storm, but a fabrication, not natural but drawn from the depths of an imperfect imagination. Natural or artificial, the wind was beyond my ability to stop, or even slow. After a few desperate and mildly embarrassing moments imaging warm sunny calm all around me, I swore and opened my car door. I tightened my 'cloak' until I imagined that I could feel its energy surge around me, and stepped out onto the street.

I walked toward the disturbance from which wiser souls still fled. Because these were people, precious few possessed such wisdom, and there remained stranded on the streets a great panicked hoard of victims, Rudy's 'prisoners,' who were not bright enough to leave. They were dying in droves, pummeled by their own fear and stupidity more quickly than they could be by the wind: people were being trampled, jumping out of high windows in the towers, or stepping in front of fleeing vehicles. I did not blame them for inviting their own deaths; I knew that in truth the multiple tragedies I witnessed were the work of one of two errant beings. Freuzre was wreaking havoc in the name of his ill-formed dreams of control and conquest, or Rudy was 'cleaning' in advance of Freuzre's offensive. Either choice was wrong, and I wished, above all else as I helplessly watched a family of four tumble hand-in-hand from the fiftieth floor of a nearby tower, that I could work a cure for their misguided war.

Closer inspection of the storm itself betrayed machinations of sympathetic humanity that truly smacked of Rudy. The debris never hit fleeing victims. Instead, entire sections of walls, or the contents of a whole dumpster, would freeze in the air to await the passage of a couple fleeing from the former drudgery of their offices. That, I knew, was not something that Mother Nature would do. She would also frown upon the easy predictability of this particular storm. I was relieved by its simplicity, because it allowed me to navigate through the detritic fog past the stronger yet hopelessly moronic victims who clung briefly to their lives, toward the center of the howling cyclone.

"Jesus," I said, "Must everything be a freaking vortex?" I steadily paced closer, fighting the powerful wind as I walked, carefully mindful to maintain my cloak. I was shortly in sight of the tightening coil of blackened wind that I believed was the center of the storm. By then I was alone on the block, probably unique in my breathing throughout this section of the once crowded city. These guys are thorough, I thought. I shuffled cautiously toward the ruins of an awful fountain that was blocking the static point from which the wind originated, or to which it homed.

I expected the eye of the storm, barely two yards wide, to have been abandoned long before my arrival. Evildoers tend to step aside when their power is thrust upon the world. I hoped that some identifiable residue would remain to guide my next move, or offer a hint about how to stop the fury. I knew this because I wanted it to happen, and seeing that residue would be as easy as understanding the warning offered by a terrified Lebanese girl. My connection with reality, or just my typical human instinct – I did not know, told me that answers lurked at the center of destruction before me.

I reached the fountain. I crouched behind it for a moment to gather my strength, and wits. When I was sure that I could step around the massive concrete structure without being blown to Kansas, I stepped carefully around it, crouching low to help fend off the wind. There was no need. Though the wind still blew mightily everywhere else, it barely ruffled the soft fabric of my T-shirt. I assumed that my understanding of the source of the storm, combined with the inadvertent power of my cloak, had neutralized the wind's effect on me. This reprieve was temporary. The vortex would eventually consume all the matter in the area without discrimination. I had seen the perfect cleansing applied to Beaver Toys and Rudy's house, and assumed that without my interruption the same would have happened to my house. I moved to within a few feet of the mighty storm's eye.

The base of a traffic controller's kiosk was visible at the tip of the vortex. It acted as a spindle around which wet, dirty air spun at a pace that would humiliate a category five tornado. The symbolic image of the pedestal compelled me to attempt to look into the opaque wall of wind. I held my hands as if in prayer out in front of my face and thrust them into the wind, careful not to expect them to be ripped from my wrists. They remained intact, but I could feel them being heavily battered by the natural forces that must have inadvertently accompanied the spell. I bore it, however, because my curiosity outweighed some collateral pain. Besides, I knew an excellent place to recover. I spread my hands apart slowly until there was enough still air between my twitching palms to form a window into the eye. It wasn't empty.

"Fuck me," I whispered.

Standing erect on the deck of the kiosk, with his arms spread wide, his eyes closed, his black hair perfect, was Rudy. I stared for a moment, enduring the pain, until I convinced myself that this was no construct, no projection. Damn, I thought, it was him. I had hoped that, should the eye not be empty, it would contain someone else, or some other obvious proof that my neighbor and best friend had nothing to do with the missing Middle East, and vaporizing environment that emanated from its placid center, its glacially calm host. But instead I encountered Rudy, entranced in the manipulation of his power in monstrously physical terms and unaware of my, or anyone else's, presence. I struggled to hold my hands apart for a few more seconds. My effort was rewarded when I saw that Rudy was not alone.

Behind him, in front of him, over him, and below him, constantly moving but always stationary enough for me to clearly see it, was a black shadow of disturbingly anthropoidal proportion. It was Freuzre, I knew, and I decided, in the instant of seeing it orbiting Rudy in a steady, dutiful pattern, that Freuzre, the evil Shadow of which Rudy lived in honest terror, was mixing up the maelstrom at Rudy's bidding. If I looked only at Rudy's face, and tried to discern his intent from the twitch of a cheek or the squinting of an eye, I would say that he was fighting Freuzre with everything he had. But I was compelled by my own nature to absorb not just Rudy's image and energy but also that of his immediate environment. I was not sure whether it was my cloak, my own innate grasp of Rudy's magic, the power I felt surging through my quivering hands, or simply the cold face into which I stared. The source of my sudden knowledge was inconsequential, only the knowledge itself: the demon I had been avoiding, fearing, and threatening to fight since Fritz's Tavern melted around Rudy's sorrow was in thrall to the man on the kiosk. It orbited Rudy in perfect subservience. The two forces were not engaged in mystical, immortal combat. It appeared that the opposite forces had successfully attracted. Rudy was manipulating Freuzre. My best friend, my neighbor, my self-proclaimed defender of all that is good, was using his magnificent power to compel the Shadow to do his evil bidding.

"Dammit Rudy," I shouted unheard even by my own ears into the wind, "It's you. And it was you all along. Freuzre's your tool, your accomplice, and your excuse! Why?" My shouts went unanswered. I was sure that if I could make the last few paces to Rudy and slammed his chest he would not hear me. It could have been my cloak, or perhaps his flawless concentration, but Rudy would not know that I was near him. Not that it mattered. The power emanating from him, cocooning him, seemed far too strong to allow my approach. I could not stop his storm and, due to the help of his apparent disciple Freuzre, anything I could conjure would have no impact on Rudy's plan. Jakarta, and no doubt the rest of Indonesia and much of Southeast Asia, was doomed. Rudy's picture was way too big for me.

In the name of future encounters I swallowed my misgivings whole and rotated my wrists to set my palms against the wall of wind. I hooked my fingers around the edge of the window I still held open. Groaning more from the pain of intense concentration than the force of the wind, I increased the gap between my hands until I had formed a space in the wall wide enough for me to pass through. Without hesitation I vaulted feet-first, spread hands last, through the hole. I fell into the eye at the base of the kiosk. My window slammed shut behind me with an

Olympian crack of thunder. I jumped to my feet, mindless of the chaotic power tapping my shoulders, rustling the hair on the back of my head, encroaching on the eye inexorably.

I dropped the cloak. I only dared do so for an instant, but during that fraction of a second I opened every ethereal pore of my soul to Rudy, to his situation, to his purpose. Instinctively, because I could not have thought of doing so on my own, I invited Rudy to define himself, his intentions, and his nature. Just once. In that instant, that microsecond before my cloak resumed its protective duties, Rudy leaned down, toward me. With wet eyes and furrowed brow, he smiled. That smile was filled with love for me, but it could not hide the admission of a truth.

The moment ended almost before it started. The eye collapsed. I was hurled by Rudy's awesome, misguided, and murderous power into the air. As I accelerated away from my best friend the single truth he had allowed himself to reveal filled, clogged, and stained irreparably those spiritual pores I had innocently made vulnerable. As I watched the streets of Jakarta shrink below me and then approach at an alarming pace I did not care, because I knew.

Knew. Idiot, I thought, you knew all along. So did Max. Hell, so did Cassie, and she's dead! Yes, I knew. But now I could no longer deny the truth because Rudy, in a flash of love, openness, and perhaps guilt, had nailed it permanently to my soul.

That truth? There was no Freuzre. Only Rudy.

Chapter Thirty-One

I wondered how many decades had passed since anyone had heard the sea from the bit of vacant real estate on which I sat, knees pulled tight against my chest by clasped hands that ached from sustained nervous effort. I rocked back and forth in concert with the dying waves' steady rhythm. For uncounted millennia the distant breakers thundered incessantly, reminding any listener that nature was nearby, and her power could be felt in the wind itself. Then humans came, lots of them, and transformed the small island to a hub for its spreading disease of technology, reproduction, and consumption. Inevitably a crowded city bearing the uncountable tonnage of technical and corporeal complication that supported their unbalanced biomass spread inexorably across the land on which I sat. It swamped its natural environment with the waste, and progress, of generations of human development. In time, in a very short time by the earth's measure, the knell of natural power that tolled wherever the land meets the sea was displaced, eclipsed even as background noise by individually insignificant but infinitely multiplied human sounds like traffic, industry, power transmission, and empty conversation.

And now, from where I gently rocked, with my head buried in my knees, the only sound that challenged the whispering warm breeze was from the sea as it slowly dissolved the same unseen reef that it had been chewing since long before humans first stumbled upon Java. All other sounds were gone; the forces that had produced them had been silenced. There were no more people where I sat. No more vehicles, no more buildings, no more electricity, plumbing, bars, dogs, doors, birds, or even bugs. Everything was gone, except the loose sand that was still settling to the tougher earth below thanks only to the ultimate influence of gravity. Jakarta, and probably the rest of Southeast Asia, was gone, in every way possible. I wondered if, like the Middle East, this once densely populated, eons-old section of the world, of humanity, would be ripped from the race's short-term memory as efficiently as it had been torn from the fabric of space.

I am not sure how long I remained fetally curled on that empty, sandy, and strangely flat island, occasionally bumping my shoulders, perhaps seeking reassurance, against the closed door of my car. When you no longer need to eat, sleep, or defecate to stay alive, time can become almost an ancillary experience, difficult to judge and impossible to take seriously. This feeling, or reversal of sensation, was compounded by the gray sky that prevailed for days as the sun struggled unsuccessfully to break through the pall generated when fifty million lives, and all their material substance, are vaporized. I think a few days passed. I wondered if a few weeks passed. I guessed that perhaps only a few hours passed while I considered what I had witnessed, and urged myself to believe there was something I could do to curb a future release of such significant power.

That image of Rudy, smiling at me through his own pain, through the veil of a million body parts stirred by the wind, the sighing breath, of their own shattered auras, and through the constant shadow of his manufactured minion, Freuzre, was all I could see for most of my stay on the newly desert island Java. It was burned into my retinas, with me whether my eyes were hooded by weary lids, or open to the emptiness around me. I could never fully digest what Rudy had done, and I hoped briefly that I would eventually forget, or redefine his destruction in an unconscious effort to preserve my own sanity. Fearing such a natural reaction to the trauma I had experienced I struggled, as I leaned against the hard reality of my mighty Escort and wiggled my shoeless toes in the soft, unbelievable dust of Jakarta's remains, to pare the experience down into a small group of imageless, easy to remember and recite words. The exercise was difficult, emotional, and may have consumed several days, but it was necessary. I needed to draw a conclusion to which I could cling before I left the horror of this place behind me. In time I latched onto the most obvious simple explanation I could present myself without benefit of counsel. I decided, established, and decreed to the edges of my frayed soul that there was no Freuzre.

There never was a Freuzre. Those were my words. As prescribed, they simply represented the truth. Max had tried to teach me the phrase, though I was not sure she believed it herself. The words had surfaced on many previous occasions, but I had dismissed my suspicions each time with the usual efficient dispatch that accompanies any epiphanous moment that dares darken my mental doorway with the threat of thought or, worse, immanent judgment. Freuzre, I decided without allowing any argument from what rational portions of my mind remained, was a construct of Rudy, a tenet of my best friend's mangled philosophy, an unavoidable force initiated by my neighbor's darkest wishes to bend the world until it aligned with his dearly psychotic template. Freuzre was the core of Rudy's rationale, but he could never be the excuse for his actions.

When I was sure that this conclusion was irrevocably enmeshed in my own battered psyche, I replaced my Nikes and stood. I acknowledged, as I turned full circle once more to scan the empty landscape, that there were no doubt other conclusions, other possibilities that wiser minds might present, but I avoided unwelcome doubt. What I saw was the truth, and my interpretation was the best that I could provide. Indeed, it was the best, period, because anyone else who discussed this would be doing so via hearsay, and it is impossible to understand the removal of life on this scale without bearing personal witness to it. No, I decided, I would work with my own counsel, and formulate strategy based on my singularly informed guess that Rudy was an incredibly powerful being bent on the slow destruction of weaker individuals because their demise allowed him to be their champion, and the savior of the few who could duck. If he were asked about the eradications he would avoid admission of his heresy to his own humanity by pointing a shaking finger at Freuzre. And, since Freuzre was him, the blame was Rudy's. Satisfied that I could remember such simple logic, I folded the thoughts into a neat wad of memory, stashed them somewhere near the base of my brain, and opened the car door. It was time to move, to gather some allies and, finally, make a workable plan of intervention before my friend allowed his messianic purpose to rip all life from my happy little planet.

I sat in the car, pulled the door shut, and sighed heavily when the sound of the ocean disappeared behind clear closed glass. I mashed the accelerator pedal to the floor, causing the car to lurch from the dust and into a dimension that was more familiar to me than nature herself. I saw the dream diner in a few seconds, floating in the sky above me as if the hand of God had plucked it from its foundations somewhere in Central Suburbia, USA. Fine, I thought as I crashed the car through charge-card-stickered glass doors, they can float a diner in the sky, but they can't bring themselves to conjure a couple of parking spaces. I shook my head and parked the Escort in the center of the main dining room.

Aside from the half dozen startled but not frightened patrons who threw themselves clear of it, nobody in the crowded diner noticed my grand entrance. I stepped out of the car, apologized to the six amiable strangers who laughed off the scene while righting their table and chairs in another location, and looked toward the wall of windows. Max and Clive were seated in our booth, waving to attract my attention.

"Will that be lunch for one, sir?" a female voice behind me asked officiously.

"No, my party's already here," I said, turning toward the source of the voice. I smiled when I my gaze settled on the hostess. It was Mary, mostly. Her eyes blazed emerald, and her hair had shifted many shades of red closer to Max's color, though she retained the Long Island Big Hair she possessed when I met her. She might have been a bit shorter, too, though I had trouble judging that due to her high spiked heels. "I thought I recognized that voice," I said to Mary as she walked me to the booth.

"Yup, it's me," she said, delighted.

"What are you doing here?" I asked.

"Um, working?"

"No, I mean, how are you here? Who brought you?"

"I brought myself, thank you."

"No way!"

"Way," Mary said brightly, "I was having a dream, and Max turned up, like she's been doing a lot lately, but this time, when she turned up, something in my head clicked and I said 'holy shit this is a dream' and bing badda boom, I discovered that I could follow Max here, as me. After I got here I decided I wanted to stay, but then I woke up back in my creepy hotel room in the city. So then I went back to sleep, knowing I would be back with Max, and here I was. So I've been here so much they gave me a job. I needed something to do."

"I'm sure you did," I said, "As long as you work here, is it okay where I parked my car?"

"Sure. Where else would you leave it? Outside in the air?"

"My thoughts exactly."

"Here we are, sir," Mary officiously declared when we arrived at the booth.

"Thanks Mary," I said. I was not sure which one of us had enabled our long conversation to be completed in the six steps to the table, so I added, "I'm also amazed that you said all that before you got us to the table."

"Pretty cool, huh?" she asked.

"Pretty. Will you join us?"

"Maybe on my break," she said, turning away after sharing a wink with Max, who slid from the booth before I could sit and threw her arms around me. She clamped her open lips to mine and held me in a kiss from which I could not escape, should I have had some unimagined and misguided reason to do so, for at least a minute. When we parted, Max held her arms around my neck, and looked up at me with natural joy.

"Nice to see you too, Max," I said.

"Yeah," she said, speaking as though I had just returned from the dead. The simile fit my mood and recent experience, but Max probably just missed me, or was relieved that I had managed another return. I wished that I could share her rich emotion. Though it was again banging on the door to my mind, happiness would not enjoy a niche in my aching mind for a while. My weak effort to present joy, or at least an honest smile, did not fool Max. She darkened slightly when my grief and anger brushed against her, but she clung to her smile as tightly as she did my neck.

"It's all right, Alex," she said only to me, "Remember that, after everything, I'm still here."

"I know," was all I could say, my vision blurring, "I know."

Max slipped her hands from behind my neck, backed away without letting go of my arm, and slid her lithe little loose-red-satin-pajamas clad form into the booth, dragging me along with her. I complied, and dropped beside her, across from Clive, and only barely a comfortable distance from that damned window. Clive tilted the fluted water glass he held in his perfectly manicured hand. I nodded back. Clive seemed a bit tense.

"Clive," I said, struggling to hold his sharp gaze against the distraction of the fruit medley that was dancing on my plate, the ripe strawberries and cantaloupe slices kicking their legs high in an effort to cheer me, "It's good to see you again. How the hell are you?" I lied twice. First, it was not good to see him again, because he was still, to me, another aspect of Rudy. And second, because I was not curious about how he was; I did not care.

"I am simply spectacular, Alex, as I hear you are now as well," Clive said. If that was supposed to mean something deep or damaging, I missed it. I did smile knowingly, though, to sustain an appearance of understanding.

"So you're aware of my recent misadventures," I said, referring not to Wal-Mart, Jerusalem, or Jakarta, but to the events that preceded them, and my last visit to the diner. I had been accidentally careful not to discuss them with him then, and wondered if he had been briefed since.

"That, I hope, is not the correct word for them, Alex, but yes, yes I have been told that your search was both successful and, um,"

"A tragic bit of poor timing?"

"That would summarize what I've been told."

"Told by who?"

"Whom."

"Fine. Told by whom?"

"That I cannot say, because I have no idea. You are aware of the rules which govern my existence, Alex."

"Yeah, yeah. Rules. But can you at least share with me what you think of the report that has been mysteriously downloaded into your mind?" I asked, my anger at Rudy sifting through my words, reminding us all of my wariness about Clive's leanings.

"I cannot say, except that I am very happy that you're still around to ask my opinion." Okay, I thought, that was a good non-answer; Clive can play.

"Thanks," I said, tilting the glass of blue stuff in front of me toward Clive.

"Okay," Max said, "Now that pleasantries have been dispensed, where the hell have you been, Alex? We've been waiting forever for you to give us something to do."

"I've been to Hell, by way of Lebanon, Jerusalem, and Jakarta. You guys ever heard of those places?" Clive stared at me blankly, and Max shook her head, her face slightly twisted by her attempt to remember. I continued, "I'm guessing that you haven't, or at least that something has helped you to forget about them.

"They were centers of population in a couple of very turbulent sections of the real world. They're not there anymore. Rudy has erased them from reality."

"You mean Freuzre," Clive corrected from behind a raised index finger.

"No, I mean Rudy. Rudy, with the assistance, guidance, or manic influence of the construct, *his construct*, Freuzre, wiped out giant swaths of humanity yesterday. He no doubt did so in the name of all that is human, but I think he missed a point somewhere in his rationalizing." Well, I thought, so much for keeping the truth to myself. Max and Clive stared in stunned silence for a moment before they both stirred uncomfortably.

"Holy shit," Max mumbled.

"I do not believe you," Clive sniffed, folding his arms, "Rudy may have his quirks, and certain questionable opinions about the World and its particular direction, but wholesale murder of millions? Why, that is simply beneath him."

"But it is true. All of it. I was there."

"Why didn't you try to stop your friend, then?" Clive asked. I felt Max's body tense beside me, and gently rubbed her tight thigh to calm her.

"Oh, I tried, Clive. I tried. I wasn't good enough. Rudy was always a step ahead of me. His power, or rather is grasp of power itself, is unimaginable. And in our game unimaginable is a very bad word. A direct intervention by me would be, was, useless."

"I still cannot believe Rudy would remove entire cities – "

"Countries," I corrected.

"Fair enough, but I cannot believe even more so that he could destroy all that he dreams to protect, and to do it on so grand a scale. You must be mistaken. Perhaps Freuzre planted certain images into our mind, to confuse you."

"I so wish that were true, but it is not the case. You assume that because a man as knowledgeable as you would certainly be aware of these places, and the events Rudy allowed to unfold?"

"Absolutely."

"Let's try something," I said. I raised my hand in the air, snapped my fingers, "Oh, hostess," I called. Mary appeared momentarily, her sharpening features broken into a huge silly grin.

"Yes sir?" she asked, "Is there something wrong with your, um, food, I guess?"

"No Mary, the entrees are performing wonderfully. I particularly enjoy the line dancing. No, I have to ask you a question."

"Shoot," Mary answered, excited to be included in my game during her dream.

"Okay. Can you tell me what you know about a place called Jerusalem?" Mary's broad grin vanished, and her shoulders slumped slightly.

"That's the place with the bomb that we saw from your car, right?"

"That's the one," I said, eyes only on Clive, "Do you remember anything else about it? Anything from the last couple of days?"

"You know, I think I do, but I couldn't tell you what it is? Something big time happened, I think. Lots of anger, lots of damage, but then there's nothing."

"Nothing?"

"Sorry. I'm a total scatterbrain. You know that. I can never remember anything. But then, we were just there, and Max keeps asking me for real world updates (I call them that – pretty neat, huh?), so I was paying attention, I thought. I should have known what happened in Jerusalem yesterday, even today, because I'm always checking on the TV and the Internet."

"But?"

"But I can't remember a damn thing," Mary said, losing all her cuteness to the frustration that accompanied her perceived failure, "I'm sorry. It's like I got erased."

"Erased?" Clive asked, finally intrigued.

"I had a feeling that the work Rudy did on Mary might have been incomplete; he forgets how close she's come to the magic that is Max."

"Awe shucks," Max/Mary said in unison, one sarcastically, one seriously.

"What about the other places?" I asked Mary, "Jakarta? Lebanon?"

"Sorry. I never really knew about them before, so anything new with them would be, well, news to me. It does bug me about Jerusalem, though. I knew about that place, I was there with you, and now everything about it is gone. What is up with that?"

"Don't worry about it, Mary," Max said, her eyes wet, "I don't think you were alone. Why don't you sit with us for a while? You're making my neck hurt."

"Sure!" Mary said, instantly cheered, "It must be break time anyway!" She joined Clive, who moved over slightly to allow her, or himself, some personal space. She smiled brightly, hands folded on the table in front of her, but then the gravity that she had previously sensed reentered her awareness and her mood decayed until an unnatural sulk clouded her features. Her swing was almost as painful to me as standing on that barren island in Indonesia. Almost.

"So Clive," I asked, "Will you be willing to concede that Rudy's remedies may have gotten out of hand?"

"No. Not yet. Something else must be behind his actions, or what you think of as his actions."

"Oh come on Clive, don't be a suck-up asshole," Max snapped, "I mean, look what Rudy did to Alex. He wanted to kill him for Chrissakes."

"That is what you told me."

"What the hell is that supposed to mean?" Max snarled, "Is everyone but Rudy lying?"

"Funny," I mentioned, "That's probably Rudy's point of view."

"Not so funny," Clive said. He was thinking very hard about his new situation, and he was not interested in angering Max any further. He rubbed the awful but tidy little goatee that capped his chin for a moment, and then looked at me closely.

"Perhaps there is some merit to your statements. Perhaps I have seen some unwanted facets of Rudy's Worldview come into play of late. Perhaps, based on what I have seen myself of his new attitude, and his general absence from the dream realm of which he has become master, I could concede that something about him has changed, and may offer some sort of offhand threat." Good, I thought, that's a start.

"So perhaps you'll listen to what I have to say?" I asked, issuing my sarcasm without humor. I was sure that Clive understood that my question was really about whether I could trust him not to share what he learned from me with Rudy. Clive paused for a long moment, contemplating the ceiling. I could feel Max grow tense again. She was ready to spring. Fortunately, Clive answered, preempting my need to referee a new conflict.

"I will listen," he said. His tone sang submission, and I knew at once that he understood me, and perhaps could be trusted. Max caught the meaning too, because she relaxed slightly. Clive leaned back, and waited. Max and Mary also sat quietly.

"Well then," I said, "Story time is nigh." I snatched a pilsner of orange stuff from a passing tray carried by Bettie Boop, took a long draw of a cold liquid whose taste ranged delightfully close to cold gin, and told them my story. I knew that Max and Mary had heard, or participated in portions of it already, but I included everything I could remember, focusing on my most recent altercations with Rudy, plus mention of my trip with Mary to Jerusalem, and the destruction of Beaver Toys and my house (during which Mary drew her foot in and rubbed the top of it while she winced). The tale took a while, and was peppered with interruptions by Clive for clarification or by Max to offer clarification. Eventually, and several rounds of orange stuff later, I pointed to the Escort over my shoulder and said:

"And that, my friends, is why my car is parked in this diner."

Max and Mary immediately fell into discussion about where they were during certain events in my story, and what they were doing and thinking, but their exchange was so fast and encoded with phrases and references only they understood I didn't pay attention to them. Instead, I watched Clive. His opinion had become important to me. He was staring at the ceiling again, so he was likely on the verge of establishing a perspective. I was not sure why I so valued his opinion, or even dared reveal the history I had previously, almost unconsciously, concealed; I barely knew the man, and had never worked with him, or even really dealt with him beyond our recent chat on the diner's steps. I sensed that his relationship with Rudy was deep but tenuous, and that Clive could become a real problem or a major asset in my upcoming challenges. Or, I shrugged inwardly, he could become nothing at all. After all, he was just a dream. Yeah, I thought, let's go there again. I waited while he considered, and leaned toward him when he lowered his eyes back to my level. He shook his head.

"That," He said, the word stifling Max and Mary simultaneously, "Was quite a story, Alex. Most impressive. The story, that is; your actions seem to fall short of heroic, don't they?"

"Yeah, well, I am new to this Cosmic Avenger shit."

"Yes. You are. At any rate, I have been in thrall to Rudy for a very long time, and it behooves me to give him every benefit of the doubt. Though your tale is probably true, couldn't it be sourced in Freuzre, and not Rudy?"

"But Freuzre *is* Rudy," Max said for me, slapping the Formica table with her open palm. Bless her, I thought.

"That is the story," Clive responded smoothly, "But again, Alex you have admitted to Rudy's staggering power. If we assume for a moment that his greatest foe is of equal power, couldn't he have arranged for you to believe that Rudy was at fault, when it truly was Freuzre?"

"I suppose he could have," I said softly, my hand firmly on Max's quivering thigh, "But you are missing one ingredient. I was there, watching the destruction take place in Indonesia. It was definitely Rudy. And Freuzre too, was definitely Rudy."

"And you were the only witness. Why are you so sure?"

"Because I was the witness. Because I know Rudy, and I have tasted his power," I spoke quickly before my voice failed me, "The man who ripped the life out of that densely populated island was absolutely Rudy, and the only shadow that accompanied him was his own."

"I'm sorry Alex," Clive said, leaning back, "I wish to believe you, and help you, particularly if so much damage is befalling the real world. But I cannot abandon Rudy so readily."

"Well then fuck you!" Max snarled. Mary slid away from Clive, but did not stand. She seemed puzzled. Max did not.

"Forgive me, Max, but – "

"Forgive this, asshole! And shut off that polite bullshit for two seconds and listen to what you're really saying."

"I am only saying that we should perhaps not so readily question Rudy's integrity."

"Which means that Alex's is up for grabs?"

"That could be true."

"So how many millions of people die before you break your precious bond with Rudy? Do we need New York, and your scum-sucking counterpart, to be vaporized before you choose to attach your good name to our petition?"

"Max," Clive said, becoming subtly agitated, "Please. There are always two – "

"Sides?" Max yelled, nearly standing on the her seat, "Come on, Clive. We all love Rudy, but something is way wrong the guy. Who else do we let him kill before you have enough examples?"

"I may have had no viable examples shown me as yet," Clive said brusquely, his voice cracking in frustration.

"Come to think of it," I interrupted, positing a thought that had burst like a nova into my mind, "Have any of you heard of a place called Kashmir?"

The three blank stares and instant silence were enough response. I continued:

"How about Korea?" Still nothing. I could not contain the shiver that accompanied my mind's eye view of the devastation, the widespread murder that defined each of their confessions of ignorance. I gripped the edge of the table. My entrée sensed my anxiety and took five. What had he done? I asked myself. Then I thought of one of the majors:

"India?"

They all spoke at once, confirming loudly and with obvious relief that they had indeed heard of India, had friends there even, and that Mary had just seen it mentioned in the news.

"Well good," I said, "At least India still exists. Hopefully China and Africa are around, too. But Clive, the bottom line here is that something has gone terribly wrong with Rudy."

"You assume," Clive interrupted, lifting that finger in the air. I was now pushing down on Max's thigh, to remind her that it would be best for all that she did not rip that finger from his fist.

"I know."

"You know," Clive said, rolling his eyes, "How can one ever know another without truly being able to see into his mind?"

"Oh, please," I said, growing impatient myself, "But I think I can draw some pretty clear conclusions here." Silence fell upon the table while the three of us glared at each other in a standoff whose gravity was based not on my need to have Clive as an ally, but by our mutual need to agree on what truly was behind the force that was currently shredding our home planet. I knew I didn't need Clive's help, beyond perhaps his keeping my plans secret from Rudy, but for reasons I did not understand I desired his sincere affirmation. To see Clive sway his opinion of his general, his god, to even slightly south of worship would have provided me with the emotional fuel I needed to incite the closure necessary to keep me moving, to help me plan. While I calmed myself to present another argument, or to at least back myself away from accusing Clive of being a hopelessly sycophantic moron, Mary cleared her throat.

"Um," she said in an attempt at humor, perhaps to break tension that she did not understand, "It's too bad you got your ass kicked last time you talked to the guy, 'cause wouldn't it be cool if you could just ask him what the hell is up with him and Freezer boy." I stared at her for a moment to sort out the feelings her easily delivered words evoked. First, I just wanted to laugh at those words to help displace memory of the last time I heeded her advice about *simply* facing Rudy down. But something else swirled in her sentiment, an opinion she might have overlooked but still managed to voice. That something suddenly caught me, shook me from my ridiculous exchange with Clive, and thrust me forward. I leaned across the table grabbed the back of Mary's head with both hands, pulled her face in close and kissed her on the mouth. Her squeal puffed my cheeks, but she returned the kiss.

"Hey!" Max cried.

"It's okay," I said after we parted. Without taking my eyes off Mary's, or my hands from her hair, I continued, "She's really just you anyway, my love. And she's a goddess!"

"I am?" Mary asked, breathless.

"She is?" Clive asked, snickering politely, if that can be done.

"Your love?" Max whispered.

"She is, and her reason targeting is infallible. Clive, I don't have to convince you, or me, or anybody. I just have to make a visit to Rudy's mind, and get the truth from the source."

"Huh?" the three asked in chorus.

"Never mind," I said. I touched a finger to Mary's broadly grinning lips, mouthed 'thank you' to her, and stood.

"I have to be leaving now," I said, alternating my gaze between Max and Mary, but gently rubbing Max's shoulder, "You guys take care, and Clive?"

"Yes?"

"Can I trust you to hold your tongue for a while? Not long?"

"Please Alex, I am a man of integrity," Clive said, as if hurt. I did not need to waste time wondering what he meant by that, because Max flashed a 'be serious' expression that confirmed that there was no chance Clive would be sharing his thoughts with anyone but her.

"Good," I said, "I'm off then."

"Where?" Max asked nervously.

"For answers to questions I don't yet have. Don't worry; I'll keep my head down this time. And I might even come up with a plan before too many of my bones are broken. Bye." Without another word, thought, or gesture I retreated to my car and backed it out of the diner. Before I could realize where I was, I was pulling into my driveway and parking the car in the garage, which was as I had left it. I got out, drew the big door closed, and made my way into the basement and the Sound Room.

I felt odd as I settled into the perfect chair for what I assumed would be the last time. The strange feeling was not a result of the chair, the room, or the fact that it was in the empty space that had once been my house. No, I had grown accustomed to surreal nuance in my life. My pulse quickened and I was slightly breathless because of my familiarity with that nuance. I had existed in a world without borders between dreams and reality for so long that I had become inured to the shock, or even anxious anticipation of, the unexpected. The chair, for my participation in that world, was no longer necessary – it most likely never was much more than a prop. So, it was of no use to me anymore, in that way. But I knew, instinctively since Mary asked her question, that I could have one more ride in the chair, this time putting it to its real use as the tool it was originally designed to be. I was going to use the chair to delve deep into Rudy's mind. And, I thought smugly, I knew it would work simply because the chair was there.

Before dipping my toes into anything Rudy, I relaxed for a moment to check the condition of my cloak. This exercise, in which I focused on the part of my awareness that I had trained by reluctant necessity to autonomically insist to my surroundings that I was not there, had become routine, almost unconscious, but my prudence brought it to the fore. Satisfied that I had some protection, I closed my eyes.

The lights dimmed in unison with my falling eyelids. Rather than imagining my purple plain as usual, I sought and found the total void that I had experienced during my first encounter with Rudy's Sound Room. After I had discovered my plain, I dismissed those first few moments of total disorientation as bad navigating by the novice that I was. What I hadn't realized at the time, and for some reason knew now, was that that emptiness had been a necessary first step for Rudy's early transitions to his World. He had initially sought to be surrounded by pure nothingness, assuming that he could fill the space with whatever came to mind. He had succeeded, of course, but I was betting that in the process his emptiness had been corrupted, and something measurable and traceable to Rudy's soul lurked unguarded in this discarded borderless mental territory.

I held myself in the void for an indeterminate amount of time, since time was also not a factor in the empty environment. I wondered as I floated, or existed, since floating is also an act of physics that would be nonsequitur in the void, how well my cloak could work in a situation where I was projecting the image of nothing into nothing. I feared that some double negative would occur in the void, thus marking my presence in Rudy's realm like a lighthouse beacon. I dared not imagine the image, though, being fully aware of where such thoughts get me. Instead I trusted in my confidence, and struggled to maintain my concentration as I searched for a trace of anything other than myself that contradicted the nothingness.

Before my focus faded again I noticed a subtle ripple in the blackness. Since to me that disturbance was somewhere, I could orient myself and move toward it. In seconds that I could feel I was at the ripple. It was no more than a bump in the nothing, a reflection of blackness whose presence I could feel only because it was real. It was also not a single locus of amplified nothingness but a ray, representing a path. I decided that it was a depression of reality embedded in nothing by the consistently, carefully, guided passage of Rudy's soul, like the dirt line worn in my lawn between the garage and kitchen. I could sense in the mar's vitality that Rudy had passed through recently. I also could sense that I could follow his trail. Either direction would work because there still were no directions in the void. I grabbed the ripple with the fingers of my mind and dragged myself along it.

Immediately, I was standing erect on a smooth, flat, flexible surface that was not purple. It also had no sky. The blackness was complete enough for me to assume that I had never left the original void, but the pressure on my ankles and the soles of my sneakers told me that I had moved to Rudy's plain, his starting point for creation. Holy shit, I thought, I'm touching the big guy's thoughts. I hoped that he would not be able to catch me there. I pulled the cloak tightly around my ethereal self, and waited for change.

It came readily; Rudy was, after all, a busy man. I noticed a glimmer of light a thousand miles away, and gradually the plain shook with seismic tremors that I had felt once before. The plain was abruptly awash in white light, and I was standing in the deep

leather valley formed by Rudy's workboots. He was in the same
scale that he held during his visit to my plain. I scolded myself for
not being prepared, but adjusted quickly by wrapping my arms
around a shoelace and holding on before he took his next step.
When his foot shifted, I expected to be swung into space, and
perhaps then crushed beneath a massive black sole. Instead I was
whipped by the shoelace into a flight that rocketed me away from
Rudy and into a stream of light, objects, and moments that flowed
infinitely in one direction – toward that distant light.

      The stream channeled the flotsam and jetsam of Rudy's
life. Its flow was random to me, but had to be connected
meaningfully to Rudy's consciousness. It was my key. I
concentrated intensely on projecting the impression that I was not
there, and then had a look at what Rudy assumed to be real. The
myriad images were uniformly gray and blurry unless I focused
directly on them. Then they became clear, washing over me like
the memories that they were. Careful not to be overcome by the
intensity of each moment, I cruised quickly through Rudy's files,
pausing at each image only long enough to formalize it and move
on.

      "Figures Rudy would set up his mind's filing system like a
bad remake of *Brainstorms*," I said to myself, careful not be
overheard.

      I recognized many of the moments. That made sense, since
I had been a major player in Rudy's life. In fact, my image
appeared with disarming regularity in the passing scenes. Not
surprisingly, Cassie appeared even more often. Max was oddly
absent, though Clive enjoyed the occasional cameo. I hoped that I
wouldn't see him in any recent diner memories. The rest was
unfamiliar – much political stuff, almost like footage from
newsreels of crowds and wars and rock concerts. Many, many
people, all of whom shared an aura of familial warmth around
them, populated the scenes. Rudy had wrapped his memories with
care, as any being with a true purpose might. Also, though I could
see only contemporary moments in this errant stream, I was
reviewing them as if from the pedestal of profound wisdom, great
age. Rudy's self-image, his belief in his fictional life history,
tempered his memories, leaving them in a wash of paternal care
whose basic euphoria was contagious. But these were but

reflections of Rudy's mind, either cast off from his consciousness, or set aside during some moment of creation. His mind, the place I needed to be, was at the headwaters of this stream.

I noticed something else as I reviewed the memories. It was a flicker, almost a disruption in the delivery of each memory's total resolution. To see the source of the flicker, I had to hold my mind steady for a profile-raising period that stretched far longer than I wished. With that extra care, I saw a shadow within the confines of virtually every memory. The personality of Freuzre was inside Rudy's past in an invasive, almost bacterial way. It occupied the space between his thoughts, his reflections, and his dreams with a brooding black presence that became manifest as a perfect shadow of Rudy himself, if I dared remain still long enough to focus on it.

Nervous about such inactivity, I decided that, since Rudy was convinced that Freuzre was an agent of all things *not* Rudy, he would never look inward for Freuzre's infestation. So, risking a loose flap in my cloak while I focused on the shadow during a recent moment outside what looked like a gothic cathedral, I joined the shadow in a memory. He, it, was standing in the vestibule of a mighty church, a church filled with Mexicans. I stood behind him, if one can in truth stand behind a shadow, and lamented once more my inability to create a plan. Then I stepped into the shadow.

Chapter Thirty-Two

My tour from within the shadow Freuzre was not a ride
that I would recommend for public consumption at Disney World.
I was simultaneously everywhere in Rudy's dream psyche,
witnessing the shadow's incessant attempts to alter Rudy's
memories, invade his fantasies, and darken his opinion of history.
But it, and therefore I, was never allowed to contact, or even
consider myself connected with, any of them. The Freuzre persona
was a pariah, cursed to the margins of Rudy's existence but blessed
with the freedom to haunt every horizon. And I didn't care.

I could not care, because there was no part of me able to
concoct compassion, or hate, or any other feeling while I was
embedded in Freuzre's essence. I could intellectualize the
emotions, but actually feeling any was beyond my purview.
Considering my recent experiences, I welcomed the reprieve.
Intellectually.

I unsuccessfully probed the shadow for any sign of
sentience. I assumed first that my failure was not because there
was no individual present, but because I did not know how to
properly conduct a search for life from the inside of an ethereal
dream being. Frustrated, I finally symbolically shouted, "Who are
you?" but Freuzre did not respond. In a short time I realized that
he, it, could not respond, because its complexity fell far short of
Rudy's other construct, Cassie. Freuzre was little more than a
projection, a psychotic appliance that Rudy kept near him at all
times, whose apparent and easily defined evil was available as
required.

My curiosity about when Freuzre's services would be
needed was short-lived, sated when the shadow, currently myself,
was yanked from our infinite locations to assemble as a tangible

unit in the sacristy of an old, nearly ramshackle cathedral. I
assumed that we were inside the place where I had last seen
Freuzre from the outside, and that no time had passed, from
Rudy's perspective, since then. Rudy was standing at the altar,
fully adorned in a catholic cardinal's vestments, and gloriously
illuminated by electric overhead light fixtures. His expression was
almost blank, save for his attempt to appear solemn. I moved with
the shadow to the edge of the altar, opposite Rudy, who stood
below a grotesquely huge carved and carefully painted wooden
crucifix. He glared at us for a moment before he chanted in
priestly singsong:

"Freuzre! You have returned. And now you are forcing
me to purge Central America of its evil infestation."

"Why?" I said, volunteering a response for my mute host.
Rudy recoiled, validating my suspicion that Freuzre had not been
programmed to speak at will, if at all.

"You question me?" Rudy whispered. His shock faded
quickly, as did his vestments and holy pose before the altar. We
remained in the church, but Rudy was back in his basic uniform of
comfortable jeans and a polo shirt. He did not need his wizard's
outfit in his own realm, I noted optimistically. Rudy held his
hands on his hips and sternly, expectantly, awaited a response to
his question. He had adapted quickly, as a dream wizard would.
He probably thought Freuzre's words were a new facet of a game
that he had long since forgotten was his invention.

"Yes, I do" I responded through/as Freuzre, opting to play
as long as I could, "And I ask again: why do I force this purge?"

"Because you must," Rudy chanted, "You must permeate
the masses here with your evil so that I can eradicate it. It is the
way of things."

"Not any more, boss," I sang back, making the shadow
shrug casually, "I'm off duty."

"Off duty?" Rudy asked, retiring his chant. He was unable,
or uninterested due to our location on his spiritual turf, to hide his
bewilderment.

"Yup" I responded as the shadow, "For keeps."

"That's impossible," Rudy said, running a hand through his
hair. Before his fingers had swept through the last of his perfect
locks, the cathedral was gone. Everything was gone, except Rudy

and Freuzre, his shadow. We stood alone on Rudy's black plain. I
suspected that Rudy was about to more thoroughly examine his
reformed shadow. Since an inspection might reveal my intrusion,
and me, I stepped out of Freuzre, careful to retain my cloak. I
worried briefly that my spell would not work in such close
proximity to Rudy, but his continued ignorance of my presence
restored my confidence before my thoughts could do me any harm.
I observed with mild irony that I was not tiny this time. Rudy's
failure to notice me could have been due to the total focus of his
attention on his shadow. I backed off a few more feet so that I
could include them both in the same glance. Though I accepted
that I could see them in the darkness, my new rules for vision
being what they were, I thought it odd that I could discern the
silhouette of the shadow. Freuzre was absolutely black, and so
was the plain. I should not have been able to see the shadow, or
even approximate its position against its matching environment,
but it was there, clearly stated in the same total hue as the plain.
The disturbing paradox almost caused me to stray from the path I
was so carefully treading. Fortunately, for me, Rudy's voice
brought me back from the verge of a mild breakdown and
subsequent disclosure by offering me something other than
blackness of whatever shade to clutch.

     "What the hell is going on here?" he asked angrily, a novel
tone for him that shaped his words bitterly, stifling their intended
authority. The shadow, bereft of my guidance, responded with
antithetical precision by hanging limply before its master. I
doubted it could hear Rudy's query, much less reason a response,
and I wondered why Rudy did not also harbor my skepticism. He
waited for an answer, arms folded in the dark. I imagined that he
was tapping his foot impatiently, but sound did not work that way
on the plain, so I could not know it. Though I could hear Rudy
speak, I was certain that his words did not reach me on the backs
of excited air molecules. After a short but demonstrably pregnant
pause Rudy stepped closer to Freuzre, as if to look more deeply
into eyes that were not there.

     "For a thousand years I've been sparring with you," Rudy
said – in this environment Rudy was a thousand years old; even I
found it difficult to question his decree, "And now, after all this
time, after I have finally established the pattern of your evil, and

established a guaranteed method for the eradication of the chaos you seek to sow, you say 'No' to me?" He waited again, but no reply would come, ever. Rudy shook his head, flung his hands in the air, and continued, "How can I counter your madness if you don't offer me something to fight?"

Oh, I thought, so that is where this is going. I wished once more that I had paid better attention in psychology class. Rudy was behaving classically, I was sure. A solution for quelling him, or at least calming him, was probably noted at length on an otherwise indistinct page of one of those uncracked books for which I had overpaid in college. Since my chronically short attention span prevented a prescribed clinical response, I could only maintain my cloak and wait for some other opportunity for action. It appeared that I had plenty of time; Rudy, hopelessly stubborn, would not accept Freuzre's silence. He circled the shadow, which continued to hold its position. It hung loosely, strangely silhouetted against its perfectly matching backdrop. It seemed incapable of locomotion. Rudy approached the shadow, stretched the fingers of his right hand toward it, poked for a moment, but then withdrew his hand quickly. He did not back away. Instead he softened his posture by slumping his shoulders and lowering his head, but he kept his eyes focused on a point where the shadow's head should have been.

"Why did you say 'No' to me?" Rudy asked intimately. I resisted an urge to don the shadow once more and offer an answer. I knew without hesitation that such a move on Rudy's ersatz turf would reveal my presence regardless of the cloak, and would also tempt Rudy to assume that I had created the shadow he currently interrogated, and that the real Freuzre was elsewhere. I continued to watch, wait, and listen.

"And now you don't talk at all, like usual," Rudy said, "But you cannot fool me, Freuzre. I heard you say 'No,' and I felt your rebellious intent. You want to break free of the chaotic course you set yourself, regardless of the consequences. How can you just walk away from the deaths of millions? How can you abandon my salvation? What kind of reflection on your image of pure evil is that? Answer me!"

The shadow did not answer, but in his hysteria Rudy had released a single word – reflection – that presented me with a slim fissure of opportunity through which I might wriggle. Before I even realized he had opened a door, I was on my way back to the memory stream that I knew still flowed, unattended by its preoccupied master, through the plain. My motion was impelled not by physical effort, useless in the confines of Rudy's plain and mind, but by intuitive visualization. I sought the pale distant light that formed both the headwaters and the destination of the stream. It eluded me, but my effort did include an easy merge into the memento flow. I decided to trust my actions in spite of my wishes, and temporarily set aside my search for that light.

The stream was the same jumble of gray memories that spanned a virtual millennium, sans shadow bouncing among the kinetic psychic debris. Rudy must have drawn Freuzre out completely for the interview. All the better, I thought. I had sought to rummage through the things that Rudy had retained to define his life until I found the as yet unnamed object that I knew was waiting for me, but I was not sure where to start. So, true to my style, I wandered aimlessly and hoped for the best.

While I did, I wondered why I could no longer see a light. This thought was as troubling to me as the definition of the shadow against its own matrix, but the new anxiety served me well by driving me to refine my search. All the while I could hear, or feel, Rudy's monologue with his shadow. His repeated requests for explanations had become shrill, almost plaintive, but I sensed that I still had some time. The spiritual machination he had created to justify his own misguided actions could not be fixed, because it was never broken. Rudy was far too bullheaded to reach that conclusion. It had said 'No' to him, thus negating the purpose of its existence, and Rudy would not stop questioning until he knew why.

"Oh," I said aloud when I noticed a complete version of his house, including its front lawn, parked upon the plain at the edge of my awareness. It was ironically positioned just outside the stream, peripheral to my search and easy to ignore. After a short focal effort it was directly in front of me, basking under a midsummer day's sunshine. I could feel my legs pump harder to accelerate me toward the house. The unnecessary physical effort was welcome, exhilarating, and reflected my unfounded but righteous anticipation.

"Now I can find the thing that will wake him up," I said to the house. I felt the warmth of the sun on my back as I jogged the brick path to his red front door. It hung slightly ajar, inviting my trespass. I entered without knocking, and swept immediately upstairs to the long second floor hallway. I felt a surge of adrenaline accompany my sudden realization of a target. The rush had to be artificial, I knew, but it sported the same invigorating symptoms as the real thing. When I reached the hall's far end I found the object I had been seeking. It was an antique full-length mirror of which Rudy was quite proud, an acquisition he had made during one of his antiquing forays into rural New England with the living Cassie many years earlier. I plucked the heavy mirror from its rosewood stand, slung it under my arm, and scrambled back down the stairs and out of Rudy's house. I stepped back into the stream for only a moment, careful not to be drawn by any images that might distract me from my mission. I invited renewed exposure to the pure emptiness that would reorient me on Rudy's plain. With the mirror fully cloaked, I found the black, and then tugged once more on that ripple in the darkness that betrayed Rudy's position. This time I remembered the scale of his ego, and found myself on the plain in about the same position I had held earlier, and I again shared Rudy's size. He was circling Freuzre, waving his arms frantically while he continued to fire verbal salvos at the unresponsive shadow. He seemed to be resisting an urge to reach out and shake the specter silly.

"Tell me now, Freuzre, why did you say no?" Rudy was asking it, "If you can't tell me, we'll just have to start all over. I know there are more of you out there; I can easily uncreate you, you know." This is not good, I thought. Rudy was winding down. Since time was about as important to him as it had become to me, Rudy may have spent a subjective century questioning Freuzre, or a period long enough even for him to surrender to the shadow's sustained silence. I had to play my card quickly, before he fell out of his pointed rant. Without another thought, and still without a plan, I put the shadow between Rudy and myself, stood the mirror at my side, and dropped my cloak.

Rudy saw me immediately, and he smiled. His smile, always difficult to read, initially could have betrayed real joy at seeing me alive, but it changed to a more recognizable expression of understanding in a few seconds. Come on Rudy, I thought intensely, careful not to speak, work with me here.

As if on cue, Rudy's attention turned to the mirror. I glanced into it, relieved that the rules of light, or expectations of those rules, were honored on Rudy's plain; his reflection appeared clearly in the mirror. I ran a hand across it demonstrably, noting for Rudy that the mirror captured my reflection as well. My friend briefly raised an eyebrow, a gesture that was his puzzled expression in its entirety, but then he resumed his cold-cast visage.

"Alex," he said, "It's excellent to see you again, more excellent than you know."

"I'm sure," I said loudly, attempting authority, "Look in the mirror, Rudy."

"You look well," he said, ignoring, or not hearing my words, "Better than I thought you might."

"They tell me I'm a quick healer," I responded.

"Are you the one who messed with my sworn enemy? Or have you chosen finally to join me in the World, in my fight?" I remained still, bit my tongue – Rudy's ignorance of my words implied that I lacked expertise in verbal communication on other people's plains. My previous phrases, as Freuzre, had been heard because I was speaking through one of his creations, and not on my own. I adjusted to my handicap by pointing to the mirror, and then to Freuzre, who still hovered between us.

"What? Now you too won't answer me?" Rudy asked, resuming the barely measurably higher pitch that his voice projected during his frantic interrogation of Freuzre, "What the hell is going on here?"

I shook my head and pointed again, first at the mirror, then at Freuzre, then back at the mirror. Rudy's eyes followed my movement. He looked at the mirror and recognized it. A wisp of the old Rudy warmed his visage while he allowed a fond memory of shopping with Cassie to surface. Then he looked at himself, then at my moving arm and its reflection. Then at Freuzre. Then at the mirror. Then at Freuzre. When he realized that Freuzre did not appear in the mirror, he understood.

Rudy faded slightly. He lowered himself to a squatting position so he could rest his elbows on his knees and cradle his head in his hands. He stared between his palms for a very long

moment, his eyes shifting slowly between the mirror and Freuzre.
His anger was gone, and I think he thought I was as well. He
looked like a teenager.

"Oh my," Rudy said softly.

Then he was gone.

So was his plain. His unifying force had left his mind, and
allowed what remained to flop about randomly in undefined
blackness. In a rush of compassion laced with unqualified guilt, I
wanted to follow Rudy to wherever it was he had vanquished
himself. Unfortunately, I could not find an exit from Rudy's mind,
so the best I could do was hope that he hadn't either, and that I
would bump into him in some dark – or possibly bright – corner of
his stricken thought patterns while I worked on getting myself out
of this place into which I had entered without regard to my limited
strength, or an exit strategy.

I retraced my steps, as it were, but could not find that handy
trail Rudy had left earlier. His moments in time had left the
stream, or the stream itself had lost its navigable pattern. Now the
symbols of Rudy's life ricocheted willy-nilly throughout the empty
expanse in which I floundered. I was not without hope, however.
Still breathing (assuming respiration existed in this realm), not in
any pain, and definitely lacking anything else to do, I allowed
myself to focus on the stuff that surrounded me, perhaps to learn a
few secrets about my insanely powerful friend.

My intent to accept the encroachment of the images around
me was a command that converted the random gray clouds of
distant memories into a blinding storm of ruptured thoughts. They
rained on me from all directions, all time, and from all points on
Rudy's surprisingly wide emotional spectrum. I would have
drowned in the maelstrom of disjointed pasts, except that there was
one unifying facet, one thread that tied each piece of the
bombardment together with the rest and allowed me to cling,
breathing, to reason. That powerful ubiquitous string was Rudy's
guilt.

I wondered whether the shadows I saw ranging his
memories earlier had been installed by Rudy to hide the guilt that
pervaded his mind. Freuzre was a vehicle for mayhem originally,
but, as the Fritz's bars and Jerusalem's accumulated, Rudy may

have used the shadow to insulate his conscience from the truth of his actions. It made sense to me, but I wondered if, knowing Rudy, any of these evil events would have occurred had Rudy faced the true Freuzre – his own ambition – and neutralized it. I would never know, but I was going to learn as much about Rudy's perception of his personal history as I cared to piece together. Perhaps in the process I would find a way home.

I wanted to start at the beginning, but soon discovered that such a moment did not exist. Rudy had so muddled his history with his delusion of fantastic age that his real memories, like those of his childhood in the 1960's, or his failed relationships in high school, meshed smoothly with vapidly glorious moments conferring with Da Vinci on armor, or arguing with Pope Urban II about the validity of the crusades. After much scrutiny, I was able to spot fundamental differences between reality and fantasy. For instance, Rudy always looked like Rudy in his imagined memories. He consistently wore the same face, the same hair, and held the same poise that I saw moments earlier. But his real memories, when they included an image of him at all, portrayed a frightened child, a skinny, acne ridden adolescent, and an adult who seemed whole enough, but one feature (a nose, an arm, maybe an ear) would be absent.

Once I could differentiate true reality from posturing, I used the guilt thread to tie events together more clearly. In time I was aligning Rudy's life in a fashion that would have riled Carl Jung, but worked to shatter his misguided ego. Because they were personal, and definable only to Rudy, most of the images I encountered were unfathomable, but a few recurring themes that I could recognize began to draw a clearer picture for me.

One primary object was the dog-eared remnant of a book that earned significance with me because it appeared repeatedly, and often as the centerpiece of archetypical scenes like church altars or girls' locker rooms. In every instance it was open to the same chapter, and it was either held by a pair of mature female hands or ensconced in female-leaning imagery. Once it was sifting through an hourglass, but I figured that counted as well. I drew myself closer to the book when it appeared in the backpack of a young woman who remarkably resembled Cassie, as if Rudy had superimposed her soft adult features on a girl he had known during his adolescence. Rudy and I clearly should have had a talk, I thought. I tugged the book from the startled girl's backpack and perused the untitled pages.

The bit of literature that Rudy posted so prominently in his dreams was an obscure text about the Merlin, his legend and his magick. Yes, Merlin with a 'the,' and magick with a 'k.' That should have spelled it out enough for me, but I read a few paragraphs anyway, keeping in mind that this was probably not a true facsimile of the original text – if there was one, but more likely the version that Rudy would prefer to remember.

The book's unnamed author claimed to historically place the death of the ancient and accomplished druid magician known to the modern world as Merlin in the 11th century, even listing the Anglican town of Surry as his final abode. It said that the wizard had lived for over 500 years and died not because of foul play or ill health, but because it was time to pass on his power to a new user.

A-hah.

The flowery paragraphs drifted into mindless literary drivel after I read the description of the hard-working young visionary from a "new world" who was the sole being on the planet capable of channeling the power of Merlin into a force for good, for creation. I shook my head, closed the book, zipped it back into the young Cassie's backpack and sent her on her way into the dark ether with a light paternal pat on her rump. I reviewed the books that appeared in three more disparate images – once as the bible clutched by an angry, impossibly tall nun corralling Rudy's first communion; another encased in the Santa Maria's compass stand, which was being ignored by Christopher Columbus who was listening eagerly to Rudy's sailing advice; and finally on the top of a shimmering golden altar, cradled in pure crystal female hands – but the words were all identical, and implied the same truth. This was Rudy's scripture, and he had based his fictional origin upon it, causing him to be born in the 11th century in south Asia. He apparently could not think of any other 'new world' from the era, so he had to improvise. Made sense, I thought, on many levels. Rudy chose an ancient but very popular myth to lay recognizable credit to his claims of magical power, but at some point he fell into thrall of his own extensive hype.

Rudy's true life history was encapsulated within a tiny fraction of the total images that pummeled me for attention. I could spot them interspersed among the more grandiose false memories and fantasies that monopolized my senses when I consciously registered their existence. The snippets of Rudy's real past were nearly translucent in the darkness, accessible only if I struggled to avoid the imposing fictions surrounding them. On a hunch I ignored the awesome moments with presidents, popes and, oddly, racecar drivers, and drew a careful mystic bead on the real things. This was not easy, especially because the energy of Rudy's imagined past was formidable, and I spent much of my own strength batting errant moments aside with a large fluffy tennis racket I pulled from his time with Pete Sampras. I waded through Rudy's childhood quickly, unsure of any of the players, or of their importance, and spotting nothing particularly unusual. I stopped in one of countless lonely records of his adolescence. A young Rudy sat on a cold step of an empty high school stairwell. I joined him, as I had Freuzre. His desperate need to rise above everyone else was tangible to me, though I had never noticed him getting physically beaten, shunned, academically or athletically defeated, or even accidentally aggrieved by anyone, in any of the memories I had opened. I wondered how he had developed such feelings of alienation.

The thread of guilt clarified that detail for me as well, because it drifted not from crisis to crisis as it struggled to collapse the real stuff under its ethereal mass, but from memories of boredom, emptiness, and unrequited laziness. Holy shit, I thought, Rudy really did pursue this power, on his own, just to make his life easier.

"And it worked," I said to poorly tiled steps that spread away from sneaker toes that were not mine, "It worked well enough that you learned to live without doing anything at all, without lifting a finger. Damn, I'll bet that alone bored you to tears. And I'll bet that you needed something to make your perfect artificial life interesting."

I browsed further into Rudy's depiction of his personal history to confirm my judgment. I found him in college, just as lazy but on the brink of 'something big.' He bragged about it, picked up girls with it, but could get no one other than himself to believe in it. I could see, while joining him at the only empty table in a crowded college pub, that he had succeeded in much, especially in amplifying the effect of his own alienation. I guessed that he must have had his breakthrough sometime after college, because all real memories, aside strangely from the ones that included me or Cassie, had given way to his manufactured past. I was not completely special: every memory of me, though bizarre to observe (like looking in a funhouse mirror) was faded, while Cassie's image still burned bright, often straight through more established images of Rudy's adult escapades in the World. Just when I was establishing a real pattern, one that held more of my wife and less of Rudy's professed sense of altruism and dedication than I felt comfortable observing, the thread of guilt snapped.

That guilt, no doubt accumulated unconsciously during Rudy's fabrication of his millennial life history, had lost its immense tensile strength when Rudy abandoned his own mind. I became nervous when the tiny unbound translucent moments faded into countless diaphanous gray blurs that grouped into a singular black thunderhead of chaotic misinformation that loomed wherever I projected my awareness. Although I could avoid the accumulated moments directly by not focusing on their content, I could not prevent them from filling the void of Rudy's abandoned unconscious with the sheer volume of their lost importance. Uh, oh, I thought, time to get my skinny ass out of this non-place.

"Easier said than done," I said aloud, but I immediately set about seeking an exit regardless of my misgivings. I quickly ran through the meager gamut of my dream-navigation knowledge – spinning 180 degrees; concentrating on familiar scenes of my own creation; imagining my purple plain, the red chair, the Escort, Max, or anything else that passed for a switch from Alex-generated reality. Nothing worked. The chaos around me multiplied and surrounded me in a confused crowd of misty mythic memories that could be focused on more easily every second. I was in trouble again, about to drown in the mostly scripted world of Rudy Frisset. A fuzzy Imax show of random memories that roamed untended by the natural controls of a rational mind obscured the once prevalent blackness. The gray finally faded completely, and I was bounced incessantly, dreamlike, between images from Rudy's history. Most of them were 'important,' all of them were somehow broken by the disarray of Rudy's exit, and perhaps my own intrusion. I noted that all the moments that rattled my awareness lacked any hint of Freuzre. His greatest foe was not included in his story. Or, I pondered as I physically ducked a nervous right cross thrown by a deeply confused and comically petite Louis XIV, perhaps Freuzre's existence was embedded in that fiber of guilt that had followed Rudy to whatever new plain he deemed it necessary to blacken.

Any humor I had summoned to help me cope had faded. Rudy's moments occupied every facet of space and time on the plain that I imagined, and I could feel myself being crushed by the weight of images and the staggering toll that participating in each was taking on my own recently healed body and mind. I had no choice but to participate, because the characters in the emancipated moments knew I was there. Unlike Louis, most behaved passively, too frightened to react to my presence, like I was a ghost.

"A ghost?" I asked aloud. Suddenly my universe petrified, as if God had hit a celestial 'pause' button. Motion resumed immediately, threatening to interfere with the response to my question.

"A ghost!" I answered, slapping my thigh in a fit of sudden hope. The other character I finally noticed had gone distinctly missing since the guilt thread collapsed was Cassie. I had already wondered why Max was not among the throng of spectral acquaintances, but assumed that she was, and I hadn't recognized her. Or, as a real creature who could roam Rudy's psyche already, she may have learned to step out of the fiction. Or, perhaps, like Freuzre, she had earned a place in the consciousness that Rudy took with him. In any case, I could rationalize and lament her absence. I had explained Freuzre. But Cassie was here before, and she was equally monumental in both Rudy's fictional and real lives. Now, she was gone.

"No, you're not," I shouted as I turned sideways to allow two passing battleships headway through the brackish waters that did not moisten my trousers' cuffs or crotch. Cassie *was* there; she had just been filed beyond my perception, I noted with jealousy-laden satisfaction. I knew it was significant, but could not place the point of my discovery. My reason was occupied by the infinite barrage of clear *Brainstorm* bubbles of memory that burst upon my senses, sometimes several at a time, whenever they were in my range. And my range spanned the entire plain. Still, I was warmed by knowledge that I recovered on my own, without aid from the cosmic mess around me. Then, its intensity increasing in proportion to that feeling of warmth, I saw an object, a point of white light that held a stationary position in the far, far distance. I was instantly euphoric. Any stationary object in this chaotic environment was a good thing, and this one was white. That had to be a great thing. I set aside, but did not forget, my revelation about Cassie, and, in the name of all the horror movies I had grown up with, I moved toward the light.

It expanded as I approached it, retaining its intensity as memories passed between it and myself. These memories did not fade in the light – my motion toward the luminescence, and through the field of dreams I forced myself to negotiate, intensified the barrage of Rudy's abandoned history. I was hit by Union musket balls on a Civil War battlefield, and nearly flattened by a freight train that crossed my path without bells or lights, clearing my nose by an inch. One of the boxcar doors was open, and the hand of Woody Guthrie passed me, outstretched. I met his haunted eyes in the shadows of the empty boxcar, but I chose not to clasp his pale open palm. I paused to watch the hand disappear, long fingers silhouetted by an orange sunset, and to thank Rudy for at least one very cool memory. I mildly regretted not joining Woody, but I had a priority.

The light had grown in the distance, and had adopted a crisply rectangular shape. I was getting close. After a few million more steps through uncounted fictitious memories depicting Rudy in every manner of exclusively Western predicaments, archetypes, and famous situations, all of which I was able to shove aside thanks to the promise of the light, I finally recognized my objective. I laughed, honestly amused by the shape that the single stable element in Rudy's shattered mind had taken. I was more than willing to temporarily swallow the bile of rage that swam into my mouth when I contemplated the dirty little secret that had fomented that stability.

Shaking my head and smiling giddily, I dusted the imagined detritus of Rudy's life from my clothes, and stepped through Cassie's open bedroom door. She was inside, wearing a pink flannel Victorian gown, knitting in her rocker. She looked up at my entrance without surprise. She was, after all, dead.

Chapter Thirty-Three

Something was different.

I had intruded into Cassie's world with enough frequency to become accustomed to her familiar acceptance of my arrival. She usually behaved as if I had always been in the room with her. Except during my unintentional attempts on her life, her emotions never swelled. They rarely appeared. This time my crossing of the tired wooden threshold into the facsimile of my old bedroom had a transforming effect on the avatar of my dead wife.

Each of my involuntarily tentative steps toward her polished away some of the standard glaze in Cassie's eyes with a dollop of living fire. I had noticed the lifeless default setting of her eyes in several instances, but had consistently offered myself a dismissive explanation for their thick plastic coating before my suspicions were aroused. Occasionally I had imagined tears moistening the empty retinas, and perhaps they had, but the real energy that sparked them declared that Cassie's eyes had been doorways to nothing more than an excellent mystical projection.

Until this visit. Something about my presence was transforming Cassie. She continued to knit with industry, but the needles clicked more slowly, and she made errors in the row she was adding to the unidentifiable violet garment she had been crafting. When I stopped beside her and rested my fingers on her shoulder, she dropped her knitting to the slate hearth. She stood, and without spoken word snaked her arms around my waist, joined her hands at the small of my back and squeezed. Her hug was tight enough to elicit a gasp from me. I did not try to stop her, because astride her hearty intimacy rode paragraphs of communication, and I wanted to listen.

Cassie's embrace told me that she was happy, relieved, that I had joined her, and that I was not Rudy. It confirmed the truth I had already assumed: she was a part of Rudy, and she never was the corporeal Cassie who was a unit of my life. But the information was not complete. Cassie had much more to tell me. I wondered why she did not speak. Speech was easy for her, and was most welcome during my convalescence. Then I noticed that I too was silent. I remembered the audio problems on Rudy's plain, and realized that perhaps she simply assumed that speech was impossible. I rolled my eyes.

"Cassie," I said, gently pushing her head from my shoulder so that I could better bask in the glow of her reignited brown eyes, "It's all right. I think. Rudy isn't here. I'm thrilled that you are, but kind of amazed that you're still in one piece. Oh, and I am in one piece, for a change; Rudy's stuff doesn't seem to hurt me here."

She unhooked her arms from my waist, but held her stare to accentuate the importance of her next gesture, which was to rest her index finger against my lips. Her touch, to its purpose, ended my sloppy speech. She had more to say, and my noise was blocking the telling. I obediently buttoned my lip.

Cassie lowered her hand, and took mine with it. Then she stood beside me, to my right, and smiled. Her chambers vanished, as did her gown, and anything else that had been accessory to her display. She stood beside me, nude and relaxed, casually drumming her fingers against the back of my hand while she waited for some additional change to occur around us. While we waited I took the opportunity to admire her form. Her breasts were rounder and fuller than I remembered, almost stylized in their perfect, matching slightly upturned shapes. Also, her hips were narrower and her legs much longer than the original Cassie, but her height and facial features were the same. I nodded when I realized that there was a little less need to feel jealous of Rudy or suspicious of the antics of my wife before she died: Rudy could perfectly duplicate the parts of Cassie that he could see and remember, but he had to defer to his imagination for the rest. And the pinup girl perfection that he envisioned in Cassie's form betrayed not only how little he had seen, but also the adolescence in which Rudy's fantasies were firmly rooted. Not that I minded. I wondered why I hadn't noticed before. Perhaps I had tainted my previous perceptions of Cassie with my own childish expectations, and in the relative purity of Rudy's mind I could see exactly what he had created.

My attention to Cassie's Barbie-Doll physique helped me to overlook the formation of the luminescent pathway on which we stood. She stopped drumming her fingers when I jerked to my toes in startled acknowledgment of its appearance. When I relaxed and let my heels fall to the hard surface she began our journey. She led me along the path without leaving my side. I followed abreast of her, um, breasts, and tore my eyes away from them to survey the environment we traversed.

The path on which we walked meandered like a backlit mountain stream through the three-dimensional sea of Rudy's mind. Ahead of us was the same gray hailstorm of the collected bursts of Rudy's past, chaotically careening about the blackness. I more knew this was happening than saw it, because the definition of light had altered itself in Cassie's presence. It was as though she walked under a ray of sunshine breaking through the morning clouds over some eastern bay.

"God," I said, "I've tried to adapt to Rudy's total lack of creativity, but the man sure can be trite sometimes." Cassie stopped, turned toward me and scowled. Her face transformed into that of a gothic stone gargoyle. She snarled, flashing rows of scythian teeth. It switched back to 'normal' before I could run screaming. I understood her message and resolved, to myself, to keep my own counsel for the rest of the trip.

As we walked, the haphazard battery of Rudy's life paused to allow us passage before the mess closed in behind us. The path remained, undulating through the shreds of memory without being effected by or causing any damage to the passing moments. First I believed that he had created a light shield of sorts for Cassie, but as we progressed I understood that the expansive dimension of her presence required no protection. It was not the path that cleared our way, or any clever contrivance that deflected the random bits of Rudy's life. It was Cassie herself. My conclusion was illustrated when I looked down at our feet. Mine were ambling along at the easy pace to which I believed I had set them, but Cassie's tiny narrow feet were still. Her world, including my presence, was moving around her, not she through it. She was not a participant, like the gray puffs that failed to transform into clear bubbles of stored time and space as they approached her. She was a hub; and she knew it.

She nodded, and glanced sidelong at me in an authentic Cassie expression that said, "Duh, Alex, I've been saying this all along," before she turned her attention back to the path. When she did I almost froze in my tracks (though I dared not, lest this incredible spell be broken) because I suddenly understood the substance of the path. It was not the literally brilliant feat of engineering that it appeared; that it was a path at all was secondary to its nature. It was the manifestation of the history-weaving thread of Rudy's guilt that I thought had dissolved with his exit. Yet now that guilt, intact and invincible under Cassie's feet, was the backlit translucent gold guide for her easy movement through the universe of Rudy. She was riding the salve, the last string of compassion that had bound Rudy's humanity to his soul, as though she had laid it there. I wished I could ask, but knew I could not, so I waited for more answers to come without questions.

And they did. Thought Cassie offered no verbal explanation, our progression through Rudy's mind continued to enlighten me. I felt myself becoming aware of, and comfortable in, the chaotic environment we were fording. The primary message I received which, after understanding, I had been told repeatedly since my arrival on his plain had finally made itself clear to me: we were not inside Rudy's mind. It had been disturbing to me to imagine myself swimming among the neurons of his frontal lobe, awash like a bug in the brain of another human being, but that was the only conclusion I could reach due to the fact that everything around me was a symbol of Rudy's thoughts and memories. Cassie clarified their origin with a graceful wave of her right hand: We were not touring Rudy's mind. We were navigating its exhaust.

In his successful quest to bend reality to his whim, Rudy had generated a substantial pile of realized thought for which he no longer had any use. Rather than forget, and subsequently vaporize, his creations, he stored them on his plain. His miserly grip on the things he had made real was a major factor in his opinion of his extreme age. His plain was haunted by so many 'real' moments of things that he had simply imagined that he had come to believe they had always existed. He probably reabsorbed some of them into his long-term memory as truth. This caused me to wonder about the truth of Cassie, and Freuzre. Cassie squeezed my hand at my thought to reassure me that it was not all that bad. But, it was. I knew.

Cassie was as unreal as I had assumed, as was Freuzre, but their existence on this plain, coupled with my existence period, had played irreparable games with Rudy's troubled spirit. These games, inspired by Rudy's emotions, were what directed his journey toward medicinal global destruction.

I was able to glean that the path we traveled was new. Cassie had recently erected it to arrange the moments Rudy preserved into a rationally practical pattern. She had intended to create the path, and some semblance of order, since Rudy had accidentally created in her a need to do so, but she had never succeeded before because Freuzre countered both her strength and her interest in keeping Rudy sane. Plus, I remembered Max announcing that Cassie had moved in with her, an abode that was surely not a part of Rudy's world. That disconnect, even if nominal and brief, could not have helped this Cassie keep in touch with the refugees of Rudy's memory. My thoughts were interrupted when we rounded a curve that passed a particularly crowded mass of memories and I witnessed the true nature of the shadow Freuzre.

There was nothing specific on display beyond that gentle twist in the path to illustrate my sudden comprehension. Rather, there was something in the curve itself, in the quality of the local ether, and in the quiet tension that coursed through Cassie's fingers that indicated we were passing through Freuzre's home realm. The proof of Freuzre's placement was asserted in feeling, not in evidence. It was more like we encountered a highway road sign than actually strolled through the shadow's neighborhood. The existence of Freuzre's home, his location, his source, depended on the faith that that sign represented something real. Cassie held that faith; I did not. Freuzre was not there, I knew, because he had disappeared with Rudy. Freuzre was, as I had suspected, like Cassie a figment of Rudy's imagination made real. However, my earlier belief that Freuzre existed to allow Rudy an excuse to do Good in the World was flawed. I had given him too much credit.

Without breaking my stride I turned to Cassie and mouthed the word, "No," to her. She was looking at me when I spoke, and was able to read the panicked, crestfallen expression that had shaded my face and crinkled my posture. Her solemn nod and genuinely wet eyes reminded me of the moment many years ago when she realized she had killed her favorite fish by feeding it too much. I turned my attention back to the path, which had straightened as it passed through an area free of all but the purest darkness. Perhaps I was being given a chance to digest the truth.

It was not an easy chew. What I learned in the last few feet of glowing path was that Rudy had fallen in love with Cassie, or perhaps the idea of her. She had overwhelmed his senses until she became the center of this universe, this singular place where he could be confident that everything was real because everything was his. So, he had Cassie, but he had a problem. That problem was me. I had Cassie, too, except that I had the real Cassie, not some construct that emulated her best features. Rudy hated that, but, in spite of all his efforts and burgeoning power, he could do nothing to diminish the real Cassie's love for me. I was amazed that I had never noticed Rudy's emotions, unveiled now for my perusal while Cassie was alive. Perhaps, I guessed, the love Cassie and I shared was strong enough that I had no need to observe Rudy's crippling interest. Or, I concluded, Rudy had no concept of his own obsession, so he could not betray it.

It was that blind desire that may have inadvertently caused Cassie's death. I had found no pod of memory to indict Rudy, but I sensed relief, almost a sublime joy, in certain memories of his home life after her death. My walk with Cassie still offered no proof of foul deeds, but it clarified his satisfaction that the created Cassie had graduated to the only Cassie. In the first few months after she died, while Rudy could still claim responsibility for her existence, everything was fine. Had I noticed anything at all during that time, and there was no way that I could have, I probably would have wondered at his sudden euphoria. But, as the surrogate Cassie's presence became more real to Rudy, he forgot her source. And then I came back into the picture, once more ruining everything for Rudy.

My revelations were interrupted by a parade of tiny black bubbles that floated across the path, near our feet. Cassie stopped our forward motion to allow them to pass. The billiard ball-sized orbs moved very slowly, and I could not resist the urge to bend down and touch one. Cassie held me back weakly, as if she were supposed to stop me, but wasn't really interested. I snatched one of the balls from its path and straightened. I held it close to my face, assuming that it was another nugget of memory. It was, but it was not one of Rudy's.

The opaque orb was reluctant to surrender information. I did not immediately see the usual memories, symbols, or historic symbols. Instead, I saw nothing. Then I squinted, and concentrated mightily. My effort was rewarded by an image. It was a moment I remembered well; a late-night poker game with Rudy and a few of his friends, about five years earlier. We were laughing, I was winning, and everything was pleasant. My nostalgia for the simple quality of bygone days is one reason I recognized the memory. But then I noticed two significant aspects of the memory that rattled my spine. First, the memory wasn't *like* mine, it *was* mine. Rudy had somehow stolen a moment of my time, and stashed it safely in his realm, out of my reach. Second, I noticed that we were playing cards at a table located on my purple plain.

I did not remember that! Anxiously intrigued, I stopped the queue of passing balls by placing myself in their path. They gently bumped my shin, then each other, until their lateral motion had ceased. They still bobbed slightly, but I could believe that they were no longer in transit. I dropped to my knees and carefully examined them. Each ball contained a memory of mine that conveyed accidental exposure to my innate ability to manipulate reality in ways that Rudy had toiled through his perceived lifetimes to emulate. He grew to hate and love me for this. He resolved to hide my ability by swiping my moments of elevation. As I matured, however, the moments became more complex, and my awareness of them harder to hide. Cassie's death helped Rudy's cause by ending my dreams, and most thought, for years, but when I began to swing back into supernatural motion, my activities became too complex. Rudy sustained his attempts to capture my insight by using his Sound Room and superior concentration, but he eventually accepted that my conscious immersion in the dream world was inevitable. He knew that his only recourse was to recruit me, to convince me that I should be his disciple. When I balked for reasons I never understood, he persisted, and brought Freuzre and Cassie into play.

Both avatars were originally created – or used, especially in Cassie's case – as carrots. Freuzre, as I had suspected, was meant to provide Rudy with a foil. The shadow was a vehicle to justify Rudy's meting of otherwise uninvited power. Because the world is a collection of independent souls, each with a unique (and mostly neutral) agenda, Rudy could not meddle in their activity, and coax me to participate with him, without a rationale. That rationale was Freuzre. Again like Cassie, the definition Rudy applied to Freuzre was so exact and permeating that eventually he grew to believe that Freuzre, and its threats, were real. By the time he obliterated his house to irreversibly draw me consciously into his realm, Rudy truly feared Freuzre's activity. He had forgotten that it was he, Rudy, who had cast the shadow initially. So Rudy's pain at Fritz's was real, though he had been ultimately responsible for the tavern's destruction. He also believed that I would be as in thrall to Cassie as he had become, so the mere mention that this magic could bring her back should have made me his dream slave forever. Unfortunately I was unsuccessful in dismissing the truth of Cassie's death, so all of his efforts, and my own half-assed attempts, failed.

By his actions Rudy had suspended two heavy albatrosses from his spiritual neck. First, he had created a mighty force that was bent on destroying the world. Second, and in serious conflict with the first, he fabricated the object of his unfulfilled love, who could never give him that breath of real love Cassie and I had shared. He clung maniacally to his fantasies and raised them, without guilt or reticence, to unanticipated, unimaginable levels of destruction until I faced him down and personally threw a wrench into his machinations. Even then he sought to destroy me, but the seeds were sewn. He abandoned Cassie, trapping her in her rooms, separating her from her role as the reasonable core of his memories, and deleting her from his constant attentions. This abandonment allowed him to act without pause on every draconian belief he had opined regarding the repair of human civilization. It was not until he saw himself in his own mirror, casting no shadow though Freuzre stood beside him, that he finally realized how far into his own abyss he had fallen.

    I gathered my memories into my arms and stood. While Cassie watched, smiling and gently nodding, I carefully placed each orb into the pocket of my jeans. Though there were dozens of them, they all fit without making a bulge. Nothing else happened; I was not abruptly deluged with forgotten memories, or handed great powers beyond my understanding. The memories just slid anonymously down my jeans and back into my possession. Maybe someday they would return to me during a dream, I thought. I gestured with a twirl of my hand that it was time to move on, and immediately felt Cassie drag me, without being in front of me, further along her thread of truth.

    So, I thought bitterly, Rudy's entire crusade, all the damage he has caused to hundreds of millions of lives, to history itself, was based on typical, petty human foibles. He couldn't possess Cassie's love, so he created another version of her. He couldn't have my power without working very hard, so he tried to trick me into ignoring it. His faith in himself and his perceived mission capsized when both efforts failed, and he erroneously locked Cassie away from her role (unbeknownst to him) as the glowing center of his dream world while in the process of permanently removing me, a potential anchor for his power, from his world. Rudy had allowed basal emotions like pride and jealousy to shred the vast structure of power he oversaw. He had achieved his lifelong dream of getting something for nothing, but never attained the maturity necessary to survive as a powerless adult, much less a god. And, when I showed him that mirror, he collapsed and retreated because he also lacked the maturity to face guilt. The blow struck by the reality of the moment knocked his mind, and maybe his being, out of commission. What a waste, I thought: all that power, all that practice and discipline, eliminated because a man couldn't understand love and friendship.

    My realization of the nature of Rudy, and my place in his misadventures, caused subtle changes in the format of our stroll. The path was no longer paved by golden light but by plain red bricks, and the chaos that had almost incessantly plagued us had faded. Countless memories-made-real had been neatly layered back into the fabric of Rudy's black plain. I smirked proudly at

my success in reorganizing Rudy's 'mind' with a thought, but a
sharp squeeze of my hand by Cassie, who still walked beside me,
still nude, wrung the immature reaction from my mind. No, I
thought, I haven't been paying attention to what I've been shown.
By taking a walk with her, I had freed Cassie to resume her
guardianship of Rudy's psychic legacy. She probably could not
permit me to talk to her because her being was focused too
completely on reorganizing what Rudy had let free by locking her
in a comfy cage. Now she was back in control, and the stuff of
Rudy's past was again filed safely within the infinite folds and
possibilities of his plain. Her resumption of control also lent light
to the plain, which I saw now was a pleasant shade of green –
remarkably close to that of the gown Mary, and the real Cassie,
once wore – perfectly empty in all directions, and bathed in the
same diffuse white light that lit my plain. All was in control again,
but Rudy was gone. Cassie and I were alone, in a place whose
nature I could not hope to affect.

"Man," Cassie whispered, shattering the silence, "Are you
thick or what?"

"Huh? What do you mean?" I asked, looking at her.
Indeed, I did more than look at her as her breasts bounced
delightfully with each step that she took on the bricks. I stared,
only noting intellectually that she was walking, and willing to
speak, again. I stared not just at her enticing body but also through
it in an attempt to see the real Cassie lurking somewhere under all
that perfectly disproportioned flesh. She let me hold my stare for a
while before responding, probably knowing that I would not have
paid her any heed until I completed my survey. She was right, and
that, I realized was the piece of Cassie I consistently identified.
Rudy, though he built this body for her, had loved her for her
perception, her wit, and her mind. He longed to touch her soul, but
his childish demeanor prevented him from tagging it. My nominal
search quickly found Cassie's true essence. It hid behind those
eyes, those gestures, and those words, subtly concealed in plain
sight behind the trappings of a comic book body. Rudy had tugged
a correct version of Cassie into his world, yet he was too dense to
notice his miracle. Or he had no idea what to look for, because in
his eternal laziness he never found the strength to fall in love
naturally. Poor Rudy, I thought, still able to pity the man while

cursing the force of nature his proclivities had led him to become. He would never appreciate his single greatest achievement, even while she organized his past and qualified his humanity for him. Eventually I refocused on Cassie's breasts, which only heaved with her breath because she had stopped walking, and came back to the moment. She smiled, and spoke:

"What I mean, you idiot, is that you have enough answers in your precious head to elevate a hundred Dalai Lamas, but all you can do is go back to the least common denominator." When I blushed and looked at her breasts again, she took my other hand, turned me to face her, and continued, "No, silly, not those denominators. What are you thinking about, right now, other than sex?"

"Well, it wasn't really sex," I retorted, "More like admiration."

"Fine," she said, blushing slightly herself, "What were you thinking, just beyond that?"

"Mostly about how Rudy shot his wad, trashed all that power, just because he couldn't have what he wanted, or thought he wanted."

"Thought so. And that's as far as you got?"

"I think so."

"Thought so," Cassie frowned prettily, smacked me upside the head without letting go of my hand, and said, "You're as bad as your friend, you know."

"What do you mean? I would never blow up half the world."

"Probably not, but it wouldn't be for seeing the big picture. You think you're trapped here, powerless, don't you?"

"Yeah, but only because I am."

Cassie laughed, lightly, like she had a thousand times a lifetime ago. Rudy did love her.

"So, I'm not trapped?"

"No."

"Why not?"

"Because you are something Rudy isn't!"

"How long does this game go on?" I asked, feigning impatience because I could talk to a beautiful naked woman for vast amounts of time.

"Until now," she said, bowing her head. When she raised it, her eyes were closed. She continued, "Alex, you were blessed with something that evaded Rudy throughout his real and imagined lifetimes. It's the power that binds all of our souls, that makes even you mighty magicians quake in your boots and err profusely. You've been so caught up in the definition of Rudy, the power of Rudy, the mistakes of Rudy, that you've failed to look beyond Rudy."

"To what?" I asked.

"To love," she said, opening her eyes. They were wet, glowing, and a shade of green that blurred my own vision.

"To love," I repeated stupidly. I held her gaze for one last minute, unwilling to break contact with Max. Then Cassie blinked, and her brown but still living eyes returned.

"To love," she repeated, dripping with wisdom, "And who, my dear living husband, have you really been thinking about all this time? Who has your heart represented while your mind worked its high school theorems?"

"Who saved my ass."

"More than once, you know. Who?"

"I don't think I need to answer that."

"No, you don't. But you know what you do need to answer?"

"What?"

"What is that butt-ugly black door doing on Rudy's turf?" she asked, nodding her head to her right. I looked to my left. There, at the end of the brick path, was the door to the castle that once dominated my plain. The castle that I had mistakenly attributed to evil, to Freuzre, before learning it was the entrance to Max's ethereal home. I never even registered the mistake, or the power that had deposited the portal on my plain.

"Oh, my," I mumbled.

"Oh, my," Cassie said, "Well I'm glad great minds think alike."

Without another word I crossed the few bricks necessary to bring the door to within a few feet of me. It was not the great black oak door through which Mary and I had passed an eon ago but an old, two-part farm door. Its top half had been flung open, and Max and Mary were leaning out, waving cheerfully. I could not tell them apart.

"Cassie," I said without looking at her.

"Yes, Alex?"

"I'm going home now."

"Yes Alex, you are."

Chapter Thirty-Four

"Alex," either Max or Mary shouted from the doorway, "You're still in one piece! Who'd a thought it?"

I sighed, thrust my hands deep in my empty but recently filled pockets, and I thought it: I was in one piece. I had returned intact to my loved ones after my epic victory in battles fought in distant lands and fantastic dimensions. I was little more than a bystander in the last rounds, and therefore I had emerged physically unscathed. I was stronger spiritually, however, because my ancillary presence had mattered. Fantastic devastation had occurred, and I had responded to successfully curb continued damage. I think. So had Cassie. I think. Still clutching her hand, and leading her for this portion of our stroll, I unlatched the gate of the white picket fence that quaintly protected Max/Mary's manicured lawn.

I held the squeaky wooden gate for Cassie. She paused for a tentative second outside the picket fence before reluctantly following me through the narrow gap I had opened for her. Consumed by the vision of two identical flaming redheads waiting for me at their door, I missed – ignored – Cassie's hesitation. I was mildly hurt that Max/Mary failed to fling the rest of their door open and hurl themselves across the lawn to joyfully embrace me. I consoled myself by assuming that they wanted to rush out, but were constrained by the rules of my plain. When I was halfway across the tidy little lawn, careful to follow the spotless white gravel path, I called to them both:

"Thanks for the vote of confidence. But yeah, I made it. Can we come in?"

"Absolutely," they harmonized. The lower half of the door swung inward, and the two stepped apart, making a path for our entrance. They remained inside, framed by the door's loosely rectangular opening and nothing else. It appeared to me more that the door was inserted into the empty backdrop of the plain than it was deposited upon it.

"Dude," One of them said, pointing to Cassie, "What is up with that green dress?" I looked at Cassie, for the first time since our arrival. She was Cassie again, in the correct proportions, and she was wearing that same silk gown that I had dressed Mary in after our flight in my house. Our presence on my plain must have dressed and reformed her without any conscious help from me. Now that, I thought, was the height of laziness on my part. I still wished I could remember the Christmas, or any occasion, in which Cassie wore that dress in life. I also freshly questioned, given what I had learned about its color, who had bought it for her. Cassie was smiling at Max/Mary, shaking her head slowly. She remained silent, perhaps proffering me the opportunity to be the center of attention.

"I don't know," I responded cheerfully, and too loudly, "I guess I have a repressed memory screaming to get out."

"Yeah; one or two," the one on the left said while they giggled amongst themselves, "Now get in here so we can get caught up."

I obliged by stepping through the doorway into Max's bright suburban condo foyer. Most of me made it inside without incident, but when my right hand, the one that held Cassie's, had its turn to cross the threshold, it didn't. Instead it was painfully crushed between the sudden vise-grip of Cassie's fingers, and jerked back from the doorway with monstrously zealous force. My attention leapt with visceral anxiety to my wrist, which I hoped had not become a stump. I relaxed when I saw that my hand was still attached. Cassie, unfazed, grasped it with her other hand, lifted it to her lips and solemnly kissed it. Then she held it close, focused on it instead of my face, and the explanations its expression no doubt demanded.

"What?" I asked reluctantly.

"Alex," she said, lifting her wide eyes to mine, "Much as I'd like to, I can't come in."

"Sure you can," I tried, "You've been here before."

"No. No I haven't."

I fully focused on Cassie, but kept Max's door in my peripheral vision, just in case. Something was wrong, and I was extremely interested in denying it. I gave Cassie another tug toward the door, but she would not budge. It was not stubbornness that belayed her; a bulldozer likely lacked adequate power to push her through Max's door.

"Yes. Yes you have," I tried again, "You were here with Max, when Rudy had her keeping an eye on you."

"Alex, please," Cassie said – I could almost distinguish a giant cartoon shoe hovering in the antique white atmosphere behind her head, preparing to fall, "Think about everything you've seen, everything you've just learned about Rudy, and about me. I was never here. The thing that Rudy made to look like me was here, perhaps, but it wasn't me. It was, for all intents and purposes, Rudy."

"I know," I said slowly, "I know. But I had hoped that if I denied hard enough, that detail would be forgotten in my world, and you could become a part of here."

"Instead of there. Now would that be fair to Rudy?" she asked, deflating my hopeful intention with her easy wisdom. She moaned tiredly when I drew a breath to protest, then continued, "Would it be fair to me? Alex, c'mon. You know that I am just a model; a thing that Rudy made in childish attempts to satisfy his fantasies and co-opt your loneliness. I'm not real; I don't belong here. Hell, I'm not sure I even *am* here."

"But you are," I said softly. She frowned, looked around at the landing upon which Max/Mary's yard perched, high above yet flush with my plain.

"Am I?" she asked, "Where exactly is here? And who is holding me here?"

"But I can do that anywhere. We should try."

"No. No we shouldn't. In there," she titled her head toward Max's door, "In there is a place governed by another independent being. Max is very powerful, Alex. You know now that Rudy wasn't keeping her around for just her awesome beauty. He effectively concealed her abilities from her until you usurped her attention, and she is only now coming into her own. Max may not be terribly interested in my company. No, don't defend her. You're missing my meaning. She's not jealous; I think she even likes me, if I can say that. She probably, honestly, wants me to enter. No, it's nothing personal."

"It's business?"

"Yeah," Cassie said, pleased that my joke accidentally made her point, "You see, if Max let me in it wouldn't be me she would be harboring. It'd be Rudy. All I am, in the end, is Rudy." That last sentence, spoken flatly and with monolithic severity, was a garrote tightening on my throat.

"How many times are you going to tell me that?"

"That's it. Last time. You have to get it now.

"So," she continued, "Because there is no Rudy around to project me into that apartment whether Max likes it or not, her unconscious can deflect me, *Rudy*, until hell freezes over. Or he comes back. Whether she knows she's doing it or not.

"In the meantime, it's only fair that I stay on his plain and keep Rudy's bubbles organized in case he should come home. Do you understand any of this?" She asked the last question while her fingers gently caressed my cheeks. I gazed into her eyes and searched one last time for a reason, for a sign that Rudy had somehow accidentally brought Cassie back from the dead, from her murder. Though they were not dull, swirling no doubt from my input with the same clean warmth I recalled the night I asked her to marry me, I knew that they truly did not belong to Cassie. Those eyes were Rudy's, and they belonged in his realm. I got it. And I felt a sudden rush of guilt for changing her, dressing her, and dragging her from her world for my sake. I finally learned. I gently wrapped my hands around her wrists, pulled her hands to her side, and let go.

"Okay," I said, "I got it."

"About friggin' time," I heard whispered behind me. I did not turn to Max. Instead, I put my hands on Cassie's shoulders. While I captured her through blurred vision for the last time, I stammered the phrase I had so rarely shared with her during her short life:

"Thank you,"

"You're welcome," she responded formally, confused by my sentiment.

"No really. Thank you. When he presented you to me, Rudy's greatest mistake was also his deepest gift."

"Hey!" Max whispered vociferously.

"Okay, second deepest," I said as clearly and without turning, then continued, "You see, Cassie, now I know, *I know*, that you're really dead, and that I didn't cause it. And now, after three years—"

"Four," Max interrupted again.

"Holy shit," I said, honestly amazed, and revised my speech to Cassie, "Now, after four years I can get on with my life with you as a memory and no longer its prime mover."

"I guess that's a good thing," Cassie said.

"It is," I said with absolute assurance leaping so readily through my tone that even I believed me: "You're dead, I know it, and I thank you. And I thank Rudy, wherever he is, for inadvertently hammering that truth into my soul. I also have to thank you for saving my life what? Two, three times?"

"More like a half dozen if you count the times you didn't notice."

"I'm three times more grateful."

"You shouldn't be. My creator was the asshole who dropped the bricks on you in the first place."

"Good point. But thanks anyway."

"You're welcome," she said, "Now stop thanking me!" We stood silently for a moment. I was mindless of anything except that Cassie, this Cassie, would never again grace my physical presence. In time she lifted my hands off her shoulders and stepped back.

"You know," she said, "I'll bet you'd never have thought you'd be thanking me for being dead."

"Nope," was the only word I could summon before lowering my head in grateful submission. She walked toward the gate at the border of Max's domain. When she reached it my head snapped up and clarity was briefly dismissed by lingering emotion. Knowing what would follow that picket portal swinging home I shouted:

"Cassie, wait!"

I heard Max gasp behind me, but she did not interfere. Cassie turned to me, her hand caressing the pointed tip of a picket. Her face crinkled in a mix of amusement and confusion. Her dress was gone and her body had returned to the obscene comic book proportions it enjoyed on Rudy's plain.

"What, Alex?" she asked sweetly, tempting me with her patience, but rejecting any desperate argument I might present simply by standing before me in her 'correct' form.

"Nothing," I said, "Goodbye, and give our – and your – love to Rudy should he ever come back. He'll need it."

"I will," Cassie said. She turned for the last time and passed through the gate. When it banged shut, she was gone. Beyond the gate was my plain, apparently empty but truly layered in infinite potential. I left it behind me, for the moment. Surrounding the doorway to Max's condo but sans big ugly birds, the black castle loomed once more. Standing on the lawn beside me, clutching my elbow, her soft cheek pressing against my shoulder, was Max.

"Welcome home, Alex," she said.

We stepped together into her condo/castle and gently pulled closed behind us both halves of the mighty oak/quaintly country door to the purple plain upon which her abode so comfortably nestled.

Chapter Thirty-Five

"Damn," I said, wiping my upper lip, "I never thought bourbon could taste so good."

"Trust me," Max said, poking my bare thigh with a long fingernail, "It's the company." She was right. A second sip reminded me that it was good bourbon, but not great bourbon. Hell, I thought, it isn't even real bourbon. My immediate, visceral interpretation of the booze, that it was smooth as single malt scotch and it neatly delivered that toe-numbing rush promised by only the best of bourbons, was of course wrong. The warmth in which I gratefully luxuriated was blanketing me long before I sipped the deep amber liquid from the simple clear tumbler; the drink provided tangible definition. The easy, deceptive perception helped, too, since the feelings invigorating my spirit were well beyond my ken. Max and I had been together in her place for only a few hours, as far as I could tell, but our reunion had been primed with emotions we had been building, hiding, and blindly promising without redemption for over a year. We did not speak for the first hour, so engrossed were we in the joy of each other's presence. Initially we silently nestled on her comfortable old couch, savoring our first moment alone that included no overhanging pressure to leave, no question of permanence. We basked in the glow of our realized love until we collapsed into an uninitiated bout of lovemaking that reduced us to a unified pile of delirious, sweaty, and very satisfied flesh. Later we showered, though we both knew the effluence of our prolonged exertion was not real, dressed in silk bathrobes, and settled back down on the couch with very tall glasses of bourbon conjured from an empty cabinet beneath a TV that had nothing to show us. We could have continued the cycle for hours, or days, and perhaps we had, given time's consistent misrepresentation in the dream realm, but our bond had passed such basal activity. Our physical consummation had occurred long ago, perhaps even before we met. So there we sat, a couple of kids acting like adults, drinking bourbon, munching on cheese and crackers, and staring without care at the blank TV screen.

"Yeah," I said, "It is the company. And of course I trust you."

"I suppose you respect me, too."

"That will have to come later, I think; let's see how you cook first."

"Ha, ha. Seriously, though, doesn't all this really seem way too good to be true? Are we getting to the part now where you suddenly wake up beside Cassie and learn that it all really was just a dream, and I'm not real, and everything we shared never happened?"

"And all those people Rudy killed are alive, and I still have my job at Beaver Toys, and I resolve to live a better, more grounded life because of the lessons I learned during my long sleep?"

"Yeah," Max said, "Something like that."

"Let me think," I said. I paused for a three-count, then finished loudly and with a firm pinch to Max's tight cheek, "Um, no!" Max yelped, playfully slapped my hand, and sighed.

"Okay, okay," she said, "It's not a movie. Everything was, is, real." I turned her chin toward me with my forefinger, and swam in the mesmerizing soup of her green eyes again.

"And it always will be," I said softly. She took my hand, ran my fingers against her cheek, and stared at the blank TV screen. In a moment, or perhaps an hour, she abruptly cleared her throat and spoke with officious clarity:

"So. Will you be telling me what happened with Rudy, and Cassie, or am I going to have to beat it out of you?"

"Tempting as that sounds, I guess I'll tell you." And I did, presenting a flowing narrative of everything I had experienced on Rudy's plain. I was careful to mix in all the ingredients required to give Max an accurate image of Rudy's mind, the extent of his power and the damage it had caused, his woefully misguided soul, and his final guilt-laden exit. I also described Cassie and Freuzre's true nature, and carefully reiterated my realization, and resolution, that neither of them was real, and we very likely would never hear from them again.

"What about Rudy?" She asked the inactive screen we both faced.

"What about him?"

"Do you think we'll ever see him again?"

"I don't know. You had to be there, but his exit sure seemed final. He is difficult to judge, but his personal devastation seemed immune to the cures of his bizarre rationales."

"Seriously," Max honestly agreed, "But you have to consider that anyone willing to toss entire races of people into the ether just because he didn't win the devotion of a couple of neighbors has got to be able to kid himself again. All he needs is time to believe in a new cover story, and maybe a third life history."

"A better rationale," I said, taking another sip of my bourbon, "That's all true. But still, you had to be there. It was as though he aged that thousand years in the three seconds that passed while he looked at his reflection. I'm sure Rudy isn't evil, and – "

"Yeah, evil guys murder billions, not millions."

"Point taken. But good hearts often cause vast amounts of damage. Just ask Harry Truman."

"Who?"

"Never mind," I said, her stroke of unusual ignorance sending an uncomfortable shiver through me that I easily ignored, "Suffice it to say that he had convinced himself somehow that Freuzre was real, and it was Freuzre who was causing all that damage as a separate, and stoppable, entity. Rudy held that as complete truth until that moment before the mirror."

"Okay, I'll give you that, but what about that place where you worked – Beaver Boys?"

"Toys. Beaver Toys."

"Oh. That sounds better. Anyway, he admitted destroying that whole place, and your house, and that mall in Jerusalem, all on his own. Just to get your attention. Are we mistakenly assigning those decisions to unrequited love instead of sticking them into the sociopathic evil drawer where they belong?"

"Point taken again. If you think about it, though, love can be a pretty powerful power."

"Point taken, Alex," Max sighed, cuddling a bit to enhance her response. Her movement stirred me, and renewed a fresh bout of a recurrent confusion that had been mildly nagging me. I had mentioned love's power as a romantic throwaway phrase, so Max and I could have a tacky exchange to help us emerge from the hell of discussing Rudy. She heard that, but a part of Max reacted far more deeply. Something in her tone, her touch, even her luscious natural scent shifted microscopically in reaction to the reference to love's power. And I had missed it. I struggled inwardly, sure that I was supposed to remember something, but it simply would not surface. I returned to the miserable subject of Rudy, sure that eventually the obvious point I was overlooking or unconsciously avoiding would eventually rise high enough above my perceptual horizon to permit even my dulled senses a handhold.

"Yeah," I said, absently joining her in her attentive review of the inactive TV, "That thought has passed through my mind several million times. But I still think that Rudy was nothing more than a kid who stumbled into omnipotence. He had all that power, but he was without imagination, and absolutely not blessed with the maturity needed to handle the power responsibly. He didn't know how to do no harm, and the unoriginal solutions he forced on the world never reaped the salvation he expected."

"And that makes him a good person?"

"It can, in the end. What if Rudy, with all this power coursing through him, suddenly realized his mistakes, his crimes, his immaturity, and his love all at the same time?"

"If he were me, his head would explode."

"Or, the myriad dots randomly decorating his cluttered slate would finally be connected in a sensible pattern. Maybe, when Rudy left, he took all that with him, but in assembled form. Maybe he didn't leave. What if he transcended into a Higher Being, disinterested in the affairs of human souls?"

"You mean like one of those Tibetan Lamas who spend their whole life meditating, waiting for nirvana?" Max asked. Her question reminded me of something Cassie had told me.

"Yes. In fact, they assume that they are the latest in a long line of Lamas contemplating their navels. And, this is all very analogous to Rudy, because he too wanted to reach perfect happiness through doing nothing."

"So the Tibetans are lazy?"

"On some level, I suppose they are, but that's not what I meant. They are after a similar thing and, since the rest of this mystical shit we've been wading through this last year (including your existence period) seems to tie in nicely with that ancient Buddhist-Hindu-God-knows-who-else bullshit, then maybe Rudy was on the right track all along. Maybe he really was a magical messiah. He just neglected to learn the rules for dealing with his new world."

"You forgot to capitalize the 'W,'"

"So I did. And, if this new world accepts him, he's learned not to capitalize – hey, wait a minute!" I interrupted my speech because the confusion had lifted. I shoved Max from her nesting spot along my left side, and attempted to glare at her from arms' length.

"What?" she asked, eyes wide but unable to keep the corners of her lips from twitching upward.

"Damn it! I've been sitting here, almost since we walked through your front door, trying to figure out what the hell was different about you! I was so happily buried in all the sex and bourbon, and then preoccupied with deciphering of Rudy, that I kept right on missing it!"

"Missing what?" Max asked playfully, bouncing her bare knees on the couch as if anticipating my announcement of an imminent trip to the zoo.

"Not it; or what. Who. Where's Mary?"

"Mary? Who's Mary?" Max said, grimacing as she looked around the room for some new phantom that I had conjured from my obviously troubled mind. I wasn't playing. I sensed the nature behind my late-blooming discovery – it was my plain we were on – and I wanted clarification.

"You know damn well who Mary is," I said, "She's—"

"Me."

"Yeah, you, sort of. And she was becoming more like you all the time."

"Alex. I wasn't asking. I was telling. She's me."

"I know. She's your other, earthly half, your material version. I'm up on all the deep stuff about you guys. Except how I didn't see her leave, and why I only thought of her now."

"You are so totally dense!" Max shouted.

"I'm getting tired of hearing that."

"Well, at least you heard something," she continued loudly, "Let me try it with a little volume this time. Mary is me. I'm her. We are the same person now, in every way, shape, and form, both mystical and physical."

"Huh?" I asked stupidly, stalling to better absorb the implications.

"We're me now. Both versions are one. I guess Rudy had it backwards, or didn't want to tell the truth for fear of making another him, or you. Our, my, soul wasn't annihilated when Mary and I met. It was assembled."

"So you and Mary are an individual?"

"Again."

"When did it happen?"

"It's been happening ever since you brought that sorry stupid and totally excellent peroxided chickie here, but the final stage was about a millisecond after Cassie, and Rudy's influence that she exuded, left this plain."

"Wow. That means that you're real now. You're not a dream."

"Well," she said, playing with her fingers, "I'd like to think I'll always be a dream. But yes, I am now just like you, and can wander both worlds at my whim, assuming that I ever figure out how."

"Wow."

"So is that all you have to say? Wow? Aren't you thrilled, or scared, or totally ready to leave this Technicolor prison?"

"There is that," I said, thinking fast and, as usual, negatively, "So I suppose now you'll want to have time to yourself, to grow and all."

"Oh please, don't turn into a man on me now."

"Thanks. I won't."

"Lose the pout, Alex. I'm in heaven here, on so many levels. And the highest level, the thing that tickles my reality most, is the level I occupy with you."

"That's good, right?"

"That's awesome," she exclaimed, taking my hands, "Listen Alex. We've got a shitload of history together, we're the only two people like us in the world, and we're crazy in love. Hell, I loved you for years, before you ever met me. I feel that not only do we have an obligation to work together to help right some of the wrongs Rudy unleashed on the world, but we also have an obligation toward each other's happiness. I would even abandon everything, should you wish to retire from this chaos, to grow old with you in reality."

"You've been rehearsing this, haven't you?"

"Mary and I went through the speech a thousand times while we waited for you to finish your walk with Cassie."

"Well bless you both," I said gruffly, standing. I headed for the front door at a stiff pace. Max jumped from the couch and ran along beside me, a real look of panic diminishing her perfect features.

"Alex, wait," she cried, rushing in front of me to grab my arms. When she did, the tie of her robe came loose, providing me with a generous view of an exciting aspect of the magical person from whom I was dramatically taking my leave.

"Sure," I said indignantly, pulling her robe closed, "That was an accident."

"Alex!" she said, finally spotting my ruse, "I'm not an idiot, you know! Well, not completely anyway."

"I know," I said, resting one hand on her cheek and the other on the doorknob, "And you know what?"

"What?"

"Neither am I. I mean, look at you for God's sake. You think I would leave you behind?"

"Looks fade."

"I wasn't speaking of your appearance," I said. That worked, I thought, as she melted against me.

"Well then what were all the theatrics?" she asked my chest.

"Theatrics? What theatrics? I just wanted to get moving as soon as possible, before you decide to not point out something this important again."

"Touché," she said, "But where are you, I mean we, going?"

"I thought maybe home, my home, for a start."

"Are we dressed for travel?" she asked, opening her robe again. She *was* taller, I acknowledged, but she had managed to retain her perfect breasts.

"Just walk out the door," I said, shaking my head. I opened it for her, spun her around and pushed her out ahead of me. The Escort was waiting, engine running, beyond the picket fence's open gate. When we stepped on the path we were fully clothed in standard suburban uniforms of blue jeans and loose cotton oxford shirts.

"Oh yeah," she said.

"Yeah. I couldn't imagine what season it is, but we can deal with that when we get there."

"Where?"

"Home. My home. Our home."

"You mean your, our, basement?"

"That's a start."

"Oh. How come you still have this ratty old car?" she asked when the door I opened her door for her groaned in protest. After I had crossed around the front of the car and climbed in my side, she finished, "I mean, hell, you could be in Rudy's Porsche. He apparently doesn't need it. Or a new Ferrari."

"Hey, don't dis the Escort, lady. We've been through a lot together. And, aside from being the mostly appropriately named vehicle in the history of vehicledom, I've grown attached to the old crate. We're a lot alike."

"You can say that again."

"I won't ask."

"Don't." We both were laughing, giddy as children while the Escort started moving. Our euphoria was a salve that temporarily masked the pain and extreme loss we had both encountered over the last year. For the moment everything ended with us, with our love, and our shared potential. We would get back to the other stuff later. When the car pulled onto my street about three seconds later, Max grabbed my wrist, and said,

"Alex."

"Yes?"

"You're not going to tell Clive about this, are you?"

"What this?"

"You know what this. The whole me and Mary thing."

"You think the same thing would happen to them? Him?"

"Honestly, no. He moves a little too close to the herd in both realms. But you know I've been way wrong about this shit before. So you're not going to tell him, right?"

"Why would I?" I asked, "I seem to remember him adamantly refusing to hook up with Cleavus, and I have to honor the guy's wish, don't I? Besides, poor Cleavus would be bored to tears." We laughed again as we turned into my driveway. The house was as absent as it was when I had first left it; no rebuild was happening on my lot. I probably owed back taxes or something that prevented my next of kin from executing a resale. I pulled into the garage, heard the big door close behind me. I opened my door, and started to get out, but I noticed that Max hadn't moved. She wasn't laughing.

"What?" I asked, masking my impatience as best I could.

"Nothing, she said quietly, chewing a fingernail in a very Mary-esque fashion. She breathed deeply and continued, "No, something. I just need to get a few things straight."

"About us? You know – "

"Not us, you fool. I'm aware that we've irreparably linked our souls, and I'll live with that, happily ever after. No, I mean the rest."

"The rest?"

"You'll have to bear with me, being that, aside from Mary's, um, puzzling scattershot memories, I'm new to this whole corporeal real-world existence. But, I know that it involves a lot of bullshit that your abilities – and hopefully mine someday if you'll teach me – "

"If I ever figure out how I do any of it, you'll be the first to know," I interrupted.

"Thanks. Anyway, your old world is cluttered with things, needs, and chores that you don't need anymore. I mean, seriously. You don't need to work, eat, shit, or clean, although I can't help but notice that you still get zits."

"Gosh thanks."

"No problem. And you don't need a permanent address. You could live anywhere on or off the planet that you want, in any style you can imagine."

"Where's this going?"

"Where it's going is this: why are we here? This is your old home, and it's mostly gone now. The only thing left is that awful sound room, and you certainly don't need *it* anymore."

"I was going to rebuild. I just thought it better to wait for dark so we don't freak out the neighbors. Not that they'd notice."

"Alex! That's not the point and you know it! It's not just your house that's gone to dust. So has the life that once gave it context. All the stuff that made this place real to you has been folded inexorably into your past. You don't need it anymore."

"That's perfectly true," I said solemnly, quietly delighted in the faith I held in my words.

"Good," she said, hearing me. She wrapped her fingers around mine and asked, "Then why the hell are we here?"

"Because, my love, we need to be. This is us. This place, this earth, these floorboards, these neighbors, this car. This context. This is where we are from. Both of us. All of us: Rudy's tragic mistake was his elevation of himself above humanity before he understood anything about being human. His disconnection was permanent and fatal for a whole lot of people, probably including him. I don't want that to happen to me or you, and I do not want to accidentally annihilate great throngs of humanity."

"So," Max said, fidgeting, "You're going to abandon your freedom, your power, your ability to help renew what Rudy trashed, and soak yourself in the mundane world again? For how long? Do we have to get jobs? Alex, I feel I must warn you that most of me is not from this dimension, and the rest is of questionable domestic and professional background. I might give you a lot of trouble."

"What about that promise you just made to grow old with me if I decided to retire from wizardom?" I asked

"Well now is a fine time for you to pay attention to my speeches!" Max whined.

I laughed, took her hand, and looked into eyes. After refocusing on the conversation, I spoke softly to her:

"Max, don't worry. Do you think I'm a total idiot? Uh-uh, don't answer that! Listen. We're going to rebuild my house, meet the new neighbors, maybe start a weekly poker game, get cable TV, and just live normally for a while. Call it a vacation from our true duties, a chance to experience, as regular people, the human impact of the damage that Rudy caused, devastation that I could easily duplicate. In time, most likely a very short time, we'll have at the universe, and we'll do anything and everything we can to make it, and ourselves, magnificent – not that you aren't already.

"We'll be creating worlds full of excitement, happiness, and awesome new things that neither of us has imagined yet, and we might just attain that wisdom necessary to truly grow, to rise honorably above that wandering herd, and perhaps in the end to give something back to the people who will listen. We'll do all that, together, I promise. Hell, the past year has proven it's unavoidable. But we'll do it later. Maybe tomorrow. Maybe next year. For now I just want us to have some time together, to suffer some arguments, to enjoy simple pleasures, to catch a few sunsets that I didn't initiate. I want us to experience being human, so we never, ever forget."

"Oh," she said. She was still silent for a minute, as though mulling my explanation. Then she put her index finger on her chin and said, "Will I have to cook?"

"Only if you want to."

"All righty then. Let's try this out." She leapt out of the car and stood at the small garage door, which overlooked the space that once lurked below my house. She already had, in the true spirit of Mary, accepted her new role. I got out of the car, joined her on the threshold. The midsummer sun was setting, of its own volition, washing us in cool orange light. I put my arm around Max. She leaned her cheek on my shoulder.

"I guess we have a plan then," she said.

"Yes."

"It's about friggin' time."

www.ingramcontent.com/pod-product-compliance
Lightning Source LLC
Chambersburg PA
CBHW020923020726
47495CB00002B/325